The Heart of Grinnwick

Second edition
ISBN: 978-0-6459960-6-7
Editing by Laurel Sills
Cover art by Angela Rizza

For myself, my family, and everyone who supported me along the way.

To Bill, thank you for encouraging me every day.

To Angus & Lachie, may you always dream of adventure.

... and now to Billie girl, my little ray of light.

Bubble in Time

'You'll all be late,' Ailsa roared in her manic tone, 'I'm off to the gardens, so you better get yourselves moving,' she added before running downstairs and straight out the door.

Scarlet stirred and fumbled out of her bed. Mornings were never easy for her; she found it easier to sleep in, sometimes even until the early afternoon. This didn't happen too often, it wasn't the way of the Amari, they used the light of the days to the fullest — as she had been repeatedly told. On her spare days though, Scarlet indulged herself. This didn't mean that some of the Amari didn't enjoy the beauties of night as she did, it's just that they usually went back to their quarters at a decent time to get their rest. Scarlet seemed to forget to get to bed early enough, and as the mornings rose it felt near unnatural to be awake at such an hour, her body begging her to rest. Finding herself alight with distractions even at a late hour, when people returned to their quarters, she searched adventure, even if it was an escape in one of the few books that she had borrowed from the elders, that was enough to spark her mind.

Lux, her best friend, was at her peak in the mornings. Scarlet could have hated her for it, the brightness Lux beamed when the sun rose seemed near intolerable. Frustration crossed her mind from the moment that Lux woke her up, for those split seconds she wanted to pummel Lux - in truth however, Lux was one of the few people she cared for, practically family. Her annoyance was only ever short lived, as Lux was one of the constant reminders that although Scarlet felt out of place, she wasn't alone.

1

Lux woke happily as usual, springing out of what used to be Scarlet's brother Flynn's bed. Lux in character was quick to get ready; as Scarlet fumbled around looking for her clothes, Lux was out the door to get something to eat.

The aroma of eggs drifted up the stairway as she walked down, with a hint of sweetness that only came from stewed fruits, a staple of village life with the Amari. The eggs were waiting for them on the table in their small hovel of a kitchen, where the dirt of the underground lay overhead, covered in a web of vines. All living quarters for the Amari were underground, Scarlet often found herself referring to everyone within the Amari as a burrow people. A joke of course, one of her overly sarcastic tendencies as Ailsa, their caretaker would call it.

'Eat up,' Lux warned, already washing her plate in their small bucket sink. Lux's dark hair was pulled into a tight bun, and her brown skin freshly washed for the day.

'The boys aren't even down yet. I'm sure it'll be okay,' Scarlet sassed. Her weariness had left her with a short fuse, even if she was only jesting with a friend.

Hudson came into the kitchen; he was laid back and cool. He tossed an apple in his hands smiling almost perfectly, 'Morning,' he said almost mockingly, sweeping his black hair up into the air. Scarlet giggled at Lux who rolled her eyes at him.

'Morning brother, eat quickly,' Lux instructed, slapping him on the shoulder as she walked past him; passing him some eggs. Scarlet thought they made the oddest siblings, especially as twins. Lux was so ambitious, and particular in every way, the organisation of even their very basic clothes in their room was just the beginning of her innate ways. While Hudson had not a care in the world, but things still managed to always work in his favour, he didn't need to be organised, he had always had Lux for that.

'What's on for today everyone?' beamed Archer, as he walk airily into the kitchen. He looked just as dishevelled as she felt in the mornings. He was fae after all, unlike the rest of them.

His stance was soft, and he moved swiftly and gently, the same senses as the other Amari had gave him a way of floating through a room, something that Scarlet and the twins could never match. One day he would be just as in tune with his natural surroundings as the rest of his people.

The Amari were keepers of secrets, that's how Scarlet saw them. Not human, but in looks they were not far from it either. Their formative distinctions were in their eyes – normal at a glance – but the colours around their pupils beamed and moved like the river flow. Their bodies were thinner, swifter, and able to move without being seen through the forest. Their inner ears curved differently to a human's; Scarlet had been told this increased their sense of their surroundings.

Their history stretched back to the beginning of Grinnwick. Their stories not alone amongst the tales of different forms of fae, each with connections to the land. Once long ago the Amari boasted their own beautiful palaces in the forest, but they retreated just as the other fae did, and tucked themselves away as the worries of the world turned on them. As wise and intriguing as they were, it was their sources of knowledge about the world around them that gave them an upper hand when looking out for themselves, and they were also known for having the gift of foresight.

The magics of Grinnwick that were reserved in the Amari, didn't pass through every individual and usually the elders held more strength and understanding of their powers. Still Scarlet wasn't entirely sure of the extent of the magic that they were capable of; it wasn't often that they would display powers in front of her, she was and always will be an outsider, that was for certain.

Scarlet didn't mind being different, but the truth was, this wasn't her true home.

Over six years had passed since she'd first arrived, and the days of wondering how long until they would return to the 'real' world faded. While they lived in their quiet village, time beyond their protective magical borders rushed by. For every year they stayed inside the bubble over 150 years passed by. Their village, a sanctuary for the remaining Amari left in Grinnwick. It spanned only a few valleys wide before it became surrounded by   the   Corazon   Forest. The insides of the forest a mystery to most as the area was thick with intertwining trees, suspiciously moving branches from what Scarlet had heard they moved around the trunks when a trekker inside of the forest wasn't looking, displacing whoever was inside, leaving them at the mercy of the dangers that lurked in the darkness. The Corazon Forest was what kept the north and the south of Grinnwick separated, only winding trails across the mountains of the Wirkswood Ranges opened up between the two, which were too long and too narrow for no more than a small group to breach, and mostly at a perilous cost for those who did.

Inside the forest there was an invisible magical barrier, or bubble as Scarlet referred to it that was what kept them safe; their bubble in time.

This ability to cut themselves off from time was no doubt why the Amari held such knowledge, with the ability to watch the wheels forever turning outside of their bubble, sitting on their perch, untouched. Letting time role by, keeping them unharmed what was outside. Scarlet didn't know who built the magics up to create such a place, or if it had always been here, all that she knew now was this life. Time was lost to her; it was nearly ten centuries ago that her life should have been lived. Never able to go back to what once was.

The Amari village offered a life of simplicity. With a freedom from the worries of the world there was nothing but peace amongst the fae. That being said, Scarlet always enjoyed the small titbits of drama that flared up every now and then. The most dramatic fae of all was their caretake, Ailsa. She was young by Amari standards, in her eightieth year – and barely looked in her mid-twenties by human age. And if she wasn't gossiping about the other faes in her circles, she managed to lose her cool generally due to the frustrations of being landed in the position to care for them as younglings. Scarlet sometimes thought she had more teenage tendencies than any of them combined.

The Amari boasted their ability to grow almost anything; it was in the gardens that Ailsa spent most of her time. Scarlet had to admit, it was aware she belonged, and the tranquillity of the garden, somewhat softened her. Every time Scarlet entered she couldn't help feel that same sense of calm.

The white bell flowers welcomed visitor over the arch entry. Lush and green plants surrounded them, and a scent that often left Scarlet calmly at ease while she picked dozens of colourful flowers.

Even though the Amari were all she knew, they were mysterious even still to her. Like they had a secret she was never quite in on. They were always looking to natural world, reading the signs of the elements as a way of knowing what was happening in the world, their way of connection to the unknown outside their village was always curious to her.

'Well, do we have anything exciting planned?' Archer asked again.

'We would know if you got a move on,' Scarlet mused, looking to Lux who was clearly getting frustrated with each passing moment.

Archer smiled at Scarlet, 'don't mock her, she's just trying to keep up with the likes of me.'

'I may not be fae, but I can learn the same as you. And I already know you would never dare face me in the practice pits,' Lux bit back.

Scarlet knew she could beat him in any physical match, as much as his fae side alluded them he wasn't gifted with a strong physical build. Where most of his kind had a lean strength to their build he somehow seemed that bit scrawnier than the rest. It allowed for them as the few humans in the village to best him, especially during their practice fighting.

The halls that connected all the living quarters were a path completely imbedded into the ground, like a deep cut out into the earth; with the earth and vines encasing the walkways; winding around the different areas of the Amari Village – from the kitchens to housing and learning areas, it was all connected like that of a beehive. The sides of the hallways reached eerily high until they surfaced topside, opening up to the valley. The deep halls shadowed by the position of the sunlight above. They had trodden on this dirt floor many times, weaving their way through the hive of Amari separate living quarters, past the underground water mill, that echoes through the halls like a nonstop running river, and just passed the room of light, which was the darkest of all the quarters and closed tight with a heavy block-out-light door. Scarlet had never entered, it was said that this was the Amari faes magical stronghold, that the light inside was a dust that had been stored up from faes long passed. Those who remained could soak up its power when needed. Scarlet barely looked at the door when she walked by anymore, that was Amari magic, something she had no right tapping into; well perhaps her curiosities where higher when she was younger, but in the years past it had just become one more thing to the mysteries that surrounded her. It was only a small walk from the room of light that they found themselves heading higher on the path to the above ground communal area at the centre of the Amari Village.

Behind a colourful cloth of vibrant reds with a patterned star in the middle, a room opened up, round and scented with a calming smoke, set up for lessons.

All the faces of the children of the Amari stared at the four of them. Their teaching elder at the front, he too was distracted by their arrival.

'Sorry,' Scarlet said on behalf of them all, pulling her hair into a ponytail as she found a seat on the ground.

'Not to worry Miss Rivers. We were just about to start. Why don't you all take a seat,' said Elder Jackson. Elder Jackson like the other Amari age didn't show, but in comparison to the others he was well into the later years of his life. Scarlet thought there was something in his face, whether it was perhaps one or two extra wrinkles, or the fact that behind his eyes he looked like he knew things that surpassed those around him. Scarlet had always respected him, yet she felt intimidated by his knowledge of all things, ideas and understandings that were beyond her. After all she had such few memories of her own life, she felt his wealth of knowledge almost intangible to herself, something she could never reach. In ways only he knew Elder Jackson always sensed what was ahead; of course this was a gift of many fae, but he tended to know things even others didn't.

Scarlet quickly rushed to a spot next to Archer, and he waited until she sat down. He wasn't an outlandish creature to the Amari like the twins or herself, he was one of them; only tainted in their eyes probably because of his connection to Scarlet, Lux and Hudson, and their lack of fae blood. Not that he ever acted like their feelings bothered him.

Archer was bound to them when his mother died while out on a mission in Grinnwick when the War of Darkness started to spread. He alone out of the four of them had always called the village home. This didn't make him any different to them. He was family, and for Scarlet, Archer was her best friend. He always found the smallest reasons to make her smile, whether it be telling her a make-believe story about the smallest insect, or about creatures from beyond the skies. Sometimes he would find the most beautiful flower in the garden for her, or share his last bite of peach pie if ever she missed out. He had always had her back, and Scarlet had always done the same for him. A simple friendship built over their childhood, when they found that all they had at the end of the day was each other. Archer in many ways had his own peculiarities of course – he was specific about most things, and repeated facts constantly. Scarlet usually took it upon herself to make sure he got his head, out of his books, and outside to enjoy himself. As she sat next to him, like she usually did in their lessons, his presence made her feel like she wasn't alone, when she most clearly didn't belong.

'As I was saying,' Elder Jackson continued. 'This morning we will cover what we can before you head off outside. Also, don't forget you're all fruit picking this afternoon. First things first, you may have noticed that some of the west watchers are back in the village. Please I know you are curious, as younglings so often are, but give the watchers time to settle back into the village. Understand me,' Elder Jackson warned, waiting for each of the children to respond, and with the nods of their heads, he continued. 'Now, let us begin.'

Scarlet unconsciously zoned out from his words, and instead absorbed every tiny detail of his presence, watching the way that he leant into his cane, the wooden beam she felt may break under his weight. Her focus moved to his face and the way that although it appeared youthful, his eyes looked sunken and weary. She imagined him as a boy, sitting in the room beside her, how many new moons, and seasons had passed since then, the rushing of time that flew by, as though a flicker she felt a surge in the room around her, the room like Elder Jackson witnessing time... Her thoughts tended to wander off occasionally when he began his lesson, she always regretted it when they did. Usually, she tried to hang on to every word he said, even if she didn't entirely understand him.

As she drifted out of her daze and the ideas of knowledge locked in time, all being seen by the walls of this room, Scarlet found herself in the midst of a history lesson of the ancient fae.

'Long ago the trees of the forest that surround us now could not only speak to one another, but to the ancient beings of the world.' Elder Jackson's throaty voice beamed. 'We Amari called it the link of Haliroot's. Some who concentrate enough can connect to that link.' As he spoke, he placed his hand on the ground, letting the children revel as the ground beneath them shuddered for a moment before he uncovered his hand to show a budding plant.

He explained that this was the magic that helped them to travel through the Corazon Forest. This skill belonged to those of ancient blood, like that which ran through the Amari veins. He insisted that this was how selected watchers in the trees knew what was happening around them.

To Scarlet stories like these were imaginative fairy tales; as real as the small doses of magic she saw before her were, her mind was swept away in the fun of them, the possibilities.

Half the things he spoke of didn't generally seem possible, but she loved to believe in the magic of them. And her heart leaped at any display of magic such as this. Especially in comparison to their previous lesson the day before where they were forced to sit down and tie different types of knots, repeatedly, for hours. Tedious to say the least.

Archer on the other hand had been scribbling onto a piece of paper beside her, Scarlet knew him well enough to know that these were his own ideas, and that like always he had been barely listening through the whole lesson. His mind Before he had come to live with Ailsa and the other orphans his mother was on the way to becoming a great Amari elder herself. She had told him stories like these, over and over, and even after she'd passed he kept studying. He knew tales like this like the back of his hand.

'Now, go on get out of here,' Elder Jackson implored as he finished his lesson.

They scrambled out the door and onto the village foot paths that mazed around the underground dug outs of passageways that connected the village. Deep into the hills of the village, winding through the path, they walked further up toward the centre of the village. Towards where the path meet the topside part of the hill that the village was dug into. Where they were met with a wide-open space. Hills green and lush as far as the eye could see, and large blossom covered trees stood out marking the entrance of the gardens; in the furthest distance their eyes could just see the border of the Corazon Forest. Its vast thickness surrounded them, and it often irked her that she didn't know more about what was inside. Most in the village seemed weary of it; it seemed rightly so, after all somewhere within was the border that ended their protected bubble. A place cornered off from time itself, safe from everything, and everyone beyond. As intriguing as life on the outside may seem, what was lost she could not get back. Her true family that were gone, and she intended on holding onto the found-family she had now. Scarlet found comfort in the fact that she had no memory of a full life anywhere else. The memories she held were here, being a part of the Amari.

Only one memory had stayed with her from before she'd arrived, like flashes of a light. Those small moments flickered in her mind, returning to her especially when she slept. The fragments were of the events moments after her head was knocked. Those same moments capturing the aftermath from losing nearly her entire family; flames, thunder, the wetness on her cheek, a hand in hers, of the only person she had left, the flicker of his young face, her brother Flynn. She had no idea of how the other members of her family died, or what they were like. She was left with nothing but a sore head, a battered and bruised body in the chaos and remnants of a home, and land she didn't remember.

Flynn now was further away than Scarlet liked to think. He had already returned to the world of Grinnwick in a strange set of circumstances nearly five months ago.

She'd remained behind when Flynn left, and not by choice; she longed to run after him. The fact remained that finding Flynn in the wide world of Grinnwick on her own was near impossible. The notion that he'd left without even a goodbye confused Scarlet more with every passing day. But to go into an unknown world seemed absurd, her friends were here, a life, everything that she knew. She would have no one to help her through the complexities of what lay outside their safe-haven. Most importantly she was only a child, going off into the unknown after him would be foolish. And with every minute, hour, day the time in Grinnwick went so much faster, and Flynn could have travelled further, already living most of his life.

His absence had taken its toll on more than Scarlet alone. Ailsa their caretaker had tried her best to return their life back to normal after Flynn's sudden departure. At heart Scarlet could tell she still worried about him. Ailsa always seemed to change the subject, and for someone who wasn't instinctively caring, Ailsa seemed nearly as affected as Scarlet.

Then there were her friends, who were her family now; Archer, Lux and Hudson. Those three tied Scarlet to the village, to her home here. As often as she would drift off with her thoughts, they brought out a silly, bubbly side to her. Together they were all each other had.

'What's our plan for today?' she asked Archer. She was getting a bit more perky as the day went on.

'Practice pits?... Dawson's back, and no doubt he'll give us some killer tips. Then we can go to the fruit field after lunch.' They all agreed and ran down past the gardens to the dirt ring that was the practice pits.

Dawson was already booming directions out to some of the other fae children. Scarlet noticed a rather dubious boy named Azra who looked too proud of himself as Dawson encouraged him. Dawson was describing the best way to stand when taking on an opponent and used him as the example. Scarlet felt her eyes roll too obviously; she didn't want attention drawn to her for such thoughts. Being different could often make it hard for her to fit in with the Amari and she did not need another reason to stand out.

Dawson was rather striking with his broad shoulders, dark brown hair, salt trimmed beard, and warm eyes. Many of the Amari ladies clearly thought so. They would often take the long way around to do their daily jobs whenever he was in the village back from one of his treks as a watcher, each of them wearing their cleanest, and brightest coloured dresses. For the little that could be done with the linen dresses they somehow managed to look lovely. Mostly each one of them longed to receive one of his sweet smiles, and to secretly gush over his well-defined jawline; the amount of times Scarlet saw them running off giggling whenever he was around was sickening. Yet, she had to admit he did have a degree of presence that not many other adult men had within the village, a smooth sense that he was not controlled by the rules or the constructs that were placed around them.

Lux on the other hand was one of the many girls who found themselves usually distracted when he was around. Scarlet could tell by the look on her face that she was trying her hardest to concentrate even though Dawson was on the sidelines giving his advice.

The practice pit was all fun and games to Hudson as he quickly jumped the fence and picked up one of the wooden swords. He was swift with every wave of his wrist; as Scarlet watched his movement, she could see his footwork came with ease. He moved towards Azra and held up the sword, wanting to try his luck. It was here fighting in the practice pit that the twins differences really stood out. While Hudson's confidence exuded out of him, every little thing was a competition to Lux, her mind was always turning contemplating her next move, a simple act that she thrived on. Most people assumed that her desire for competition came from needing to be better than her brother, Scarlet felt it was more her desire to prove herself as an outsider within the Amari people.

Like Lux, Hudson was persistent with learning whatever they were taught, but he didn't care if he was the best. It did usually come naturally to him, even as an outsider. Hudson mainly enjoyed besting his sister when he could. Even so, there wasn't a time that Scarlet could recall that he'd ever been anything but fiercely protective of her. If anyone else tried to pick on her he was ready to stand up to them, no matter how many he had to take on. The same was said if they ever tried to terrorise Scarlet or Archer; Hudson was there if they ever needed him. The twins were a year older than Scarlet, who was twelve, and they had taken her under their wing like another branch of their family, as they had with Archer. The two of them were haunted by the memories of their parents from the day they arrived. Scarlet sometimes saw the twins flinch or jump at a loud noise, they never said what had happened, and she never asked but there was times that genuine fear crept into their eyes. Scarlet knew their parents were heroes of their time, and whatever happened stuck with both Lux and Hudson.

When they arrived it wasn't as long ago as her own time, but it must have been just as terrorising and daunting time to be a part of the world she thought, if not for just from their own reactions, she could also tell by the reactions and respect that the Amari showed the twins.

Hudson's sword knocked against Azra's fiercely, gaining Scarlet's attention. There was a mutual respect in each of them. Hudson kept up with Azra's effortless movements. But he was no match for the Amari-born abilities. Even at a young age as swift and strong as Hudson was, Azra's' sleek motion kept him one step ahead. His eyes were sharp as Hudson approached him, concentrating intently. He had a natural edge and with

14

practice and training it was imbedded since the youngest of ages that the Amari learned to arm themselves.

Ivy, Cooper and Meena were three Amari children that they practiced with, each always impeccable in their skills. Their footwork was quicker than theirs, and their foresight could not be matched. It would be children of the Amari like them who would work their way to becoming watchers just like Dawson.

They may not be watchers, but in their teachings it had not mattered that they were outsiders, they had been taught the exact same set of skills, honing them as their own, pulling on their own strengths. Scarlet, Hudson and Lux may win against the others every now and them, but their differences meant a life as a watcher of the woods was never in their future. Their blood did not have the same connection to help them protect the borders. Sometimes Scarlet wondered why they practised if their training was for nothing, yet she also enjoyed the fun of it, with the spike of energy that brightened her, intoxicated by the joy of the game.

Scarlet jumped right into the practice pits, grabbing her own wooden sword, pointing it at Archer, who did the same in return.

Scarlet and Archer motioned back and forth, knocking each other until they were out of breath. Dramatically she threw herself to the ground, and covered in dirt she began to laugh. Archer laughed back at her, 'We will never learn if you keep throwing the fight,' he said.

'You're not going to learn anything down there,' Dawson chimed in helping her up, pausing for a moment as he held her hand.

'I get this is a game to you, little one. But one day you will grow as the trees around us do and you may need skills like these. You are quick, I'll give you that, but you need to think like a warrior. Be mentally prepared like some of your other friends are already, this is no game.' He nodded towards Lux as an example for her; she managed to take the compliment in her stride while still knocking Ivy's sword out of her hand.

'It's just a game sir. How long has it been since the Amari were involved in an actual fight?' Scarlet replied.

'Yes, just a game…,' he said ominously, with a lingering stare at Scarlet before he drew away, 'then why don't you go up against Jules?'

Scarlet looked to Jules, who was twice her size, and nearly three years older than her. Not to mention the muscle that he had, and the fact that he moved effortlessly with Amari foresight. It was one thing for Hudson to take him on, but another for her. It was not that she wasn't good, but she was nowhere near good enough for this.

As they stepped towards the centre of the pits, everyone around them was silent. Scarlet could not believe she was doing this. She was going to get her butt kicked.

Looking into Jules' eyes, she wanted to be sure she wouldn't tremble the sword in her hand, holding it as firmly possible. She could see he was ready for blood; Jules was always ready to take out his opponent.

He was quick, his legs moved effortlessly, without a thought about them. His mind was transfixed on her, his actions building ideas as he stepped into action. Scarlet was quicker, she dodged his advances sliding underneath his arm, quick enough to slice her wooden blade across his slide. The small win didn't last long, Jules turned and knocked Scarlet to the side rattling her for a moment.

Regaining herself, Scarlet crossed blades continuing to move her feet lightly to keep herself in front and out of harm's way. In a swift motion Jules forced the blade straight from Scarlet's hand. He swung his blade through the air toward Scarlet's leg, tripping her up in a quick motion, and her head banged against the floor. Scarlet moved to sit up when he knocked her back to the ground with a kick to finish her off.

'Not all a game now is it?' Dawson said, and walked out of the pitch leaving them to themselves. Scarlet sighed while Jules walked off fully impressed with himself.

Archer helped Scarlet up. 'You okay?' he asked.

'Yeah, just battered my confidence is all,' Scarlet said sarcastically.

'You did well, don't know many other kids who would have lasted much longer against him. Don't worry about Dawson either, my mum always said he was a bit off with the fairies,' Archer said, and flinched at the mention of his mother. His loss was fresher than the others.

'Anyway, let's get out of here before the other watchers come down for their training,' Archer said.

'Good Point, we don't need to cop it from them too,' Hudson added.

'You know I heard Elder Jackson say that Dawson is the sharpest warrior he's ever known,' Lux said, cutting into their conversation. Scarlet scoffed, she knew he probably was, but didn't feel like this was a pivotal moment to admit it.

'I mean it sucks he put you up against Jules, knowing full well you'd get your ass handed to you. At least now you know what it's like getting a proper thrashing,' Lux noted.

'Lux I would have been dead in under a minute if that was a real fight,' Scarlet retorted.

Lux rolled her eyes, ignoring what she said. 'Dawson is pretty scary up and close, isn't he? Still, it's nice that he makes time for us kids. I swear every time he's back, we run into him. I mean how lucky is that.'

'Lucky you didn't make a fool out of you I think you mean,' Hudson said teasing Lux.

Pondering Dawson, his peculiarity and brass nature, Scarlet didn't think he was all that scary. He was familiar to her, and although harsh his presence was comforting in a way. Part of him reminded her of Flynn. He would have loved to grow and be just as unforgivingly astute as Dawson was, how he always found time for her and their friends in his spare time. Sometimes when she pictured what her brother would be like grown, the two weren't all that dissimilar. Dawson would have been another twenty or so years older than Flynn, but Scarlet believed their hearts were the same. The only time when Dawson seemed uneasy was in the centre of the village, whatever glimpses Scarlet caught of him, he usually looked incredibly alone. Part of her felt sad for him; did he not call anyone family?

Usually, the watchers had more important things to be doing, especially when they were in the village back from their watch rather than hanging out with a bunch of kids giving them fighting tips. In Scarlet's opinion, the reason Dawson seemed somewhat scary was because he was distant from nearly everyone in the village. It was only the times here at the pit that he seemed connected to the lives of anyone else.

Lunch was eaten without a second of silence as they talked about who had the best moves out on the pit. Hudson was trying to explain how if he had his right footing, he might have beaten Azra. Archer insistent that next time he wanted to fight one of the other two because Scarlet gave up before either of them ever had a chance to win. She rolled her eyes when he said this; it didn't matter to her who won, the thrill of the moment when someone might win was her favourite part, if someone won it seemed like there would be a finality to the game that she didn't enjoy. However, after her embarrassing encounter with Jules, there was also no way Scarlet was going to let that happen again, she was going to be prepared.

The afternoon had cooled off and Scarlet journeyed out into the gardens, on their way to the fruit fields walking side by side with Archer, behind Lux and Hudson. They passed Ailsa on the way, as she was tending to the gardens.

Ailsa quickly pulled them aside. 'I hope you four are behaving yourselves,' she said sternly.

'Of course, we shall not leave one fruit unpicked today,' Archer responded, his voice full of character with a touch of sarcasm. He knew as well as any of them that the question wasn't directed at him or the others, but to Scarlet. Ailsa had a nasty fixation towards focusing on her, somewhat passionate, but mostly hovering over what she was up to. Scarlet didn't know why, but over the years any mischief they got up to always seemed to be her fault, especially in Ailsa's eyes. Scarlet loved Archer for always trying to deflect Ailsa's snide comments.

As Scarlet slyly laughed at his ridiculous response, the day was thrown into chaos.

Dawson rushed over to Scarlet and Archer.

'Hey kids,' Dawson said stiffly. His eyes shifted between them, and another watcher named Milo who had just reached them. Milo was already frantically talking to Ailsa in a hushed tone, as Dawson kept Scarlet and the others out of ear's reach.

'What's going on?' Scarlet awkwardly asked Dawson.

'There is news from outside the Amari Village. I can't explain to you here, but we must wait for Ailsa and Milo and get going,' Dawson said.

'But we've got fruit to pick,' Archer said, as more of a matter of fact this time. Both had lost sight of Hudson and Lux to call them back while they waited with Dawson.

Ailsa quietened, looked to the two of them, then at Dawson. She came over and placed her hand on his shoulder, then grabbed both Scarlet and Archer by their arms and motioned them back towards their home in the centre of the village. Despite Scarlet's demand to know what was happening, Ailsa remained tight lipped.

All around them whispers from people seemed to break out in the gardens.

On their way back Scarlet was stopped by one of the eldest women in their village who usually worked away in the kitchens cleaning. She hugged Scarlet from out of the blue. Scarlet looked to Archer who shrugged in confusion. He scoffed that the woman was a crazy old bat as Ailsa hurried them all along.

Reaching their quarters, Archer and Scarlet were left by themselves to discuss what they thought the news could be.

'It has to be about Flynn,' Scarlet said. 'Something's happened to him, I know it. Why else would the old bat hug me like something bad had happened.'

'I don't know. It could be anything. Maybe there is something dangerous, maybe they're putting everyone on lockdown. Dawson said he was going out to get the other kids in the fruit fields too,' Archer said.

Lux and Hudson soon made it back to their quarters and were both questioning all the commotion.

'Something bad has happened, that's for sure,' Hudson said.

'You think?' Archer sarcastically replied, ignoring the glare that Hudson gave him return.

'Like what, you think the fighting out in Grinnwick's gotten close to the village? I didn't think that the men of Grinnwick could find us here,' Lux said.

'They can't,' Scarlet bit her lip. 'This place is protected. Even if not for the bubble, they'd have no chance getting through the Corazon Forest.'

If any of them thought Ailsa would give them answers they were wrong. She didn't talk for most of that evening. Her wine glass was her solace as she pottered around the room, cleaning things that didn't need it, heading to their small kitchen to get more food for them all, even after they'd eaten.

Hudson and Archer couldn't help but take full advantage of the extra food and managed to eat three jacket potatoes each. Lux was a bit more nervous about it all, wondering if they were in trouble. She was going over all the silly things they had gotten up to over the years, sure that one of their escapades had been discovered.

'The great bear debacle,' Lux cautioned; Scarlet smiled at this fondly... they disobeyed direct instructions and entered the containment zone to find out what the watchers had brought back from the forest; an extremely disgruntled bear, which was caught too close to the village. Scarlet couldn't help but release it, causing a wake of destruction in the orchards. '...We always skip our chores, maybe this is to be our punishment for not helping the village enough?', or 'The clock. We changed it, well you and Hudson did...' Lux berated, albeit quietly. Scarlet knew there were over a dozen things that they shouldn't have done over the years, her favourite included a large amount of pheasant feathers, and honey from the hives; a brilliant spectacle at an elder gathering. She laughed softly to herself in memory, yet found herself trying to keep busy while the time dragged on, and the unknown only grew. It would have been an hour that passed when Scarlet finally couldn't stand the anxious look on Ailsa's face, and once the second bottle was well started Scarlet decided she needed to confront her.

As soon as she started to pry into what was happening it was nearly too easy, Ailsa crumbled. The extra time to consume another bottle of wine also seemed to help her willingness to share.

'I made a promise to Flynn, to your family, and the elders never to tell you the things you've forgotten Scarlet. I promised. And you've forgotten so many things; some wonderful, some not; things we never speak of, because they're too sad. I wondered if you'd ever suspected your life is not as it seems. You learn many stories in class, it only seemed like a matter of time,' Ailsa spun her words out, frazzled like one of the blabbering elders who spent too much time with their heads in books.

'Well, it'd be Lux or Archer who would have caught onto anything in class, the rest of us completely zone out,' Hudson said, resting back from a food coma.

Scarlet wasn't sure what it was that she was supposed to suspect but helped Ailsa onto the couch so she could calm down. Her worried eyes looked up into Scarlet's. 'Look at you now, a child whose gained the scent of endless summers, filled with so much life. You'll never lose that. None of you will. As Amari, Archer and I are born to this life; intuitive with nature. All to serve Grinnwick, now bound in the time loop protecting everyone as best we can, holding the secrets only time knows. You three aren't, you should be free; you have lives you need to live. Many things have been hidden from you, so many lies. And now someone's dead,' Ailsa practically wailed.

'Gee, she's lost it,' Hudson noted, looking extremely uncomfortable.

'What do you mean. Who's dead?' said Lux. Scarlet's fears built up – was she talking about Flynn? Was that the news, what all these secrets were about, had they got word about him?

She felt the rain echo on the ground above their quarters, the mere memory of it happening just like this when she found out Flynn had left for good.

'The princess,' sighed Ailsa. Scarlet breathed out in relief at the simple words.

'That has nothing to do with any of us,' replied Scarlet.

'But it does, you see Flynn left because he heard she was alive. That was the reason he left, to try and save her. He obviously couldn't do it. But he knew out of the two of you that you were in a much safer position than she was, and he only wanted to help her. A fool's mission, many before him had failed– he was just a boy, a boy in a world bigger than him,' Ailsa's eyes drooped further with each word, tears falling gently down her cheek.

'But he doesn't know her. Why would he find the need to save a princess? How do you even know she's dead?' Scarlet found herself rambling. It didn't matter what Scarlet had to say, Ailsa had quickly fallen asleep. The drink had taken over and lulled Ailsa into a world of dreams. Scarlet pulled the blanket over her and turned to the others who all sat in silence. The boys didn't touch any more food, they were just as unsure about what Ailsa had said as Scarlet and Lux.

'The princess is dead. Great. I still don't get why that's a big deal for us; why now? I remember her from before, she was a prisoner, she was eternal people said. Old bat had to fall off her perch sooner or later,' Hudson said, standing up from the table. 'I'm off to bed.'

Scarlet watched him walk up the stairs, as Archer too stood up. 'Don't worry too much you two. You know Ailsa, she gets like this sometimes; dramatic. You both know this princess, we learn about her in class all the time; she was old, I mean they say she looked young, but she's older than any of you would have been if you lived out there all this time. Imagine living for near a thousand years, it was well past her time. It takes old, old magic for her to even live that long, she should be happy she saw centuries beyond her time,' he said, before heading up to bed too. Eventually Lux went to bed as well not long after the boys. Scarlet remained downstairs, and even with Ailsa asleep softly snoozing on the couch the room echoed of blank space; the feeling that everything was about to be pulled out from her feet surrounded her. Remembering this feeling from the moment she found out Flynn had left – like her insides had dropped and the reality of every little thing seemed big, scary – all Scarlet could do was find her way to bed too and close her eyes.

Dawn had barely begun when she heard voices downstairs; Lux was still fast asleep in the bed next to her, Flynn's bed. She often grappled with his loss of presence in her life. His wit matched hers perfectly, he always knew the right thing to say to bring her out of any mood. If he was here he'd undoubtedly tell her to buck up, carry on, a new day is here, and the world awaits with a gleeful smile. It was reminiscing like this with herself that enabled her to get up and go on. After being on edge all through the night Scarlet hesitated to go down and find out who was there. Her weariness of the early morning an added weight for an already curious string of events.

Eventually she succumbed to finding her feet and found Dawson with Elder Jackson in the doorway entrance. Their presence didn't seem as much of a shock to her as it should have. She greeted them politely. Elder Jackson woke Ailsa and helped her to a glass of water.

'You look frightened child,' Elder Jackson said. Scarlet waited for a moment before replying.

'Can you tell me what's happening? Why is a princess's death making everyone go crazy? Was she really the reason why Flynn left? He's just a kid, how could he even help her?'

'Hmm,' Elder Jackson frowned, and looked unsteadily at Dawson. 'Child, I don't know what Ailsa has told you. We were mistaken, the High King Geoffrey Thorn's daughter Princess Ava has not passed. However, it is a wakeup call for myself, and the other elders. You see it would be ending the line to the throne in their world, a blood link that is tied to the fabric of everything as we know it. And perhaps it's loss will leave more damage than foreseen, but for now it remains. Flynn, as I said not long ago, followed his own path. Something called to him, and he believed he needed to answer it. You sweet child. We find you on the edge of all of this. Orphaned and lost in a world you never would have known otherwise. Stars fall out of the sky; the sea flows with an ever-changing current all the way around our world, and you are the heart that holds a missing piece, a piece that needs to be returned to Grinnwick. It is something we cannot hold onto any longer.'

'...I'm leaving. Why does some princess supposedly dying make you think it's time for me to leave?' Scarlet said interrupting Elder Jackson.

He sighed. He looked again to Dawson, who sat down beside Scarlet.

'This is not your home anymore. It never should have been. It may sound silly, but there is a balance to this world. And part of it is askew at the moment, the elders believe that they have taken too much from the world, which now needs to be restored,' Dawson said.

'Then what home do I have? They should have just left me there in the ruin all those years ago.'

'Do not feel as though you are losing out by leaving here but remember what you are gaining. You are re-joining the world you were always meant to be a part of. You have been safe for some time. But time comes for all of those who are not from here, we can't be greedy even when the hearts are as kind as yours, dear one. Besides you are not the only one who doesn't belong here, two others time has come to join the world and live the lives they are meant to,' Elder Jackson said.

Even through his whimsical manner Scarlet understood what he was saying. But was it silly to think that maybe they might not belong out in the real world either?

When Flynn left and Ailsa and the elders had said it wasn't her time to go into Grinnwick, they convinced her to stay, to not chase after him. The desire to run after him was overwhelming yet extinguished by their reason. The elders believed that this was now her time to go, but being convinced was just as utterly confusing as it was when they convinced her to stay.

There was no choice in the matter, the truth being that this was the Amari's home, and she was subject to their ruling. Practically she felt she was much like that of a pet that they no longer wished to care for.

Lux and Hudson were subject to their decisions too and Elder Jackson explained they would join her and return to Grinnwick.

He also issued that she needed to with Dawson first as only a certain number of people could leave at once.

In what seemed like a blur Scarlet walked hand in hand with Ailsa. Not questioning any further – any fears she had kept her in silence. While her friends were still fast asleep, they may as well have been on another planet while she was being swept off, none of them aware of her departure, or their departures to come. Unaware if she would even be able to say her last goodbye to Archer.

Hours ticked by and Scarlet waited, in a cold room near the elders book storage, with a case sitting next to her. She had been given different clothes which she now wore; a heavy skirt, and ruffled top, with hard leather shoes that made her feel oddly constricted. Itchy and uncomfortable in the fabrics Scarlet wanted nothing more than to rip them off, but instead did her best to ignore it, as an overwhelming numb feeling consumed her; paralysed by the unknown. She hadn't heard when or how Lux or Hudson would be joining her. Stupidity filled her mind; why didn't she ask for Dawson and Elder Jackson to allow her to wait with Hudson and Lux? Why did she need to wait alone, was this notion of it being her 'time' a ruse for abandonment? Why did they tell her separately, why not wake them all? An emptiness filled her, everything she knew was about to be taken out from under her, and a great unknown was ahead.

Centuries had passed since she left Grinnwick. She would be journeying into a world so different from this one; How could she know how to act – how could any of them?

And Scarlet was racking her mind for what could connect her brother to an old princess. It was near pointless trying to pry answers out of anyone, no one seemed to tell her the entire truth. She had been taught to respect the memory of the Royal Thorn family of Grinnwick. They were from her time after all, the time where the Amari once flourished through the world. To many here the notion of their presence was second nature. Yet the idea that Flynn left because he was connected to the princess seemed completely ridiculous. And why was it that he alone thought he had the capability to save the last remaining princess. Surely, he was led to these choices, to the fool's errand.

Scarlet couldn't help thinking that if Flynn had gone to save the princess and they believed he possibly failed, did that mean something bad had happened to him?

Ailsa finally returned to Scarlet, with Dawson in tow, her face blotched and her hair a mess. Dawson took the case that sat by her side and waited at the door. Ailsa ran straight to Scarlet, hugging her and bursting into tears. 'I'm so sorry, I thought they might let me come with you.'

Scarlet almost sighed, that would have been the last thing she needed. The overly emotional woman before her, a newly caring version of Ailsa was strange enough. There was no way she could journey on having to look after her too, or deal with her snide remarks once her random burst of empathy left her.

'Where are the others? Aren't they coming with me? Why haven't they been brought to this room with me?' asked Scarlet.

'In time dear. They're back in our quarters, you remained here for your own... safety.' It was clear to Scarlet that she was holding back information.

'For now Dawson is taking you. He'll keep you safe. He will stay with you from now on,' Ailsa said, sounding like she was convincing herself more than anything. Scarlet on the other hand found she had no problem trusting Dawson. His smarts felt like the exact thing she needed outside in the real world.

'That's right, the other two will meet up with us on the other side of the veil,' he nodded back.

'I didn't think the Amari liked to leave the Village for long periods of time?' Scarlet asked him.

Dawson bent down and whispered. 'True. Lucky I'm not one of them.' He gave Scarlet a wink. With a clearer look into his eyes, the flow of energy that could be seen in the Amari wasn't there. How had she never noticed it before? Scarlet scoffed a laugh; it was a surprising fact, and one she wasn't sure made too much sense considering he was a watcher. Only Amari could be watchers, and they would need one to be able to navigate the forest.

'Not everything's as it seems, kiddo,' he said before leaving the room.

Scarlet went to question Ailsa instead, but before she could start the sentence Ailsa built up into a series of stuttering statements that began to jumble up through the tears.

'You'll be safer... so much happened back then; light and dark, and you... Stay out of trouble... Please,' Ailsa wiped away her tears and pushed Scarlet's golden wavy locks out of her face, finally pulling herself together for one last hug.

Scarlet searched for words to say along with the build-up of her own tears that were near impossible to hold back. 'I promise I won't forget you.' It seemed like the most important thing to say.

Secrets from the Other Side

'Move over,' whispered Mason, his stocky body squishing Bastian uncomfortably tight between his two friends. Sticks was on Bastian's other side and Bastian couldn't help but notice him glaring over at Mason, motioning him to hush. Bastian ignored the pair, peering down into the gap that opened in the ceiling below. He knew if he got caught, he'd pay for it one way or another. If not from Winslow himself; then more dauntingly, his mother. After all they had scurried their way into the ceiling above Harvey Winslow's private office not just for laughs, but because of what was unfolding inside.

Winslow was pacing, his brow sweaty, and a thick scent of sweat drifted up to them. There were three other men in there too that Bastian didn't recognise. Plus, one other; a man who was on a chair, passed out, beaten, bloodied, with his arms and legs tightly bound.

'He won't give us anything else,' bellowed one of the men below, he sounded more than a little aggravated.

'Tell me again Markus, how did you get him?' Winslow questioned the same man. Bastian got a small glimpse of the man named Markus, his dark locks atop of his head all tied up, and the small whisps of hair that crossed his dirty and bloodied face. A fierce look in his eyes.

'It was a camp, east of River Tundell—' Markus started, before he was cut off.

'At the turning point. That's barely three days' journey from here,' the second man said.

30

'Yeah, there would have been dozens of them.'

'What happened to the rest?' Winslow asked.

'Well, I gave them the benefit of the doubt, I listened throughout the night to their whispers. They thought they were hidden in the thickness of the woods. Their notions were warped – no man I know would ever think that way. Thinking that it is their right to take our children, to leave the remaining people torn and ruined in their wake. The sheer enthusiasm some of them showed at causing monstrous devastation, all in the name of Van Helm. The men and I showed them mercy; a swift death... lost two of mine but only this one of theirs remains,' Markus rubbed his knuckles.

Bastian could see Winslow thinking as he remained quiet. He was sure he wanted to know more about those conversations, Bastian himself wanted to know every snippet. He felt himself edging closer to the opening of the crack in the roof, but as the lights flickered, he paused, still as possible, not wanting to draw attention.

'Did you hear any specifics?' demanded Winslow, as terrifying as Markus seemed, Winslow wasn't backing down to him. Bastian hadn't expected him too.

'I heard them speak of what they had done to villages south of here. Of how they had twisted the people against each other before they even infiltrated. How when they finally did take a town, they didn't care what state it was left in as long as the people were subdued enough. I heard them say the commander wanted more, he wanted his presence felt everywhere,'

'Well, we already knew he wanted that,' chimed in one of the other men.

'Did you? So, you're prepared then for when these men take us all for fools. Don't you question what he wants from us once he gets us all in his grasp? What he intends to do with all of that control?' Markus asked.

'Your families will be torn apart, they will leave their most seasoned killers to keep any eye on things, you will work only for them, you will work only as part of their plan, and any resistance will be met more harshly than any of us could imagine,' Winslow noted, almost conceding to the inevitability.

Winslow stepped closer, crouching down to be at head height with their prisoner. He stared at him for a moment then smacked him over the head; stirring awake the bloodied man.

'What's your name soldier?' Winslow ordered. The man before him stirred back to consciousness. Bastian almost felt bad for him – as he awoke, the Grinnwick Guard soldier seemed a lot younger.

'Percival,' he said, still unsteady, gathering himself and taking in his surroundings.

'Percival. How long have you worked with the Grinnwick Guard?' Winslow said.

'What's it to you?'

'Answer the question.' Markus pressed, taking a firm grip on Percival's shoulder, increasing the pain from a bloodied wound.

'Three years,' Percival winced.

'And what are your scouts doing this far north?' Winslow demanded.

Percival said nothing, he just looked around at each of them. Bastian could tell he'd already endured some brutal beatings. So why was he hesitating?

'NOW,' barked Winslow.

'You think the worst thing you could do to me is anywhere near as bad as what will be done to me if the Guard finds out I talked?' Percival spat on the ground.

Markus pulled back for a moment, looking around the room then turning back.

'Why do you fight for them?' Winslow asked.

'There is no choice. Southern born and strong, we are taken to training as soon as we are old enough – that is how it has been for generations now, we don't know any different.'

Winslow looked across to Markus, Bastian wished he knew what they were all thinking.

'Your family boy, what of them?' Winslow asked.

'We don't hold family names. We are one of the Guard and that is where our loyalties lie. To be bound to the Guard, and only the Guard.'

'We know this Winslow. They've done this for centuries, those who aren't of the court are sculpted into their perfect soldiers. These boys become the men who feel elevated amongst the rest of us. They are shells of the boys they use to be, and to them we are savage, worthless, a dent needed to be smoothed out,' Markus said.

'I know, but we have never had one of them so young at hand, have we. If he can remember where he was from, maybe we can get a better picture of how far they've spread. How many villages they have picked off. We haven't had word from south of the rapid rangers for years, and there are at least a dozen towns spread through there,' Winslow bellowed, his frustrations rising, and fear creeping into his tone.

Bastian felt shivers down his spine – the reality of the world outside their town had seemed so far away. He had heard that children were always taken; but this fear never sparked so true than right now.

'You won't hear anything from the rangers, we poisoned their water; forced them all out,' Percival sounded almost proud.

Bastian felt his whole body go rigid. It had been true; he hadn't heard of a traveller passing through from the rangers since he was six. He hadn't thought much of it till now, only that they weren't travelling for the past few seasons.

'You think it wise to sound proud boy,' Winslow warned.

'Do with me what you want, I am dead either way,' Percival nearly growled at them, spitting blood out of his mouth.

'You think we are going to give up so easily?' Markus pressed.

'You sliced the throat of every soldier I travelled with… don't see why I'd be any different.'

Bastian could tell that no one was pleased with this retort, if not by the way their bodies stiffened, but from the hard punch that Winslow gave him.

'It is mercy compared to what you would have done. The protection of our people was worth every man we took. Looking at you, your complete lack of empathy for the people outside of your realm, what would be left of our own people?' Winslow said.

'I've seen other towns. I've seen the piles of bodies. I've seen the men take women, brutal and disrespectful, then cast them aside. Horrors like that aren't one a good society should be built on. You call us savages, but I fight to protect the ones I love from the madness you and men like you set out to inflict. There is no honour in fighting, but surviving your world brings out the monsters in us all,' Markus said.

34

'You talk in circles. Any effort to go against the Grinnwick Guard is futile. You squashed a small group of us, but you aren't truly ready, in time more will come. They are smarter than the oafs you think us to be. Some may have even infiltrated your community, staking out the area, you will never even see them coming,' Percival mocked.

'Give us names,' Winslow demanded.

'You think they would give a low-level soldier like me names… that would be way above the knowledge we have access to.'

Bastian felt himself frustrated, he couldn't even imagine how annoyed Winslow and Markus were becoming.

There was a knock at the door, a shift of bodies as it opened. Bastian felt Sticks knock him, a stupid notion considering Bastian was well and truly aware that the person arriving was none other than his own mother.

She glanced at the soldier in the chair. 'Markus, Winslow.' She said in a proper voice to the rebel fighter.

Bastian couldn't believe she was there, what did she know about rebel fighting? She would have smacked him raw for even being in Winslow's Hall; he had no clue what she would do if she found him watching them. The townspeople of Bellevue Point thought she was a witch, her garden remedies signalled her as an outsider to many; that was until they needed her, not that they acknowledged her in kind after benefitting from her cures.

'Liz, did you bring what I asked?' Winslow said.

She handed him over a small bottle. 'You won't have long. Get what you can out of him, and quickly.'

'How's the boy?' Markus asked her. Bastian was hanging on to every word. It was a whole life he didn't know of his mother's. How did she know this man, who was he to her? Why did they trust her so much to let her in their interrogation room?

'He's good. Will he be safe here?' she asked Markus, who looked over to Winslow before he spoke.

'We don't know. I can't make any promises, it doesn't look good though,' Markus replied.

Sticks was hitting the side of Bastian so much that Bastian had to push him to stop. He knew they were talking about him. How did this stranger even know his name?

Bastian wanted answers, he didn't want to move. He wanted to hear the rest of the interrogation.

'Be safe,' Liz said before she made to leave the room. Bastian's eyes were fixed on the door even after she left.

Winslow moved to pour the contents of the small bottle down Percival's throat, even as he squirmed to try and avoid it Winslow became firmer with his grip around his mouth.

They waited a moment; it must have needed time to take full effect. Bastian was curious to see what it was his mother had concocted.

Winslow sat on a chair in front of Percival.

'Tell me, are you scared?' Winslow asked.

'Of course,' replied Percival.

'Do you want to live?' Winslow continued.

'Yes,' Percival answered.

'How many have you killed?'

Percival paused, 'More than fifty.'

'Do you regret anything?'

'I cannot regret actions committed in the name of our Commander; it is for the good of our world.'

'What are the names of infiltrators known to you?' Winslow asked, waiting heavily on the answer.

Percival looked like he did not want to answer but was bursting to blurt out what he knew…

'Rick Walsh, Desmond Creedy, Juniper Reidddd…' Percival stated before he paused suddenly. His words jumbled together, and he looked fearful for a moment. Bastian could see his body start to shake ferociously; he was not in control, something was coming out from his mouth, and with the shaking his chair fell to the floor. Still, limp, Percival didn't move.

Bastian's senses jumped into overdrive; shock hit him until Mason motioned backwards beside him. He and Sticks both followed. Climbing back down the outside of the hall and climbing into the large opening, which could only be describes as a whole opening dedicated to sleeping; it was tidy enough – each tarp like bed had blankets draped over the top and scattered belongings underneath them. With the light shining in the whole room was noticeably empty. This was where Sticks and Mason lived, a shelter for kids like them with nowhere else to go. Bastian was almost bursting to discuss what they'd seen; he didn't have the words though.

'Can you believe it?' blurted Sticks, 'that was one of them; a real soldier of the Grinnwick Guard. Well, he was.'

'What in the Corazon Forest was that? He just died.'

'I can't believe it,' Mason whispered, as gobsmacked as the rest of them.

'Bass, your mum,' Sticks noted. 'I didn't realise she was helping the rebels. Every time I'm there for dinner she's always dead set against you hanging 'ere,' Sticks added.

'Yeah, I had no clue. She must be worried if she's helping them out.'

'Worried wouldn't even begin to explain it,' a familiar voice snapped from behind them.

In the doorway his mother stood. She wasn't yelling. No this was beyond being in ordinary trouble.

'Come here now,' her voice was calmer than it should be. Bastian led the three of them closer to her.

She took a deep breath. Bastian was waiting for her to start shouting. His fear kept his head down, he couldn't even look her in the eye.

'Do any of you think that was a good idea; to witness what happened up there?' she asked almost curiously.

How did she know? She always knew, it was silly of him not to think about it before. Her senses and abilities were what gave her the nickname of the Earth Witch by the people who grew up in the town of Bellevue Point. Sticks always teased him by calling him the son of a witch. In truth it was old remedies and concoctions of herbs that she provided that the people feared, but her overall sense of knowing was something he had come to accept as her gift.

'That soldier you saw was a young man, his mind warped. You may think nothing of it, but he was killed by those he serves, the Grinnwick Guard's ability to shut him down at any time is in their hands. Does that not scare you?' she asked them all.

Bastian thought that Percival was mad, he knew something bad was happening to him, but he thought that perhaps he had taken some potion before he was captured, that he ended it himself.

'Can they do that to anyone?' Bastian asked.

'We are finding out more every day, but it seems to be an update of their younger generation of soldiers, some form to harness them to their cause. And think about it, if they can cause their own people to die, if they can use their systems to force out chaotic behaviours and manipulate boys, what respect do they have for those not under their command?'

'If they came here…, would they turn us into them?' Sticks asked.

'There could be worse fates, but in truth the closer their strength reaches, the more of the unknown lies ahead,' she replied. 'Now, if the three of you don't want me to inform Markus and Winslow that you were watching them, please get your butts moving, I'm putting you three to yard work.' She motioned them towards the door.

'Let's go,' she bellowed when they hesitated.

Bastian, Sticks and Mason all rushed out the door. When they had finally moved down to the main hall and out into the exit the three of them followed her out. None of them were willing to question her punishment. Sticks and Mason probably respected her almost as much as he did.

Bastian moved up to her side.

'Mum, how do you know that Markus man?'

She didn't stop walking, but he knew she was working out what to say.

'He's your father,' she said simply.

Bastian stopped, but then quickened to catch back up.

'Why didn't you tell me he was here?' he asked. He had only ever had little comments of his father here and there. There was no hate between them, he could always tell by the fond way she spoke of him. But she said when she found out she was pregnant with him, her priorities changed. She left his father so he could fight the Grinnwick Guard… she often called him impulsive and fearless. But overall that she had no idea if he was even alive.

'I should have told you. I don't want you to hate him, he stayed away because I wanted you to have a better life. You're the future, and you deserve more than either of us can offer.' She answered. 'But it seems that there might not be escape from things to come.'

'What does that mean? Will I be able to meet him?' Bastian asked, almost nervously, the idea that the ferocious man was his own father was barely tangible. The opportunity to meet him would be incredible. He couldn't wait to tell Sticks and Mason.

'You may. In time though, he doesn't visit often. But I think perhaps you will be safer somewhere further away,' she said more to herself than to Bastian directly.

'Where to?' Bastian questioned.

'Somewhere away from all this rising tension,' she said, lost in thought.

'Mum, you can't protect me forever.'

'I know, I need you to be able to protect yourself. Your fathers too busy for that, and I can't provide you with more than my senses. I feel your future depends on you becoming more than this little town can offer.'

Into the Wild

The idea of heading into the unknown brought on a fear within Scarlet that she had never felt before. The notions of what her future would hold seemed daunting.

Trying to focus on her horse, Scarlet quickly found her new case had been packed onto its back. The horse itself had a jet-black coat that felt like silk as she brushed her hand across its back. Dawson looked exhausted, more than any other time she'd seen him in the practice ring. 'Just you and me kid,' he said, as he helped her up onto the back of the horse before jumping onto his own mare. 'Lux and Hudson are meeting us outside the Village, Milo's bringing them out,' Dawson started, but quickly jumped in to answer the question on Scarlet's lips. 'We can't all head out at once, the Veil can only stand so much displacement at a time.

'Now, come on. Better get going, or we aren't going to make good time.'

Scarlet had ridden before, but never for this long. There was never that far for them to go, and the slow pace made it feel like it was going to take an eternity to reach the forest's edge. Looking back toward the Amari Village for what she could only assume was the last time, it looked empty and quiet. She felt an eerie sensation that perhaps Archer would run out from a hill, waving to her to capture their last goodbye. While the twins would follow, she would never laugh with him again. Never wander the valley or climb a tree. She thought of the nerdy, neurotic boy, her best friend, who she knew would no doubt be an elder, just as his mother was, and that his life was laid out before him. There was a comfort in knowing exactly who he was. His absence now only marked the moment for Scarlet that all she knew was behind her, only to be held in her memories.

Only when Dawson urged the horses to quicken their pace towards the trees of the forest did Scarlet turn back to the path ahead.

Knowing that Dawson was a man of few words usually wouldn't stop her from the delightful thrill of trying to spark something that he could talk to her about, but for some reason this didn't seem the time. This point in their journey Scarlet kept to herself, with too many of her own concerns on her mind to bother with such antics.

'Don't know if you know kid – we'll be heading into the Corazon Forest of course – but beyond our borders is where the forest thickens, and the danger really begins. It's no picnic in there, so be vigilant. Notice anything out of the normal, don't hesitate to let me know. Might just save our necks,' Dawson said. He was curiously staring at Scarlet's lack of reaction. She may not have been that far into the forest before, but she knew of its abilities, its curious nature, the way that it had a mind of its own. The stories they'd been told never scared her, the forest if anything seemed like it was misunderstood, that its nature to turn people away was a part of its beauty.

The blue sky soared above them as they rode on swiftly, its light disappearing but for a few rays that broke through once they were surrounded by the thick forest, allowing the path before them to be seen. Goose bumps quickly rose down the back of Scarlet's neck from the icy chill that blew their way. Quiet and in thought, as they passed an opening by a steady stream, Scarlet remembered all too clearly being with Flynn when he used to take her fishing at that exact spot.

Drops of tears fell from her face, as she thought about how it seemed so long ago that Flynn too left, but how it only felt like yesterday when she sat in this opening with him. Like him, she was to go out into the wilderness of the world. In the moment that she found out he had left Scarlet wanted nothing more than to follow behind him, to keep their family together. In her heart she knew Flynn would have wanted her to stay behind. She wondered if he would have expected that not long after she would follow his same path.

Slowly the forest thickened as they reached the edge of the Amari lands. The ground underneath them became rockier, leading Dawson to slow down their pace. Scarlet unsteadily was tossed around on her horse's back, her sides brushing across the rough branches at their side. Focusing on keeping upright, as she clenched tightly to the horses neck. Her head banging abruptly into the horse when Dawson came to a sudden halt.

'We're about to pass through the time veil. You won't see it but by the gods you will definitely feel it.'

As he slowly motioned ahead of them, Scarlet looked to see the veil. The speckles of light that broke through only captured the dust particles that blew up around them from the horses' steps. Dawson's mare moved ahead, Scarlet watched closely as his horse began to shake its head and nearly throw the usually skilled rider Dawson off balance. Dawson's eyes were clenched shut and he appeared dazed holding onto his mare.

Scarlet hesitantly followed; she noticed her horse's reaction as it became agitated underneath her. Unsure of its own motions her horse became restless on the rocky terrain. A wave of her own confusion swept through her. The woods began to spin. Her head heavy, and her horse's movements were not helping as she swayed around. She held onto him, keeping her eyes shut, and waited for the feeling to pass. A feeling that seemed to last a lot longer than it should have, but eventually she felt Dawson take her reins and lead them onwards. The feeling seemed to pass over him quite quickly; Scarlet presumed he had no doubt passed through multiple times, so he was likely used to such a strange feeling. In time she too opened her eyes, but it may have been an hour later as her head was still spinning. In the time that passed the rocky terrain had ended, and the path ahead looked longer than ever before.

Dawson suddenly climbed down from his mare. 'We're leaving them here. They won't take us any further,' he said, helping her down and looking at her confused face. 'This forest has a way of bringing out the craziness in any beast. Drives the narrowest of men mad, in the end. That's how we keep so well protected from the outside. The horses will only slow us down and draw attention from other beasts,' Dawson explained, while taking Scarlet's bag off the back of her jet-black horse and strapping it up onto his own back. He then directed the horses back to where they had come.

'Why bring them through the bubble then? It seems stupid to have brought them this far... Will they be able to get back? How do you know we won't get lost without them? And we won't be driven mad either?'

'Ah, there is the trickery of things isn't it. You see, I don't know. But the forest, while it drives others out or even to madness, it knows a true heart when one is inside. It'll let us find our way, you just have to know where to look. As for the horses, they will find their way back, they are drawn to the safety of the Amari, their speciality lies in generations of being a part of the Fae's world. Besides, with them we have already travelled quite far. I think you were knocked around from the veil, or bubble as you call it. Possibly you haven't noticed or couldn't tell through these trees that the light beaming on you now is from the moon and not the sunlight,' he said walking on.

Scarlet looked above, she had not thought about it, light still shone through, albeit not that much light. Knowing if the sun or the moon caused it truly perplexed her.

'Do you know where to look then? You have a map of some sort? Because you said you weren't one of the Amari, and I thought it was only people with their blood who could navigate the woods. That's what Elder Jackson said in class,' Scarlet asked, only to be responded to with a heavy laugh.

'Can't map this forest. It'd just end up different the next time you came back. And I may not be one of the Amari, but they aren't the only ones who can talk to the forest, and they're not the only ones with connections to the ancient beings. You see long ago there were some people who could speak to the forest directly.

'They are said to have spoken with a woman called Niamh, the Heart of the Corazon Forest. She's not much use to us though, thing of stories they reckon. Some people do believe that she is real, that her descendants are witches with dark powers,' he said laughing. 'Don't know if I believe that myself, but out here I have my own tactics.'

Leading the way, he continued down a form of path and came to a stop, pulled out his knife and cut into a tree. Dawson placed his hand on the opening he had made. He waited; for what, Scarlet didn't know. Closing his eyes for a moment he opened them only to lead the way further into the forest.

Scarlet wondered if it was magic that helped guide Dawson. Was it like that of the magic that Elder Jackson had shown, or something entirely its own. They had been told several stories about ancient magics that used to be associated especially with the forest, but that within the world of Grinnwick these had been long forgotten.

Dawson saw Scarlet look upon him strangely.

'Whether or not Niamh is real it doesn't matter, her heart – the heart of the forest's power – still remains true where vibrations run through its roots. I may think I know every bush and root that has buckled up inside of the Corazon Forest, but it is best to be sure we are heading along the right path. Especially when this forest likes to play ticks, even on the best of us.'

'And you can feel the movement?' Scarlet asked.

'Here,' he said, ushering her towards a tree near where he stood. He showed her where to place her palm into the bared part of the tree.

It was instant, a strange wave through her. Not like when they passed the invisible veil but a warm sense that she felt beneath her hand. The feeling of pressure inside her palm escalated, like all her blood rushed to that one spot, a surge of energy all converging between her palm and the tree. Looking at her hand on the tree a white glow began to bloom behind it. The same light then began to turn into forms of leaves falling from the tree. They floated down as though the ghost of the tree was laying a path out before her in the direction of where they needed to go, and a growing confidence inside her moved towards its motion. She looked around her, a surprise gift of magic lit the darkness. It's power continued surging, as she moved to follow her hand came off the tree and the leaves slowly disappeared.

'Magic,' she whispered.

'You feel it?' Dawson said, beaming through his crooked smile, as he knew exactly what she felt.

'Sometimes you need to believe in things, even if you don't understand them little one. Trust in the unknown, that always leads to the greatest adventures.'

'It was beautiful, is all magic like this?' Scarlet put her hand back to the tree.

Dawson looked at her curiously, 'Tell me, what do you see?' He asked.

'The light of the tree? The forest dropping leaves to light the way. It's incredible, do all the watchers see this all the time?' Scarlet asked.

Dawson rested his hand on her shoulder, 'No one will ever see the world the way you do.'

'What do you see?' Scarlet asked.

'Unlike yourself, I feel the path; like I'm being pulled towards the right direction,' Dawson answered.

'Is it strange that I can see that power?' Scarlet didn't know much of magic, but from what she did, it was something a human like herself didn't often possess. The forest allowing her to experience only made it that much more intriguing.

'Perhaps unusual, but not surprising. The forest trusts you enough to show you it's purest forms.'

Both of them followed the path that had been laid out ahead. Scarlet noticed that even though she had let go of the tree the feeling that it was the right way stayed with her. She longed to move towards it.

Dawson eventually started slowing their pace, looking for a tucked away opening to set up a small camp.

It wasn't long before Scarlet sat by a raging fire listening to Dawson hum as he prodded at a stew of freshly caught rabbit that they'd trapped. She was sure she knew the song, but didn't know where from, perhaps when she was a child, a spark of memory that was only held by her forgotten past. It reminded her of Flynn, of being rugged up and cosy while the cold from outside echoed. Scarlet couldn't remember the words. 'What's that song?' she asked.

Dancing on water, a fealty to offer.

The light of an ocean, and the heart of one man.

Once a flicker now a flame, time holds no love for those to blame.'

Dawson sang out the lines.

'I can't quite remember the name, nor the rest. Always been terrible with words. Suppose half of those lyrics aren't even right.'

Scarlet moved over closer to him, cosying into the side of his jacket, allowing herself to feel comfortable. 'I thought it sounded marvellous.'

The constant breaths of her new companion eased her. 'Best get some sleep, I'll keep an eye on things,' he said quietly. Throwing water over the fire.

'Will Hudson and Lux meet up with us soon?' Scarlet asked as she found herself closing her eyes.

'In the morning, I should think. Now get some sleep or you'll be useless tomorrow.'

Only after making Dawson promise that he would wake her if there was any sign of trouble did Scarlet fall quickly into a deep sleep.

***

The following morning dragged on with more trekking. Scarlet was sure that she was slowing down their pace. Part of her worried that because of her they would miss their meet up time with the others, whenever that was.

Dawson on the other hand didn't hurry them; he even stopped mid-morning so that they could practice some fighting techniques. Scarlet didn't mind the change of activity; at least these techniques required her to focus on something other than her thoughts and the endless path ahead of them.

Dawson was quick with his movements, always one step ahead. Talking them out before quickly taking action. They each used a broken twig as their weapon, but no matter how hard Scarlet tried she never once managed to get ahead of Dawson to attack.

'You're getting there,' he said, a sly smile on his face.

He didn't mind that it tired her out. The thrill of a practice fight made him laugh and working on honing Scarlet's skills made him glow.

Scarlet on the other hand felt determined to prove herself; she tried to keep up with his movements, even in her skirt. Usually, her practice fights ended in laughter because she never took them too seriously. This time she wanted Dawson to really see she could handle herself, even if everyone else didn't think she could, and especially since he saw her miserably lose to Jules.

The idea that they would be in the wide world was an overwhelming concept and the ability to fight would be a handy talent if she ever needed it. Her desire to prove herself to Dawson took over. Considering Dawson was a fully-grown man three times her size she thought that there'd be more of him to hit, deluding herself that somehow it would make it easier. But at every one of her misses he laughed, and Scarlet tried only harder to think ahead of his movements. A couple of times she even found herself close to knocking him with her stick. Still, she wasn't fast enough.

'Don't worry. You're doing well. You know what I think; I think you don't really want to hurt me, that's why you keep missing,' he joked, leaving himself wide open for Scarlet to knock him on the side.

'Maybe you shouldn't have looked away,' Scarlet said cheerfully. Dawson did nothing but laugh at this, while pulling out water from his own sack for them to drink. Taking a seat, she was relieved for the rest. Scarlet sat opposite him, taking the water after him.

'Do you usually come out here on your own?' Scarlet took a great gulp of the water.

'Not too often, or I would have aged out long ago. But most of my time is out on the edge of the forest. Guess for a watcher like me, it's a lonely life,' he replied.

'Lonely? But you must have all sorts of friends back home. I mean you're Dawson, one of the best watchers on the western borders. I've heard Milo talking about you to Ailsa all the time... and why are you a watcher if you aren't Amari? I thought their fae blood was what made them watchers,' Scarlet rambled.

'Full of questions aren't you. In many ways you are right. I'm not Amari, so my senses can't classify me as a watcher. The bottom line is just because I wasn't Amari, doesn't mean I had less respect from their people. I have my own ways, so they saw me very much like a watcher. So much so that in time, I took the name, more as a sign of respect given by them. Still, more often than not people keep their distance. They know I'm different, much like they always knew you were. At the end of the day the ones who were usually excited to see me were you kids at the practice pits. Most of the Amari don't see me as a person anymore, but as line of defence; a relic from a time they would prefer to forget. I offered to take you kid, not only

50

because it was important, but because I get to go back out into the world as my own self again, something I never thought I'd get the chance to do.' Dawson looked off down the path.

The lines on his face that Scarlet had once thought to be youthful and full of joy now seemed older – there were added wrinkles against his eyes that looked strained from concern. The salted colour of his beard had increased, his grey eyes looked saddened, and his usually strong body looked weak as he hunched over sitting down.

'Out here will be different won't it, for both of us.' Scarlet said. It was the only thing she could think of that sounded hopeful. Part of her wanted to say that everything was going to be alright, it's what she wanted to hear.

'There is hope wherever our path lies as long as you believe,' Dawson said. Before Scarlet had a chance to question Dawson further an echoing noise from the shadows behind them caught both their attention. Dawson was up and standing ready to take on whoever waited.

Standing behind Dawson Scarlet was ready for whatever came, her practice fighting stick in hand.

'Scarlet,' called out a familiar voice from out of the shadows. It was Lux; she came running from the darkness, followed by Hudson and… Archer. Each of them was beaming at the sight of Scarlet and Dawson.

The three of them jumped right on top of Scarlet with a large group hug.

'I can't believe this, I actually thought I'd never see you again,' said Archer. 'We packed everything as quickly as we could, but Milo's given us a decent load extra I tell you that. My pack ain't light,' Archer continued, still beaming.

'What are you doing Archer, I didn't think you could come?' Scarlet said, gobsmacked with his presence, elated that they were all here.

'Couldn't let one of us stay behind, while the rest of us go into Grinnwick. Besides, imagine he had to stay back with Ailsa on his own,' Hudson said, his eyes shocked in fear of the thought.

'It's insane, but I love it. I mean it's the real adventure that we've always dreamed,' Lux said, continuing to talk a million miles an hour.

Scarlet listened to their version of events from the moment they woke up to a quiet house; finding Ailsa sitting on her bed, blubbering on. It only took them a few minutes after finding out she had left. Ailsa had told them that Hudson and Lux were going to meet up with her, but was met by a barrage of pleas for Archer to come too. They were delayed in leaving by the time they got the okay from Elder Jackson for Archer to come along.

'Okay, Okay,' interrupted Dawson, a stern look covering his face that would have scared Scarlet had she not known him. 'I thought this would be the case young Archer Baines. Whatever you were thinking leaving poor Ailsa alone like that; I don't want to be the one to tell her you've all ended up dead, so turn your little shoes around now. She should at least be able to keep one of you.'

'What? No. He's not going anywhere. Ailsa sent us on our way. See she packed us rations of her fresh cob loaf and told Milo to give him a fresh set of clothes too. Besides, she's mostly being dramatic, having us around does her head in most of the time. She'll be happy for the peace,' said Hudson, opening his backpack to show the wrapped bread.

'Yeah we are all going, I mean what kind of friends would we be if we left someone out of the adventure?' Lux boasted.

'The worst,' added Archer, with the slyest of smiles.

52

'Where's Milo anyway? He would have had heart failure, trying to get all three of you and him through the veil,' Dawson said looking out for Milo in the distance. 'Mr Baines, I understand you think this is an adventure, but you're not a watcher, you've not yet been subjected to too much time displacement, you can still go back and live a happy life. Who knows what will come of you out here? The Amari are creatures of habit, there are traits to you that will not sit well out here. That others will not understand, or even tolerate.'

'Yeah. Yeah. I know. It's not like time slows down out here though… I can always go back when I'm older if I want,' Archer said.

'Time displacement doesn't always work like that boy. As Scarlet likes to call the Amari village, it's a bubble. A place cut off from time itself, everything inside its own; the ecosystem, the seasons, a safe haven for those inside. You were born there, so naturally once you leave that bubble, your safety is gone, time as it's meant to be resumes… you can go back, yes. But time has found you now, your already being factored into its wheelhouse. If you find you want to return, it may be harder than you think,' Dawson warned.

Archer looked at him almost fearful, then with ease he said, 'what will be, will be. These guys are my family, I can't see a reason I'd ever abandon them.'

Scarlet looked curiously at Archer for a moment – he was giving up everything to be here, his desire to follow in his mother's footsteps would be hindered if he followed her.

'You sure?' she interrupted him.

'It's okay. You guys are my family, there is nothing left for me there.'

53

'An eternal life boy, you know that. Fae blood like yours lingers longer than that of the people out here. Coming out here your life will go on. You will outlive all those you say you love,' Dawson warned, his serious manner more intense than they had seen before.

'But I will live,' he smiled.

A Way Out

Every one of them welcomed the fear of the unknown. They stood tall and gave in to the fate that was about to befall them. Bastian was taught to question everything, but this wasn't the time for questions; he would only find out what was to come by keeping his mouth shut.

Strangers to each other, waiting in silence, seven in total; five boys and two girls. Three of them kept their heads down, looking at their feet. Bastian's was one of the ones who didn't; his eyes were wide open, looking around the underground complex. Nothing too engaging was placed in the room around them, except for a single painting that was a blur of autumn colours spread across the small canvas. The rest of the room was a plain steel structure with the only light coming from the harsh flickering lights above.

As hard as it had been to leave his mother, it had been her constant urging that led him to make this decision.

The past few months an eerie knowing began to consume her mind. Taking caution at the smallest incidences. Looking to the signs; food shortages, missing persons, heaving taxes, most uncommonly a turn in the summer weather as the skies fell endlessly. Her belief that the safety in their small town had been warped since the Grinnwick Guard soldier had arrived in their small corner of Grinnwick, and a lurking sense that the Grinnwick Guard was spreading closer towards them had left her fearful. She felt their days were numbered, that the Guard would reach them, that they would get their paws into him, her only child.

Bastian wasn't a child anymore though, nor was he a man. He understood his mother Liz's reasons for refusing to allow his father to take him in stride in all honesty he didn't know the man. It was his own fathers' choice to leave them, to allow them to run off. If they had not, Bastian wouldn't have grown up in a freer land dreaming of adventure with his two best friends. Both of which he wished could have joined him now. Sticks would be growing lankier by the day. There wouldn't be a bigger goof around, but he had always been there for him. His mother would say he was her second child, the rate that he ate her out of her kitchen. While Mason was a little quieter, stockier with less charm. Bastian often thought he reminded him of a muscle dog, that the more you got to know him the more you liked him. He was always a little rough at first, his gruffness often turned others away. They would be spending the remaining of the warm days by the beach, and journey to the swimming hole. He wondered how they managed without him, that they'd undoubtedly still be standing up to the bullies who hung around the markets of town. As well as dodgy travellers who lured in unsuspicious townsfolk to buy their fake goods. Sending all on their way, slowly claiming the streets as their own, even if the people of the town didn't know it. It was in these back streets, and by the Market places that Bastian had grown to find his own courage.

Still, Liz had other ideas on her mind and the joys of his youth were now being left behind him as she followed her gut. Turning to the only other man she had ever trusted, her father. A man who she barely knew, or who she barely spoke of, yet seemed she respected all the same.

Wanting Bastian to follow a path better than she could offer him, a life that would keep him safe. Knowing that her own father would help Bastian get through whatever dangers the future had in store.

'Not as reckless and foolish as you father. It'll be structured, you'll make something of yourself,' she'd assured him.

In truth, Bastian wasn't sure what it meant, and as hard as leaving her behind was, it was all she wanted, and she gave him little choice. In his heart he wished this meant they all stayed together.

So Bastian readied himself to leave; he didn't question his mother any further, he had heard her cries late at night; if this one thing he could do that would help keep her worries at bay he would do it. She wanted him to be able to survive any storm that came their way, and his grandfather was the person she trusted most to help him be that man. Not just anyone was able to go and study under men like her father she told him, it was one of the things she herself wished she could have done. Promising him that it wouldn't be forever, and that before he knew it, he would return to her, to their home.

Both Mason and Sticks' faces had been in shock as the black engine mover showed up at his front door. Neither of them whole heartedly wanted to believe that he was leaving. Bastian himself hadn't quite believed it. He had imagined the world outside of their town since before he could remember. As much as he loved the breeze of the sea, the bustling forests and noisy yet calm atmosphere of the town, it always seemed so small, so confined from the outside. Now that he was finally taking those first steps, he found he wasn't ready to let go of what was behind.

The driver didn't get out, he wound down the window of his huge van and said Bastian's name, telling him to get in the back. At fifteen Bastian still felt like a small child as he turned to his friends, both who he had come to know as brothers. Sticks as tall, lanky and awkward as ever waved, kind of in shock, while Mason nodded in encouragement, even behind his serious face.

Then he had looked to his mother, the best mother he'd ever known. Her face was a mess, he hadn't even left yet, and Bastian already felt a world away from her. He did this for her. No words escaped him, just a gentle nod to his friends and the need not to tear up as he embraced his mother one last time.

'Say hello to my father, won't you?' Liz said as she let go of Bastian for the last time. 'I'll see you soon boy, promise.'

The door of the steel room creaked, bringing Bastian back to the present, and with a quick jerk it opened.

A man entered not looking at any of the seven strangers who stood before him, but was transfixed on a list in his hands squinting at it through his glasses.

'Verne Greenleaf,' the man said.

The tallest of the boys, third in line standing beside him stepped forward, and the man in front of them glanced up for a moment then straight down. He seemed to be judging the boy, and writing down notes next to his name, making the confident looking boy seem uncomfortable as he looked around at the others.

'Gertrude Bell,' he said again, peering up from his glasses at a red-haired girl who'd stood forward wearing a hood that covered part of her face from Bastian's view. Her eyes were still at her feet.

'Felix Grovedale,' the man said next. A snobbish boy stood forward like he was a peacock on show, and Bastian would have rolled his eyes if he felt like that would have been acceptable in this situation.

'Bastian Conway,' the man said. Bastian stepped forward, he did not often use his father's surname and it was strange to hear it after his own. Brushing his messy brown hair from his face he tried to look as respectable as he could. Looking into the eyes of the man before him who seemed to peer at him a moment longer than he had the others.

Quickly he stepped back in place. Following him was Rudi Westford, a sharp cut looking boy who seemed to be shaking more than any of them. Mandy Ross was next. A tall, lanky girl, who looked like she was about to cry. And finally, Russ Kemp, a rounded cherry-cheeked boy, whose face was covered in freckles stepped forward, not blinking as the man peered over at him clearly looking at the size of his belly.

The man ahead took out a briefcase that held a small tool. He stepped up to each of them and one by one he inserted a chip into their wrists.

Pulling Bastian's hand towards him when it came to his turn, he quickly injected a small black chip, without giving Bastian a chance to stop him. Bastian looked down at its wrist, the pinch of pain was small and left no scratch, no blood, no trace that it had ever been inserted; yet he could feel it beneath his skin. Bastian had heard of these. He'd seen dodgy sellers try and sell discs in the markets that were supposed to do all kinds of things like strength boosters, and sense heighteners, but he himself had never trusted them. He had tried his best to stay off the grid as best as he could, here and now it didn't seem like he had a choice.

'These are your trackers; don't confuse them with whatever nonsense you've seen before. This is the real deal, and they'll help us follow you through the task ahead. Know this; it is only the beginning. If you all make it through the following task it will help us determine that you can manage any possible tasks or objectives that could be presented to you. No further questions will be answered until you pass, so please one at a time enter the door behind you,' the man said, holding his hand out towards them.

Bastian turned around as the others did. He was next to Verne and Gertrude. They all stepped in a line following Felix through the door.

Whatever he expected to face (not that he expected to face anything as soon as he arrived), this wasn't it. By the looks on Verne and Gertrude's faces they didn't expect this either. It didn't seem like anyone was prepared to admit it.

They were stuck out on a thin ledge, barely wide enough so that they could all fit on it.

The room around them was a vertical, narrow cylinder that would have been just as cold as the room they'd been in except for the heat coming down from above.

'A furnace?' he heard the boy named Russ question under his breath.

Bastian stared up; he could see the red embers beaming through a charred vent. It looked like the flames behind it were getting stronger and a rumbling made the hairs on his neck stick up. Because of course it should have been obvious… it was going to explode, it seemed almost ridiculous to not have thought that whatever this place was, it would've meant business, and endangering the lives of its applicants was a part of its plan. He at least had no concept of what he was going into, what were the others thinking coming to this place?

'Quick,' Verne called to them all before Bastian even got the chance. The others' voices were echoing around them in fear as they too realised the heat above them wouldn't be contained much longer.

'Follow me,' Verne said, and quickly took a step back into everyone before leaping off the ledge and to the other side of the large air cylinder.

Verne didn't fall, relief overcame Bastian; they had all expected him to fall but instead Verne grabbed hold of a ladder on the other side. He descended quickly, and it wasn't long before Mandy, Gertrude, Felix, and Rudi all jumped across after him. Bastian went to go too but noticed Russ quivering by the locked door behind them.

'Hey, Russ is it? We don't have many options here. We have to get out of—' Bastian was cut off, as part of the fire above exploded making them both duck down as close to the ledge as they could.

'I— I— I just can't,' Russ said his face covered in fear. He was frozen. The confident boy from the main room was gone. Bastian knew he wasn't going to get Russ jumping off this ledge, and in truth he didn't know what was down there either but the idea of burning to death didn't seem like a great idea.

'Look, I'm not leaving here without you, so we are just going to think of a new plan.' Bastian assured him. Without another word he looked around, thinking of the next best option if another burst of flame came at them. His heart quickly sank as he spotted a small square vent. He knew the pain of getting closer to the heat wasn't going to be their best chance, but it was their only option.

'As soon as I get up, I'm going to break that vent open. Then quickly jump up on my shoulders and you need to jump in,' Bastian said directing Russ towards the vent ahead.

'You're serious. But if another flame comes we'll burn,' Russ said.

'So, move quickly.'

He stood up feeling the sweat on his brow. He banged on the sealed shut vent.

'Will this help?' Russ said, handing him a flat metal bar.

61

Taking the bar he used the ends to unscrew the corners of the vent and pry it from the wall.

'Come on.' Bastian pushed Russ up and helped him into the vent above, feeling the ledge beneath them start to rumble and the heat above them increase.

Pushing the edges of Russ's feet in Bastian started pulling himself up.

He reached inside inch-by-inch as Russ moved deeper. Not quick enough. He winced in pain as another explosion reached his ankles. The heat in the vent was only building, and it didn't give Bastian the time to worry about the pain, his focus was on moving forward; or downward, to wherever the others were.

Making their way down the vent shafts wasn't any easier. Russ clearly didn't find it easy to manoeuvre his round belly through the tight space. However, after they made a quick right turn the shaft provided a vertical downward option, and as they moved their way into it Russ's roundness prevented the two of them from sliding directly down, avoiding a rather nasty fall.

Bastian found himself placing his feet on Russ's shoulders as they inched their way downward. He wondered what the others were facing at that moment. Bastian was happy to give his ankle a rest and take their time, but that relaxing feeling only lasted a few moments up until they saw a light at the bottom creeping up on them. Russ managed to kick out the tray beneath, and with the help of Bastian who pushed Russ from above they both pried themselves free, landing at the bottom of the cylinder room. The light from the fire was now so high up above, leaving them well out of danger and in the dark dusty cold.

'Oi, where have you two been?' Called Felix, grabbing their attention as they were both overwhelmed with the darkness around them, barely able to see a thing except for the small flicker of light from above, which did little to light the area they were in. Adjusting to their new conditions they saw the two corridors on each side. Each with glass black tinted doors covering their entrances.

Felix held in his arm a half a dozen books and handed two to each of them. Bastian looked up at him.

'What's this for?' Bastian asked. He was half distracted by his ankles, checking he was able to stand and move properly, they hurt but they wouldn't hold him back.

'Well, if you came down with the rest of us you'd know wouldn't you,' Felix said glaring across at Russ, who looked more than guilty for keeping them behind.

'Two groups, each with a pile of books. There was a note on top of each pile that said *Mission: Return the books to the library*. Verne took Rudi and the girls with him, leaving me stuck to wait around for you,' Felix sighed.

'You could have just gone on without us,' Bastian said, already sick of Felix's attitude.

'Nope. The doors track our sensors, and they would only let four through at most. They walked through first; doors wouldn't open again for me. They're tracking us remember, guess they knew you two would need an extra pair of hands,' Felix said dryly.

'Okay. But, how did the others know which way to go?' Russ piped up.

'Yeah from what I can tell it looks like there are two corridors out of here. Two doorways. How did they know it was right?' Bastian said.

'They didn't. There are no signs anywhere, but Verne was sure it didn't matter. That there would be obstacles both ways,' Felix said.

'That's true. But both groups can't go the same way, or we will just run into the same tasks. There'd be no point having two groups. Which way did they go?' Bastian asked.

Felix pointed to the corridor on the left and the black doors remained still as he led them all in front of it.

'The trackers probably have sensors to the doors. That's how they're forcing us to go separate ways, those pricks,' Felix said.

'Yeah well at least we don't have to choose which way, yet,' Bastian said, leading back to their door.

They waited in front of their door, and a red laser scanner horizontally scanned each of their wrists and allowed them in the glass door one at a time.

Bastian held his head high as he walked into the room; he wanted to be aware of everything, every part of him was alert.

They were faced with two large men standing at the end of a very small dusty room. Neither of them looked remotely friendly and they clearly weren't there to help give directions.

Bastian knew he could deal with this; he had done so on a number of occasions. He was used to having Sticks and Mason back him up, but he knew exactly how do deal with brute force when necessary; his years of experience on the streets, alleyways and down at Winslow's every now and then gave him his fair share of run ins with shady figures like these two. Always wanting to take something that didn't belong to them. He couldn't help it – whenever he saw thick-skulled bullies like these taking advantage of the people of his town, he was happy to have a go at them. Now all he had to do was protect a bunch of books against these knuckleheads.

'Who are you?' he asked, trying to find out exactly what the men wanted from them, apart from the books in their possession.

Neither bothered to answer. The first one instantly attacked. The vast size of the man only increasing with every step he took closer towards them.

Bastian pulled Russ to the side, close beside him as the man made to jump at them both. Keeping them both in the clear, for the moment. Felix was caught on the other side of the room.

Bastian could see his eyes were focused clearly on their books – their task was to retrieve them by whatever means it seemed necessary.

The two of them kept on dodging the one man. Bastian looked for a way out of the room. It wasn't until he saw that the other man hadn't budged from the moment they walked in, that his focus was drawn to why. There was a small square hatch above him, the kind that needed to be pulled down.

Bastian grabbed his books ready to use them like a swinging bat.

'Russ, give Felix your books,' Bastian yelled.

Doing as he said without question, leaving Felix with a very concerned look on his face, Russ threw him his additional books. Felix fumbled them all for a moment as the large brute of a man smiled at him in a menacing way.

'Drop,' Bastian barked to Russ.

As he dropped Bastian stepped back and took the small run up, taking a step up onto Russ's back, using the motion to lunge him at the man. With the books in his hand, Bastian swung and hit the man over the head with the force behind him. The man caught off guard turned to him, away from the others – he went to punch him, but his reflexes were slowed. As Bastian landed, he turned quicker than his opponent, punching him across the face, waiting until he was down before he knocked him out one last time.

'Wow,' Russ said.

Felix was slower to return the favour, Bastian hadn't realised he hadn't gotten to him in time to at least cop one punch from the first attacker. He would have felt worse, had his concentration not been taken by the other guard.

This man would have been double their age, muscles twice the size of the man they just faced and shaved sides of his hair that only made his jet-black eyes look mad.

'See that hatch boys, that's what we have to get to,' Bastian said.

'Get him out of the way, and I'll open it,' Russ said before they all took a step closer towards the jet-black eyed attacker.

Bastian was confident as he walked forward; he was already strong for his age and he stood up tall knowing that all he had to do was draw him out, away from the hatch.

Walking up Bastian went for the hit. But the man just ducked them with ease, even with his huge size he was even more agile than Bastian had suspected. Still Bastian could tell the man wanted to squish him like an annoying fly that buzzed around, and the more he tried to take him down the more he moved away from where the hatch stood. One of the swings that the attacker took at Bastian struck the left side of his shoulder pushing him across room, another impacted right across his face, leaving his cheek bones aching. The man swiftly kicked Bastian, and his already injured leg collapsed beneath him.

Bastian on the ground remained calm, panicking wouldn't help. He knew that. He held his focus as he went to get up and jump back in again to lure the man away, only to be relieved by Felix who came from behind.

Felix came out of nowhere and slammed their attacker – it wasn't strong, but it knocked his head against the wall. Confusion hit the man, and with a quick burst of luck Russ pulled down the hatch stairs which finished the man off, knocking him out.

Looking at the blank face of the large man Bastian took a deep breath; thankful he didn't have to endure another hit.

'Here,' Felix said, holding out his hand, pulling Bastian up and helping him up the stairs. 'You know I'm kind of glad I got stuck with you now. Don't know if Verne would have it in him to let himself get bloodied up to protect everyone. Wait, let's be honest, I've known that guy five seconds, and he definitely would have done that too. He wouldn't be able to help himself but being the fearless leader sort of guy – guess it seems like you might be one of those too,' Felix laughed.

'Guys, hate to break up your blossoming friendship, but I found a map,' Russ said from the top of the stairs. Bastian and Felix hurried up to Russ who was facing a complex looking map on the edge of what was an indoor infirmary. The infirmary itself was all set up but completely empty. Bastian sat on the end of a bed while the other two looked at the map. He grabbed a bandage and bottle of rubbing alcohol and pulled down his socks, pouring it over the burn on his ankles, closing his eyes tightly as the pain intensified. Wrapping the bandage around it carefully he managed to pull his sock up before Russ and Felix came over to him.

'So, where're we going?' he asked, pulling his shoe back on.

'The library's not too far from here. We'll be there in no time,' Russ said.

'Yeah, we just need to get through two secure doors. It looks like the map's been adjusted, someone's added a room in that we need to pass, something called the red room. Sounds delightful,' Felix quipped.

'Well let's get going. I don't want to miss out on the fun,' Bastian added.

Bastian didn't pay attention to his surroundings as much as the path they took; two lefts, through a steel door, and a right up a flight of stairs and down a corridor. The hit he'd taken from their attacker was starting to fog up his head, but he remained steady as he walked behind the others.

'This is it, the first security door,' Russ said excited. He started looking at the lock on the side of the door. 'You still got that flat metal bar of mine Bass?' He asked.

Bastian looked through the pockets of his jacket and pulled out the bar. Handing it to Russ he watched as Russ pried open the key numbered lock on the side of the wall.

'Do you know what you're doing?' Felix asked.

'Kind of, I once had to break into a distillery in Port Angeline and well, long story short; that was a very good winter for Dad and I,' Russ said brightly, looking at the wires now that were behind the number pad. Bastian stared at the door and with a flick of a couple of wires within Russ's hands the door opened.

Bastian was filled with an unsettling feeling as they stepped inside of the pitch-black room. He was unable to do anything about it as the door behind them sealed shut.

'This doesn't seem like such a good idea now,' Bastian said, feeling like all the walls were closing in on them.

'What happened to Mister Confident?' Felix said. 'Look I can see the door over there. it's black glass like the first corridor.'

Stepping forward Felix cried out. They quickly realised why it was called the red room.

The darkness lit up with flashes of red from multiple heat lasers that beamed across in every which direction, covering the entire room. None of them had seen such a thing.

'Magic,' whispered Felix.

'Don't be silly. It's just really high tech,' Russ said, looking at the walls around him.

'This is a little over the top. I mean, I don't think anyone has this sort of power outside of this place,' Felix said.

'I don't know. If the Guard doesn't use this type of stuff, I bet I'd know some pretty shady guys who would definitely love to use it,' Russ answered looking blankly ahead.

'What type of people do you know?' Bastian asked.

Ignoring Bastian's remark Russ continued, 'Even if we get to the other side, we have another problem, that's a touch pad code, I can't break it or something worse might happen in here. We need the password,' his frustration was evident as he burnt his elbow on one of the red lasers banging his hand on the wall.

Bastian was still in the thick of a headache, the knock from the man downstairs was really making his head heavier with every moment, and exhaustion was gripping him quickly. Glancing at the books in his hands he felt bad for what they had endured so far. He looked intently at them, his mind drifting off into them, unfocused on the two new friends at his side. Why did they have to do all this for some stupid books? What was so important about them? Then he noticed something peculiar about the two in his hands.

'Pass me your books,' Bastian said, feeling his head pinch with pain as he spoke. 'Hurry up.' He his hands out for the books.

He shuffled them, moving them about. He had to be right; or quite possibly his mind was playing tricks. Looking at the six books Bastian felt stupid for not even thinking of doing this earlier.

'Look. The spine of each book has a letter at the top. The letters don't have anything to do with the book's name or the author, and they are the only thing on it that's embedded, but why...,' he questioned. Handling them all looking at the letters all together.

'An anagram, if you reorder them all you get... R. A. V. E. N. S,' Bastian beamed at them showing them the spines placed in order.

'And you think that's the password?' Russ asked. Bastian nodded.

'What other option do we have,' he replied, a little careless now.

'Okay, but we still need to get through the laser death trap before we try and fry ourselves entirely with an incorrect password,' Felix said.

'Well only one of us needs to go. Hold the books while I go through,' Bastian said, steading himself as he took his first step into the laser field before either of the others could say a word. In hindsight his exhaustion meant he was indeed the least stable candidate for the task at hand.

He ducked his head and moved on his side, taking note of every read beam that he was yet to cross.

Taking a step across one, he carefully pulled himself straight up again before manoeuvring his legs over two lower laser lines. Followed by multiple moving lasers coming across forcing him to go as close to the ground as possible, with a slight climb over an incredibly low one in between. Both Felix and Russ were silent as he moved through the beams.

Standing back up he needed to move past a set that crossed over each other; he had to time it perfectly. Careful, but still lightheaded, he unconsciously fell back into at least three of the lasers, each burning his back in multiple places. Screaming he fell forward. Trying to protect his face with his hand from another beam but felt the sting of the deep cut across the side of his face. Gathering himself he only needed a few more steps as he rushed through the last beams at just the right time. He faced the touchpad and glass door in front of him, gasping for breath in relief.

'You okay Bass?' called Felix.

'Yep,' replied Bastian, taking deep breaths as he leaned on the wall. He tapped the password into the screen, waiting for it to load He hoped more than anything he had been right, that ravens was the correct password. It had to be; he just knew it.

He sighed as the doors before him opened and the library was revealed. Relief took over as the laser lights all turned off. The room was quiet; the engines of the lasers were no longer humming. Russ put his hand out to test they were off and smiled to Felix when his hand wasn't burnt.

'Mate, you are one hell of a guy,' Felix said, helping him into the library along with Russ on the other side of him.

Curiosities of the Corazon Forest

'Three. Three kids, I got them here, and all you had was one. Please try and explain that Dawson. I mean, I understand, but by love of the old queen may you know I never need that sort of responsibility again. They ran off as soon as they heard your voices. I wasn't exactly in a position to go running after them either, nature called if you know what I mean,' Milo said, glaring at Lux, Archer and Hudson.

'I don't suspect Elder Jackson will force you into any more unspeakable tasks in the future. Ailsa I see has lost all of her children though, and her empty nest may need filling. I suppose you may be the one up for the job. Or should you be taking the boy back…' Dawson said sternly.

'Ah yes. About that, Elder Jackson agreed to it, "the boy's best chance is on the same path as his friends."' Milo recalled with a hint of sarcasm. 'So, here he is. Now if you don't mind, you're not wrong Dawson, and the perfectly lovely upset woman is waiting back at the village and if I hurry, I may look like an appealing option to rest a shoulder on, but I do hope she doesn't need any more children,' Milo said, patting Dawson on the back like an old friend.

'You kids behave. Look after Dawson, he's one hell of a champion you've been given.'

Dawson gave the kids each a moment to say their goodbyes to Milo before he headed back to the Amari Village.

'Alright you lot, if you're about done with it, we do need to keep moving,' groaned Dawson as he walked on. 'Don't be too loud; you never know what's lurking out here. The more of us there are the more naturally loud we will be, so tone it down.' Scarlet couldn't help giggling though as Lux rolled her eyes at Dawson's caution, but very quickly gave an understanding nod when he looked back at her.

Hudson and Archer wandered up with Dawson, hitting him with a dozen questions while Scarlet remained behind them with Lux. Most of them Dawson never really had to answer, and the boy's ability to fall off onto another tangent only increased his agitation.

'Do you always come out this far? I mean it's safe, right?' asked Archer.

'Don't be ridiculous; he obviously knows where we are going, so of course he's been here before. He probably knows every inch of these woods. I hear the other watchers call you the master of the heart,' Hudson added.

'Master of the heart? Whose heart out here is he going to master? I don't see anyone, do you?' replied Archer, head high and exaggerating with his arms the lack of others that were around.

'It's just a name four-eyes. The forest used to be known as Corazón forest a thousand years ago, meaning the heart. Thought you out of all of us would know that one,' Hudson stubbornly pointed out. 'I heard some of the other watchers say its old name was a convenient play on words, because Dawson has always been so unlucky in love, and this was his favourite place to be.'

Dawson stopped at this, Hudson and Archer did too a moment after only realising what they'd said. Archer self-consciously pushed his glasses closer to his face as Dawson turned to them, 'You two, behind the girls. Now,' he said, watching as they both retreated behind Scarlet and Lux.

Scarlet watched the look on Dawson's face – he showed the hint of a smile, laughing to himself as he turned back to lead.

73

Scarlet had been listening to Lux's version of leaving the village; it didn't differ too much from her own. According to Lux, Ailsa spoke of their path… 'She described it as the greatest adventure we would all ever have. And of course, it's bigger than anything we would ever be able to do back at the village. We have access to anything, to everything, we can explore, find out more than the barriers of our cooped up little village. I mean I've read books about the world out here, and heard updates at the Amari gatherings. I know there's awful fighting going on with the Grinnwick Guard these days ramping up their take over, but I mean that's one part of a whole world to explore. It doesn't sound half as bad as when we left Grinnwick anyway, when they were killing towns left right and centre. Geez Hudson probably would have been one of their soldiers by now if we'd stayed,' Lux said, her enthusiasm boosting Scarlets spirits, realising how much having her friends here made moving away feel easier.

'Not to mention if we'd all stayed we'd be long dead by now,' Scarlet added.

'Right… minor problem,' Lux laughed.

Hudson and Archer had joined in on pondering what type of life waited for them all at the end of the forest. Archer thought they would be put with a family on a large property, especially now there was an extra person; they were going to need a lot of space.

'I bet there's miles of land, and a large house for us with two nice people to—' he said before being cut off by Hudson. 'You're joking right? As if it'll be that easy, they would have let us stay at home if they wanted us spoon fed somewhere like that. We'll probably end up in some sort of group home; didn't you hear the update on those institutes for all the orphaned children, and I doubt Dawson's going to want to stay with us. We'll get put

74

into some system, and lost in it like the other orphans, having to do what we're told every second of the day.'

'Stop it Hudson, I'm sure it won't be as grim as you're making it out to be. We'll find a home. All five of us. Why would the Amari have spared us from that sort of life to only send us right back to it? Besides, Dawson knows where we are going, he just hasn't shared those details… yet,' Scarlet said, trying to keep looking on the bright side. Scarlet realised she was unsure how long Dawson really was going to hang around for, he seemed to want to have his own life. She only hoped that included them.

'I hope you're right Scarlet,' Hudson replied.

'All of you be quiet,' Dawson hushed them all, completely disregarding their conversation. Holding his arm out, he kept them all behind him. 'Whatever you do, stay close to me. And be quiet.'

'What is it?' whispered Lux, looking out from behind Dawson.

'Be quiet,' Dawson snapped back.

Lux looked anxiously at Archer as they all steadily followed behind Dawson.

What Dawson sensed quickly became obvious to them all. The ground beneath them began to tremble.

Swarms of birds flew out into the sky from every direction. A loud grumbling noise shuddered all around them as the wind flung twigs and branches their way. Dawson stood in the middle of them all holding his arms out while the ground shook, bracing himself so they could grab hold to him to steady themselves. He winced as he copped the brunt of the debris that flew around them.

Scarlet was standing behind him holding onto the bag on his back, looking at Lux who had her face buried into Dawson's side protecting her face. Archer and Hudson lent on each other crouching down while holding a strong grip on Dawson's arm. Scarlet remained silent and steady as the other three screamed when the shudders of the ground gathered momentum. Dawson lost his footing and they all nearly fell to the ground in one large pile.

In the trees out of the corner of her eye, a cloud of dust like a thick black mist moved with force, an entity of its own. It stopped to the side, as though it had reached its prey – them. Feeling herself gasp for breath Scarlet tried to remain motionless as it closed in. It evoked a sense of doom and sadness within her. Head down she used her arm to protect herself from the force as it descended on them. It swirled faster and faster. Scarlet felt the pressure of it as she closed her eyes. The darkness enveloped all of them; Scarlet tried with all her might to push back against its pressure. It felt inside of her like she was moving against a brick wall, stopping wasn't an option if only to keep herself from falling apart. Not unlike the build-up of power under her palm when she touched the tree, Scarlet felt an increase of the same energy inside of her. As the fear of the swarm surrounded her it built, pulling on the pressure until she felt it burst out of her. In a way Scarlet felt as though her whole body burst, falling to the ground, only to realise the entity had scattered.

Dawson recovered himself and turned to Scarlet to make sure she too was okay; she'd already pulled herself up to standing alone. Exhausted and sore from the debris that had scratched her, Scarlet tried to gather herself as best as she could. An empty quiet filled the opening they stood in, debris laying all around.

The ground finally stopped trembling, and the commotion finished. Whatever it was, it had moved on. Archer and Hudson were both panting out of fear, covered with scratches from the branches that had hit them. Dawson too bled from his cheek. Lux lay on the ground, she held her leg, tears sweeping down her face.

The boys rushed to her side,

'I think it's broken,' Lux cried. 'I felt a rock, or something fly into it.'

Dawson had not yet joined them; he was focused on Scarlet who was still staring into the dark forest after their attacker. She sensed its patterns as it moved through the forest, its ferocity and violent nature. Somehow she felt connected to it.

'What was that?' called Archer.

'Here help me get her up?' Hudson ignored the questioned, ordering the others to Lux's side.

'Whatever it was, it was warning us off. That close, within its reach, why it didn't finish us is anyone's guess,' Dawson questioned, moving to help the boys with Lux.

'We all need to get moving. Now,' he beckoned.

He didn't show fear, but concern was present in his voice. Helping Lux sit up, he assessed her leg.

'It's not broken, its badly bruised, and it looks like the kneecaps popped out' Dawson noted. 'Hold her.' The look of fear breached all over Lux's face. The boys held back her arms and waited; it was like a switch that turned Lux to scream in pain. Dawson then found two branches, and a cloth from his own bag, wrapping it tightly around to keep it straight.

'Can you stand?' Dawson asked.

Lux nodded, but Scarlet wasn't sure it was wise for her to stand just yet at all.

Dawson helped her up before motioning Hudson to help him carry her once she moaned in pain.

'We won't be able to go fast, not with Lux like this,' Hudson called to him.

'Unless you want to be close by when that thing comes back, we better get going,' Dawson barked.

'You'll be okay, we'll have you better in no time,' Scarlet assured Lux who still looked in agony. There was nothing Scarlet could do for her, she almost wished it had happened to her so she could bear the pain.

'If we ever get out of this place, it's a dead man's trap in here. My mother use to always tell us stories about monsters that lurked here, about the magic that conceals everything waiting to be unleashed. Beasts bigger than bears, and more teeth than any shark. Sources of power that lay uncontrolled and dormant only revealed to those who got in its way. She would say there would be creatures in here you'd never see coming. That the small creatures too were the deadliest. And worse than that, she spoke of witches who cursed the land, who would trick those around them into their lairs. When she first told me those tales, I don't think I slept for months,' Lux rambled, fear still struck in her eyes mixed with pain of the non-stop movement.

'We'll get out, don't worry. I don't know how true those tales are, besides I don't think we have much longer to go now. Do we Dawson?' Scarlet called out to him as he led with the boys.

'We'll stop soon for the night, but the journey's end is not yet in sight,' he replied.

'You'll be able to rest soon see,' Scarlet reassured Lux, smiling gently at her. But she wasn't entirely sure she believed that Lux's pain was going to end anytime soon.

Hudson hadn't spoken another word for hours following the attack, his usually pleasant disposition completely changed by the terror making him withdraw from everyone. His only concern was Lux.

Archer had been going through it out loud, 'We've made good distance between us now; it was the one to turn from us, clearly it wasn't a true threat to us, or we'd be dead. Although perhaps it's watching us, tracking us,' he said on a continuous ramble.

Night fell and the group's dampened spirits grew more as they sat quietly beaten by the day, the rushing sound of the close-by river echoing around them. Dawson left them to rest as he pulled out a small boat that was stored in some bushes and dragged it down to the water's edge. Only when he was close did Scarlet and Hudson help him put it in the water. Neither of them cared to ask how he knew it was there. Continuing in silence they helped Lux in first before jumping in and beginning their journey down the river.

Each of them was nervous, not knowing what would be around each bend.

'Are we sure we're safe?' Lux finally broke their silence.

'You need to relax Lux, do not fear what we haven't yet met. Look after yourself now, you need to heal,' Dawson said.

'How's that supposed to calm her down? Her leg barely works right now, what is she going to do at the next attack if she can't fight anything off. Why didn't you fight that thing off eh? Isn't it your job to keep us safe?' Hudson barked at him.

'I'm no magician. You saw it plain as day, it had its own inner workings, things we couldn't begin to understand. Even if I had access to some old magic, it would be nothing to take on something that strong,' Dawson explained coolly.

'I think I did,' Scarlet said, almost too softly.

They all stared at her.

'What do you mean?' Archer asked.

'I mean I felt it, not at the start but afterwards, I sensed its movement.... like the connection we had to the trees; except it was fear instead of confidence. That power that I felt in my palm at the trees, I felt like it was in me. The pressure from that thing, it only made it stronger, bursting out—' She knew she sounded as though she was talking nonsense. The looks on their faces didn't help, it was like one of Elder Jackson's lessons about old fae magic, but it was real, she felt it.

'This makes no sense, why could she feel something like that. How could she,' argued Hudson plainly at Dawson. He ignored her completely, looking at him like this was all his fault. Scarlet couldn't help but feel like it was no one's but hers. 'There has to be something here that is not adding up.'

'Our lives don't add up brother. Think about it, all those years ago why save us, why save Scarlet and her brother too; we aren't normal. Then they go and expel us from the place they forced us to call home. We are the things that don't add up. If Scarlet is somehow feeling like she is sensing something within herself, maybe it was the world who was being protected from us.'

'Don't be ridiculous Lux, there are plenty of other orphans that were taken to the Amari. I mean I'm one too,' Archer said.

'But what, a dozen non-Amari children retreated there. And four of us are orphans, no parents to speak on our behalf to tell them to choose us. What made us so special to be swept away? There were no parents keeping them to their word,' Lux posed to him.

Scarlet had wondered this — what brought them into the Amari's presence, the safety that they were granted seemed too kind. How did her parents know them? How had they come to trust them? the moments before she lost her memory, maybe there were even answers there; residing herself to that fact that she may never know. Flynn had been by her side, but it was Dawson who took them to the Amari Village. Dawson, who wasn't Amari... 'You,' Scarlet accused Dawson. 'You're not one of them, you took me to them.

Why?'

Everyone stared at Dawson.

'It was a plan your mother had organised in any event that the worst may happen. When I found you and your brother the night your parents died, I knew that it was the only option for you. I had no other tethers to that world, so l left with you,' Dawson explained. Scarlet suspected more emotion was behind his words than he let out.

'You knew my family; you knew my mother. What have these last year's been then, just keeping me at a distance, why didn't you take us in?' Scarlet felt herself heat up.

'I didn't think it was a good idea, Flynn didn't either. But I'm here now,' Dawson affirmed.

'So what is this in me, you must know. You felt it too with the tree.'

'I don't know. Perhaps it is the forest, it plays tricks on minds and hearts, even kind ones like yours. Or remember what I told you about the witch Niamh, the heart of the Corazon Forest, maybe what you're feeling is a reflection of her old magic, I cannot say. This forest is probably the one thing in the world that hasn't changed from the day we left Grinnwick, yet it is still a mystery to me,' Dawson said.

'You brought us to the Amari too...' Hudson added. 'Why us? Did you know our family too?'

'No, yours was after our time, probably a century or so. Elder Jackson sent me out to get you all, your whole family. Something dark came for you, a sort of shadow creature... the last of the magical creatures left in Grinnwick living in the shadows. I was too late for your parents. I blame myself every day; if only I could have travelled faster. But both of you were unharmed. You where both the children of a Lord, I don't know if you remembered he was one. Distant relatives to some of those closest to the High King and Queen of Scarlet's time. Both warriors, both stupidly naive. Those details at the time could be said of a number of people, but it wasn't who your parents were that brought you to the Amari. You yourselves both showed promise, and the Amari as kind as they seem are schemers. Stuck on what the world was like when they left, hoping one day magic will be brought back and they can thrive once more.

'The two of you, they felt a connection to the future in your destiny. They searched far and wide, continuously for those they believed had the strength to change what was, what would be,' Dawson said.

'And me?' Scarlet added.

'The very same. To let you out of their safety, they must believe now that it is time for you to live out your destinies in the hope for a golden future, as they believe,' Dawson said.

'And what is it you believe?' Scarlet asked.

'Me. I believe in the woman I once loved and the world I knew. But like yours it burned down in front of me. Unlike you I am stuck with the memories. I believe hope lives inside of us, and it is scarce, but to pin the hope of an entire world on small children is unnecessary and cruel. I told you I look forward to being able to just live a normal life, and now I think that's what we all need.'

As much as they usually would have jabbered on at him, they were silent. Scarlet assumed the others were deep in thought like her. The forces inside her felt foreign yet natural to her, she didn't want to ignore it but thought it best to leave it with the Forest, with the notion that that is where such things belong. She was going into a whole new world – she didn't need to be worried about what might be, like Dawson said they needed to take in what is, and find themselves their own normal. The idea that the hopes of magical creatures like the Amari were on them, the idea of a destiny, seemed absurd.

Eventually, the water calmed, and the soft rocking motion of the boat soon sent the others off to sleep. Dawson had given up rowing the boat and allowed it to flow with the motion of river. He tried to stay awake, but Scarlet watched as his eyes slowly drifted. Tired but still awake, Scarlet embraced the river's beauty by night.

Scarlet was stuck in thoughts of an unknown future. Why had the Amari not let her follow Flynn? Was it not the right time then for their agenda? She pushed away the anger and the fear that her life decisions were being pulled at like strings. The only truth she knew right now that she cared to understand, was that they had looked after her, and that the village had been her home for as long as she could remember; her life there was what made her free to be herself.

Gazing upon the stars above she twisted and turned her hand through the water. The moonlight reflecting along the ripples and the stillness of the trees overhead was its own form of magic.

With her head resting on the side of the boat Scarlet watched as the motion of her hand sparked the water with an unusual light like the stars she had watched above. It was as though the water was alive whenever she moved her hand, the luminescence mesmerising her. Staring into its light something unexpected happened, a spin of her head rocked her, and the glowing light turned to a flickering memory. One she was sure was not hers. The shores of a clear never-ending beach with the same luminescence in the waves of the water. She'd never having been to a beach before, only had the blue waters described to her by the elders. This new experience mixed with the possibility of a memory unveiling before her was nothing less than exciting. As she felt herself soaring with happiness inside, the lights from the water around her rose from the river and swirled into their own form bouncing along the breeze. Perplexed at the sight before her, Scarlet turned to the others to see if they were watching, but they were all still asleep. Instead, the luminescence began to form into a path, as though they were small flowers atop the water. More light swirled and the form of man stood before her. She didn't know his face.

He moved closer, his face kind. He stopped, waiting while the lights brought forth more figures towards her, but she couldn't make out their faces, only that they waved to her.

'Hello,' Scarlet whispered, not wanting to scare them off.

The boat shuddered, catching her attention as it got caught in the river's edge. Balancing herself she realised as she looked across the water that the figures she saw in the distance had run off down the river while the man remained. He looked at her, similar to the way Dawson did. He reached out his hand for her face, every bit of her at peace that he was there by her side. She smiled and reached out for him, hoping that he would speak, that he would tell her his story, who he was. She was left with only wonder as he looked in the direction they headed, towards those who had run off in the distance. Their light trickled sparingly across the water and Scarlet now followed it too. As it settled it formed into a giant creature across the river. Double the size of a bear, like an ape of sorts with tough green fur, and charcoal scales down its back. It was just resting on the river's edge, pulling at the roots of a bush and stuffing it into his mouth. It didn't seem to have noticed them nestled on the other side of the riverbank. Peaceful, sweet almost. However, there was no saying if it felt threatened it may not hesitate to attack them. She turned back to the man, only to find herself disappointed that he was gone, as the light swirled around and back into the moving river.

Scarlet's attention went back to the creature; she needed to think of a way for their boat to float away unseen before it caught onto their presence.

She shook Dawson awake, worrying that the creature would notice them as he slightly rocked the boat beneath them. Hushing him fiercely Scarlet's eyes turned his to the creature, guiding him to its presence.

Thankfully it remained nibbling at its root. Doing his best not to make a noise Dawson pulled a blanket out of Scarlet's case and slowly covered his back as well as Hudson and Lux's, who both lay sleeping on the creature's side view of their rowboat.

'Push off the bank' he whispered to Scarlet. She waited, so that when the creature decided to pull up another root, she would perfectly time the echoing noise covering any sound she would make.

As the creature pulled the root, Scarlet pushed with all her might. Making it as smooth as it could possibly be. Taking hold of an oar herself, she pushed off to get them further down the stream and out of sight.

Trials of a Raven

Back burnt, head and side sore and ankle throbbing, he realised they weren't alone. Mandy, Verne, Gertrude and Rudi were already on the couches in the library, each resting their own wounds. Mandy was fast asleep.

Gertrude came straight over to him helping him to the couch so he could lay down properly.

'What happened to you guys?' she asked, shocked as she got a closer look at Bastian's wounds, using the edge of her sleeve to wipe the blood off Bastian's face. He focused on the delicate curve of her pale cheek, and the deep red of her hair that he wanted to reach out for but felt like this was neither the time nor the place. Instead, he smiled and thanked her as she passed him some water.

'If these people wanted us dead, they definitely went the right way about it. We had to take the other door and apart from some swine trying to attack us we had a great time taking on a mind puzzle to prevent a laser death trap. And when I say we, I mean him,' Felix said.

They nearly laughed as Rudi looked gobsmacked by their comment. He looked like he was going to ask them about it before he wailed in pain; Verne had just popped his dislocated arm back in.

'What about you lot?' Russ asked Verne who took a seat next to Mandy now that Rudi's arm was back in place.

'Well, I don't even know where to start – as soon as we walked into that corridor we were ambushed by dozens of robotic spider-like machines. Like your lasers I guess, they shot them out of their eyes,' Verne said, shaking his head. 'I've got at least ten burn shots on me, only small shots though. Anyways there were a couple of weapons in there that I managed to grab a hold of, got these guys out with only a few hits to them. Then at the end of the room the door led us up some stair to a garden.'

Bastian looked to Russ and Felix when Verne didn't continue.

'There was a man in there,' Gertrude said, gaining all of their attention. 'He was smart, a real egghead you know. We didn't know if we were outside or if the plants had been grown inside so we asked him. He was pleasant enough; he handed us some water and told us the answers we seek lay in the books. That's when Mandy fell asleep; she drank the bloody water. Verne got a bit annoyed at the guy after that, and that's how he got the red cheek. Meanwhile, there were tentacle plants creeping up on us trying to strangle each of us. Rudi quickly got hold of the shovel to start hacking them off while I looked at the books for the clue. *Ravens.*

'Anyways, I saw a path with ravens tiled onto it leading one way out of the gardens, so we followed it. Verne had to carry Mandy the whole way out so we made sure the plants stayed clear of them, but Rudi didn't fair too well with one of the plant attacks, and they got his arm before we could get clear. I only got tripped up and hurt my knee but got out before it could do any more damage.' Gertrude took a breath, pulling her red hair behind her ears.

'So, this place really is next level isn't it? No wonder you never really hear of Guardians anymore, how can anyone last doing shit like that all the time,' Felix said.

'Guardians?' Bastian asked. The little his mother knew to tell him about his grandfather's work was only that he was a teacher, a professor of a kind.

He had adjusted to the trials, but as to the foundation of where they were, he felt completely out of the loop.

'Yes Bastian, I thought your mother would have told you all about us... Then again knowing her probably not,' came the voice of a man standing at a large wooden set of doors that was now wide open. He was tall and broad, wearing a fitted dark grey vest and jacket with a loose tie. Overall he looked rather handsome, in a refined sort of way. His white hair sat neatly parted, yet despite his dapper appearance he couldn't help giving off the impression that he was a man who'd been on the most daring quests.

'Maybe not, well I don't know what I expected her to tell you. But something about me might have been nice. I guess I should introduce myself to you all then. I am August Harker, and I will be one of your teachers.

'Welcome. Each group has found their clues I see. Ravens: This is your squad's name, all seven of you.

'Being a Guardian isn't an easy task, but it's a life you will never forget. You all come from different walks of life, but here you are family. You may wonder why we separated you if you are to be a squad together. Well so you know, the task is formed to our benefit, not yours. To identify your qualities, your skills, and to find what will make you be the best Guardian you can be.

'I can see that most of you took the challenges of the first task head on, and I applaud you. You will all need to go to the infirmary before we continue, and you will need to be shown to your rooms,' Mr Harker said.

Bastian had sat up on the couch looking intently at Mr Harker from the first moment he saw him, but the shock of who he really was still didn't sink in. His grandfather. The man his mother had spoken of, the one she wanted him to learn from. She mentioned nothing else, nothing about the Guardians, and nothing about what she thought he would be faced with. He wasn't sure she had any idea. Did she even know he was being sent into this chaos?

Russ and Felix helped him to the infirmary following the others. They were taken a different way there by his grandfather – apparently the maps they had seen earlier had shown a non-permanent access way to the infirmary.

Bastian took to the bed he had sat on earlier and waited for the short, perky nurse – Ms Madlyn – who looked like a bag of lollies with the colours of make up on her face. She quickly lathered some cold solution on his back, hands, and ankle to relieve the pain of his burns and lay him down, giving him a sedative, and mentioned a cracked collar bone and concussion to his grandfather who walked his way before the drugs finally kicked in and he slipped into sleep.

Waking to expect a chill Bastian was shocked to find he felt ten times better and was cosier than he thought he'd be. His ankle was still bandaged, but there was barely any pain, his back felt like new and the hit he took on the shoulder and head were well rested. The room he was in was dark, minus a blazing fireplace that sparked at the centre; a room that held six other beds. Each was made up with blankets like his, but all were empty.

He pushed himself up, feeling the small aches in his body, but it was nothing compared to what he expected to feel.

'Ah, you're awake pet,' a middle-aged woman came to his side. She had a kindness in her eyes, something not too dissimilar from his mother's. Her long woollen jacket was wrapped around her, and she placed her steaming cup of tea as she tended to him.

'You fought well boy. Not many take charge in a beginner's task so easily. I haven't decided if some choices were brave or plain stupid yet, but I doubt it matters now.' She seemed both impressed and underwhelmed at the same time.

'You're Ms Madlyn, yes? Where is everyone else?' Bastian asked.

'That I am. As for your new friends, that's hard to say. Although by this time they are probably up eating their morning meal,' she said before leaning over and checking his back. He winced for a moment but again the pain was minimal. Then she looked down at his ankle, moving it in her hands. Finally, she got so close that he could smell her floral sent that sometimes older woman preferred; he always thought it was nearly too overwhelming.

'The burns were bad. I can't say if they'll fully disappear. Some men like to show off their scars, so I'm sure you won't differ too much. That one on your face is deep, I suspect you'll be stuck with that scar for life. Your ankle burn like the others is doing well – keep them all bandaged, and as much as I'm clearing you to join the others a slight hint of dirt or water gets into them you come back here for me to clean them,' Ms Madlyn said.

'Thank you, they barely hurt anymore.' Bastian was still in shock.

'Why should they, this is the best infirmary in Grinnwick with the best sources of books. And I am the leading educator in medicinal treatments, from forgotten magical and herbal remedies and those created. You feel no pain because I wished it, and with the help of a rather handy gel formed from a weed; a weed that is very hard to come by in these times. Still, August Harker's grandchild is tended to with only the best,' she posed, perfectly impressed with herself.

Bastian didn't really know what to say. He thanked her again, and after he managed to climb into the clean black shirt and pants by his bed, she let him go.

He wandered down a hallway, lit with lights but no windows in sight. The hallway led to another ten doors. A couple had been left open; they too were filled with beds, but these ones were set up like a cosy dorm room. At the end of the hall he walked upstairs to a large open room that had dozens of sculptures and artefacts placed in glass around the rosewood and glass wall cabinets.

'You're awake,' Gertrude said beaming, walking through a door to his left. She seemed happy to see him.

'Yeah, how long has it been?' Bastian asked.

'About three days now, I was starting to think you'd never wake. Come on. I was going to get my notebook, but I can do that later – the others will all be so thrilled to see you,' she beamed, grabbing his hand and pulling him behind her.

Taken aback by how polite and welcoming Gertrude was, Bastian followed her. For some reason he expected to have his defences up; to be friendless.

She took him through a door and around a corner to a hall-sized dining room, again no window in sight. Several sets of tables filled the space, and the five others he now knew as the Ravens all sat at the second table in. Passing by the other tables he felt some people look at him. He noticed two large guys at the end of the dining room on a far table who were unmistakably the two men he had fought during their tasks. The bruises still evident on one of their faces gave him the chills – this was not the way to make friends. Keeping his head down, he sat at the table.

'The dead has finally risen,' laughed Felix, clapping Bastian on the back. He winced, yet again surprised that it didn't hurt that much.

'Welcome back mate, ' Verne said, 'So much to fill you in on, and so much for you to tell us. First, how in the hell does Mr Harker know your mother? Don't think for a minute I missed that one.'

Bastian laughed awkwardly for a moment; they were all staring at him, even Russ looked up from a mouth full of oats.

'He's my grandfather. That's why I got sent here. I didn't know anything about the Guardians, she just knew he was in a position to teach me how to protect myself,' Bastian said.

'Ha. Like you need it. You were awesome during the first tasks,' Russ said swallowing down his oats.

'Doubt my small-town tricks could help stop the Guard or worse. What's the deal anyway with these Guardians? Is that what we are now? Are Guardians not just a form of the Guard? Where exactly are we?' Bastian kept his voice down. His confusion was spiralling…

'Well, it's an underground operative, and quite literally we are underground too,' said Rudi, 'Out in the middle on damn nowhere,' Rudi said.

'The Guardians, which is what we'll be trained to be… They are meant to follow missions to help the people of Grinnwick. An age-old group that predates anything the Grinnwick Guard has ever done,' Russ noted.

'So they were around when they Grinnwick Guard got started and didn't think "hey these guys are kind of crazy maybe we should send one of our teams to stop them?",' Bastian mocked. He was sure Felix grinned, but the others didn't have the same reaction.

'I know, it seems ridiculous. But teams within the Guardians have done great things too…. Everything we do is undercover, not known to anyone. There's even an old photograph with the High King in the main hall working with one of the old Guardians long ago. Our teams can be seen rescuing people from attacks in the fall of the Kingdom. The bombs that went off in the main streets of Old Town Burbank near the kingdom, there's heaps of those shots. You can see them searching for survivors. Even the raids during the Van Helms rise, there's a whole spread sheet of names of people the Guardians managed to help escape. The Grinnwick Guard don't even know we exist,' said Verne.

'Okay, but who do they answer to. Who gives them the missions or calls them out for help? Who decides who the bad guys are? Not everything is black and white. And I mean with all these resources surely they have enough power behind them to overthrow Van Helm and his men,' Bastian said.

'From what I can gather, they have people all over the country. Anything suspicious or curious they send word back, and the Guardians like your grandfather clear what's worth a mission, and what squads should go. The Guardians don't have the same power in the sense of holding stores of Cor-Marinium. Their advances are just too good, even with everything the Guardians' learnt over time. Strength in numbers, the ability to spread people out through Grinnwick makes change in smaller way, but none less effective,' Verne said.

'All I'm saying is if we are here to protect the people… we aren't doing a very good job. Outside these walls, they're hurting. Families are still being torn apart, and what we just watch?' Bastian argued.

'Well…. We haven't exactly learnt all that much yet,' Russ chimed in.

Bastian turned to him; Russ was right. He was getting ahead of himself. He wasn't ready to take on a whole city of people, a way of life that had suited the lavish for centuries. To them he was no one'

Taking in what he could of their new life, Bastian took some of the toast from the plate in front of him lathering it in jam while mulling over what Verne had told him. He knew nothing about the Guardians, only that he needed to gather every little piece of information on his new home, and sitting back and listening to his new friends as they spoke excitedly would be the best way to find out as much as possible.

'Eat up Bass. Trust me you're going to need it,' Felix said, finishing off his own toast before taking his dishes to the kitchen.

Bastian barely knew what he was getting himself into, his mother only described going to live with his grandfather as being a part of a life that would protect him and help him grow into a stronger man. After the first task he expected the first thing they did to be some sort of physical training, that the focus would be to begin shaping their bodies to be able to protect themselves and to complete whatever missions the Guardians required of them, or maybe learning the equipment that they'd use. Instead, the first place Felix led him was back to the library.

Verne, Russ, Mandy, Gertie and Rudi were all ahead of them, seated on both sides of a long table, facing towards a man at the head of it.

His grandfather stood behind a grand oak desk, looking at them all.

'Welcome,' his grandfather said, while Bastian stood there awkwardly.

Bastian looked at Felix who was already heading to the far end of the long table and taking a seat, grabbing one of the rather large books from the centre.

Bastian followed suit taking a seat opposite Felix next to Mandy, accepting the book she passed him. *History of the Guardians* was its title. Bastian looked up, unsure of what to do as the others all started looking in their books.

'Now Bastian, I know you've still been on the mend the first few days, so what you need to know is that first thing in the morning – unless told otherwise – you will come here and read from the book provided. Each day of the week will focus on a different subject. Today's class is history. Knowledge is key. It is from this we can grow, understand, and think beyond ourselves. That is one of the main priorities here – you may have thought yourself and the other Ravens are the only ones here, but through the morning you've undoubtedly seen others. They too will look through books they want to read, a choice in time you will all be able to make. For now, you focus only on the ones given to you. It's important to start with a base as there are so many incredible things to learn. So, dive in,' his grandfather encouraged.

Bastian looked at his sprightly face, and around at his new comrades. Their faces already deep in thought as they'd jumped into the pages of the books.

Bastian opened his book titled *Legends of Grinnwick*. He felt uncomfortable as he sat, unsure as the others so easily fell into the books. And he sat there wondering why he still didn't have more information on this place. Still, he made an effort to read, taking his time; reading about how the original founders of the Guardians came to be. At least this was about answers he wanted, about what on earth was happening around him.

The founders' names were Liesel Miller, Fredrick and Dempsey Jones, and Melvin Huw. The first chapters described how each of them grew up.

Noting that Grinnwick first came to be only with something called the Heart of Grinnwick. The legend said that at one point the heart came into their lives and that because of it, it became their life's mission to protect it, and as such to protect all of Grinnwick. The Heart of Grinnwick was described in the pages as a power stronger than anything the world had ever known; a source that was purer than any resource.

Bastian read on about how they took charge looking after the heart. Following their journeys with it, passing the charge onto their children when the time came. At some point, the knowledge of the Heart of Grinnwick's location was lost. In time the Guardians became what they were now, a hidden institution to shape the generations to be their own force for good, to help Grinnwick and the people of the land.

The early generations of Guardians were described in the chapters. Each chapter had its own title, just as his squad had been called the Ravens. These chapters detailed the missions each squad had been on, and the good they had done, leading up to about twenty years ago. Bastian read across the chapters titled the Eagles, Kingfishers, Brown Bears, and so on until he noticed under the Hornets was an old picture of five people. Three of them were wearing jackets with hornets on the side of their arms. Underneath was captioned with his grandfather's name, August Harker. Along with two other names he didn't recognised; Gregory Dash and Copper T. They were pictured helping a woman and her son, wrapping them both in blankets. His grandfather looked so young, younger than he himself was now. Yet, Bastian's main thought was how terrifying it must have been for that woman holding onto her son, the fear in her eyes couldn't be squished by the hope that the three men brought her in that darkest time. He couldn't bare knowing that not too long after that his mother would have been a similar fearful woman, fleeing from an impending disaster with a small child in tow. Slamming the book shut on the faces before him, he made a promise to himself; if this was going to be his place in the world, he would do better than just rescuing them from disaster, he would stop those from causing it all together.

'It seems your done for the day boy,' said his grandfather, placing his hand over the cover of the book Bastian had just been reading, seeming lost in thought more than any of them.

'Our personal history focus as you have all been reading is the legacy of the Guardians. It is not to go unnoticed as some of you may have read. We turn up when we need to, and not any more, or less. We do what we are called to. Protecting Grinnwick has always been our number one priority, looking out for the people. But we are not soldiers. It is not our place to step in and fight a war, and we do not start them either. Still, when opportunity strikes, we act; in a way that keeps us hidden out of sight like a shadow while restoring Grinnwick; helping those who need it.

'Many of you may have been reading stories of older squad's missions, where we helped people, where we looked like heroes. No one else but those people, and us know their stories. We stay out of the public eye, they don't know about the Guardians, they don't know the work we do. In those stories, those men in their squad that helped them escape, their images are here only, no one else has seen them. We are a part of the shadows. Also, a lot of you will have read that the Guardians' beginnings derived from finding the Heart of Grinnwick. Now, there is much speculation that this was a treasure so pure and beautiful to behold that it needed a village to protect it. It is believed by some that it is a jewel or statue, some even believe whatever it may be is cursed with magic. Whatever it was that our founders discovered, it's unknown to us. It is now as much a myth to us and the world as it's a part of our history. Some speculate its last location was within the walls of High King Thorn's Castle some near thousand years ago.

'Since then each mission that our squads have been sent on are under the lines of protecting the Heart of Grinnwick, which now is the people, the history, and the future. It is important to understand that the Guardians derive from a small group of people who believed in something; that hope was a light for them, so let hope's light be the same to you.

'Each and every one of you have been affected by the darkest parts of our world; you were each chosen for different reasons. Many of you may think it was random or by chance that you are here. You may not yet know each other's stories… when you do share them they will only bring you closer.

'Guardians have had their eyes on you all. We know when someone has the potential to become something bigger than the lives they were given. Being here now, you may find more than knowledge and strength but a reason to believe in something more than yourselves. If anything, remember you will always have each other.

'Now. I have jobs for you all,' his grandfather said. He turned to the board against the wall. Intrigued by Harker's words Bastian felt like there was so much more his grandfather wanted to say. Distracted, he only then noticed four other students walking out from a row of books. They each glanced their way for a moment; Bastian ignored the stares seeing that it wasn't their arrival that distracted his grandfather from continuing their lesson but a man waiting by the door.

A man in glasses, the man who met them at the beginning of their first task. Much younger than his grandfather, the greasy haired man looked up from his glasses like he had no time to wait for Harker's speech. Bastian felt a similar distaste for him as he had done when they first met. His eyes squinted in a way that Bastian didn't find trusting. Yet, as Harker returned to talking instead of writing on the board, Bastian quickly returned his attention to him.

'So, until lunch I'd like you all to take this book on *More than Greenery*. And head to the nursery and identify as many of the plants in this book as you can. Detail in your notebooks the ones you've found and rewrite the details of the plants if you could. Gloves are on the wall, and Miss Mathison is in there if any of you need a hand,' he said, handing Mandy the rather large book that was much too heavy for her.

'After lunch today, I need you all to head to the armoury where you will begin further studies under Sir Gregory Dash, a friend of mine. He doesn't take to insolence, so do your best to pay attention. Then afterwards you will all head to the fields for training. Until tomorrow, Ravens.'

Bastian Felt his grandfather's eyes linger on him as he picked up his own notes and left the class on their own, walking past them and following the greasy haired man out the door.

'Come on guys. Let's get this done quickly, I don't want to be in that place any longer than I have to,' Gertrude said, standing up and leading the way. Bastian didn't have the same uneasy feeling towards the nursery as Gertie. He hadn't been there during the first task and his curiosity as to what was held within excited him.

Walking into the lightly humid room, it didn't feel dangerous. It was bright and colourful, full of dozens of flowers and bright green plants. Mandy walked straight over to a patch of flowers that looked like yellow buttercups.

'I wouldn't get too much closer to that,' Verne said. 'We have those back home, and we've always said they're a gift for only your biggest enemies.'

Mandy took a step back, alarmed, then made her way over to a desk. She placed the book down in the centre for them all to see while they grabbed notebooks off the shelf to write in.

A group of girls behind them a couple of tables back, only a year or two older than them, started looking their way as they took a seat.

'Looks like this place isn't all too bad,' Verne said, half turning around and eyeing one of the rather pretty girls whose blonde ponytail swung around as she too turned back from looking at him.

Bastian said nothing, he couldn't help catching his own glimpse of the girls before quickly returning to his notebook.

'Right, so teamwork. Split up everyone into pairs and each of us find a flower from the book. Draw it, then come back and we can swap and share,' Verne said. His voice was full of authority that commanded them all to get up and get to work. Bastian paired with Verne; they were looking for something called the Phillius Root. It was only described as a greyish green root that had no flower, noticeable for the brown spots on it. It was specified as a medical plant, that when chewed would relieve pain, which led them to search the medicinal area of the nursery.

'Where abouts are you from?' Verne asked him as they looked around the benches of plant life. Bastian put his gloves on so he could move aside a leafy plant that had overgrown.

'Small town a long way from here about a two-day mover ride north I'd say,' Bastian said, not wanting to be too specific. He wasn't too sure how safe it was having others know about their town. It was after all still one of the only ones this side of the outer districts that the Guard had no power over.

'Nice. I'm from a farm in the central valleys. We ran a dairy cattle station; it was beautiful out there. There are hills for as far as the eye can see, and its calving season; my absolute favourite time, can't believe I'm missing it. They are always so cute when they are small, the little tykes,' Verne boasted.

Bastian appreciated the sweetness behind what Verne said, not many guys ever really appreciated the beauty in small things, and Verne seemed like the last person to do just that.

'Yeah, I get you. There's nothing like being at home. I miss my friends and my mum mostly. But for me I don't think it was really just the place, as beautiful as the beach or the woods could be, I'd give it all up if my mum and friends could be here with me now,' Bastian said, as Verne agreed. Strangely Bastian felt that Verne understood where he was coming from. How could this tall headstrong boy be so kind? It was mindboggling to him, and yet also comforting.

'Hey Verne, do you know anything about the guy—' Bastian began. He wanted to know if while he'd been recovering they had learnt anything about the greasy haired man.

'—Look, is this it,' Bastian said cutting himself off, pulling up a spotted root that was nearly grey with his hands.

'Finally. Come on, lets sketch it and get back,' Verne said, quickly pulling out his notebook.

Bastian drew the Phillius root the best he could – unsurprisingly they were the first ones back.

He wrote down the notes in his book underlying the fact that it was for medical purposes and that when chewed it could relieve pain for up to two hours. However if it is used in conjunction with the leaves of the plant then it could send the user into a deep sleep. A high dose itself could be deadly to a frail patient.

By the time he'd finished Gertie and Felix were already back from finding a flower called the Hellfire. According to the book, the red flower spread quickly, yet it favoured light. Places kept in the dark all the time made it impossible for the flower to grow.

After sharing all of their works including Russ, Mandy, and Rudi's when they returned they barely had any time to get to lunch.

'You were asking me something before Bastian?' Verne asked, as they finished up Mandy and Rudi's fiddle frog flower notes.

'Oh yeah, just if you knew anything about the guy who was there when we arrived. The guy with the glasses?' Bastian said.

'Yeah, Emmett is his name. He's a bit shifty, not great in social situations, but harmless enough. He's a real egg head. I think he deals a lot with the admin side of the Guardians from what I can tell, the guys in Phoenix said that he never really got sent on any missions. From what I've seen looks like he's taken a bit of a power trip with his job here,' Verne said, shaking his head.

'Yeah, needs to relax doesn't he,' Bastian mused, happy he wasn't the only one given the creeps by Emmett.

'How'd you guys go? I mean, it must play on your mind being back here after being attacked,' Russ asked Rudi, Mandy, Gertie and Verne.

Gertie looked at him horrified. 'I'm just glad whatever it was they sent after us doesn't want to kill us anymore,' she said.

'Don't be certain of that,' said the girl with the ponytail who sat at the table behind them, walking past them but not before turning to Bastian with a sweet glance as she walked off.

'That girl is going to be trouble,' Verne said. 'By the looks on your face, you don't get many girls like that back home either.'

'Well, most of them wouldn't exactly look my way, not for that reason anyway. Anyone in town thought I was a witch's son, and decent girls didn't end up outside of town,' Bastian said, his eyes trailing after the girl who'd now left the nursery.

'A witch's son? I didn't think they existed anymore. But when it comes to girls some of us do have experience in that area. While you two sit there, I'm going to go talk to her,' Felix said smugly, picking up his notebook and following her out of the nursery.

Bastian and Verne stared with astonishment at Felix in action – he was just as smooth as he let on. Whatever he was saying to the girls made them giggle annoyingly, but he held their attention completely.

'Well, aren't you two going to go over and try your luck too?' Mandy said, looking at the two of them staring over at Felix.

'Yeah they're pretty, and they seemed to like you guys,' Gertie said, but Bastian noted a tone to her voice.

'I don't know. I mean, it's my first day out and about. Think I'll just lay low you know. Already recovering from my last few punches,' Bastian said, scared of making a fool of himself.

'Yeah, besides we have you guys to keep us company,' Verne added. Bastian was happy he did too because it turned the conversation around to be much cheerier.

Russ naively chimed in, 'I heard from one of the serpents that Sir Dash is one of the fastest gunmen. No one's ever been able to beat him. They said he knows every weapon in the armoury like another limb; that he's a legend amongst the Guardians.'

'Eh, you never know Russ… give us time, and even you might be able to beat him.' Bastian boasted.

'Welcome Raven squad, I believe we have delayed the start of your weapons and teamwork training, to make sure everyone's present.

'My Name is Sir Gregory Dash,' Sir Dash said, his voice echoing in the against the steel walls of the armoury. His loud voice rattles the racks next to him. And the harsh light of the armoury glared across the side of his face. He was taller and broader than any man Bastian was yet to see within the Guardians, a gun underneath his jacket that Bastian could see clearly from his seat.

'Today we will assess your fighting skills before any real training begins; be ready to show me what you've got,' he said and instructed them all to follow him to the armoury. When they got there through a series of doors and hallways, due to his extreme height Sir Dash had to bend and turn to fit through the door. His presence amongst them made the rather large armoury look quite small.

'Let's begin,' Dash started, his voice tired and croaky. He showed no sign of interest in getting to learn their names.

'You each need to start off knowing your weapon. We will begin our studies with staffs and spears, moving onto bows and swords before moving onto mechanical equipment like firearms, which as you know aren't always readily available, even to us. For now, I want you to grab one of the staffs on the back wall. You are using these to show me what skills you each have so far,' Sir Dash said, unlocking the door behind him. 'Once you have your staff, head upstairs onto the fields and show me what you've got.'

Bastian grabbed the centre of a wooden staff, still taking notice of the variety of firearms locked up behind another metal gate. There were at least a dozen different types from what he could see, some looked old and beat up, like relics. While others were filled with green Cor-Marinium. Bastian could only imagine the power behind those ones. They barely had many Cor-Marinium powered devices back home. There was no chance his mother would let him near one of them, not even one of the small technology devices that was run off it either. He always had a particular interest in wanting to see the power behind them, it was said to be incomparable. His town didn't hold stores of it like others, they firmly believed it was this that kept them off the Grinnwick Guards radar. His mother wasn't opposed to these thoughts either, and if he'd been caught handling such a device that ran green with its power she would have scolded him something shocking.

Bellevue Point had always run off energy from a dam just outside of town. And his mother's little house was run off her own windmill that caught the oceans breeze. The countless days and nights though that they spent with only the fireplace for light, due to the drop in the breeze was enough to have them use to using nothing but the heat of the fire to cook with. He had gotten so use to lighting the flame and boiling water that he forgot when their power even worked, he still used the fireplace.

Astoria on the other hand, the largest city of the south, the home of the Grinnwick Guard. Held the largest stores of Cor-Marinium, and every bit of it was said to power the whole city. Rumours of their own large mine west of the city of Astoria where they held complete control of the resource. Bastian often wondered what it would look like in person, with endless supplies of power to support whatever want or need, the constant energy lighting up their entire city. He was sure it was a spectacle of sorts, and that those who surrounded it were drawn like moths to a flame. That it was its vast power, and consumption of their resources that drew so many people into their world. He had heard of tubes of the green liquid that ran through the streets, connecting every house, apartment and building. Travellers would visit Winslow's Hall and say that if you travelled even at a distance to Astoria you could see the city lights beam into the night sky; like a beacon. He often heard Winslow warn it was more like a lighthouse, and they should be like ships, warned to stay away from the shore. It was a notion his sure his mother would have agreed with.

It was clear to him however that it was the stores of Cor-Marinium that the Grinnwick Guard held that was their largest weapon of power. He was sure it enabled them to rally people behind them over the years, to be sucked into their delusions of power. He didn't understand why they had to expand their forces, or their need to take over other towns, other cities and enforce their dominance. They seemed like a large-scale bully to him, and bullies weren't uncommon back home. They were easy enough to beat, you only had to wait for the right moment to strike.

Bastian had allowed him too much time drifting off in thought as Felix nudged him, passing him a black rain coat. 'Come on space cadet,' Felix laughed. 'Get your head in the game.'

Up the rickety metal stairs, breaching up and outside onto the fields they were met with a rainy afternoon. He hadn't been outside above the compound; it was desolate to be sure. Sparce grass that was drenched from the rain, and hilly terrain making it hard to see what was in the distance. Even though he stood in line with his new team of friends, it gave Bastian an overwhelming sense of being completely cut off, and facing a reality that he truly at the mercy of the teachers who wanted to shape them into warriors.

'Hold the staff with intent, it is to be one with your movement,' Sir Dash issued. 'Remember that for each weapon we handle, they all are a part of us. Every action they cause, every infliction is because that is your will; it is your responsibility. You use it with purpose, as one.'

Sir Dash made sure each of them held their grip properly, walking along each of them as they stood spaced out in a line. Using his own staff to smack the hands of each of them as he walked past making sure they held it correctly.

'This is no toy, even if it is the first stage of are armoury training it may be the most useful, when things don't go your way. The ability to find what you can and use it not only in defence but in an attack is pivotal,' Sir Dash cautioned.

He began setting them up against one another. Bastian was placed against Rudi, who as far as Bastian could tell was as skilled with a staff as he was at being quiet. Rudi quickly combated every movement Bastian made; he only managed to keep himself out of harm's way by remaining a step ahead.

Rudi got in a strike to Bastian's side. The sharp pain wounded him, making him step back from the fight for a moment. He was still sore from the first task, but he managed to gather himself quickly to return to the fight.

Out of the corner of his eye he saw Verne taking on Gertie with a quickstep movement that left her on the ground. Russ was taking on Mandy, leaving Felix waiting on the sidelines to take on their winner.

Knowing Rudi was ready to continue, he had a sense he wanted to prove himself. Bastian wasn't quite sure why? They were a team. All this wasn't about who was the best, but about getting to work together… at least that is what he thought. Perhaps he should be trying to one up the others but knew that wasn't something instilled in him.

Bastian stepped closer, initiating he was ready to continue. He took to watching Rudi's footwork, without thinking he stepped quickly to the side. Moving himself ahead of Rudi a sharp movement of his own staff knocked Rudi's staff out of his hand.

Rudi stepped towards him this time, taking hold of Bastian's staff. The force tugged on Bastian's arms. Bastian pulled back, using momentum from the hold Rudi had on his staff. His own tug towards him stronger the weight of it throwing Rudi off balance and forcing him to the ground. Bastian took the opportunity to hold his own staff at Rudi's chest, pinning him down.

'Good. Rough and a little stiff but we'll work on that,' Sir Gregory Dash said to the two of them before going to watch Felix's fight against Russ.

After helping Rudi up, Bastian shook his hand. The annoyed look that Rudi had at the outcome could not have been more obvious.

Verne and Felix on the other hand were alight with excitement after the practice fights were done, but their afternoon was far from over. Sir Dash walked them down a valley and into an open area of muddy grass that looked as though it had been cut out of the landscape some time ago. There were other squads down there too. Bastian could see the Serpent and the

Phoenix squad wearing red, and green raincoats. Bastian only then noticing how obviously theirs were black for the ravens.

The valley came to an abrupt halt as the light beyond was blocked by wired gate with black mesh covering the rest of the valley behind it. Through the mesh Bastian was able to glimpse what looked to be messy, overgrown grassland, filled with some sort of set up, an obstacle or sorts. Something told Bastian that whatever obstacles lay behind weren't going to be easy. He could see the closest entrance was just one of many along the wired gate. The Serpents and the Phoenix squads at two separate entrances each of them stretching before entering.

'As Guardians in training, every afternoon where possible after your lessons you are to complete the challenges in the gated fields below. Today you will be introduced to it before we start you on your team building training – you will not return to the fields until after your initial team building training is complete. After that you will get to know these fields quite well. Starting from level one – we have over thirty fields... you'll have forty-five minutes to complete the challenges. You will complete the level together until I deem that you're ready for the next level. Be warned most of you won't finish, not yet anyway. Don't fret though, there's a team of guardians watching the field, including myself. You will most likely be too busy to notice us, still we are there to keep an eye on you. We'll open up the gates at your position when the time's up,' Sir Dash instructed.

Bastian was next to Gertie and Verne, and Felix and Mandy were right behind him, followed by Rudi and Russ. The moment they stepped inside, leaving the clearing behind Bastian was blinded by mud in his face by two boys on the field next to him running by. Wiping it out of his face he saw their own course in front of him. Verne and Gertie were already down in a dirt ditch, charging underneath the netting into the watery mud.

Following their lead Bastian was down underneath the net, crawling along as fast as he could, covered in mud from head to toe. He felt the watery mud beneath him begin to rise against his arms, getting deeper by the moment.

'On your back, grab hold of the netting' he called, before pulling himself through the slosh of mud upside down. The muddy water now rising to his shoulders, with his mouth close to the net as it filled his ears and covered the sides of his face, making it harder to gasp for air.

Calming his breathing, trying to get use to sludge surrounding him. It weighed down his body, as though if he stopped it would swallow him whole. Bastian stretched his arms wider trying to pull his head up away from the mud, he managed to look back to see that everyone got his message, only just being able to see all their heads above water. Relieved, he continued stretching out across the netting. The lines or rope dragging across his face as he pulled himself slowly along. Slowly they all moved through, Verne who was first out helped them all out one by one.

It wasn't over yet. After everyone was out, dripping in the brown filth, not one of them looking comfortable at all.

'Down there,' Mandy said, pointing out a gate down the end of the rather long thinning field. Running down to the gate there seemed to be some sort of contraption at its side. A hanging copper basin, quite large. If he'd had it at home, he'd use it as a firepit. The fun he would have had with Sticks and Mason roasting sweets by it side. Bastian eyed it off, it looked as though the basin was connected to the gate, and that weight would unhinge it open.

'The rocks, back there,' Russ said. 'We need every last one.'

There were three rocks that they each needed to carry. They weren't the lightest either. And the mud was quickly starting to dry to their skin, making moving even harder. Bastian lifted a large one, and carried it awkwardly down. He had to make two trips overall. Verne only had to make one trip for his three but went back to help Mandy with hers. It took every rock for the basin to fall. With a creak in machinery the gate opened.

'They're really throwing as much as they can at us…' Felix noted, as they all faced with a rock wall that needed to be climbed. Looking up it looked uneasily high, and not straight.

'Come on Felix, you charmed those girls. Don't want them to think a wall got the best of you,' Bastian Laughed. He was used to climbing; the higher the climb, the bigger the splash was always his Sticks moto when they'd go cliff jumping.

Bastian was halfway up the wall, scraping his muddy hands across its surface trying to get the dry mud off so that it would stop pinching his hand. It was only in that moment that he realised that Mandy, Verne, and Felix were still on the ground below. Looking up at the wall confounded at where to even begin. Verne looked like he was trying to grab a hold of the wall, he seemed so unsure of how to even lift himself. Rudi continued up past

Bastian, and soon disappeared over the top of the wall, Russ and Gertie both stopped and waited when Bastian didn't move.

'What's wrong?' Gertie asked.

'We can't just leave them,' Bastian said. 'Aren't we supposed to be a team?'

'We won't finish in time,' Gertie replied, but Bastian was back on the ground before she could say another word.

'Get up the top both of you and stay there to help if you can,' he said to an annoyed Gertie, she was fixed on doing her best. Russ followed her up. Bastian had helped Russ climb into the vent, so he was surprised how well he did. He was slow and careful making a few missteps, but he didn't stop trying.

'Okay. We are going to get you guys up the top,' Bastian said assertively as he landed beside the others.

Felix was covered with fear. 'I'm a city kid, golden boy. I can't climb something like this; ledges and ladders and rooftops sure, but dirt and rock, no.'

'Don't be stupid, this is the same sort of thing. You've just got to grab the rock face and I'll show you where's best to place your feet.'

Bastian showed them the easiest way to get up the wall. Verne was up in no time getting the hang of it before the others. It took him a while with his large feet, but once he got the hang of it, he managed to think his way through. Gertie and Russ were both up the top ready to pull him up as he got closer.

Mandy got the knack of it too. She stumbled by stepping on a loose bit of rock, but Bastian steadied her and helped her back up showing her how to test the rock before she put her full weight on it.

Bastian went side by side with Felix, talking him through every movement. Seeing the nerves in Felix's face with every inch he moved, it was the most unsettled he'd seen him so far. Bastian was nervous as they gained height that Felix was going to lose his nerve and fall, talking to him to distract him.

'Go on, tell me. What did you say to those girls?' Bastian asked as Felix climbed.

Felix laughed, 'As if I'm telling you. Your face, and your courage. You don't need any extra help,' Felix retorted.

'Sure I do. I wouldn't have a clue what to say,' Bastian tried to explain, but before they could say another word Felix grabbed onto a piece of rubble that fell out from under him, leaving him unbalanced, where he started to freak out, hugging the wall tighter than ever. Bastian knew he wouldn't get any further, not this time, so he climbed ahead of him.

'Grab my hand Felix,' Bastian called down to him.

Felix inched up so that Bastian was in reach and grabbed hold of his hand. He called for Gertie to come down and reach out for Felix's other hand.

'Now, I'm going to hold this side of you, use my momentum to swing up to the others. There's another step up for your foot just here,' Bastian said, eyeing a small dent in the cliff next to him. 'I need you to pull yourself up as far as you can, and Gertie will catch you,' Bastian said.

Knowing how scared Felix was, as he swung him up made it only an even bigger relief when Gertie finally caught his hand. Russ took Felix's other and soon enough he was on top of the wall.

Followed by Bastian who was the last one up, who couldn't help but clap a now joyful Felix on the back. 'Nice work, reckon tomorrow you can do it yourself?' Bastian asked, half laughing. He looked at the remaining field ahead and was exhausted at the thought of it but continued on all the same.

***

'How long do you think it'll be until they send us all on a mission?' Felix said from the comfort of his bed. They were all getting ready, and slowly making their way tucked into their beds after filling up on as much roast as they could handle.

'You might have to get through that field first mate,' Bastian joked.

'I don't know,' said Mandy as she got ready to jump into a top bunk, 'I asked some of the guys from Serpent Squad, they've been here nearly a year and they still haven't been sent out on any missions,'

'What do you think our first mission will be?' Russ asked.

'I think we just need to focus on getting through the training we have ahead of us. Or none of us will make it to the first mission,' Gertie said.

'She's right guys,' Bastian added. 'We need to learn all we can, today was hard enough for us all. If this is just the start, we have a long way to go. So, lets rest up.'

'Too right,' came his grandfather's voice as he pushed their door open.

'Before you get some rest Bastian, do you mind if I have a word?' his grandfather asked him. Bastian looked around at Verne who encouraged him to go. He knew that the others where all staring at him as he left the room, following his tall grandfather out and down the hallway.

At the entry hall his grandfather led him up another flight of stairs to a set of doors. When they walked inside a room that was quite small, or perhaps a large cupboard. Bastian wasn't quite sure. His grandfather closed the doors behind them, enclosing them in. Then he moved a metal lever on the side wall and pushed it up. Bastian was interested to what it would do. With a shudder and a jerk of movement Bastian felt the room around him shift, as though it wasn't stuck in place. He wasn't sure how, but the room was moving. When the sensation stopped his grandfather waited a moment before opening the doors leading to a round room. Curiously staring out to the round room, Bastian took a quick step out, cautiously not wanting to be stuck in the moving cupboard. This must have been his grandfather's quarters. There was a grandeur about the room, his furniture was of the highest leathers and looked finely made, it put the rest of the Guardian's compound to shame. A capsule of warmth, and a nod to a life of adventure. A shirt and tie lay over the side of a couch's arm. There was a large map that covered most of the back wall, and next to it a small arch that led to his bedroom.

'Bastian, have a seat son,' his grandfather said.

He sat down as his grandfather took a seat at his own wooden desk that was twice the size of the one in the library. It too was covered in an array of books, letters and paperwork. The weariness that was set in his face couldn't be covered; not even by his intrigue of having Bastian in front of him.

'What am I doing here?' Bastian asked, remembering his mother always said his grandfather exuded confidence and pride during conversations.

'Well, we haven't had a proper chance to talk, you and I.

I am your grandfather after all. Shouldn't I want to get to know you?,' his grandfather questioned.

'I don't think that counts if this is the first time that we've had anything to do with each other. I'm only here because it's what mum wanted. Unlike you, I listen to her. I think maybe somewhere along the line you decided that we weren't good enough to be a part of your life,' Bastian said.

'Ah, you have her spunk. Don't be fooled boy, I love your mother very much. She will always be my world. Yet, my duty has been ever so important, she knew that. However, over the years I expect she forgot me, and the love I have for her. It seems she never forgot what I did, that's why she trusted in me to take you on,' Harker said.

'Yeah, well how would you know what she's like?' Bastian said, wanting to protect his mother's feelings more than anything. 'She barely knows you. Whose fault do you think that is?'

'That's true. She was much younger than you are now when I last properly knew her; she was so young and full of life, always questioning everything and wanting to learn. She was meant for so much more than I am sure has become her.

Still, I had a mission back then; it was a stupid mission. But it took me very far away from your mother and grandmother. I was gone for so long that by the time I got home they were both… gone,' Harker looked directly at Bastian. 'I tracked them down and found my wife had passed. I could see the sadness my arrival caused Lizzy. She was grown by then – to her I was too late to save her mother. I left, she seemed happy with her husband, she didn't need me anymore, and so I returned here. From what I've heard he turned out not to be too different from myself.'

'What mission, what took you all that way away?' Bastian asked, not expecting the silence that followed as his grandfather stayed in thought. Harker's hands grazed over a letter that had recently been opened in front of him. The bottom of the letter from what Bastian could see read:

She's alive, and alone. Tell me what can be done,

Bastian couldn't make out any more of the letter once his grandfather broke the silence.

'There are bad people in this world. And no, not just the Guard. But my mission was to take care of something much more than just our family – to protect our world from forces that you can only imagine. There are those out there that need to be stopped from causing any real damage to our world. And others who need to be protected.' A haunted look crossed his face.

'Well, that's wonderful, you didn't even think of us as people who needed protecting,' he'd had enough of his grandfather's answers.

'Please Bastian; I'm only here to help. There is so much you still have to learn, to understand about Grinnwick, and even amongst the Guardians safety isn't guaranteed. Knowledge isn't safe. All I want is to protect you, and I will do everything I can to ensure you are prepared for whatever this life throws at you.'

'Why wouldn't I be safe here? That's the main reason I was sent here, to be safer than I was.'

'Not just you, all of us are in dangerous waters. As Guardians we have a high degree of skillsets that if uncovered will be highly desired by those in power. Sometimes I don't know if they have uncovered that knowledge, and I feel this place losing control of what it once was. There's a niggling feeling inside of me that perhaps the guard are more than aware of our presence, that they are strategic in their plotting. Their aggravation at having a long running organisation placing their own form of soldiers throughout the world would most definitely make us a target. As your teacher, and your grandfather, I only want to tell you to look after yourself and your friends, okay? Keep your head down, just like today and I will do my best to look after you. Curiosity is smart, I would encourage it even. However, your safety is vital to me, and I know to your mother… So just make sure you are smart in your time here.' The calmness in his voice eased Bastian but also made the alert even more significant.

The Quiet Man Inn

Waking with the sun, Scarlet didn't feel the need to reveal to anyone else the presence of the river ghosts. She decided that was the only explanation for them, that the river must have held their memory. And if anything, she was lucky that they arrived to bring her attention to the creature.

'Not far now, you lot,' Dawson said enthusiastically.

He wasn't wrong, by lunch they were off the boat and on a real path.

'Land,' Archer hugged the ground, leading them all to laugh. Even Dawson managed to crack a smile at that one.

Hudson and Scarlet both helped Lux up, and with them under each arm she hobbled on one leg.

'Look, I know we got a bit scared back there, but that wasn't too bad. I mean you'd think four kids and a man would attract some scary stuff. Isn't that what this place is famous for?' Archer mused.

'Geez Arch, don't jinx us now. We're still in here you know,' Hudson replied.

'But the Corazon Forest is supposed to have a bunch of scary things in it. And all we got was a dust ghost,' Archer replied.

'You call that a dust ghost, more like a spirit demon,' Lux noted, gasping as she accidentally knocked the leg. Scarlet had been helping her walk, but the weight she put on her after that knocked forced them both off balance.

'Let me,' Dawson insisted, helping Lux.

'Just because you didn't see anything else, doesn't mean there wasn't anything there. I have a feeling we had a couple of friends following us on this trip keeping trouble at bay,' Dawson said. Scarlet felt his gaze follow her at those words. 'If it were me, I wouldn't be running back in here any time soon,' he warned, at least not on your own.

The late afternoon drew near as the forest began to thin. The sight of a small town came up ahead. Lamps lit up the few wooden buildings that were at the edge of the forest.

The largest building was the first they came up to. Scarlet had never seen such a structure like this; the Amari Village rooms were all embedded into their land; she had never seen something so obviously protrude like this. The wood was structured into the shape that she'd seen in books, a real house. The wood was worn and warped, and at the front of the house a ragged sign hung, *The Quiet Man Inn*.

From the moment they stepped through the large heavy door, the warm light was comforting. Inside, was not too dissimilar from the common room back home. Except for perhaps the large, long table that they faced on entry. Their looked to be bottles and glasses stored behind it. And the room was covered with tables and chairs with four built-in table settings, that had chairs hugging all the way around it. Hudson and Scarlet both helped Lux settle her leg up across the seat of one of the built-in tables. A man behind the bar who appeared from behind the kitchens with a large red handlebar moustache and a round belly.

'Ello there,' he greeted them merrily. His jolly smile made it easier for them all to relax.

'Doesn't come every day we get a family like you lot in here. Mostly get hunters, lone travellers, and the odd soldiers in these parts. But I gotta say it is mighty nice to see a lot of fresh happy faces here. What can I get for you?' The rounded man asked before his face turned to Lux's leg.

'By the gods, what happened to the wee one. Let me grab a few things and I'll have you sorted in a moment,' he said.

The notion of gods wasn't foreign to Scarlet, the Amari's beliefs were stemmed in natural beings that built Grinnwick into what it was; the stem of all life. They also taught them in their lessons of how the human world of Grinnwick often held a significance to a god.

He returned to them with proper tape and stirrups to hold her leg and passed them to Dawson who helped Lux rearrange her bandages.

'What else can I do for you?'

'They'll have some water, and I'll have a beer. And we'll get some of your meat to share,' Dawson said.

'I can do that.' The rounded man smiled and returned to the bar for the drinks.

Dawson turned to Scarlet and the others.

'Now, we have a few things to discuss. And no, this isn't following any agenda that the Amari want. It's some logistics, there's another one of you here so things might get a bit tricky when it comes to finding a place for us to stay. I do have somewhere in mind which should still work, so let's just hope that pans out.

'It's also time for you all to know a few things about life out here. The elders may have had you sheltered from too many things; I couldn't say, I wasn't a part of their teaching. However, the moving pieces of this world are complex, and these changes have never meant much to the Amari. Here and now, you need to know what to expect.

Scarlet ears were enticingly perked, she wanted to know everything.

'There are those in power here that would end our time quicker than not; what a waste protecting you all would have been, wouldn't it. So, let's stay alive. Not for anyone else but ourselves.

'Caution to the south, is one you need to remember. That is where the Grinnwick Guard hold most of their power. In the city of Astoria. It's there that for centuries they have built up their defences, through flames and terror.'

'What exactly is it that they're doing? Are they worse now than the people who led the War of Darkness? How do you know any of this if you've been with the Amari too?' Lux interrupted.

All of them were a little shocked that she interrupted Dawson, but he didn't seem to mind. Scarlet was glad for it, she needed so much more clarity with what was going on. She had heard in the last couple years mentions of The Grinnwick Guard. They definitely weren't an organised group when she first came to the Amari, that much she knew. In that regard they could have been in Grinnwick still for a few centuries. She was nearly overwhelmed at the thought of all the small titbits of information one gathered in a lifetime that none of them had, the knowledge of the way of the world as it currently was that they had no clue of. The unknown nearly too large to comprehend.

Dawson thought to himself for a minute.

'I've had contacts keep me informed through the centuries, generations of people passing messages through the Corazon Forest. Their messages sent by burrows in the trees, an old magical form of communication that the Amari set up before they retreated to their Village. It's all hard to say for certain if they are worse than those who left our lives in ruin; for what was and what is are two distant realities. Back then, once the angry mobs stormed the southern towns after they took the kingdom when we left, it was like the land reacted. Storms were reported from every corner, the ground shook at the furthest reaches of Grinnwick. Even the Wirkswood Ranges succumbed to the events, from what's reached me is that there is a great tearing through the rangers, as though the land has tried to pull itself in half. The seasides were met with ravaging seas, destroying many seaside towns, while lost to landslides from the hundred-year storm. While the south was devastated the north became consumed with heat. While Grinnwick has never fully stabilised, the people here have found ways to rebuild, to adapt. It is how they have become what they are now.

This Cor-Marinium substance that they have found powers their development. I had heard of the substance years before we even left, it used to be called Agma. We didn't use it for power then, we wouldn't have known how, but small villages of fae used it for the aroma. The Cor-Marinium starts off as a green rock, and they would throw it in with their woodfires. Its smoke causing them to "see the future." Doubt anyone uses it for that anymore.

'Non the less, I think we will all be met with the unexpected in the way that these people live. Where perhaps magic and faith in our world was at the forefront of our time. Since we left little is known to this world of magical entities, or faith in a power beyond their own means. The Amari, your kind are one of the few I believe who still interact with the living world. Not a creature or a relic elsewhere has been seen. Apart from the Amari it was as though the day we first left I felt their presence dwindling. The

124

smallest creatures, even yellow lobbed hares soon started being scarce. Their yellow tails once spread seeds of the garden as they ate on the dried gums. 1 I didn't think much of it until Elder Jackson casually mention the lack of sighting. Even then at the beginning, I'm sure he knew. I thought the Corazon Forest being is own entity we would come across more than we did. But it is quiet, nearly too quiet even for the Forest. Although, perhaps we were more than just lucky....'

'I wouldn't say it was silent,' Lux interrupted.

'Not silent,' Dawson laughed in agreeance, 'but as though it's been asleep for a very long time. The same must be said for the creatures of Grinnwick. That they've retreated into the deepest, darkest depths of the land that they too have found no need to rise.

'As for the Grinnwick Guard themselves I was informed as they began. Word came to me from a distant relative of our close friends whose family I'd written to over their generations. He said that the Guard took the children off the surrounding families and killed those who fought against them. Their drive to do this, I couldn't say. But the greed of men is strong, and from what I heard few families in the south escaped. Those that did joined towns and cities north of the great divide that formed what they now call the outer districts. I do not know much about those lands; I never them visited before my time out here ended.

'In time though, those children were lost, brainwashed to become the Grinnwick Guards soldiers. Those boys were turned to men too quickly and released back onto their own people as machines. Girls and women alike became property if they were not already a part of the rising families,' Dawson stopped. Scarlet didn't understand the concept, how could a person be property... Dawson just stared off for a moment.

125

'Things have changed,' he begun again, he spoke in a way that was drawn out and slow like he was wrapping his own mind around the realities of the world, 'as is expected with such a great time having passed. I understand it's strange and foreign, but these are our new realities. Those in the south who respect the Grinnwick Guard and honour them for protection, pretending to be oblivious to the actions the Guard take outside of their bubble, as they live in a delusional lavish world. Assumingly there would be those who work there too, ensuring that their life style is catered to. We may never know the ins and outs of how they work exactly; it is not the path we are on.

'However, ultimately those who attacked the king and queen centuries ago had a goal, which was to drain Grinnwick of its magic, so that magic was nothing but a tale one tells children. Their goal seems successful, especially as the rise of the Grinnwick Guard has led the worlds focus to this sense of science and machinery to guide their lives forward.

'Some of the wealthier families who remained over the centuries hold some sort of power in the eyes of the rising Grinnwick Guard, perhaps it is their legacy their personal riches and idolised sense of a higher society that let those families remained intact. People who gave into the monstrosities over the generations to solidate their livelihoods. Part of me reckons they sold out, sold their soul sort of thing... you know.

'Of course, there are outcasts who work against all of them, for hundreds of years they've tried. Rebels and others just alike, and probably not so distant from my contacts – descendants of royal allies who fight against the Grinnwick Guard in their own ways. Some live in hiding or have been chased towards the outer and desolate lands of the north undoubtedly taking small actions, small wins to keep those they love safe.

126

'The Guard's leader from what I've heard is a man named Van-Helm. His strength supposedly comes from what his immortality. The belief from his people in his everlasting power. Taking whatever means they can to ensure his rule, they are still trying to spread their reach, and get to that goal to this day. And while they do, their demoralised soldiers ruthlessly inflict horrors on innocent people, from the sounds of it, they want to squash the light of hope out of every corner where it sparks.'

Dawson took a breath, he needed it. They all did frankly. Scarlet was fully absorbed into his tale of what was; what is. It didn't seem real, so much pain and suffering.

'Maybe....' Scarlet started. 'Maybe their rumours, that's all they are you know. Maybe we don't know the whole truth,' Scarlet said.

'Maybe,' Dawson answer.

'The truth is we together know so little of what the world is like now, its problems are not our own. The events that led you to be sheltered, your memories from life outside the Amari are from so long ago, what you remember – or don't remember – is nothing but history to people now. History that they may not even entirely recall. So, I don't want to hear about any of you getting involved in what is happening. It isn't our place to involve ourselves, no matter how much you think you can change it.' Dawson finished.

'But what if something happens and we need to defend ourself,' Hudson asked a little too enthusiastically. Only to be eyed down by Dawson, until he chuckled.

'In all honesty your lives always needed to be led properly. Not hidden away like little trinkets, ignorant to the reality of things. As much as it was safe for you with the Amari, that world wasn't yours. Well apart from you

Archer, you're one of the few Amari who will ever venture out of their comfort zone in all these years. Anyways, it has been a long time since your kinds been seen by man. You need to do your best to blend in. We don't know how easily recognisable you will be to the current people of Grinnwick; how they'd react to such difference. There are still many things about this time that I don't know, which means that we need to tread carefully as we move to find our place. So just don't go looking for any fights, is what I'm saying' he directed not only to Hudson, but all of them. He stopped curtly as the barman came back over to hand out their drinks. Dawson thanked him kindly as did each of them when they received the jug of water, and Dawson's beer. Dawson waited for him to return to the bar before Dawson continued.

'Caution is the key, we're strangers to everyone, and everything,' he added seeing the four of them ready to butt in. 'Trust in each other, and don't let that stray. I need you to trust me too and go along with any lies I may tell people to keep us safe. I'm jus' saying cause I know if I don't one of you'll do or say something stupid. Okay?'

'Okay.' They all replied.

'One other thing' Scarlet asked. She felt shy, not wanting to press further. 'You say we aren't safe. But that we need to live our lives. Our lives technically should have been lived nearly a thousand years ago. To these people we are part of the dead. How are we supposed to protect ourselves, not stand out and understand what the hell is even going on out here?' She saw her own confusion on everyone else's faces.

'Day by day, we'll learn. We are not staying in a city, but in a small town far from strife. A town not under the Guard's rule, and easily able to go under the radar. And although we will take precautions, you are here to live, to be happy. Do not dwell on the cautions I have given you for now. Just keep them in mind. Probably best others don't know where we are from, and even though your training like at the practice pits will continue, best not to go attacking people without proper cause.

'Think that's all enough for now. Why don't you dig in?' Dawson finished as the barman came back and dropped off the large plate of delicious smelling meat and vegetables, covered in a thick gravy. Scarlet's stomached just about reached out ahead of herself, not realising how much she was craving a hearty meal like this.

'We'll get some sleep, I'm sure this gentleman's got a room for us,' he said as the barman came back with another large plate full of meat, and a side of roasted veggies.

'I think I can manage something for you lot. Just the night then?' he asked.

Dawson nodded and joined the others digging into the food.

'What even is this?' Hudson said picking up his meat playing with it foolishly.

'It doesn't even matter, I could eat all of it and more,' Archer added.

'As if,' Lux butted in stiffly but still swiftly swiping his leg of meat out of hand.

'I'd watch out Lux, don't steal from the hands that have to lug your butt up to the room,' Scarlet laughed.

Lux looked at her a little annoyed, but it wasn't long until they were all laughing at Archer for being completely covered in food, and continuously inhaling what was in front of him. Sitting with her friends, with Dawson, Scarlet couldn't help but enjoy the company around her. It was relaxing to say the least. Although they weren't at their new home yet, the exhaustion that they had felt from their journey through the Corazon Forest was beginning to fade. Their tired bodies finally resting.

Even Dawson finally looked relaxed amongst them all as he playfully fought over a large bit of meat with Hudson while drinking his beer. He was already looking like a stronger man.

'Please, come on. Tell us about it. Where is it?' Scarlet started.

'What does it look like?' Lux added.

'Do we each get our own room?' Archer questioned.

Scarlet was sure Dawson mentioned a place he called Bellevue Point. But missed it over the others rambling excitement.

'Most western point along the Golden Coast, far from any city. A quiet town at heart; the towns people are true to their roots. sprung to life with the people who came from all over to find shelter from the surrounding wars,' Dawson said, warning them too that the people who lived in town had undoubtedly been from families who had lived there forever. He had been informed that some of them considered themselves extremely sophisticated and didn't always care for outsiders. That close by there was a market town where travellers passed through. That's where his intel came from, the head of the marketplace; a man named Winslow.

Even though Dawson was warning them of the ways of the world, his tone Scarlet noticed was enthusiastic as he spoke of their new home, his excitement at what lay ahead didn't go astray and stayed with him the rest of the evening.

Scarlet jumped into the one large, quilted bed that was in the centre of the room they were given with Lux, Hudson and Archer, all knocking each other out of the way trying to get the most space on the bed. After settling down, and somehow managing to find their heads on a pillow, Scarlet turned to face Dawson who was sitting in an armchair beside her reading an old worn book. She realised how much she had grown used to his presence.

'You'll always stay with us Dawson, won't you?' she asked. The steady breathing of the others quietened as they listened for the answer. Waiting for what seemed the longest moment, he slowly looked up from his book.

'You couldn't get rid of me kid,' he replied softly with his crooked smile. A simple comment that managed to put them all at ease, and soften them into a world of dreams.

***

Scarlet didn't know how to describe what she saw in front of her – it was like a cart, a very large cart indeed. It had metal on the outside and had a large tray on the back. It rumbled like as though it emitted its own power, however she wasn't really sure of the purpose.

The Quiet Man didn't have too many differences to the world she had known, but perhaps they were still far enough from civilisation that those differences weren't prevalent. But this machine, this beast had them all gobsmacked. She heard Dawson talking with the man who owned the machine and heard him ask how it ran. He seemed nearly as unsure as she felt by the contraption,

'What you mean, this old mover?' It's how you travel around, where you been hiding, in a hole?' The owner cursed. His rough retort, was mildly off putting yet Dawson followed through with hiring him.

'Alright you four, get your things and back here in five minutes,' Dawson instructed. Looking at their blank faces. 'Come on.'

Scarlet shut her case; it was twice the size of the others backpacks, so Archer helped her carry it down the stairs. 'Geez, what's packed in this thing? They gave you this much?' he asked panting from the weight of the case.

'I hope there're other outfits than this,' she replied, pulling at her skirt.

'Yeah, I was going to ask you about that. But I just assumed that's what girls out in Grinnwick wear. We didn't really have time to change into anything, but it does look a bit like some of the clothes Milo gave us to put in our bags. Guess we'll probably need it to blend in,' he said.

'If only it didn't weigh so much. Your stuff fits into your normal pack, why'd I get this old thing?' Scarlet gasped struggling to pull the leather handle of the case. 'Plus doubt I'm going to be able to do anything too fun in these clothes.'

'Eh come on, you've just trekked through one of the scariest forests in that outfit, haven't you? I'm sure you'll be able to pull off any adventure no matter what you've got to wear. And I think it's the case that's the heaviest,' Archer replied, finally passing it over to Dawson who was at the back of the mover waiting for them.

'See Scarlet, River is written on the bottom there, that was your last name yeah,' Archer stated. Scarlet realised Dawson turned quickly at the mention of her last name, a name she didn't often use. 'The "S" for Scarlet must have faded off. Would have been the case you came to the Amari Village with, or maybe Flynn's', Archer pointed out, and it was the first time on the trip Scarlet had noticed it. She felt bad that Dawson had carried it so far for her, she could have just had a simple bag like the others.

Adrian they had come to learn as the name of the owner of the mover. He wasn't exactly talkative. He had a thick neck and billowing moustache that didn't move as he helped the four of them onto the tray of his mover. He quickly returned to the driver's seat, not looking any of them in the eye.

'They're a bit skittish this far out,' Dawson assured Scarlet as she was sure her faced look nearly as uneasy as she felt, 'probably finds it strange that a group like us has made it so long out here. He probably thinks we aren't exactly desirable cargo.'

'Then why take us?' Hudson asked.

'Elder Jackson left me with more than you kids, and packs to ensure our safety,' Dawson replied, and pulled out a bag that jingled. A form of payment for his services was obvious, but Scarlet had no idea what was used to barter with, whatever the contents of the bag it must have been something of value.

Scarlet had Archer next to her, his face poking through where Adrian controlled the mover, trying to catch a glimpse at how the machine worked. Dawson encouraged them to sit back as they got moving.

'There's water and snacks in the tub. don't you eat it all at once,' Dawson added, eyeing Hudson. Unfortunately, he was already hands-deep into the tub and pulled back at Dawson's words. With a thud, Dawson hit his head on the side of the trailer as the mover started, with a snarly glare and the rub of his head he shifted further down into the tray so it wouldn't happen again.

Their ride was far from easy; it was the first time any of them had ever been in something like this. Scarlet found herself wishing for her horse. A most uneasy feeling overcame her as they tried to hold on. The constant grumbling noise, mixed with the vibrations not helped by the rocky road underneath knocking them all around.

The queasy look on Archer and Lux's face after the first hour or so didn't go unnoticed, and the tub of snacks soon turned into a vomit bucket for them both as Adrian carried on down a valley.

Scarlet started to feel ill herself and the fumes from the tub weren't helping one bit. Resting on her back was the only way to get through the journey as they jolted along the road. She kept her eyes closed trying to zone out from the gross noises that Archer and Lux were making.

The mover came to a halt a few hours into the journey. Adrian had stopped to top up their fuel from a can he kept locked up inside the trailer. Scarlet couldn't help but dry retch as he opened it up while they were all still inside.

Archer raced out of the trailer, not far off hugging the steady ground below him. Hudson helping Lux and her injured leg out was blissfully unaware, appeared with an apple clenched in his mouth, as Lux squirmed to sit steadily on the ground, just as relieved as Archer. Dawson too looked like he had just awoken from a peaceful nap. Scarlet enjoyed the air as much as any of them, the rumbling of the mover's power still rocked her, doing her best to try focusing on the horizon. Her head still dizzy and her stomach queasy. The uneasy feeling was drowned out by what was before her.

From where they stood a large valley was in sight, it went on for miles, ending only when it reached a vast ocean that could be seen across the horizon. The sea spread along the coast for as far as Scarlet could see right up until a hill of overgrown woodlands began. The height of the woods restricted her view of the sea from that point onwards. The ocean itself was breathtaking, finding herself looking with longing into the deep blue colour, Scarlet never did she feel such a rush for seeing something new. Dreams and paintings of a sea would have never compared. She'd spent years isolated, reading about the hidden depths of the ocean in their classes and yet never actually seeing or touching it. The idea had tested many of them to believe in something they had never seen. Now that they were so close to its shores it seemed to be the one place on the outside that called to her the most. And it was only another stinky, bumpy ride away.

As the others began to take notice of the view, they too couldn't look away.

'That can't be real,' Hudson gawked.

'Just you wait mate, I'll be the first one of us to jump in.' Archer teased.

'You couldn't beat me in a race if you tried,' Hudson retorted.

'Ha,' Scarlet laughed, 'You've got to be kidding. When have you ever run a race against him?' she beamed, completely bemused by Hudson confidence. As lanky as Archer was, and as more of a bookworm he may be in comparison to Hudson's strength; when it came to speed, and agility Archer had Hudson beat.

Lux, as sick as she was from the ride in the mover, still managed to find her eyes nearly falling out of her head at the sight of view; the one lake that they had back at the village was nothing compared to the sight down below. Scarlet, Archer and Hudson begged Adrian to rush and get back on the road, hurrying Dawson up to help them get back into the trailer. Hudson and Archer had practically scooped Lux up on the spot wanting to jump right back in the rumbling machine.

Not one of them seemed to mind the rickety ride as they talked about the sea. Lux still looked a bit queasy, but at least now a smile was spread over her face.

'That's where we're going Dawson; Please say yes.' Lux said, drinking some water to ease her belly.

'I know you said we were going to be on the coastline, but I didn't think about the sea; a beach. This is amazing. I mean I never imagined I'd ever be this close to the ocean,' Archer beamed, 'Did you guys know thousands of years ago there were a group of Amari that came from the sea? It's pretty much like me finally going home,' he boasted.

'Did you see how long it went on for? it's incredible,' Scarlet claimed, pulling herself up to the window looking through past Adrian and the cabin that controlled the mover, peering out to the picturesque hills that where in the forefront of the ocean and the deep blue that was only getting close. Feeling Lux, Archer and Hudson all climbing up behind her too peering out

'This is going to be amazing,' Scarlet said in awe.

'Alrigh', relax. All of you.' Dawson said, pulling them back down to sit in the movers tray properly, trying to quieten them down, the smile on his face was the biggest they'd seen yet. 'I knew you'd all get like this. Yes, we are heading to the coast like I said, and there will be the ocean, and plenty of space for you four to explore.'

'You're kidding, this is the best.' Archer said, 'We're going to live at the sea.'

'Hold your horses now boy. You'll all need to behave; the sea isn't to be meddled with. It's not like the lake back home, there are rips, tides, it is a beast in its own right.' Dawson said steadily. Each of them nodded enthusiastically yet completely distracted in their own excitement, leading Dawson to sigh at their lack of attention.

'Okay, well. There's a house, on the edge of that woodland up near the cliffs.' Dawson stopped, holding his hand up as Hudson and Lux both tried to speak. 'There is a beach below, a bay of sorts from what I've been told.

But I do need to talk to my contact before we can put claim to the house. I'm hopin' it's all good; the place is small and well hidden; perfect for keeping you lot out of trouble.' Dawson said.

'Why this town Dawson. How do you know this place?' Scarlet asked. The fact that this was to be their new home was nearly too good to be true.

'A friend told me it was there a long time ago. The main idea is that this town isn't known by the Grinnwick Guard, or at least it isn't on their radar at-the-moment. Their forces haven't been reported to be taking nearby locations, or as I most recently heard. And as we would like to stay hidden from any problems, a spacious unknown town like this will be exactly what we need. We do still need to be vigilant, so no exploring through town without my say so. We keep to our own little place on the edge of the forest; that's if we can stay there,' Dawson said.

Scarlet's excitement beamed internally, she tried to contain herself while the others continued to question Dawson. She couldn't believe that this would be their new home; even the word sounded strange, like it couldn't be real. Archer, Hudson and Lux made the village as much a home for her. But out here, she felt that they would make their own together.

***

They drove through the centre of town, where the buzz around them was booming. Scarlet couldn't help but be fascinated by the fancy outfits many of the women had on, her outfit was similar, yet it paled in comparison to some of the dresses the women here wore. They looked lovely as they walked in and out of shops. Each of the towns people noticed the mover as it rattled through the town. The streets also had other children playing not unlike they would have done with the Amari. Lux grabbed Scarlet's attention pointing to a sign above a building named St Augustine's

Home for Girls. An iron gate stood tall out the front of the large red brick building, and about a dozen or so girls could be seen in the courtyard within. Each of them were different ages, sitting in small groups listening to their elders within.

Archer's nose knocked into the side of the tray as he closed his eyes breathing in the scent of fresh bread from a bakery store that they passed right before they reached the town centre.

In the middle of the road, in the centre of town up ahead they saw a round fountain with a statue of a large bird with wings spread in the centre. Their mover had now attracted more than a few glances as they drove along, but their fascination at every detail of the town distracted each of them from the attention; Dawson seemed weary the whole time, sitting as low as he could in the tray.

Once they were outside of the town's gates and the overwhelming sense of excitement eventually died down amongst them, Hudson and Archer still talked about how there might be different types of food here. Both of them of course insisted they needed to try every single thing. Dawson ignored them; he was concentrating on the path ahead. It wasn't long until they arrived. They jumped out while Dawson handed Adrian the driver some coins, the likes of which Scarlet had never seen. From what she could tell the coins were silver with crosses on.

'All right you lot. Out.' Dawson said.

Scarlet was quick to jump out of the car dragging her large case behind her; Dawson took over for her once he helped Lux out, before she had a chance to pull it off the back of the tray herself.

'Are we here?' Scarlet asked.

'Of course not, this is a marketplace. It's not a house,' Hudson said. He was right, they had been dropped at the end of a path that led to what looked like a nestle of market stalls in front of a large hall.

'You four, wait here. I'm going to ask about the house. Okay?' Dawson said, concern covering his face as he left the four of them with their bags alone.

He made his way over to the hall, while Archer, Lux and Hudson began wandering towards the market stalls.

Scarlet however was transfixed on someone else. A man, who watched her from afar. Beyond the market and in a patch of trees she saw him standing alone, as though he was there yet not there at the same time. She blinked quickly trying to make sure he was really there. His blue eyes reflected in the sun; he carried his jacket over his shoulder and stood stall, stretching one of his suspenders across his chest. Even from the distance she was sure he was smiling, he moved with confidence and a sense of cool, chewing on something as he walked through the trees. It was as though he was looking straight at her, yet through her at the same time. But no one was behind her. His brown hair wisped to the side as it moved. Scarlet moved across as he too did.

Knocked to the side by a couple of small kids running past, she stood up to find the man had now disappeared. Her eyes dashed over the market stalls looking for him, but he was gone. Had he ever really been there? She had no clue.

First the light people at the river, now a disappearing stranger. What was going on?

Her gaze cast across the stalls of the market looking for the stranger as she got close to a wooden craft stall, that was filled with finely made chairs and tables, with an elderly man sitting in one of his own rocking chairs.

'You alright young lady?' he asked.

'I just thought I saw someone.' Scarlet looked back to the spot where she first saw the stranger.

He looked towards the same spot where Scarlet's eyes lingered. 'Think you're seeing things kid.'

Scarlet turned away from the old man, ignoring his remark. Shaking the feeling that something was off, she spotted Lux at the stall opposite speaking to a woman in charge of a veggie and herb marquee. The woman rummaged out the back and gave her a pair of sticks to help her walk; Hudson was joining in on a ball game with some of the boys near the large hall; Archer wasn't to be seen; he seemed to have vanished just like the mysterious gentleman.

She felt her breath tighten as she panicked from his disappearance. Where was he, how far could he have wandered? This wasn't a part of her imagination, and his absence from them all was a bigger deal than a random stranger disappearing.

Scarlet realistically knew that Archer had to be here somewhere. But they were all so far from what they were used to, the reality that there were so many unknowns around them made a small separation from her friends in this gigantic world almost unfathomable.

It took a moment with a tight chest and an anxious string of eyeing everyone in the market for her to finally relax when he popped up next to a bin of broken trinkets, she could see popping out some forms of machinery and smaller much more obscure items.

Archer looked fascinated by all the trinkets he was rummaging through. Just as quick as Scarlet had lost him, he came running towards her holding what she could only call rubbish, intrigue all over his face.

'Look at this Scar, I mean they just chucked it out. I can't wait to get my hands on it and see how it works.' Archer beamed.

'I bet. Do you know what it is?' Scarlet replied, sighing in relief that he was back by her side.

'No idea, but looks pretty cool, don't you think? I mean if I move this that way, and this the other...' He started to play around with the junk. Scarlet wasn't too sure what to say to that, the rubbish was a black box that was broken in half, and inside was an empty vial surrounded by layers of wires and metal sheets. She nodded in agreement with Archer but didn't find the piece interesting one bit.

Dawson returned with a man in tow, who looked fierce. Scarlet and Archer followed as he and Dawson made their way through the marketplace back to their bags. Dawson called Hudson and Lux over to them and quickly grabbed Scarlet's case and his own bag before continuing.

'I guess we are staying then,' Hudson whispered excitedly as they followed behind, grabbing his own pack along with Archer and Lux. Dawson caught onto their whispers dropping back to them.

'This here is Winslow. Anything happens to me, you four are to come back here and see him. Got me?' Dawson said. Winslow curtly waved from ahead but didn't stop moving. Dawson caught up to him and they started talking softly, with serious tones that Scarlet couldn't quite make out.

The Kindness of Ravens

The morning air was crisp, and the light just started to shine over the Valley atop of the compound. Ice reflected in the light glistening atop of the harsh grass of the valley. And The Ravens stood together huddled up in their black jumpers,

'Ravens,' Sir Dash issued from in front of them all, gaining their attention.

'I understand that you may not have known each other that long. However, you need to depend on each other, you need to have each other's backs. Teamwork is the most essential part of being a part of a Guardian's squad, and as such your confidence in each other needs to be flawless. Trust is key.

'Look around you. These are you brothers and sisters now. If you lose one of your team, in time it will feel like you've lost a limb,' Sir Dash said, capturing the weight of how important they were all now to each other.

'Work together and you can achieve anything. Today we will start out small, but at the end of this training you should feel confident in your team, knowing that if you're ever faced with a task that'll push you to your limits your squad will have your back.

'As I said, each and every one of you need to believe in each other, need to be able to rely on the person standing next to them. That is what we are building here.'

Quickly Sir Dash grouped them off into pairs and handed each pair a blindfold.

'This task should be relatively easy… you and your partner will work together. The one blindfolded in the pair will be guided by the other through this next task. Treat this as a real-life situation, because it is.

It is a master of the elements sort of situation. There will be threats that you come across that are dangerous, you must trust in each other to pass through.

'The course for this is up on the edge of the mountains, along the Cliffs of Bo. The trail is narrow and edges across the southern peak. Your goal is to reach the end of the trail by nightfall. Don't let the sound of this task fool you into thinking it is easy. The trail is difficult at the best of times. And the risk of walking it holding your teammates' hands in yours can make it even more nerve-racking for our leaders. While the ones being led will have to trust in the other, to have strong will in their friend to get them through. Remember to keep your partner blind folded the whole time, and don't take it off or you will just be sent out here again. We will give you a bottle of water, and a knife for precaution. When you reach the shelter that will be your stopping point, you will stay there the night and wait for extraction at first light. There will be instructions there on the extraction process,' Sir Dash advised, and nodded to them all good luck before a large green people mover appeared.

Bastian turned to Gertie who was his partner.

'Guess I'll wear the blindfold,' Bastian offered, picking it up from the ground, while she took the water bottle and knife. No one really seemed sure about what to do as they jumped into the mover.

'Are we really going to be out here all night?' Russ said as Mandy tied up his blindfold.

'Don't worry, we just need to find the shelter to sleep for the night and we'll be fine,' Verne assured him.

'Wait, do I put this mask on, who's guiding me?' asked Rudi.

'Put it on, or Dash will probably make us all do the task again,' Felix said, 'I'll guide you and Verne.'

'Look you lot, why don't we all just stick together, we just have to make it through the mountain pass. We will all be together, we'll be okay. Surely you lot have spent time outdoors before, this'll be a synch,' Bastian said, hoping that he was at least facing some of them. Feeling the rumble of the movers engine beneath him as they headed to their task.

'Alright, everyone. You heard our fearless leader, let's get to it,' Felix heckled, Bastian couldn't help but smile, sometimes his ridiculousness reminded him of Sticks.

***

When the mover stopped, nearly an hour or so after a small hand moved across his back, and another pushed against his shoulder as he got out of the car. Gertie's hand.

'Wow,' Gertie sighed in awe.

'Yeah, this isn't the walk in the park you made it out to be, Bass,' Felix added.

'What's it looks like?' Bastian asked.

'Well… It's a proper cliff face amongst the mountains. And from the looks of things, it's a long way down,' Gertie added, he could hear the echo of her voice, undoubtedly from the mountain terrain.

'Go on, I promise I won't let you fall,' Gertie laughed.

Bastian stepped ahead into the darkness, a different sort of grin covering his face.

'Alright. Guess you two are going first,' Felix said to Bastian and Gertie.

Bastian didn't want to step too far out of step, he could only go so far to assume it was a narrow track. He moved slowly; much more so than he thought he would have.

'What are we just going to stand here all night?' Rudi asked, his breathing seemed somewhat quicker than usual.

'You, okay?' Bastian called back.

'I just don't like not being able to see,' Rudi snapped.

'None of us do, just take your time,' Bastian said.

'It's my fault, I can't seem to move too fast,' Verne admitted.

'Look, how about you stand behind me, just hold onto my shoulders and we will take small steps,' Felix noted. Bastian could hear the three of them shuffling around on the path behind him.

'Ahhh!' squeaked Russ, causing Bastian to stop. He heard the trickle of stones and a thud. 'He's okay,' called Mandy.

'You're okay, hold onto me,' she insisted.

With a sigh of relief, they all moved on slowly for at least ten minutes or so.

'Do you guys think we'll be safe out here all night?' Russ asked.

'I hope so, cause if you four have to stay blindfolded, don't think we will have much of a shot defending ourselves. Not without plummeting to a miserable death,' Felix added.

'Don't worry Russ, we'll be fine. Think they just give us the knife in case, more of a fear mongering sort of task. Besides Sir Dash made it out like we got to get to know each other better, this is probably his roundabout way of trying to make that happen,' Gertie said.

Hoping she was right Bastion slowly continued with a few slight jerks from Gertie every now and then, helping to guide him.

The heat of the day started to tire Bastian; he felt his cheeks flush with would inevitable be burn. His stops for Gertie to give him water became more frequent. As it did with everyone. Slowing their pace entirely.

His steps kept on inching further and further forward.

'How'd they know if we took these blindfolds off?' Russ asked.

'No Clue, but I'm not risking doing this all over again, so don't even think about it,' Rudi replied.

In an attempt at distraction Mandy started to describe their surroundings. Bastian hung onto her creative descriptions, 'the shadows turn the clay-coloured rock grey with the lack of light. Its texture looks...'

'-Like it might crumble at any minute,' added Bastian.

Bastian could only imagine how severely Mandy was scowling at him.

'I mean his not wrong though, I'd be more concerned about the path under us crumbling beneath our feet,' Felix said, it was the slightest stir but brought out the biggest silence. Bastian almost gladly relished in the fact that he couldn't see the drop of the cliffs edge, it would have made the comment all the more daunting.

'Don't listen to him, Gertie laughed. 'This path been here for longer than any of us have lived, it's not about to collapse now.

Eventually a chill from the shadows reached them on their trail. And Mandy had returned to her descriptions, 'purple and orange light is reflecting of the small clouds ahead,' she described the setting sun. Once night fell, she told them of a tale of the stars.

'When I was younger my mum told me a story of the stars, the ones you can see now. Ma would say that Grinnwick was once a dark and scary place. That creatures before man, before the spark of magic even ruled. She said that the Heart of Grinnwick exploded and broke off into a million pieces and reflected into the night sky. That when this happened it used its power to cast a light over Grinnwick, and to bring the land back to life. The stories of old can be seen in the shapes the stars make too.

'There,' Mandy called-

'We can't see...,' Verne reminded her--

'Oh well if you could see you would see the stars of Farrah the fire goddess and bringer of peace, you can see her fiery necklace form in those five stars,' Mandy pointed. 'And Madalyn the Water Goddess; Right there,'-

No one bothered to remind her again, her voice was calming as they continued.

-'It makes the shape of a rounding shell that sat in her hair. And Helga, the Earth Goddess. That crisscross over there is her crown of thorns. Mum said that something happened to our stars, that the Gods and Goddesses were dishonoured, so they allowed the Guard to take control, and force so many people into a life of fear. But that a kind heart can always make a difference. So, we should always be nice to those around us,' Mandy said, and continued telling more tales of other stars.

The calm in her voice put them all at ease as the night went on, no fear struck them as she spoke. He thought only of his home and the stars there, if they would be looking up at them just like Mandy was looking at now.

They talked through the night about nothing too serious, mainly of bedtime stories that each of them could remember. Verne sung rhymes of sheep; Felix told tales of fat old men who ate too much; Each of them was

147

tired from the day, their conversation had dwindled with their weariness, when a large gust shocked them all.

The gust echoed down the pass, thundering the rocks onto the cliffs path; its force knocking them all off balance.

'Down,' called Gertie, pushing both of Bastian's shoulders heavily towards the ground. She forced him to drop as low as he could as the wind only increased and flung stones and dirt at them all. He had braced himself, yet his face copped a pelting. When it finally stopped, he didn't dare move.

'You, okay?' Gertie asked him. He nodded.

'The others?' he asked, she paused for a moment.

'Think we took the brunt of it,' Gertie said. 'Here, sit up I'll get you the water.'

Sipping the water, he felt a wetness on his forehead that could have only been from blood. He felt Gertie wipe it away with something before helping him up.

The next hour or so seemed to drag on, the small motions continued, and Bastian was feeling not only defenceless, but useless too. With no clue of what was before him, he only had Gertie to put his trust in.

But he did, he trusted her.

'Is that it? Is that the shelter?' Felix called out.

Gertie kept on guiding Bastian but called back, 'Yeah it looks like it, but there's no one else in sight.'

Bastian kept on moving along until Gertie tugged him to a halt.

'There's a sign,' Gertie said, and began reading.

'It says, *A leap of faith is only increased by your faith in each other….*'

'What does that even mean?' Felix called out.

'I don't think I want to jump off of anything?' Verne added.

'Not a chance,' Russ called out.

'You may have to but, we still have a few hours before first light so maybe we should try get a couple hours sleep,' he posed to the group.

'Good thinking, I'm exhausted,' assed Rudi.

'You guys really think you're going to get any sleep?' Verne asked.

'No harm in trying,' Gertie said.

Bastian felt her hands move across his body forward – the path must have opened up wider, she seemed confident in her movements now. There must have been plenty more space with less concern for falling.

She told him to sit helping guide him to the ground.

***

The whole area began rattling around Bastian, shaking him awake. It took a moment for him to realise that he'd actually nodded off. But he was still in the dark, blindfolded unaware of what was going on around him. The motion around him, the shaking of the path beneath him was cause for concern. However, this wasn't being caused by a gust of wind, but that something was close by.

'That's next level wicked,' called Felix over a loud propellor noise.

Bastian wanted to peek so badly, but Gertie quickly reminded him to keep it on. Slapping his hands from his face.

'You ready?' came a voice from his right. A familiar one, Sir Dash.

'Look, it's not that far, it's only a little jump,' Gertie encouraged him.

'It's a giant mover, hovering above the ground just next to us. But you need to make the gap.'

'The gap?' Bastian asked.

'the black nothingness that drops right off the cliff,' Felix nervously said himself.

Bastian was almost glad he couldn't see it but imagined the darkness below.

'And if I miss it?' Bastian asked.

'Don't,' added Gertie.

I'll put you in the right spot, all you have to do is jump up and ahead,' Gertie said.

He followed her cautiously; this did not seem like the sanest idea.

He had to trust in her though, there was no other choice. He stood there… 'When I say go jump as far out as you can,'

'Ready…

Set…

GO.'

Bastian couldn't remember jumping, his heart pounded. Feeling arms pull him closer when his jump into the unknown. Feeling as though he should be falling he collapsed heavily onto the floor of the hovering mover. Like a dead weight. A rush of energy and a blur of light as his eyes adjusted from Sir Dash removing his blindfold. He took in the sleek surrounds of the mover, the vibration of it under his feet. It was large and spacious inside, with braces across the world that would have been used to strap passengers in. It took a moment for him to adjust but he soon realised he was needed, and he dove right back to help Gertie into the hovering mover. As he pulled her in, his attention diverted back to his surrounds. While he was impressed by the piece of machinery they were in, the slickness to the metal, the softness to its curves. He had no idea the Guardians owned anything so advanced. He could now see the Cliffs of Bo, and the narrow path Gertie had managed to help him pass. He was almost glad he never saw the plummeting drop off the edge of the already rough and winding trail that hugged the cliffs. Normally it would be absurd to even take the path. A fall from the edge would leave you not only fatally injured, but lost; unclaimed, left to be consumed by the mountains of Grinnwick, forever. They both continued helping the rest of the team, mind you for all his talk Rudi was the one who took the longest to jump, making Bastian more than a little smug for the trip home.

***

Half lost in thought in class Bastian was knocked over the head by his

'You're not paying attention boy,' his grandfather said.

'These creatures may be lost to the known world, but they are still very real.'

Bastian looked at the page below him, it seemed utter nonsense to him. A little green lady on the side of a riverbank, her skin lined like that of a leaf, coarse to be sure. A clearly defined outline of wings completely whimsical and that of storybooks, not of reality. The description in the book noting 'the ravine are a small group of fae, that once flourished in the heartland of the rainforests, and their stature depicts our current form of fae in storybooks.'

on the page opposite, was a rather grave looking form, not man yet not entirely bone – it was illustrated as though dark burns ripped through its skin, and its eyes pointedly sharp, yellow and black, dagger like.

Underneath it was titled – 'shadow dwelling daemon – wraith: beings of the old world, a time before time itself. When the light of this world did not yet exist, and the flames and darkness consumed all of existence.

These creatures now hide in the shadows, they are still said to be messengers for the old gods – Ezekiel, Thundas, and Magna, the Kings of the shadowland. These wraiths carry out the requests of the Kings. To this day they lurk in shadows, hidden, to squish out the light that maintains our existence.'

It was a dark tale; the sort of thing you'd read that was for sure. And the look of disbelief must have been all over his face.

'You don't believe in such things boy?' his grandfather mused.

'It's just… it seems, impossible.' Bastian answered.

'What is possible? Things you've seen before you. Things you can hold…. is that what makes it real?' he asked.

'I guess, – these wraiths, the notion of ancient gods it just seems otherworldly. I mean I can't read it in a book, and instantly believe it because you say so.' Bastian said.

'You're right!' his grandfather beamed.

'A view you should always hold tight, all of you. The ability to question is your greatest strength.

'If these beings are real, then why is it that no stories are told of them? That the first you learn of them is from an old book, and who is the writer of this book, why are they to be trusted with sharing such information?' Is there parts of their mythology that we are missing, how can we know if we don't have the full story?

'They aren't the only stories told,' Russ chimed in.

'I heard stories on the ships with my father, about the dragons of the underworld. The manipulators of our world, trying endlessly to send it back into an eternal night. Father said it was said their power is what brought on the great War of Darkness.'

'Ah huh! Great example Russ,' his grandfather beamed, making Russ go red.

'So, there are other stories throughout our world, that correspond to the stories before us. And this book, its words have been passed on for generations through the Guardians, each adding witness sightings of shadow creatures like these.'

'So, these are tale of men long ago, men I have never known or trusted,' Bastian replied.

'You are correct, and I say to you boy your questioning is valid – but here we have a chance to believe.

'Believe in faery tales -,' Felix called out, 'I don't know about that sir, we aren't little kid.'

'You are not, but sometimes there is merit to the tales you were told as young kidlets. And belief is something bigger than yourself, it is an acceptance of possibilities in the world that you may never thought imaginable. And I'd say this to you, to be open to the inexplicable that life offers you.'

Bastian noticed the cheekiness, almost boyish look in his grandfather's eyes.

***

'Do we really need to do this?' Rudi asked, as he and Russ tied a rope to connect their hands, and then Felix did the same on the other side of Rudi. They weren't the only ones; the whole squad were connected by ropes forming a line.

Each of them was desperate for a break; ever since they'd arrived it had been a massive change of pace to their normal lives, and whatever group bonding task that Sir Dash had concocted now was just another barrier before they got to enjoy a day off.

'If you shut up and wait for him to tell us what we are doing, we might get done sooner, and if anything, be thankful that we're not covered in shit for the day, ' Gertie snapped back from the other end of the line to Rudi, surprisingly as she was usually the calmer minded of the group, 'And besides, we get through this task, that's our beginners group tasks done, and we'll get tomorrow off.'

Bastians ears perked up, a day off. He couldn't even remember the joys of just doing nothing. These few weeks had been taxing on them all, and all he wanted was some time to breath. Frustration had been building up in each of them. The exhaustion of a whole new world and no reprieve had been turning them all crazy.

Still, tired and annoyed and ready for a break as they were the Ravens lined up, each with their hands tied to each other in a line. Russ was so fidgety that he kept on pulling on Bastian and Mandy's arm.

It was their first time in this field, it was on the northern end of the topside valleys above the Guardians compound. It had been stripped back to look even more desolate than the whole area usually did. Mounds and holes had been formed, and mover tires, haybales, and rusting parts of large ship containers were placed.

Sir Dash stood ahead of them, calling out to another squad coming down the pathway.

'Phoenix Squad. Welcome, thought you might be able to help me whip these guys into shape,' he said with a daring smile.

'As I suggested to you last night, these guys need to feel the pressure. They need to know what it's like to make their way through enemy terrain. I want you lot to grab a rice bag shooter. Head out into the field behind me and hide behind something, stay out of view so they don't know where you are. Don't be easy on them. Watch out on your way out too, there's a few traps and holes set up to make this task a bit tricky,' Sir Dash said to Phoenix Squad, who all seemed to take on their task with ease, none of them questioning their orders.

Sidney, the Phoenix squad leader grabbed one of the bean bag shooters and led his squad out into the field carefully, he was as sure of himself as anyone in the Guardians. Bastian admired his confidence. He walked like he owned not just the field but his team. Noticing Mandy blushed when Sidney walked past, and the slight giggle she tried to hide as he spoke to his squad quickly made Bastian draw his eyes over to Gertie who couldn't help but stare at him too. Undoubtedly, he was a good-looking older guy; somehow their interest in him only increased Bastian's desire to win.

'Get to the far end of the field Ravens, you only have to reach the red line painted on the ground and still be attached and you're done for the day. If you don't…If even one of you gets hit by the Pheonix squad; if you hit a trap, I will blow the whistle and back to the starting line you come,' Sir Dash said, as a clear warning.

'One step forward,' Bastian called, and they stepped out, so far out of range of the Phoenix squad.

They were only a mere ten steps ahead, when Bastian called for them to hit the ground —he'd spotted one of the Phoenix Squad in the distance on their right. Unsure if the guy would be able to shoot them from his vantage point, Bastian didn't want to risk it. He called for them to start crawling along so that he wouldn't spot them from his angle.

'Ouch' cried Felix, who'd taken a hit on the side of his neck on the far-right side of their line.

Sir Dash Blew the whistle. Bringing them all back to the start.

Felix was on the right, so they stuck to the left when they first dropped to the ground. They veered towards a hay bale, still staying out of eyesight of the first Phoenix squad member that Bastian saw earlier. They stood up behind the hay bale. Verne edged out, trying to see if he could see anyone from Phoenix who'd have a clear shot of them. They went to run up to the next hay bale when Verne copped a bean bag in the chest, and Russ fell into a camouflaged hole.

'Again' called Sir Dash. Bastian could see a slight grin could be seen on his face, he was taking too much joy in this, that was for sure.

They were caught in the middle section next time around, Bastian taking the full blow when a dozen bean bags came at them, protecting both Russ and Mandy, while Verne stepped up to stop Gertie from copping any. She was preoccupied with a cut on her leg from a bear trap that had just narrowly missed shutting on her entire foot. Rudi meanwhile had fallen down a hole and Felix was trying to get him out. They were a mess, and they'd only just begun.

Exhausted, they returned to the starting line. Gertie looked clearly in pain, and Rudi had a scrape across his head from a fall. Bastian could feel his bruising but didn't say anything.

'Stick to the left at the start. Don't go right until we reach that hay bale,' Bastian said, thinking about what the next move was, if only they had a shooter of their own it would make it all the easier to move through the field. This was like a board game to him, and Bastian's mind focused intently on laying out a path to make it across.

The closest Phoenix member that they could see was a tall long-haired ghostly looking boy, who was now hiding on the far side of the hay bale just out of their view, to the left.

Getting to him and taking him out was Bastian's new mission, it was the only way they'd be able to fight back. He stepped out but was tugged back by Mandy.

She pointed at another Phoenix Squad shooter further ahead, aiming directly towards them behind some barrels. If Bastian was separate from the group, he would have swung across the field and taken a chance to force the ghostly boy's weapon out of his hand, taking it for his own.

He didn't want to risk the group being a target again, he felt his own bruises and knew they would welt soon. Standing up, he turned to the others, ready to organise their next step.

'Get down,' called Felix, using the force from his wrist to the pull them down along the line.

Ducking just in time Bastian and Mandy missed a couple of bean bags that came flying overhead.

They moved further around the hay bale, keeping themselves tight knit so they stayed clear out of shot.

'We've got to get to the shooter over there, grab his weapon; that one on the left,' Bastian quietly said to everyone, nodding them all to his direction.

'What, how the hell are we going to get over there in one piece?' Rudi barked, agitated he pulled at his attached wrist that was connected to Felix, 'shouldn't we be going forward?'

'No, Bastian's right. If we can get his weapon, we can use it against the others, and force our way over the line,' Verne added, his brow viably sweating, and his demeaner was quieter than usual Bastian noted, he must have been hit quite painfully, doing his best to hide it.

'Question is, how are we going to get there?'

Russ looked from Verne to Bastian. They stood there awkwardly for a moment, neither of them had an answer for this. They looked at each other, both as confused as the other.

'Well, if I'm the only one with bright ideas, we really are screwed,' Felix said. 'Come on you lot. Grab hold of the hay bale and follow my lead,' he dropped down to pick up the bale, each of them following in suit, hugging the bale as much as they could holding it as protection.

Moving across the field, grappling with the hay bale Bastian couldn't help but smile. They had managed to get it right up to some barrels and crouched down.

'You're not the only one with bright ideas Felix… peer out and distract him,' Bastian whispered to him, a smile in cheek.

'Oi. Over here,' called Felix, poking his head around the side of a barrel.

The ghostly lanky boy pivoted around with his shooter as Felix quickly ducked back. The boy came towards Felix's side of the barrels, not realising they were already long gone around them and with Gertie at the front of their line they quietly snuck up behind the boy. Bastian nodded to Gertie and Verne to take him from the back, ready with the others to pull them back to safety if he attacked.

Gertie tripped up the boy as he went to step back when he noticed Felix wasn't there anymore. He stumbled, but had a firm grasp on his shooter. Verne knocked it out of his hand, forcing him down while Gertie picked up the shooter and handed it to Bastian.

There were still a dozen small bean bags left in its canister. Bastian passed it to Felix who was edging around the hay bale that they'd carried to get a better look at the field ahead, leaving the lanky Phoenix shooter a bit dazzled at what had happened on the ground. With nothing but an empty field between them and the next shooter, they needed to move on quickly before Phoenix squad realised they had taken one of their own.

The ponytail girl that they'd previously met from Phoenix squad, named Harriet, positioned at a trailer ahead, was right onto them.

Again, they picked up their hay bale as a team and moved forward.

'They're coming,' he heard one of them call.

The force of bean bags hit their hale bale; all of their arms trembled from the hits as they pressed forwards.

'Drop,' Felix called to his squad, who all instantly dropped the hale bale and sunk towards the ground behind it as close together as possible. Bastian looked to Felix too, who held the shooter ready. They edged around the hay bale as much as they could while staying out of view, allowing Felix a clear shot at the next Phoenix squad member.

Heart racing, and adrenaline pumping Bastian wanted to see what happened, but he was just out of view. Sir Dash hadn't called them back to the start line, so Felix hadn't been hit.

'Their shooting from this side,' Gertie called over. She was squishing up to Verne and Mandy as close as she could.

'Let's move,' Felix popped back around to tell them all. They picked up the hay bale, following in the direction that Felix led until he stopped.

He moved around and pulled back a girl with a rather tight bun and pointed nose who looked like she had smelled something foul, as she evil-eyed their squad. Rudi tied her up with an extra bit of rope that had been around one of the hay bales. Felix passed across her shooter to Gertie while he went back for a shot at Harriet.

'Don't know if she'll date you now mate if you're taking shots at her,' Bastian said a little too gleefully.

'Ha, ha, very funny. Any bets she's just impressed with my skills. Wait… Guys, looks like there are two of them shooting from the left, Gertie can you get a shot in from your end? Oh, and Sidney up in the distance with another one of theirs too, but we are well out of their range for now at least,' Felix said.

'Yeah, I can see them,' Gertie took a shot at the two on the left forcing them to take cover.

'Any traps?' Russ asked.

'Looks like there are two holes so we have to make sure we clear them, they are about twenty steps out at about ten and two o'clock,' Rudi chimed in, pointing in the direction of the traps.

'And another at forty steps at about twelve o'clock,' he pointed. 'Can't see any others, but make sure you watch where you step.'

Bastian felt their eyes on him. 'What are you waiting for? Shoot at them Gertie and that will get us clear run-up to those barrels.' He pointed at a group of broken barrels.

Filled with momentum, Bastian's mind ran a million times a minute. Gertie took a few shots at the shooters on the left, forcing them to hide, giving the Ravens the chance to run part of the field up to the barrels.

They dodged a couple of holes and scraped by two more animal traps that snapped up as they passed by, the noise alerting the last two Phoenix squad members that they were gaining on them, one of whom was their leader Sidney, forcing the Ravens to lay low as they snuck in behind the barrels.

Pressed against the ground, Bastian felt the vibration of the ground motion underneath him. The last two Phoenix were on the attack.

They were the only thing between them and finally finishing the task. Bastian poked his head up to gain sight of where they were headed. He saw them climbing atop a burnt-out mover. That was just a few meters ahead of them.

Gertie fired her rice bag throwed at them before warning the team. And they flung off the roof and behind the car as the bean bags landed right in front of them.

They all scrawled across the ground together, going around the far side of the group of barrels, following Gertie. Bastian in line with everyone, pulling himself across the ground. Felix ducked his head in the corner of his eye, narrowly escaping one of their returning fires. From there, they all pulled up to run. Aiming for a mound of dirt with a skip bin on top of it, they all began ducking up and down as the shots from Pheonix came at them, it was only a by luck that they all reaching the bin, sweeping behind to use its cover.

Russ was breathing heavily beside Bastian. Mandy collapsed against the bin too, pulling Bastian's hand to her face as she used her arm to wipe muck from her eyes. The same muck from crawling across the field spread across everyone's exhausted faces. He felt it, he knew his friends were faltering. He wouldn't let them be pulled back to that starting line to go through all this again. There had to be a way.

'So how are we going to do this?' Felix made sure his shooter was ready to fire.

'We've got just as many shooters as them, this shouldn't be a problem,' Rudi said, his patience wearing.

Pulling Russ and Mandy off the ground Bastian turned around.

'Get up. We've got to give this a shot guys, that's it. That's all we can do,' he called, feeling his own weariness in his voice.

'We'll stay low and quiet for as long as we can. Look at Sidney – look at them all – they are so serious. Let's not be like that, in the end, this here is only practice, it's a game. So, let's enjoy it. That's all we can do.' It was the last ounce he could muster in the moment and for the most part he believed his own words.

'Let's go,' he whispered with the slyest of grins.

***

Lying on the dirt, forearm over his face, feeling his own heavy breaths, he was unsure of the past few moments as his head still spun. He could feel every inch of his body in pain, and the sweat from his face forcing his arm to slip.

'How's about a hand mate.'

Bastian wanted to ignore the voice, he was exhausted, the idea of opening his eyes seemed like too much effort. He could sleep right where he lay.

Grabbing the arm that was offered to help him up he saw Sidney from Phoenix smile behind it. There was no doubt Bastian was more than a little confused, he didn't remember even getting past him.

'You've got one hell of a squad kid. Leaving Novak and I, just shooting at us to keep us hidden while you ran for the line. You could have put an end to us, but you didn't,' Sidney said.

'Yeah, well what was the point of taking you two on when all we needed was to finish the game. Besides I think I left Harriet quite stunned back there too,' Bastian said, wiping the sweating dirt from his brow.

'She's not happy about that, that's for sure. She'll be scolding your name forever,' Sidney laughed.

Bastian allowing Sidney to help him down the path, feeling the bruises from the bean bags starting to sting.

'You called this a game?' Sidney said amused. 'I like the way you think. It's a hard task that one. Most squads don't get through it on the first day.'

'Yeah, well they weren't the Ravens,' Bastian said.

'From what it looked like to me, they had a pretty good leader. Even if he thought it was just a game,' Sidney complimented.

Bandaged and covered in ice didn't stop them from a night consumed with celebrations. Relieved and ecstatic to be the first squad to complete Sir Dash's task on their first try. As well as the weight off their shoulders having gotten through to having a day off. Bastian couldn't help but feel like every single one of them moods had already lifted.

Felix was teaching Verne the best ways to talk to girls. Rudi jumped in with his own bits of advice every now and then too. His gleeful banter surprised Bastian with his new-found confidence and happiness amongst their team.

Russ was explaining to him how to make a compass by magnetizing a needle. Bastian was intrigued by his craftiness, as he watched Russ make one in front of him. They played with the trinket for a while, fiddling with it until they soon found north which turned right to the kitchens. As the night drew on, and they had eaten more than any of them could handle they each became captivated by each other's stories about their life before being at the Guardians Compound.

'There was a time I thought I wouldn't make it,' Mandy said, trying her best to keep smiling, brushing away her bushy brown curls that fell over her face.

'My dad worked for the Guard before I was born, he was young and from a long line of the Guard. But he quickly realised their actions weren't that of any respectable man, that he couldn't condone what they did. We moved around the outer districts a lot after. I don't think I ever called anywhere home. There were nights in the freezing cold on empty stomachs that made it near impossible to move onto somewhere new. That's how we lost my mum to her illness out in the wilderness a few years back, we weren't close to anywhere to get her help. Dad had said, 'she likes her sleep the old girl', he didn't want to say it but kept her full of enough medicine, so she felt no pain.

'The guardians found me when we stopped in at the city Bohdi. Have you heard of it?' Mandy waited to see if they had but continued when everyone shook their heads.

'It's a dead land, nothing too eye-catching but home to one of the largest underground city markets. Everything is imported by traders from the other districts, there's a tunnel system below the ground where everything's traded from, mostly from the south to supply everyone in the outer districts with supplies.

'We organised a stall, I was the eyes of our operation. I figured out who was the best targets before they even approached us. We conned people into buying all sorts of rubbish, pushing all sorts of gadgets on them. I spent my spare hours stealing from other stalls too, I have a good knack for being unseen when I want to. Well, that was until a Guardian found me trying to pick pocket his friend. I thought I was done for, but here I am, he told me I should put my tricks to use,' Mandy said, a sigh of relief from the worries of her past.

'Wow, that's one hell of a story. Don't think my dull farm life even compares. Apparently, they had their eyes on me for a while, came to my mum when they heard I'd won our local woodcutting contest. Don't know what they saw in me from that. Still, here I am.' said Verne, nudging her to get even the smallest smile; which he managed.

'Yeah well, my life wasn't dull. I lived in the heart of Astoria. At least for the most part,' Felix boasted.

'Well, that explains your sense of entitlement,' Gertie rolled her eyes.

'I lived a high life once, so what. It was great being at the centre of everything. Every want and desire cared for at a moment's call. And honestly, you don't realise the horrors of an establishment like the Grinnwick Guard if you're at the centre of it. The distractions of the high life are endless, and the food... oh I could have a delicious poach duck and apple puree right about now. But, I ended up as street scum anyway. My mum and dad were in deep as spies in Astoria working for the rebels, not that I knew. But one day, they didn't come home.'

Felix allowed an appropriate amount of time to enjoy the looks of shock on their faces. As shocked as Bastian was, he did take a certain enjoyment in the theatre of Felix's story, noting to use this trick.

'My sister and I fled to the streets; if they'd been caught there wasn't much chance for the two of us against the guard. They'd either kill us or line us up to be part of their new army. A life neither of us was made for, mind you. I knew the streets like the back of my hand soon enough, but she was too good for that life. She older than me, but still young, and pretty enough, I guess. I hear she married a highborn under an alias. Quite the scandal in the world of the socialites. Wherever she is now, I doubt she remembers my name.'

Bastian found it somehow sadder that Felix's own sister abandoned him as well. So far, Felix seemed truly alone before he came here.

Felix continued after another theatrical pause, 'A Guardian found me after I hung around waiting outside of windows of the different commander's homes, wanting to hear if any of them mentioned my parent's whereabouts.

'I was heading back to an abandoned building to spend the night when I was caught. Usually, I'm pretty slippery and could talk my way out of the situation. This guy just picked me up and pulled me inside without a sweat. He pulled out a bowl and gave me some soup. Think he felt sorry for me. I looked scrappy then, my rich clothes didn't look so classy anymore.

'Still, he barely said much, I had no clue he was a Guardian. Without fail though, every night after that he had a bowl of freshly made soup

166

waiting for me if I returned. He called himself Wally. It was about a month until we trusted each other enough to really talk. After learning about me he told me about the Guardians, said if I wanted, he would send me here. Didn't really have any better-looking options did I.' Felix ripped into his roll like and stuffed it in his gob like it was the last bit of food he'd have for a while.

'What about you Gertie?' Felix asked her from across the table.

'Well, I didn't live as fabulously as you did. I lived in the outer districts too; in the wealthy city of Langford. I was a slave... to an elderly woman named Marietta. It wasn't that bad really,' she added, seeing the astonished looks on their faces.

'She was kind enough. I had my own room, and a fresh meal every day. I was on the streets coming back from the market when a man tried to rob me, and well it doesn't matter what else he tried; let's just say he ended up worse off than where he started. I didn't know that someone out there had been watching me take down my attacker.

'Anyways times were tough, so the day came for Marietta to sell me. I can't really explain what that's like. There were already bidders lined up, none of them were at all who I could imagine life would be pleasant to work under. But when the time came and my number was up for sale, he was there – not that I knew it – and he bought me just like that. His name was Frederick, he was rough around the edges with a scar down the side of his cheek. I could tell he wasn't like other owners, he didn't really understand the concept of owning someone, he was sweet; once he bought me I waited for instructions, what to do, where to go, but he walked straight to a highspeed transport station, me trailing behind him clueless as a lost puppy. Finally, he tells me that he saw me out on the streets that time. He saw me handle myself. Said that he knew a place where someone who stood up for themselves would be of great value. Over a week later he dropped me topside here where Dash met me and brought me to the first task,' Gertie said.

'Remind me never to get on your bad side,' Bastian said, struck by his newfound respect for Gertie, and the others.

'Yeah, that's hectic. I mean if my brother wasn't a Guardian already, I honestly don't know where I'd be. My village was just outside of Astoria, some of the guys I grew up with went off to become Grinnwick Guards, I probably wouldn't have had the chance to consider another option – it was just what was done within the village. And if you didn't put your hand up, they would eventually cart off to join them. Luckily, my brother sent me down this path, from the moment I knew he was coming here it was my goal to get here too,' Rudi said, 'what about you Russ?'

'Me. I'm not your typical guardian am I?' Russ tapped his belly, and bit into his chicken wing. 'I'm good with gadgets, and handy with any system. But my story's pretty boring really. My dad dropped me off here himself. You see he didn't have any time to raise me, we lived on a ship for most of my life. He was a smuggler, mostly helped people get to the outer districts unnoticed, people who escaped their town's demise at the hands of the Guard. Or ones that the Commander was after specifically. Good man, my dad. He's the best at moving people and keeping them hidden. I traded with most of the people came aboard. My room was filled with dozens of books and gadgets. I was good at hacking into anything; I'd make coin every now and then trying to hack people's discs, get them off the radar of whoever was following them. One of the people he was smuggling was a Guardian,

I never met him. But he gave my father a map of how to get here, and when we pulled into the closest port, he took me straight here.

He just wanted what was best for me you know. Honestly, I just hope he's alright out there on his own,' Russ finished.

'He sounds like a good guy,' Verne said to Russ, 'He's right to help those people. That's all any of us are here for, right? To help.'

'Really, cause it doesn't feel like it. Didn't my grandfather say we don't get involved in the war, that we are an undercover operative, from what it sounds like there are dozens of Guardians out in Grinnwick, and with all their training shouldn't they be doing something to stop those bastards from attacking everyone? All those history books only had stories of the guardians after a strike or attack, how they helped people only once they were stricken down. What's being done right now to keep people safe while there are Guards out there already damaging and ruining so many people's lives?' Bastian said, his frustration boiling over.

'You took it too literal mate,' Verne said, a half-grin on his face. 'We are a hidden operative yeah, you have to read between the lines. No one is ever supposed to know we are helping. There is no record of any missions because we don't really exist. I'm guessing you've always taken pride in winning a fight Bass but from now, outside of the Guardians, no one will know what we'll do. Do you think they've got us doing all this gruesome training for nothing? It's so that when we can, we will be able to slip in and do what needs to be done together, as the Ravens,' Verne said, clearly proud of what they were a part of.

'You believe that don't you?' Bastian finally broke a grin.

'If the Guardians have been around for so long, then why didn't they stop the War of Darkness, or the rise of the Grinnwick Guard just to name a few.' Bastian posed.

'How were they to know at the start how ruthless the Grinnwick Guard would be,' Rudi added.

'You both aren't thinking large enough,' Mandy noted, 'our foundation is to protect the heart of Grinnwick.'

'Yeah, the people.' Verne agreed with her.

'Yes, and no. The Heart of Grinnwick is a form of myth, a stone or a relic that the organisation was built to protect its secret. Don't you remember those first books we read. We need to remain a secret in case it surfaces, and it needs protecting.' Mandy said.

'You can't be serious. That's just a story.' Felix replied, rolling his eyes.

'It doesn't matter if it's real or not, that is why the Guardians have always stayed away from prying eyes.' She noted.

'Look it doesn't matter anyway, why don't you tell us about your home Bastian.' Verne said kind of frustrated, his tense face made Bastian feel like he didn't like the conflict that was building. Bastian didn't mean to accuse the Guardians as such, he was one after all. But it was perplexing that the Guardians for all the notions of helping the world, did make a bigger deal when it all came crumbling around them.

'Well, not much to tell really, I lived outside of a small town with my mum. We had a quiet life, me and my friends, we sort of took it upon ourselves to make sure that the community of kids a lot like us – you know, not townies, those who were a bit rough around the edges. Well, we just tried to make sure they didn't get up to too much mischief as we got older.

Some of them needed pulling into line every now and then, you know. And the townies, they didn't exactly have the desire to deal our sort of riff raff, as long as we kept away from them.

I kept an ear out for the Grinnwick Guard… you know, how close they were getting, and any close by attacks. The town itself was a haven for so many who had already escaped the Guard. We haven't been on their radar; I mean not really. But my mum, well the growing stories of towns, and families getting torn apart if they didn't surrender to them played on mum's mind to much, so she sent me to the only man she trusted. I didn't want to leave, but it's all she asked of me, and I couldn't say no,' Bastian said.

Bastian still wasn't sure that Verne was right about this place, but after what he'd said about them working together and being a part of a team, he slept much easier that night, even with Rudi and Russ's snoring. Knowing that he had the Ravens beside him was comforting, he was proud of them all, proud of their effort.

It didn't stop him missing his friends, and his mother most of all. It was in these quiet moments that he found he missed home the most. Sticks' deep and quirky laugh, his mother's kind and calming, yet authoritative voice, even the thought of it made him smile. He knew that any training he had would help him if the Guard were to eventually reach his home, only hoping that they weren't in trouble without him there. All he could do here and now was embrace his team. His friends would help him if things turned south.

A Cottage Called Home

The white wooden structure was covered in vines. Old and worn, it was small, yet perfect for them all.

Racing inside for the very first time, even Lux with her new walking sticks taking the weight off her leg came in quickly. The four of them stood in the main room looking around at the walls; it was dusty and had fallen into disrepair, still to Scarlet it was perfect in every way.

Archer and Hudson ran up the stairs to a second floor, that overlooked the open area of the bottom floor. Both calling out to her and Lux to come and see the view. Lux got a helping hand from Scarlet as they climbed up.

'Come on' Archer insisted, his energy filling them all with excitement.

Upstairs was even better. The room wasn't enclosed at all, a small balcony was all that separated it from the room below, but it had a view of the incredibly close ocean. The sea caps could be seen from their window and the soft swaying movement lulled them all. Scarlet helped Hudson lift the window up, and the rush of waves echoed into the house, taking their breath away. She had not in her life ever heard a sound that was so calming and inviting.

'Incredible, isn't it?' said Winslow from behind them. His harsh voice and surprising presence turned them all in his direction.

'You kids, you've come a long way,' he said, his eyes lingering strangely on each of them. 'I expect you don't know much about the sea growing up where you did. Spectacular isn't it, like a song the way she moves. Controlled by none, and a trickster to those who dare face her. I doubt there is anything more beautiful in this world,' Winslow said. He was talking more to the sea than to them.

'We are very grateful to you, for this.' Dawson interrupted, arriving at the top of the stairs standing behind Scarlet, placing a hand on her shoulder – she couldn't help but beam up at him.

'No worries at all… I only mean you are all quite lucky to finally be able to call somewhere home. Each of you has quite the story,' Winslow said, with a sort of longing towards each of them, like he was reading each of them, as though they were a story, before consciously pulling himself out of his deep thought.

'Well, you know where to find me Dawson, if you need. But I expect you will keep to yourself,' Winslow said, flustered. Dawson nodded.

'Yes. We will probably need a fair bit of adjustment to this… life. But, thank you again,' Dawson said, guiding Winslow back down the stairs. The way Dawson moved around Winslow was almost cautious, as though he wasn't too sure of the man that he supposedly called his friend.

'Ah, yes, I should be off,' Winslow said, following Dawson downstairs and outside.

Enamoured with the motion of the waves before her Scarlet nearly forgot one of the most important things she needed to do since leaving the Amari. She quickly dashed outside, catching Winslow and Dawson off-guard.

'What's wrong?' Dawson questioned her. Dawson may have thought they weren't here on an agenda or any other notion but to live their lives. But she had her own task at hand, and she was dead set on following it to its end.

'Mr Winslow, I wanted to ask you. I mean I hoped you might have heard of someone; he may be quite old now… my brother, Flynn Rivers.' It was the burning question in her stomach, looking into his eyes she desperately watched for a sign of hope. Ever since they had left, it was the only question she wanted to find the answer to. The answer she thought she might finally find. He was out here somewhere; he had to be, whether he had lived and aged or met his end, someone had to know something.

'His face is sweet, and hair curly and dark and he's a great tracker.'

Dawson sighed, giving in to helping with the questions he knew Scarlet wanted answered. 'Actually, he'd be in his thirties or something now.' Dawson said, 'He'd have strong dark features, with a warmish complexion, light eyes, tall as well. He'd have popped up out of the blue around twelve or so years ago – trust me you would know if you ran into him, he'd have taken you by storm with some of things that he knew,' Dawson added.

Struck by the questioning, Winslow looked from Dawson to Scarlet.

'I have had so many boys and girls come in and out of my halls, and that description can be said of dozens. And unfortunately, the name doesn't ring any bells, but in saying that it doesn't mean he was never there. I sometimes get swept up in my work and don't get to know the people who stay under my roof. People come and go, you know. And as for the name I haven't heard of it, but if he was wise and wanting to go unnoticed, I doubt he would be using his own name,' Winslow said.

'Are you sure?' Scarlet had an uncomfortable feeling in her throat.

'Look, you may have just met us. But you know where we've come from, you know that what binds us to this world isn't common. One of these youngn's is true born Amari himself, you know this. The rarity of being in the presence of a fae in this time is almost a gift to this world; to an understanding of what was. And he is only one gift, they all have their own strengths that are relics from the age of kings. And all of them grew up living the way of the fae. The way they walk; light as a feather, and the feeling of happiness and calm that rushes over you just by being in their presence, it's almost intoxicating. And the three that aren't fae, they had to be ahead of those who were. I tell you this; they're wiser than any others you would know; and the scent of the wilderness follows them. That life is a part of them.

'Flynn, he was just like that, if not just that he would have been more wary than most. So, you may not have known his name, but if you interacted with him, you would have known, you would have understood the difference to his presence from your everyday runaway.' Dawson said persistently. Not able to hide his own desire to know what had happened to Flynn, it was the first time in a long time that Scarlet had felt someone else in the world still cared about his whereabouts.

'Look. I get what you mean, my family has passed on the stories of you all. Impressing how important it was to pass on your connection to the outside world. I myself dived into those tales as a boy, and without a doubt your presence is indeed captivating. It's as though you all move to a different calming rhythm. It's a strange sense, a feeling that I can't put words to. But that same sense, that same overwhelming calmness that I can feel now, I have not sensed that before.

'If I hear or see anything, I promise I will let you know as soon as I can.' Winslow said,

'Know this, times are much different to the ones you left behind. From my records you left Grinnwick in the beginning of the royal collapse, as you said the age of kings. The flames undoubtedly would have engulfed your happy memories of that golden era. That time is lost to tall tales now, I would be one of the few who holds any true understanding of the past.

'That devastation that consumed your world has been forgotten with the centuries of passing conflict, continual havoc of the natural world; hurricanes violently bombard the north-eastern coast, the outskirts where many have fled to in the north would have been a lush area in your time but are now utterly desolate from what I've heard. And under Van Helm the rise of powering technologies has formed a form of greed that can lead even the most genuine man down a path unforeseen. It was the rise in them that left the notion of peace behind, led Astoria and the Grinnwick Guard to control as many as they can, under Van Helm and his blood-thirsty soldiers devastation continues to spread.

'Don't get me wrong we have tried to fight against their greed, we still try to fight for peace against their persecution of those they deem less than worthy. Generations of families have been lost or torn apart; they still are. Women deemed lesser are enslaved to the Grinnwick Guard and the socialites of Astoria, while the men they find are brainwashed into a life as a soldier,' Winslow took a breath.

'Where were your people over the years, any of you, you all abandoned us. It was your choice to leave. To live a simpler life while the rest of us have been left to try and pick up the pieces. You are the ones who left the people to fight your war.'

Dawson looked taken aback, Scarlet could tell he wasn't prepared for such an outburst. It had seemed as though a lifetime of frustrations of fighting had come out in Winslow's rant. Yet, he wasn't wrong, they had left this life so long ago, what was their right returning to it.

'For that I am sorry. I did what was right at the time. Others remained, they fought just like you continue to do, and I imagine their whole lineage is gone because they stood tall. What they fought then was heartbreaking, but in your heart, I see just as much pain as we experienced. Nothing I could do could ever repay those who remained, but we are here now. I am here, to help you in your time, you must only ask,' Dawson firmly stated.

Winslow shook Dawson's hand, and bid them farewell one last time before finally heading off back down the track.

Scarlet couldn't help but feel bad for fleeing all those years ago, the generations of terror and pain that had been experienced out here. She felt the pain coming from Winslow about the generations of terror that had been experienced bestowed a heavy weight on her. Should they have run? Would staying there have turned her into a different person? Would things in this time have been different without the fall of the royal family, and the retreating of magical beings? The truth was, she'd never know. The choice wasn't hers.

Dawson gave it a moment before he spoke to Scarlet. 'Don't fret; he'll be out here somewhere. But we aren't in any position to go searching, not just yet.'

'I know, I just miss him,' Scarlet said, turning back to see the others at the door, listening in.

'-How is it that Flynn would be in his thirties, if my calculations are correct, and he got out here five months ago, he should have aged into his eighties or nineties.' Archer said abruptly.

'You kids ask too many questions,' Dawson pushed through back inside, trying to change the subject.

But he wasn't wrong, Scarlet thought.

Scarlet joined Archer in facing Dawson on, forcing him to sit down. 'Tell us?' Scarlet added, more than a little adamantly.

'The thing is, he didn't leave nearly a year ago... He left just over a month ago. He was with me in the Corazon Forest.'

'But you said. You said he was gone.' Scarlet felt herself fuming.

'Why would you lie to everyone?' Archer asked him.

'I had to okay. Your brother, he wasn't made for a life in the Amari. And, if it weren't for you Scarlet. He would never have even come with us to their Village, he would have stayed behind after the fall of your family. He would have fought. He had been mad at himself since the moment he was taken from their lifeless bodies,' Dawson said.

'-wait why was he mad at himself,' Scarlet asked.

'At losing your family, at not being able to save them, being kept from those he wanted nothing more than revenge on, I mean you never would have known it, but he was battling his own inner demons. He shielded you from everything, from his mindset, from the truth about your life before.

'And I, well I might possibly have let him stay... but you, I couldn't do that. I wanted to do what was best for you, and ultimately you needed each other' Dawson explained.

'But the Amari, Lux, Hudson, and Archer, they are our lives, we were his...,' Scarlet posed.

'No kiddo, they're yours. They were all you knew. His memories of your old life, the devastation and loss a young boy should never be met with – with the Amari he was merely going through the motions, all except when he spent time with you,' Dawson answered.

'He was all I knew, and you helped him.' Confused, and agitated, Scarlet felt flush with tears running down her cheek, flushed with adrenaline, she could hardly believe what she was hearing. She knew in her heart Flynn loved her more than anything, part of her hated herself for not seeing his pain, she tried to think back to moments, but he always had a smile for her every time she saw him.

'…What was I supposed to do, he wanted go back, and he would have done it with or without me. He had no care for what the Amari thought. He knew they'd stop him if he tried, that they'd use you to convince him to stay. So, he came to me. Should I have told you the truth; that he was training by my side? That we were working together; that we had never planned for him to return?

'I knew how much he cared for you, and you may hate me for it, but staying by your side was a distraction from his mission, and he needed to focus. He needed to learn things that he may have forgotten and prepare to be the man he was setting out to be. Our idea was that he wouldn't go until the opportune moment, gathering intel on the princess before he officially was ready to leave,' Dawson said.

'What intel, what was his connection to this princess?' Scarlet asked, almost pleading to know.

'Like I said, he remembered his life before. You weren't rescued from flames because you were nobodies.

-Yes, I lied, I do that sometimes. Flynn had a select set of skills along with the Black Forest tricks… much like the ones I showed you Scarlet. You may not be Amari, or even fae, but your family had its own power, beyond anything else anyone had ever seen before. It was one I'll never understand. Your brother knew how to access his powers. However more advanced, more connected with the earth, it had still been some time since his teachings from your parents, and it took many full moons for him to finally hone in on the princesses whereabouts.'

All of them looked at him, completely stunned. Scarlet could barely speak, 'but I don't have any magic.'

Dawson focused entirely on her, 'not that you know of, but you will. They have been restricted from you since you were brought to the Amari. Now that you have left the safety of their bubble they will slowly grow,' he assured her.

'Why didn't anyone tell her that before now? Wouldn't that have been something the elders should have helped her harness?' Lux asked.

'It was magic beyond them, and in truth they wanted to keep that sort of power hidden from others who may wish to wield it for themselves,' Dawson answered.

Scarlet felt the cautious eyes of her friends staring at her from the side. She didn't have the brain space to think about the fact she may hold some sort of magical abilities, like she was a form of fae, it seemed absurd. Something you heard in a story book, but not in real life. Her mind remained focused on Flynn, and why a princess brought him out here on his own.

'I don't care about that. Just explain, what's the life of a long-forgotten princess have to do with him?' Scarlet asked, more than a little flustered by his truths. 'Why did either of you even care so much?'

'He knew her, we both did,' he stood firm, 'I am not Amari; I left the same life behind at the same time as you both. And she was close to us, him especially.

'Her survival had always been a rumour to us, we could never pinpoint if it had been true, so by the time we did it was word that she may have been killed. We knew then that if she had lived what she would have experienced over the centuries, alone and used if we didn't put a stop to it, they would only continue to control her.

'None of you could understand, in our time, to our people the royals were everything, they were more than our leaders, they meant the world to us. The queen's grace itself was beyond magical; it was a spark of light.

'Anyway, Flynn he wanted to, he needed to help just as much as I did. She was our past that we wanted to save. She was something that we may actually be able to control after all these years.

'And, he knew you were safe, but what about her, what about the centuries that she has lived captured, an image of hope being controlled and living several life sentence for no crime but being herself?' Dawson said, his passion towards one life so far away was so astounding to all of them that it kept them quiet.

***

Scarlet was flushed with anger as she paced up and down the path in the darkness, no one had dared to come outside, she was glad of it; her mind running in overdrive. She couldn't even put into words her frustrations; all she knew was she hated all the lies.

The build-up of thoughts whirling around inside her was nearly unbearable – all she wanted to do was. Smack. Shoving the outdoor tin shed it echoed all around her forcing her to close her eyes from the noise.

Finding herself on the floor, and the tears down her cheek when she felt a hand on her shoulder.

It was Archer.

'It's okay,' he said, helping her up.

'You're allowed to be mad, sad, literally anything your feeling, get it out.'

Scarlet looked up at him, his calming demeanour was soothing if anything. Taking a big breath, she hugged him.

She stayed there for a few moments; it was like home.

Stepping back from him she smiled, 'thanks, I just – I don't understand any of this.'

'I know you don't. But don't let it worry you. Focus on the good things, Flynn is younger than you thought, and hasn't been out here for anywhere near as long. The chances of finding him are probably so much better. And as for these powers, take it from me being different isn't so bad,' Archer explained.

He was right, she knew he was.

'Whatever changes you face, we'll all face them together. Don't worry. You've got us. Dawson too, if you let him,' Archer added.

Following him back inside the others had begun on a stew, made from leftovers from The Quiet Man Inn. It was tough to say the least.

'We won't eat this type of grub every night will we?' Lux broke the silence, looking disgusted at the spoon as she went to eat.

'It's not my finest. You four are more than welcome to pitch in too you know. We'll have to get a garden growing and maybe a few live bait traps in the woods,' Dawson added.

'We could fish?' Hudson suggested.

'Yeah, we'd catch some real tasty ones out here, surely.' Archer noted.

'Alright, well I'll get us some rods rigged up,' Dawson said.

***

Scarlet ate quietly, still processing all the Dawson had said, that Flynn had helped a princess because she had meant so much to him, in their life before. If she remembered that time herself, would she know the Princess too, and perhaps this would all make sense. Even more curiously, what magic was it that Dawson was on about… the river with the ghostly lit figures? Perhaps she was the one who brought them to life, and not the forest as she had previously thought.

Scarlet helped Lux upstairs, but they were both determined in a claim to the upstairs level that they would sleep there from the get-go. Winslow had left mattresses, that although dirty were relatively comfy. Meanwhile Archer and Hudson both were in one of the downstairs bedrooms, and Dawson in the other. Thinking that she would be up for hours still going over Dawsons conversation, it took mere moments for her to drift off after the exhaustion of their travels.

***

The sun broke through the large top levels window as Scarlet woke up. Her enthusiasm for whatever the day held almost outweighed her dislike for mornings. And for the realisation that Lux would need her help again getting downstairs.

Archer and Hudson were nagging Dawson to let them go for a swim. After he poured himself a tea he finally gave in, 'Go on then.'

'Scarlet,' he said much more politely. 'Can I talk to you?'

Scarlet waited while the others went to get ready. She didn't look him in the eye.

'Don't be like that, kid. I know I should have told you I helped your brother earlier, but that was between me and him, he didn't want you knowing. And truth be told my mind's kind of been on getting you lot here.' Dawson's heartfelt honesty shined through; he was hard to be mad at in that way.

'You could have told me ages ago, I thought he left months ago. I nearly went after him. I was so confused; he just left me. He's my only family. And now I find out you knew, all along, you helped him get away from me, leaving me stupidly ignorant,' Scarlet stammered.

'It wasn't like that,' Dawson said bluntly, 'Look, I'm here now, that's what matters right?'

'Cut him a break Scar,' Hudson called out from his room, 'he told you eventually yeah, no harm done. Now let's get going, come on.'

Dawson awkwardly smiled at Scarlet. She smiled back. 'Alright, but don't hold back from me again. Promise.'

'Promise,' he replied.

***

Searching her new case for some swimming clothes, Scarlet thankfully found her same old bathing suit, pink with orange polka dots. Leaving Lux to slowly make her way down the rest of them ran out the back of the house, the breeze on their face as the path wound around towards the sea smelt amazing.

Archer ran the fastest, beating them all there, stopping right at the top of the beach.

The water was still and the sand white and soft. The sun glistened on swaying water. There were small waves further out, and every part of it looked more inviting to them all.

Hudson tumbled over a branch, pushing straight past her heading for the water, it barely slowed him down though, and as soon as he was in Scarlet followed. She couldn't even compare it to their lake back at the village. From the moment she stepped in, to the first time her head went under every part of her felt alight with energy.

Glistening sunlight reflected on top of the water. The motion swayed them as they floated above the small waves that moved in and out of shore. The feeling of swimming with ease underneath the waves, and around the calm patches looking at these under water formations of living rocks that were bright and colourful and had a whole world of fish each with different colours swimming through them, every moment seemed like a dream.

She couldn't imagine anything ever being more colourful than underwater world beneath her. There were fish of blue with teeth twice the size of their face and big googly eyes; small yellow fish with black dots and rounded purple ones that looked like they had fur.

The peaceful beauty calmed her as she gazed above the water to see where the others were, spotting Lux sitting atop a rock with her good leg dangling in. She got a glimpse of something that didn't belong standing up in the shallow water, an outline of another, but it wasn't Dawson.

Thick dark brown messy hair wisping through the light wind. For a second she thought it was Hudson. As her eyes adjusted, clear as day she saw Flynn, he was standing on the shoreline.

But it couldn't be him, it was just a flicker of a ghost amongst the waves; a memory, he was calling to her. Boggled with confusion she made to move closer but in a splash of her paddling he disappeared.

Since leaving the Amari she was seriously starting to think something was wrong with her mind, it was playing countless tricks on her, perhaps this was a form of the magic that Dawson was talking about, it had to be.

She stared at the spot where she'd seen him, as if he would return, finding it hard to ignore her thoughts of him. Her heart ached with confusion.

That they were so much closer to answers, to finding him, distracted in her thoughts, and Scarlet didn't take notice of Hudson waving her down.

Every bit of her mind felt like a haze.

Archer's sudden tug at her arm pulled her back to reality and she noticed they were staring at something too… but it wasn't the ghostly shape where Flynn had stood.

'Move! Come on,' Archer screamed, terror across his face.

Scarlet's face dropped; she was stunned.

Smoke had overcome a large area of coast to the south, flecks of black and red looked as though they burst within it. It was far away yet right in front of them. An explosion.

Fear struck inside of Scarlet, a terror she had never felt before. This was surely the power of the Grinnwick Guard.

Scarlet moved quickly into the shore as Archer held her hand tightly. His eyes reflected the fear she too felt.

The far distance swelled with smoke, and none of them were able to look away. Imagining the devastation that would have been happening in a not-too-distant place now seemed too close to their new home. The blue sky and glistening water didn't look the same as they all stood on the beach; it had darkened as the sun became hidden behind a smoke cloud that moved closer as they stood in silence on the beach.

Not one of them needed to tell Dawson what happened as they quietly made their way to their cottage.

He stood waiting by the cottage; he knew, he'd seen the smoke.

Scarlet didn't say another word about their fight, she was just glad to have Dawson by their side as she ran up squeezing him tight in fear. The others joined in, they all turned back up to face the darkening sky. all.

Dawson left for a couple of hours the next day, visiting Winslow and making sure the place that was attacked was okay. That they would be okay. Scarlet hated to think what happened to the people there. She couldn't understand why so many people helped cause so much grief towards the world.

When he returned, they were finally ready to bombard him with questions.

'What could those people have possibly done to deserve that?' Lux started.

'Can we help them?' Archer added.

'Yeah, can't we just tell this Grinnwick Guard we don't want to fight them? No one does,' Scarlet asked.

'I'll take on the lot of them,' Hudson added sternly.

Dawson sighed.

'If only the answers of four children would make the changes the world needed. I'm afraid that's not how the world works kids. People are weak, insecure and their fears make them defensive. Many of the men who work for the Guard believe that they are keeping structure to a troubled world. They have forgotten themselves, brainwashed to the fact that people outside of the circles are the enemy. They have forgotten that the world is naturally flawed, and that's what makes it precious. They are overpowered by the manipulation of their superiors. But like I said before, it is not our war, and we will not get involved.' Dawson said.

'I mean it sounds like something someone needs to get involved in,' Hudson commented.

'Of Course, and there are plenty who fight against them. We won't be one of them,' Dawson answered, 'Those people in that village that was attacked had people making too much noise about working against the Grinnwick Guard, that's why Winslow thinks they were attacked.

'Winslow said we are still safe, so we will remain here. He told me that that town was full of fishermen who had retreated there from one of the surrounding towns of Astoria, each of them working together to revolt against the Commander Van Helm. Winslow advised me that unless the Grinnwick Guard saw reason they would not come to our town.'

The days after were free of any signs of attacks so they continued to explore the coast and woods around them. Every bit of the coastline they'd seen was just as beautiful as the spot right below where their cottage stood. It didn't take long for them all to find themselves in a routine. Mornings were spent practicing their fighting skills with Dawson. He insisted, saying that they needed to keep sharp in case he couldn't protect them.

Followed by a beach swim. Dawson would leave them to explore more of the shoreline and sometimes parts of the woods. The trees were perfect for climbing, and they reached higher heights than any of them had climbed before. Hudson was able to reach the highest out of them all; climbing up one of the thickest oaks he could find during their fourth morning. He left Scarlet searching for him as he'd disappeared into the part of the tree where the branches thickened, only to realise he somehow found his way up on a slender branch five feet above her.

The two of them usually found themselves in separate trees close by to each other so they could still see one another, it was one of the things that they had done just the two of them. Archer should have been brilliant like the other Amari at climbing trees, but he never ventured too high, he always reminded Scarlet how he fell when he was a boy, that he didn't need to get too high to feel connected to the land. Lux on the other hand plainly had no interest in sitting still in the trees, not that she could currently even climb the smallest ones.

Hudson and Scarlet however enjoyed the small amount of alone time they got while being a part of the serenity, both whistling along to the bird's tunes, taking time out from everything around them. Checking in with Archer who usually hung in the low branches playing with one of the gadgets he'd taken with him from the market.

Days turned into weeks, and weeks to months, and their cottage soon felt like a home. They had built themselves proper beds from felled trees. They visited the market to purchase their own mattresses and blankets instead of the ones donated by Winslow.

Archer and Lux had been planting an array of veggies right out the front; Lux – whose leg was now all mended – constantly nagging him not to drag dirt into the house reminded Scarlet of Ailsa. Scarlet helped out whenever Lux's plants needed repotting. Lux would always swear that her help made the soil lucky for them.

'Wow, can't you wipe your feet?' Lux scowled, eyes narrowing on Archer on a slow Thursday afternoon.

He washed his dirty hands in the sink, Scarlet could see on Lux's face she was about to burst in a rage as Archer splashed the dirt across the wall. Grabbing an apple from the table, Archer did nothing but ignore her frustrated stares. Hudson and Dawson were both ignoring the others' spat (a common occurrence between the two of them these days), instead they were organising their fishing gear to head to an inland watering hole deep in the woods they'd found. Scarlet still sensed the boiling point Lux was reaching, as Dawson loudly piled the gear onto the table.

'Look, why don't we all get out of here tomorrow? We can head into town, and have a good look around? Maybe go explore something new for a change. See something other than the woods or the marketplace,' Dawson Suggested. It was perfectly timed to distract Lux from her current mood, yet he was not nearly prepared for all of their excitement at finally being able to properly explore the town.

'You mean it?' Lux said her face alight.

'Really. I wonder what sort of shops they have; I bet there's a book shop,' Archer beamed.

'Yeah, and a place that sells great throwing knives. I'm going to need extra if you keep dragging mud in,' Lux added, this time with more of a glow in her cheek.

'Hey maybe if we catch enough fish, Dawson, we could sell them in town one day,' Hudson said gathering the rods together.

'You better get better at fishing then Hudson,' Scarlet said, enjoying the glare that he was now giving her.

'Alright, Alright Alright…. Listen up Kiddos. Bellevue Point is only a small snippet of what's out there, so don't pin all your hopes on it. Everything will be new to you, to us all. So, take it in slowly. It's still bigger than what you're used to, so if you think you can't handle something, or someone you run into, think smart; not everyone is going to be looking out for your best interests like back with the Amari. Know that I'll be there if you need me, it can be easier for me to have your back first then dig you out of a whole lot of trouble later. And before any of you say you know how to handle yourselves, that's not my concern. My concern is that you'll draw attention, and not the attention we'd like. Probably best you wear a hat or something Arch, to cover your inner fae ears and shade your eyes too,' he said, his tone serious before turning to the rest of his fishing gear.

'Now, Let's head off and catch some fishes Hud, before they decide to swim off on us.'

Scarlet and Archer both joined Hudson and Dawson as they carried their gear to the fishing hole. Lux waved them off, taking advantage of the rare empty cottage for some peace and quiet on her own.

***

Archer walked like he had finally got rid of a weight off his shoulders and talked incessantly on all the types of books he longed to read. Scarlet vaguely listened along with Dawson and Hudson. Her mind raced with excitement, the possibility of getting into town, seeing what life was like there, and finally being able to reach out further to find Flynn; part of her knew that somewhere out there, someone knew where he was.

Diving into the water first thing was a refreshing feeling. Running water trickled down the cliffside above the water hole. The waterfall was the only motion at the watering hole apart from them. The hole was wide enough that Dawson could set the rods up further away from where they swam.

Scarlet moved the clear blue water through her hands and looking up at the stillness of the tall trees that circled in the sky around them. Laying on her back she slowly spun. This undoubtedly had to be one of their favourite spots.

Her serenity was ruined as Archer jumped in from the cliffside. Ripples of water flowed from where he landed, leaving all of them covered from the wake of his splash. Hudson jumped in after him, trying to cause a bigger splash, and even Dawson joined them.

It turned into a fun filled game of splashing in the water between the four of them. Sprays of water lashed each of them. Before Scarlet knew it, they were all ganging up on her, water flying at her face from every direction.

Her eyes winced from the glare of the midday sun reflecting on the water all around her. An unexplainable tension built up inside of her, a happy eagerness.

The tension carried through to what she thought was a playful splash. She had only wanted to get them back. But an unexplainable force formed her force through the water to splash four times bigger than she had intended, covering each of them unaware in one hit, sending them backwards into the water.

Shock hit her.

The power inside her had been so intense, that feeling foreign yet completely natural. In that one moment for a split-second she had felt out of control in her own skin; a feeling that had gone nearly as quick as it came. Was this part of the magic she held. The looks on Hudson and Archer's faces were both broad with smiles; they didn't see issue with the innocent splash as Scarlet had felt it. To them it was merely upping the ante in their game. Both of them instantaneously came and jumped on top of her, dunking her under the water. She took their tackles with a sigh of relief that what happened wasn't as big a deal as she thought.

Dawson pulled her to the side once the boys were done goofing around.

'You alright kid,' he asked her.

'I am, I think that must have been whatever power you were talking about, but I don't know how it happened,' Scarlet answered.

'Don't let it scare you, alright. We'll work it out; you'll feel more confident with it in time.

'Alright guys,' he said to them all, 'Let's get to fishing.'

Hudson and Archer each cheekily splashing Scarlet as they got out.

Hidden Treasure

A buzz of anticipation filled their cottage from the moment they woke. Scarlet was sure Lux had been up for hours and could have even been convinced that she'd slept with her shoes on, ready to go.

'Hurry up Scarlet.' Lux pestered, as Scarlet tied her laces.

'The boys are already eating breakfast. Let's go, let's go.'

'You head down, I'll meet you there,' Scarlet replied. Lux's bruising had subsided, and she was managing to get up and down the stairs on her own, as awkward on her leg as she still was, she was focused to get more movement on it.

Scarlet found everyone around their small round table scooping up some fresh oats Dawson had cooking on the stove. They were all wearing some of the finer clothes that had been packed for them. Scarlet and Lux both wore black skirts, with white stockings and white frill shirts that they had put off wearing knowing how dirty they would get. While the boys wore suspender pants and a collared shirt. Scarlet personally thought they all looked sweet, yet uncomfortable.

'Here you go kiddo,' Dawson said, placing her bowl in front of her then moving onto the others.

'Get in as much as you can, it'll be a big day, for all of us,' Dawson said, packing a bag full of apples as well as a sack that rattled full of gold and silver pieces.

'Hurry up now, we've got loads to see and do.' Dawson polished off his own bowl of oats.

Lux's enthusiasm had nearly died out after the two hours of walking it took them to reach the town of Bellevue Point. Archer on the other hand ran straight inside the main gate toward the main street.

Scarlet's eyes were being torn in each, and every direction. She had never been so overwhelmed and excited at once.

A mix of Wood and cobblestone buildings stretched along either side of the street with hangers above each door, naming the shop inside.

Jessie's Manor of Fine Design & Haberdashery; she had no idea what it meant, but there were jackets and a dress on a fake body, so she concluded they made clothing. Then there was Potts and Co.; it had a very basic exterior, grey in colour with black window trims. She could not see inside it, but by the boring look of a woman who stepped out it was not a very interesting store. Monroe's Books was painted a deep red, with charcoal trim, it looked a bit lopsy at the roof as the tiles looked uneven, like the store was off centre from its base. Inside a mess of books filled the whole window. Bellevue Point Corner Store looked full of people each carrying a number of household kitchen items, a young boy jumped from their steps onto the path, crunching on an apple while his mother wrangled a large bag full of her food. Deswell Bakery was next; the scent, Scarlet had remembered the smell from when they first drove through, and it was still so deliciously inviting, never having more than bread back with the Amari, the notion of possibilities inside was nearly impossible to resist.

Her face, along with the Lux, Hudson and Archer were all touching the glass of the perfected baked treats inside. There were buns, in round shape, hook shape, some that swirled, others that were decorated, some that looked like they'd been filled with extra delicious goodness.

Dawson called them all away as nearly every one of them stared hungrily at the treats in the window. Right on the corner of the street stood out a large black brick building named On The Pint Bar & Inn. A place that looked busy for such an early time of day. Scarlet tried to sneak in a peak as a lady walked by the window with a tray of drinks, but Dawson moved across and blocked her view.

'Alright, go on have a wander. Don't go too far, and stick in pairs at least.' Dawson handed each of them two gold coins, while they stood in front of On The Pint Bar and Inn. 'Only use the gold if you really need it, okay? And meet me here in let's say, three hours.' He looked over at the large clock tower above the corner store. 'Yes, that'll be good timing. We'll be able to find some food then and can head on home.'

'Don't you want to come and explore with us? You said you would be there if we needed?' Scarlet asked.

'I won't be far, and I know how much you all want to explore. You don't need an old man like me holding you back.'

Scarlet hugged him then turned to go with the others, but felt oddly comforted feeling Dawson watching the back of her head as she left. She went to look back, but he had already disappeared.

'Look at these coins, they've got strange markings on them. It looks like a sun almost, with a large G. Wonder why we never really learnt about money back home,' Hudson said.

'This is home now,' Lux butted back.

'Besides there were no stores with the Amari, everyone worked together so there was no need for coin. I think I remember coins from before, but they were different, not as shiny. Don't forget what Dawson said though, they're only for if we need them, so don't go spending on the first thing we see,' Lux warned.

'Okay, Mother,' Hudson said sarcastically, 'Well, where to first then? I think I saw some more stores just around the corner when we first drove into town. We could have look there first.'

'I want to check out the book shop first, anyone else want to come?' Archer noted.

'Alright why don't you and Lux go have a look around, and I'll head with Archer to the book shop,' Scarlet prompted. She wasn't fussed about where to explore first, and a bookshop seemed like as good as any a place to begin.

'Yeah. Good idea. If we don't run back into each other, we can just meet up later with Dawson,' Hudson noted.

They went off in opposite directions. Lux was loud, and her voice carried even as they walked around the corner away from them.

Archer didn't take notice of their carrying voices but was focused on Monroe's Books.

'Come on Scarlet, hurry up,' he said, as she had to double step to keep up with him. A mother and her young son had captured her attention as they walked by; both quickly walked down the street. The boy was covered in mud, and his mother had handed him a hanky to wipe a part of it off his face.

'I've told you a hundred times Dean those boys aren't your friends. How are we supposed to show up at the Mayor West-Moore's Party looking like that? I'm going to have to take you home and scrub you down before we even think about showing your face,' the boy's mother said, frustration basically steaming from her forehead. The little boy looked abashed from whatever had led to him being covered in mud in the first place.

'Scarlet. What world are you in? Come on.' Archer dragged her up the stairs into Monroe's Bookshop.

Never had either of them seen so many books. For a small town like this, it probably wasn't that many books, but to them, it was the most they had ever seen. There had maybe been a hundred books between everyone with the Amari. That wasn't including the history recordings that the elders kept, those ones went on for ever and were basically a room of messy papers filed into years. Nor did it include the special book Flynn had given Scarlet called *The Star and the Sea*. Flynn had read it to her a hundred times; it was about a couple deserted on an island, trying to get home. It had pirates, swordfights and a magic light that the couple needed to light up the lighthouse to help find their way home. It was the only thing she wished had made it into her case, but sadly it was left behind. Scarlet imagined the hardcopy bound book with an imprinted image of a lighthouse on the spine, golden etchings of stars, and mermaids on the cover still laying underneath her bed back in their quarters a whole world away.

Walking around the stacks of books, Scarlet read the titles. Passing her hands over the spines, none of them were as finely made or looked anywhere near as wonderful as her copy of *The Star and the Sea*. Still, she pulled out a couple of storybooks to read.

Archer on the other hand continued roaming for books containing information to help him with his broken tech box, specifically looking for communication devices and mechanical books. He'd decided that the box he'd found was a communication system that had been smashed.

Sitting alone in a cluttered yet quiet corner, Scarlet flicked through the pages of the first book she'd picked; a tale about a boy with a pointed nose and draping long hair who didn't seem to fit in wherever he tried. Diving deep into the story before she heard the faint sound of steps, she expected to see Archer pop around the corner with an armful of books, but instead a shadow was cast over her by a man who could only be Mr. Monroe, the store owner.

He stood short and slightly hunched, with so many layers of colourful clothes you might have thought it was snowing outside. Wearing too-small round spectacles that nearly fell off his nose, and a black beanie that covered his scrappy white hair.

'Little Misses don't usually come into my store. Not to read anyhow, usually just have their noses up in the air while their mothers buy something. Or they have too many problems and don't understand the value in a good book. What're you reading anyhow?' Monroe asked, pushing his spectacles closer to his warm brown eyes.

Scarlet showed him the cover. It was a green hardcopy with the title *The Weeping Woes of S. Knight.*

'Ah yes. Good tale that one. I believe a long time ago before even the beginning of Grinnwick there was a man that this story was based on. Curious man, never too happy or kind, but he loved more fiercely than anyone. If you'd like to finish it though, I think you ought to pay for it.'

'Yes, sorry of course,' Scarlet said, poking around the pocket of her fancy skirt. 'Here' she handed him the gold piece.

'This is much too much for that old thing. Come with me,' he said, taking hold of the gold coin in his hand rather tightly. Scarlet followed him down to his desk, which looked cluttered with all sorts of papers with scribblings she couldn't quite make out.

'Scarlet, there you are. I thought I left you back in the first row. Oh, you're getting a book too,' Archer stood waiting at the counter.

'You interested in tech are you boy?' Monroe asked, eyeing his copy of *Working with Data boards.*

'Well, yeah. I thought I'd give a crack at restoring a few broken pieces,' Archer said, curiously staring at Mr. Monroe.

The bell over the door dinged as it opened, a lady stood in the doorway in a bright wrap dress that was red with white spots. Cheerfully she walked towards them. Her lips were coloured red like her dress, Scarlet thought they stood out wonderfully, and her dark hair curled into a fancy style.

'Uncle Joe!' she cried with joy. 'I've had the busiest day with the girls, thought I'd drop by before the party and see if you have that book I asked you to look for?'

Archer's eyes couldn't help but stick to her; Scarlet was even in admiration of her beauty. 'Nora, can't you blooming see I got customers,' Monroe cursed.

'Well, yes you do. Sorry Joe. I'll wait,' she said, taking off her white gloves to look at the books on the shelves closest to her.

'Here you go little miss,' Monroe said, handing Scarlet her change of a large silver piece with the hammer crosses on it and five iron pieces embedded with two lines.

'Sir, you don't have any books called *The Star and the Sea* do you?' Scarlet added.

Mr Monroe's grumpy face turned to a look of curiosity.

'Never had a book here by that name. What's your name kid?' he asked.

'Scarlet. Scarlet Rivers,' Scarlet replied uneasily. He looked at her much more intensely than he had a moment ago. 'Can I check your book for a moment miss?' He looked over her copy of *The Weeping Woes of S. Knight* then passed it back to her.

'Here, my money for this book too sir,' Archer said. Mr Monroe took the money and rustled in the register before practically throwing his change on their side of the table.

'Oh Joe. Be nice to the kids, look at them. Don't think I've seen any of my girls in class that interested in books,' Nora said.

'You're an elder?' Scarlet asked curiously.

'An elder? Gee don't think I'd be classed as an old lady yet lil one. What I am is a teacher,' Nora explained, 'There is a girl's school, St Augustine's, for girls with nowhere to go and no family to look after them.'

'Don't you teach boys?' Archer asked.

'Our school is more than just for learning, we keep girls safe from the world outside, girls who don't have any homes to go to. You know?' Nora said, 'Who are you two then?'

'I'm Archer Baines and…' Archer started.

'This is Scarlet Rivers,' Monroe said introducing Scarlet to his niece, like they were old friends.

'Well, welcome both of you. Nora Monroe's the name. Joe heres' niece. I don't usually look so dressed up, but with the Mayor's party and all. See how long I last among the stiffs you know. Never mind that, you two look like you must have just moved here. I haven't seen your faces around, usually recognise most of the kids, even the little mischief-makers who hang around Winslow's place. Where in town are you staying?' Nora said.

'We just moved here with our... uncle,' Scarlet said, a little delayed, trying to think of what they should call Dawson. 'We're living in the woods, by the cliffs outside of town.'

'All the way out there, are you?' Monroe said, his gaze intently on the two of them. 'Must be running from something bad, if you've decided to hide yourselves that far out.'

'Joe,' Nora gasped, shock across her face. 'Don't mind him kids,' she said, eyeing her uncle down. 'He's naturally suspicious. Don't take his rudeness as a sign that we're all like that around here.'

'Rudeness got nothing to do with it, Nora. You know not many people take to the outskirts beyond our little town or the market village. Most who already live here are hiding from the Grinnwick Guard and their bloody destruction of the world we used to know.

'So, if these young'uns are resorting to living that far out, then there's something a bit peculiar about that. No doubt about that, they're hiding something. But not to worry you two...,' Monroe said now closely to Scarlet and Archer, '...I deal in more than just these books, and I keep a few secrets of my own. So, don't be frightened by the likes of me. I have a feeling you both have plenty to tell about your travels when you're ready.'

Neither Scarlet nor Archer knew exactly what to say to Mr Monroe. Did he know something about where they had come from? Did he know about them, about the Amari Village? About the likes of magical beings still very much being a part of Grinnwick. She had no clue. Scarlet did however see his gaze cross Archer's eyes and the irrefutable movement within them. Nervously she felt their visit was up.

'Look Joe, you've gone and scared them silly. Pay no attention both of you. You're safe now, wherever you're from, and your whole lives are ahead of you now. It doesn't matter where you've come from all that matters is what's ahead,' Nora said, her red-lipped smile beaming at them; she was a burst of cheerful eagerness that was nearly the complete opposite of her uncle, even as her eyes frustratingly darted towards her uncle who stood behind her.

'That's not exactly right though… is it?' said Scarlet.

Nora looked at her curiously. 'What do you mean hun?'

Archer nudged Scarlet, trying to edge them out of the shop.

'Sorry Miss, I just meant that we aren't exactly safe here are we. It wasn't long ago there were attacks down the coast, who's to say the Grinnwick Guard won't come looking this way thinking someone here is a threat,' Scarlet said. Noticing in the corner of her eye Archer looking a little shocked.

Monroe was the first to break the silence.

'You are a smart kid. We've been clear of their rath for centuries, let's hope new changes around here aren't the reason that that changes too,' Monroe ominously stared at the two of them. 'Why don't you two get out of here, enjoy the sun,' he finished.

Archer took up Monroe's offer quickly, and made for the exit, still uneasy with the whole bookstore experience.

The street outside had built up by three times the amount of people. Many of them were wearing brightly elegant outfits as Nora wore; if anything they were even fancier. The heels of the women clapped along the stone ground, echoing along the street.

Scarlet and Archer walked down to the corner where they'd last seen Hudson and Lux.

'Do you think Mr Monroe knows anything about us, and where we've come from? What about the secrets he spoke of. What do you think he knows?' Scarlet asked Archer as they walked down the street.

'He seems to know something. But it's probably nothing about us, he probably says that to all the new people. Who really cares anyway, he seems a bit loony,' Archer commented. 'Probably didn't take kindly to you being all doom and gloom… He does have a decent book collection though,' he added, mainly to himself as they went on searching for Lux and Hudson.

'Look over there,' Archer motioned towards a small alley that was full of market stalls. 'If I was those two, that's exactly where I'd have gone,' he said, heading straight there.

Scarlet knew that the others were likely to head for the alleyway, but she felt an eerie sensation that they shouldn't go down there.

The shadows of the building made the whole alley cooler and darker than the other parts of the town of Bellevue Point. A black metal sign was stuck to the side of the brick wall labelled Steel Circuit.

They came across smaller stems of laneways that led off the original one, winding between all the other buildings. Most of these locals here were not the fancy people that were in the street. These were rough, worn and scrappy people who gave off a sense of unease. None of them clean and most wearing tattered clothes, some with trench coats hiding the goods they were there to sell – or as Scarlet suspected they were used to help them steal products from other market stall holders.

'You two interested in West Land Rot Figs? great for syrup,' voiced an old hook nosed purple haired woman as soon as they entered. Scarlet didn't believe it was the same sort of sugar syrup she was used to by the looks of the woman, her worn face made her look as though she was under the influence of a high strength tea that was given to them when they were ill.

'Location Displacers: the best on the market,' called a rather young man, smiling broadly in front of a cabinet full of small greenlit-filled discs. 'They'll keep you off the grid, and out of any Grinnwick Guard Soldiers tracers. Implantation for a fixed price,' he noted.

Scarlet could see Archer's eyes beam in interest to this; neither of them had ever seen such tech, it wasn't the sort of thing that they had back home. His broken communicator was the most advanced piece of technology they'd truly come across – if not for the light room back at the Amari, but she suspected that sort of power wasn't used here.

Her knowledge of a disc's or something that could be implanted inside her body seemed utterly alien, not natural to their way of life at all. She pulled him by his collar away from the stall, and quickly squirmed between people; barely escaping other sellers who tried to vie for their attention. Instead, she tried to focus on keeping an eye out for the twins.

Scarlet saw many other stalls for other types of discs or 'updates' as they called it. Each claiming to do something she wasn't too sure they could. Whether it kept them off the radar, wipe the person who used it memories clear, or update them with knowledge. A large weapon stall also seemed to be hidden in one of the deeper corners. Scarlet's eyes flashed from the swords she knew in various sizes too well, but with the addition of guns which she had only ever seen pictures of, some older and released a lead bullet, while others contained the greenlit liquid. There weren't too many weapons, as was to be expected in an off the grid town like Bellevue Point, but the stall still had three great brutes standing guard at the front of it.

None of them even bothered looking down at Scarlet and Archer as they passed by.

A knock across her back quickly grabbed Scarlet's attention; two kids had swiped passed her, nearly knocking her off her feet.

Intrigued, Scarlet followed them at a distance. One was at least twice her and Archer's size. She thought that they might have an idea of where the twins were, but realised after glimpsing the looks on their faces that they were up to no good.

'I saw them go down this way,' she heard the larger boy say.

'Get them Amos,' The other called back.

Scarlet watched them spot somebody at the end of a skinny side laneway. She felt Archer bump into her as they reached the opening of the lane.

'Hey,' Scarlet yelled out to the two boys. They turned to spot her with dumbfounded expressions on their faces, nothing about them screamed kindly by any means. Quickly she noticed two other boys behind them. The boys ignored her and went after the boys behind them. One of them was pushed into the wall by Amos; the overly large, muscly, and extremely dumb looking one. But the boy being shoved into the wall didn't look scared at all. None of them could have been much older than Lux and Hudson were. A couple years older than herself. By the looks on the faces of the two boys being attacked she could tell they weren't too eager to have her there either.

'Why don't you guys get out of there, before I call someone down here,' Scarlet yelled out.

'Scarlet. Stop it. Let's leave them to it,' Archer muttered, careful not to make eye contact with the fight about to break out before them.

'I don't know who you are, but this town is ours now. So if you've got any smarts, keep outta our way.

'What is this Sticks... you got yourself a girlfriend now do you, she going to fight for you? Probably punches better,' said the smaller of the brutes.

'We don't even know her. You think we're scared of you fools... we'll take you on any day,' the boy up against the wall said and pushed himself out of the situation with all his might.

'Big talk especially since you don't have your little leader Bastian around anymore,' Amos the large bully mocked.

'Best run off like he did, if you keep getting in our way you won't last long... even with a girl on your side,' Amos warned.

'We don't need her, and we are strong enough without Bastian to keep you out of trouble,' the boy argued back.

'Don't worry... I'm sure he'll end up in the slums back with us before you know it, answering to me. Or better yet, he won't make it back at all,' Amos boasted, his menacing laugh echoed the laneway only before the two boys overthrew Amos, casting him to the ground. Leaving the two buffoons stumped for a split second, giving the boys a moment to escape.

They ran down the laneway past Scarlet and Archer, and Scarlet followed them joining in and catching up with their pace until they were finally clear of the bullies and could all stop to catch their breath.

'Clean cuts like yourselves don't want to be caught down here, doesn't end well,' the boy warned as he passed Scarlet.

'I think we should listen to him Scarlet,' Archer said, following the two boys.

'Wait. We could have helped; I mean we can handle ourselves,' Scarlet noted, following Sticks and his friend, keeping up with the fast pace, ducking in and around the crowd of people to keep up.

'You don't catch a hint do you girl. Listen to your friend, this isn't the kind of place you make friends. This isn't a life you want, stick to the main street' he snapped and ran off quickly down the alleyway out of sight before Scarlet could follow.

Pulling her to a stop, Archer made sure the two bullies weren't close by, 'Well, that was interesting. Can we get out of here now?' He panted.

Scarlet walked straight out of the alleyway, not taking notice of anyone trying to grab their attention, but focused on her own annoyance built up from their unwanted presence. She knew perfectly well how to handle herself, and Archer may seem like a cowardly pup at the moment, but she knew he would have had her back if the need arose. After all, in the practice pits back home, he was always ready to take on anyone, even if he didn't win.

This must have been written all over her face as she bumped right into someone, now out on the street.

'Scarlet. Look where you're going why don't you.'

It was Lux; her face was shocked and beaming all at once.

'Where have you two been?' Lux asked.

'You don't want to know,' Archer said, his face glaring, annoyed at Scarlet.

'Don't be ridiculous Archer. We just ran into a bit of a fight down the alleyway is all,' Scarlet said, brushing off the situation, her annoyance fading with it.

'Oh yeah, its wild down there isn't it. We went and had a quick look earlier. Thought you guys would get stuck with Archer looking at all that tech. I dragged Hudson to sit by the streets edge; we were watching the parade of people walking down in their outfits. Those dresses, the hats, and the fur. It was mesmerizing, I've never seen people look so pretty,' Lux said in awe.

'It was boring,' Hudson piped up, rolling his eyes. 'I ended up in the corner store buying these,' he said holding a paper bag full of gummy looking treats. 'Try them, the purple ones; Pop one in your mouth. Think they called them Shooting Blue Drops.'

Sitting on the sidewalk, Archer told the twins all about their run in with the boys down the laneway.

'Lucky I wasn't there, I would have had that big guy on the ground before any of them spoke,' Hudson said.

'Scarlet nearly did,' Archer retorted. Scarlet couldn't help roll her eyes.

'It's not that you couldn't of, it's just that we don't know the ins and outs of how things work around here. I mean, those guys could be into some real bad circles. You just don't know,' Archer said.

'He's not wrong Scarlet,' Hudson agreed. 'This place isn't like the village. People have survived out here, they weren't provided for, we don't know what those kids have had to do, or what they are involved in.'

'But they're kids, they're just like us. I mean we can't let nice people get beat up,' Scarlet noted.

'You're right Scarlet. But this is what this world is, and we can't save everyone,' Hudson replied.

'We should try,' Scarlet said, more to herself than anyone else.

It seemed like no time had passed as they reached the bottom of the treat bag that the clock tower showed it was only ten minutes away from the time to meet up with Dawson.

Making their way back Scarlet saw in the distance Sticks and his friend, in another laneway giving a bag to another boy, who she couldn't see properly from the distance. Catching their eyes for a second leading them all to stare at her, the third boy looked familiar. But as she walked with the others and they turned into the main street, Scarlet still looking back as she walked leading to her running right into someone. Again.

'Miss Rivers, are you okay?' asked Nora Monroe.

'Yes, sorry. I didn't see you coming around the corner,' Scarlet said helping her pick up the bags she had dropped, as did Hudson.

'Not to worry, I was just heading to the school, I got word a bunch of girls at St Augustine's have been misbehaving, so party's over for me,' Nora said, 'Looks like you've found a couple of friends,' she added smiling sweetly at Lux and Hudson.

'Oh yeah. These are the twins, Hudson and Lux Watts. They moved here with us,' Scarlet said handing Nora back her lipstick and pen from her bag.

'Nice to meet you,' Lux said, her finest and most polite version of herself coming out. Scarlet and Hudson both looked at each other rolling their eyes.

'Well your uncle has his hands full with four of you, doesn't he,' Nora said.

'Dawson,' Lux said, confused for a moment before spotting Scarlet's face. 'Yeah, Uncle Dawson is the greatest,' she added.

'That's the first time I've heard you kids say that about me,' Dawson said, walking up behind them.

'You must be the infamous uncle,' Nora said politely.

'I am?' Dawson said. Looking at the kids. 'Oh, their uncle. Yep, I'm Dawson. And I'm sorry you are?' he asked, the most flustered any of them had ever seen him.

'Nora Monroe,' she said, smiling. 'I was just saying it looks like you've got your hands full with these four,' she added.

'You have no idea,' Dawson said, his eyes awkwardly looking around at Scarlet. She couldn't help but giggle under her breath by how uncomfortable he looked. 'You work here in town Ms Monroe?' Dawson asked.

'Nora, please. And yes, I've lived here my whole life; I'm a teacher at Saint Augustine's Home for Girls. Just around the corner,' Nora said beaming at Dawson, seeming more than a little flustered in his presence.

'A teacher, well I might have to get you around to get these four up to scratch,' Dawson noted.

'I don't usually do home classes; but I'm sure we can organise a time to help keep this lot up to date,' Nora said. 'Scarlet and Archer mentioned you're up in the woods on the cliff out of town. There's an old cottage there isn't there? I can pop by after class on a Friday, I usually have those afternoons off.'

'I'll make sure they're all there,' Dawson assured her, then insisted they all say their goodbyes to Miss Monroe. They were unsure what they'd be learning, but the idea that soon something other than fighting practice would be taught to them excited each of them their whole way through dinner.

They ate their way through mince burgers trying to find out what Dawson had done with his day. He was used to dodging their questions by now, a skill he had become quite good at over the weeks no matter how hard they prodded him.

'I spent years protecting the Amari boarders. Keeping a watchful eye out, and you four think I'm going to break just because you keep asking. And, don't think that just because you don't know where I was doesn't mean I didn't know exactly what you were all up to,' Dawson said, his roundabout of words confusing them all. Scarlet smiled at him, whether he was bluffing or not she didn't know. But if he had been watching over them, it only made her feel more at ease.

The Last Page

Heavy rain pattered on the roof and wind whistled by their cottage for what seemed like days leaving them all stuck inside. Scarlet had been reading her book *The Weeping Woes of S. Knight*. Archer read his tech book that had sent his brain into overdrive. While Lux, Dawson, and Hudson had been in a never-ending game of snap, a game that Dawson had taught them where you had three piles of cards in your hand, each card had a different colour of black, purple, red, and blue. As well as symbols in the centre, hammers, water, crown, and crow. Each placing one card at a time on the pile to your right, and on each pile clockwise, and if the card matched the players had to snap the pile before the other. The trick was, other players were putting theirs on the same time, so you had to be aware of every card played.

Dawson even taught them a few other games, one even required making a board that he called Galant. The more resources you tried to gain in the game the more likely you wouldn't make it to the centre of the board as someone would try to steal them from you and you would end up back at the beginning, yet you needed them to help you build your city to the middle of the board, thus winning.

The tale of S. Knight was a sad adventure; the character had escaped many harrowing monsters only to lose the love of his life. She was about halfway through the book when a small piece of paper fell out into her lap.

It was torn at the edges and read 'Don't read the last page.'

Scarlet stared at the piece of paper. First unsure how it hadn't fallen out sooner, then really taking notice of the words, not believing the small thing she held in her hand. The circumstances that a piece of paper with these words would be here couldn't be accidental, could they? The last time she had heard those words, they came from her brother Flynn. That very last night she saw him after he had ventured out into the Amari woods to his last watcher training sessions. Which she now knew was a ploy to go off with Dawson to find the princess.

***

'Excuse me. I seem to have misplaced a very small, annoying, and incredibly cute little sister,' Flynn teased.

The mask of night covered his face in a way that led to uncertainty of who he was. Peering down Scarlet saw dashes of moonlight swiped across his face. She sat perched up in a high tree on her own, far away from the village, away from a terrorising Ailsa. She wiped her tears, not able to hide her smile as Flynn held out his hand, helping her down out of the tree.

'How did you find me so quickly?' Scarlet asked. 'I thought you left this morning for joining in on their watcher's classes. Wait, how'd you even know I would come out here.'

'You forget; I have ways of making Archer talk,' he laughed shyly with his half-smile, helping her to sit down by the foot of the tree. They were in the gardens of the village, a quiet place where the stars above shined so clear, and the beauty of the blooms somehow made all the things that upset her a little better.

'What are you thinking running off, where did you think you're going to go? I know Ailsa is a bit… difficult at times. Trust me, I know. But she tries, and most importantly she's here, she's looking after us,' he explained.

'She doesn't try,' Scarlet butted in, wiping away her tears as slight anger built up.

'She looks at us like we are a problem. She misses her old life; she misses the fact that she could never be a watcher now. That's why she fawns over you going to your classes. I don't even know why though it's not like you're Amari; you could never be a true

214

watcher. I mean I don't even know why you go…. But still she watches you go off and hates that she still needs to take care of the rest of us. She barks at us all the time.

The way she looks at me sometimes. It's like she can't deal with the fact that I even exist,' Scarlet cried, hating herself for sounding so ungrateful.

'And you know why I go to train, I want to be my best in case anything ever arises like it did back in Grinnwick, I want to be agile enough when and if I ever need to be,' Flynn said, followed by a rather exhausted sigh.

'What am I supposed to do around here grow up twiddling my thumbs. I'm no book worm either, need to be out on the move, keeping busy. You of all people know that; you'll probably do the same thing when you're older.

'And Ailsa, she's a tough cookie to crack. Hard on the outside, but I think she's really just as alone as the rest of us. Try and see through her hard shell okay? You don't know your past, nearly just as much as you don't know hers. How do you know she doesn't need someone to bring her some light.

'If anyone has a heart of kindness to give, it's you. Try sharing it with her, maybe she thinks you don't like her and she's at a loss… After all this time we've been here do you think our family, do you think our mother would be happy knowing that you're sad, that you're not trying. They would want you to embrace others, to bring them joy,' he told her.

Scarlet looked at Flynn, feeling foolish for running off now. She had only wanted space, only wanted someone to truly care for her, it was hard every time that Flynn left. Even with Archer there, she had felt alone. Not realizing that maybe the others including Ailsa felt just as alone as she did. Maybe they needed her to care for them instead.

'I'm sorry. I should have been better,' Scarlet conceded, hugging Flynn.

He laughed. 'It's okay. You're a kid. And you've forgotten what it was like, what they would have wanted for you. It's easy to want to have people look after you, to care.

Sometimes others just care differently, and are the ones who need to be cared for. Just like I will always look out for you, little sister,' Flynn said, putting his arm around her.

Scarlet looked up at him. 'Tell me more about them. Please. Having no memories of my own, it sucks,' Scarlet pleaded.

Flynn looked at her, his smile was fading but he moved her hair out of her face.

'You look like our mother, even now as a little girl. Although our sister she was her clone,' Flynn started.

'You never told me we had a sister,' Scarlet said, surprised at the notion of family beyond that of an unknown mother and father that Flynn already barely mentioned.

'We did. I don't know why I didn't tell you; I guess… It hurts to remember,' Flynn said, his own face seemed lost in a sadness, a familiar sadness Scarlet often saw in him.

'Unlike you I hold those memories, but it's painful to look back… the most recent memories of them aren't so nice. But I do remember; I remember our home before this place, before the Amari. It was more than you could have imagined. As lush and green as this garden is, ours was beyond beautiful; it was enchanting. That's what our mother called it, and it was. Our home was a place full of love and magic. Our home made you the adventurous kid you are today. You were mischief from the get-go. Before we were torn away from it, before you hurt your head and your memories were gone, you always managed to find yourself in the strangest of situations, and still do.

'I recall when you were half the size you are now, absolutely no one was ever allowed in father's office, that was except you. I found you inside there with our giant dog Ned and you had managed to draw all over his office wall. I thought he was going to be furious. He just laughed, patted the dog, sat in his chair and let you keep drawing. I don't think he ever took it down either,' Flynn said, his face going from the light of his memories to a solemn brood.

Scarlet didn't say anything, she was trying to imagine a man whose face she didn't remember being delighted to see her drawings on a wall, she wondered what she would

216

have drawn. Imagining that they couldn't have been too good if she was even younger than what she was now, and she wasn't exactly a talented artist.

Flynn. Do you think they'd like me now?' Scarlet asked.

'So many questions from a troublemaker,' he laughed again, 'Of course they would, and I know as much as Ailsa gives you grief, she likes you too.

'Don't let the fact that you can't remember bother you. So much happened back then that a lot of people are still affected by, including Ailsa. You're free from that, so it's up to you to look out for them,' Flynn said.

'Including you. I've got to look out for you,' Scarlet gloated.

'We've got to look out for each other,' Flynn replied, softly laughing. 'You know what, you are still the same kid you always were, being able to forget has made it so nothing has been able to dampen your spirit, and every time I see that I'm jealous. You see my memories of our life then as unattainable, but they keep me stuck in that time when I thought anything was possible for us and stuck with the harsh memories that followed. But you; you're free from that, free to follow any path you like, and have nothing in your heart stop you,' he said, half lost in his memories and half ensuring Scarlet knew she was better for being in the dark of her past life. Not able to hide his sad eyes behind his smile.

'Does it make you sad because our family is gone? That it's just you and me,' Scarlet asked.

'It does. It makes me sad that you don't remember them. You were always everything to them; to our whole family. There is so much of them inside of you. Nothing mattered more than our family to us, even now that they're all gone, they will be all that I hold close to my heart,' Flynn said.

He helped her up and they headed back home to their quarters.

Closing in towards the hill above their quarters in the Amari Village where rows of windows stuck out of this side of the hill. The windows were from the second stories of each individual's quarters on this side of the village. Scarlet slowed her pace. Never had Flynn told her so much as he had tonight, she still didn't even know her parent's names; Flynn never told her. His answer would usually go along the lines of 'Another time; when you're older; I just don't know where to begin,' Tonight, the way that he had begun describing what their life had been like was more than she had ever wished for from a family. If only she could remember. Besides Scarlet also knew once she was back in her quarters, it would mean Flynn would be off again, he would be on his trip with the watchers, and when she woke it would be over a week before he would return.

'There you go,' Flynn pushed open their window. 'Maybe I'll tell you another story about our family when I come back okay?' Flynn holding the window open for her. He stood steady on the hill, overlooking the village. 'You know that book The Star and the Sea. It's under my bed; it's all yours now. Just, don't read the last page. Promise me,' he said, hugging her tightly.

'But it's yours, you'll want it when you come back,' Scarlet noted.

'Think it's about time you had it kid. Now hurry up and get inside. If anyone asks where you were, say you went out fishing. I saw Archer and Hudson heading down to the lake on my way to find you, gave them the heads up to tell Ailsa you'd be fishing with them,' he said with a wink, and after a warm hug, he waited as Scarlet jumped through their bedroom window.

Scarlet quickly looked for the book; its old, beautiful hardcover was embedded with beautiful gold embellishments of fairies and mermaids. She brushed her hand over the top feeling the details. She held it up to the window, looking out at Flynn and showing him its cover. His smile was brighter than ever, then with a wave goodbye he looked out over the village for a moment before walking away. He disappeared down the hill, and Scarlet returned to her bed, opening the first page of the book, noticing written inside was what Flynn had said, 'don't read the last page'. She had never noticed it before, but he usually *read it to her before now. Slowly drifting off she looked over at Flynn's empty bed thinking of the stories she might finally hear of her family.*

***

Scarlet had never looked at the last page of *The Star and The Sea*, it was her last promise to Flynn, and she never wanted to break it, the last little thing she had to hold onto. Reading those five words here, now so far away from the Amari village, she felt like maybe it meant something more, and maybe, just maybe she should have looked at the last page of the book, that now sat underneath her bed abandoned a whole world away.

The little piece of paper stared at her like Flynn was saying it to her all over again. This time however she didn't promise him that she wouldn't read this last page; quickly she turned the pages of the book, flicking them through her fingers. The motion brushing a soft breeze across her face, and on the back page was something she didn't expect, another page had been slipped into the book. She felt silly for not noticing it earlier.

Don't cry if I'm gone. Don't dwell on what you've lost. I once said you are lucky to be unburdened by the past, that will always be true. Remain as kind and bold as the sister I left behind. Your life will never be the same. Many secrets lie in the lighthouse, yet your answers are right where you stand. F

It was a message from her brother, she was sure of it. 'If' was the only thing she focused on, *If* he was gone; it meant there was a chance he could be alive. He had to be; he'd left the letter. How did he leave the letter? It must have been the bookstore owner, Mr. Monroe who slide it into her book. When he'd written this note he wasn't sure what was to come it seemed. So, he wasn't sure of what his fate was to be, still the truth was he hadn't returned to them. But he was close, he had to be. Maybe he was still here.

His words, *answers are right where you stand* – that had to be the bookstore. Mr. Monroe knew something. Maybe he himself had seen Flynn. And what did the lighthouse have to do with anything…

She was unable to comprehend what she'd read. Unable to fully believe it was all real. Scarlet kept it to herself. It played on her mind constantly, not paying attention to anyone as they spoke to her, ignoring requests for what she'd like on her toast or if she would like to join in their morning fighting practice. Instead, she remained inside, off in her own world.

However, by the time their actual first lesson with Nora came around the next day Scarlet beyond excited, as were the others who finally got to learn real-world knowledge from Grinnwick, not the stuff that they had just been taught in their village. Scarlet was on the verge of exploding trying to pry out information about Flynn, since it would be a while before Dawson would allow them to go back into town. She wondered if it was at all possible if Nora had seen something or heard anything about him while he visited the store. However, not having said anything about the note to the others, even Dawson made it difficult to ask straight away.

Nora herself seemed to be bursting with excitement for the lesson.

She'd brought with her a mound of books, that nearly seemed impossible for her to have carried the whole distance from the town. Dawson quickly helped her lug them in the door. They realised that her enthusiasm to be taking the class outweighed all of theirs. She had a childish grin spread across her red-lipped face.

'Oh, we'll learn about space, area, velocity, and even about music too. It's going to be a ball,' Nora was giddy with enthusiasm. None of them really knew what half the words really meant besides music, well except perhaps for Archer.

Even for Dawson enthusiasm for the lesson entered a steady decline as the day went on. Nora appeared to have developed a sweet affection towards him, and Scarlet wasn't sure he felt the same way, as he awkwardly tip-toed around whenever he needed to grab something from inside the cottage. Spending the majority of the time outside, in the rain.

The class itself wasn't very interesting, as much as Nora tried. She started off talking to them about photo-sin-thesis, at least that's what Scarlet gathered was the name. Truly she wasn't quite sure. She gathered that it had something to do with plant cells, and light. Scarlet drawing useless pictures of flowers in her notepad. Which didn't help when Nora decided to pull her up for a question.

'How do plants make their own food?' Nora asked, clearly aware Scarlet hadn't been paying attention.

'Umm, you said the sun,' Scarlet said, hoping it was right.

'Close, the process is called photosynthesis, remember,' Nora continued talking for what seemed like ages about plants. Scarlet had nearly forgotten about Flynn's note, and her need to find out more as Nora went on and on. Dawson finally reappeared and Nora's train of thought drifted as she was instantly drawn to him. Scarlet and Hudson sighed in reprieve. She started gasbagging about a girl named Olive in her class who had gotten into trouble for not showing up for dinner the night before at St. Augustine's. Their curfew was seven at night. Nora had run all over town apparently looking for her. Only to find her cooped up down at Winslow's ready to join some rebel crew wanting to retaliate against the shooting of a small family in a town about a week's ride away from where they were, all because they couldn't afford to pay the Grinnwick Guard for some fee due to crossing a river under their jurisdiction.

Dawson seemed pretty upset by the whole situation; it was the first any of them had heard about it. It wasn't until Nora went to leave that Scarlet decided to ask her.

'Wait. I was just wondering; I mean you probably don't know him... my brother Flynn Rivers, he might have come through Bellevue Point,' she felt herself relieving the moment when they first arrived, and their conversation with Winslow.

'It's just I found a note in the book I purchased from your uncle's shop from him. So, I wondered if maybe you saw him, my brother that is. I think he'd probably be in his thirties now, he had wavy dark hair. You'd know him if you met him,' Scarlet was very aware of everyone staring.

'The name does ring a bell. From a while back maybe, I don't think I met him. But I remember Uncle Joe maybe said something about him. But then again I could be dead wrong, he can drab on about things that I don't always pay attention to,' she said apologetically.

'Thanks, well I'll ask Mr. Monroe next time. See you later,' Scarlet said, trying not to look at Dawson's face. Now he knew she was keeping secrets of her own. They needed to return to town to find Mr. Monroe, and ask him straight out about Flynn and this mysterious note.

***

Bellevue Point was not the same lively town it had been the day they visited. The rain still poured, and most people were inside hiding or scurrying under rooftops. It had a dull, depressing sadness to it as Dawson and Scarlet walked down the main street basically alone. He still wasn't happy with her for keeping the note to herself, for not trusting him with something so important.

The moment Nora left he had glared at her for what seemed like an endless silence, then asked calmly where the note had come from. After Scarlet had explained, all he had said was, 'Something like that, something that important to you. It's just as important to us. The fact that you didn't share it, well I'm disappointed you didn't trust in any of us as soon as you found it. I mean I know I'm just your caretaker, but these guys, they're your friends. And from the looks on their faces they too had no clue.'

Scarlet had been speechless. Every fibre of her had felt awful.

'You're not just my caretaker, you're my family. I just hadn't wrapped my head around it was all. I didn't want it to not be true,' she had told not only him, but all of them, but was disheartened when she had seen the look of disappointment in all of their faces.

The bell rang as they walked in the door, but Monroe didn't come straight out. Scarlet hadn't expected him to. Dawson walked around a bit as they waited; he looked in the adventure book section. Stories where bravery tended to win out in the end. She wondered if he enjoyed the mushy parts of the books just as much.

'We have to wait all day for this old bat,' Dawson said to her, still clearly grumpy.

'Am I the old bat?' came Monroe's voice. He was draped in about four scarfs as he came out of the back room, each one thicker than the next.

'Sorry, Mr. Monroe is it? I'm Dawson. This is…' Dawson began.

'Miss Rivers. Welcome back,' Monroe said.

'Yes, well we are here because we have lessons with your niece, Nora. And she told us you might know a boy named Flynn Rivers. And then there's also a whole question retaining to a note that ended up in my niece's book that she purchased from your store.'

'That blasted girl. She's trouble, never keeps her trap shut,' Monroe said aghast. 'At least she blabbed her mouth to the right person this time. I'm glad you got the message young miss,' Monroe said, nearly ignoring Dawson and talking directly to Scarlet who felt nervous and unsure of where to look as he stared at her. She wiped her palms on her skirt.

'Yes, that message. How did you know it was for her?' Dawson said looking at Scarlet.

'Well... Flynn wrote it for her. Didn't have much time either so he only got the basics down. I had strict orders from him, to get it to Miss Rivers here any way I could – mind you he didn't say when you'd be coming. When you said your name I wasn't entirely sure, but then you asked if we had that book. And I know the title, your brother spoke of it too. Anyway, I asked for your book back, and slid the notes in. He was your brother, wasn't he?' Monroe said.

Scarlet nodded. Dawson looked at her curiously, she regretted not telling him about the message, she couldn't really believe that it was from Flynn, not until now.

'So, where is he?' asked Dawson.

'Who, the boy? No idea. Left here in quite a hurry, this was years ago, maybe five or so. Grinnwick's a large place, and that's not including the isles off the western front. Or the mysteries to the north. But he did tell me about you, young lady. Oh, he did. I mean for a scrappy little kid he's put a lot of hopes on you I'm guessing. Left a couple of things here for you too,' Monroe said.

Turning around to the wall of books behind him he pushed the case across like a rather large door until a hatch was shown behind it.

He encoded a combination onto a small screen, and with a huff of stale air it opened.

He pulled out four objects from the safe and placed them on the desk. The first was a long round canister with F.T embedded into the top; a small notebook that was loosely wrapped in paper; a golden necklace that had a beautiful locket at the end of it, the locket itself was sealed shut but the front of the round locket it was engraved with the initials E & G in the middle of a heart shape. And finally, a photograph. Scarlet picked it up. It was of two people. Their faces couldn't be made out, but it was clear it was a celebration of sorts – amongst a forest of blooming vines and streams of light showering them from above as they stood together. On the back of the picture was written *Mum & Dad*.

This had to be them; her parents.

She dropped the picture for a moment, looking up at Mr. Monroe, who looked at her with a kindness, a kindness from him that she did not expect.

Dawson meanwhile picked up the photograph, silent as he stared at it.

'Where did you get this?' Dawson demanded.

'I told you, the boy. Flynn left it here for her,' Monroe replied, clearly not appreciating the accusation in Dawson's voice.

'Why did he leave this here? He never let this picture out of his sight,' Dawson said.

'I don't know. He seemed very intent on having Miss Rivers be the one to take them off my hands,' Monroe said, snatching the photograph from Dawson's fingers and placing it with the other Items.

'Now Scarlet, I'm leaving these things with you. There's also a note here that he left for you.' He handed Scarlet a small envelope with her name on it. Scarlet took the envelope, looking from Mr. Monroe to Dawson, opening it slowly before them.

Scarlet,

I find myself writing to you in fear that I may not see you again. Bellevue Point was always the back-up location in case something happened within the Amari Village. We were not meant to be there forever, as beautiful as it was, and as precious as that time we spent there was, it is not our home.

I know at some point you will find yourself standing in front of Joe Monroe, just as I did. He was a needed friend at a pivotal point since leaving you. He helped me where others could not. I know that Grinnwick is stranger and vaster than you've ever imagined, but you're not alone; we were never alone. Don't rush off and try to save every single person you know; wait, allow time for yourself to grow up, and in time you will discover that you are more than anyone at the Amari could have hoped for you to be. You will notice things that make you different, don't fear them, never fear them. Embrace every part of you, just as this world will in time. I know you've always enjoyed the moment, sometimes though you must be prepared for what tomorrow will bring. So, in time you'll be ready, and you can take everything I've left you. Hold these things close. Go on the journey I wish I could have followed you on. Read the map, listen to yourself and you'll find things that no one has seen for years. Be brave my beautiful sister, and live.

Your brother and friend, Flynn

Scarlet handed the letter to Dawson, who read it much quicker than she did. He read it twice from what she could tell. All Scarlet knew was that those words came from her brother, and she knew he wouldn't have left them to her if they weren't important.

'I'm sorry that I can't give you both any more answers. I tried asking him to hang around longer, to wait and see if you would come retrieve these from him yourself, but he insisted that there was no time. He stayed with me maybe a couple of weeks before he left,' Monroe said.

'So what you just take items off any stranger who walks in this door do you? That seems like an odd business my friend,' Dawson handed Scarlet back her letter, still looking quite unhappy.

'I owed him a favour, and I can now say I've paid my debt,' Monroe replied honourably, standing tall to try and align himself with Dawson.

'And why'd you owe him a favour?' Dawson asked.

'You think I'm leading you astray… I told Scarlet here that I dealt in secrets; Flynn not only gave me a hand on the street against some thieves when we first met, which gave him a roof over his head. The boy also revealed a secret to me that I found most valuable. I think *you* would find the secret he gave me most interesting, but I also assume that is why you are here today,' Monroe said puzzlingly to Dawson.

With a face as still as the piles of books around him and a stare that sent a chill down Scarlet's arms, she stood silently until Dawson said to Monroe, 'Whatever he told you, remember he was just a boy. His knowledge of things was only the tip of things. He obviously trusted you, but I know him, he never would have given you any real leverage, just a taste of the world he knew.'

With that Dawson piled up the items on the table into his bag, grabbed Scarlet's hand, and they walked out of the store. Scarlet waved and tried to say thanks as they walked out the ringing door behind them, but she didn't get to see if Monroe waved goodbye as well.

'So what do I do?' Scarlet asked as they gained on their cottage. Dawson stopped and took her shoulder in his hand.

'We'll have a look at the map and the other items a bit closer, but I think no matter what's on the map Flynn was right; it's best you give it time, wait to follow that path until you're older. Just, make sure you hold onto that picture, I knew Flynn treasured it, so it's your responsibility now. Look after it for him,' Dawson said.

'You were with him before he came here, did he tell you about these things, did he tell you he would leave them for me? How well did you exactly know him?' Scarlet asked.

Dawson gazed down at her; she could tell he held so much in. 'You know I was with him; I knew him well enough, but these trinkets, I knew nothing of. All I can say is he was a good kid. And I bet he's just as good of a man now. Probably nearly my age now, which is strange to think about,' Dawson pondered for moment, 'Truth is he cared about you Scarlet, and I promise if he's out there we will find him. So just know I want to help, I want to believe he's out there.' Dawson pulled her in for an embrace before they took their newfound treasures inside to the others.

Lux, Hudson, Archer and Scarlet all looked over the letter, necklace, map and notebook. Archer and Hudson had sat down and gone over every inch of the map with Dawson quietly tracing his finger over a star like emblem in the top corner, lost in thought.

The map had Grinnwick clearly outlined in the centre, with islands and an offshore land around the edges; main cities and sections of the districts were named. With the tree separated area of the outer districts; *the grey plains* to the east, *the moors* of the west, and to the north the city of *Sildor*. South of the border of the outer districts a mass portion of the centre of Grinnwick was covered in Greenery, this had titled *the Corazon forest* in the centre, somewhere in amongst the Corazon forest, the most treacherous terrain in this word hid the valley of the Amari village, perhaps the forest held more secrets than just their small villages. To the south there was *Astoria* right at the very bottom. To its west was *Serina*, just inland from the coast it seemed. Another further north of it called *Airedale*. And to the east, a city titled *Woodwark,* it was much more central inland. Scarlet had only heard of Astoria, and of course Bellevue Point outside of the Corazon Forest, and Bellevue was much too small a place to be titled on this map. There were no roads or paths that could be made out on the map either, only Scarlet felt she saw some vague lines, but when the others didn't mention it, she thought it must have been a trick of her mind. Archer was convinced there was a secret to the map, and he was intent on finding it. She left him to it and joined Lux focusing their attentions on the notebook.

Gently opening the notebook, Scarlet hadn't been prepared for what to expect. The insides looked like the ramblings of a mad man. She couldn't understand the writing at all, and the more she tried to read it the harder it became to look at. It was full of codes, seeming a language she didn't understand at all. The pages that were written on also had images drawn on them, and Flynn had been quite the skilled artist. Each picture was detailed and perfect; some of the pictures were just of creatures he'd have come across more than likely in the Black Forest, one resembled the green ape-like creature that she'd seen by the riverbank. Others were of people; the face of a man who looked weathered and scarred, a small child holding a bucket, and a woman carrying a baby. Under each picture in the far-right corner was a single word, mort. 'It means the dead. I don't think the futures were too bright for these people,' Dawson said from behind, leaving a solemn silence at the table. Scarlet touched the cheek of the woman on the page in front of her. Flipping over to the next page held another picture.

'That's definitely you Scarlet. Look at the shape of the eyes, and the way the hair falls,' Lux said.

'I don't know,' said Hudson. 'I know it's hard to tell from a drawing but that looks like an older lady, not the Scarlet that Flynn would have remembered, you know. Besides I don't remember Scarlet's hair ever looking that tidy. Yours is always a mess or pulled up into a ponytail.

'What about there, the writing? Can anyone make out what he's written on the page?' Hudson piped up from across the table.

'It says a face I've never forgotten. The rest is in a language I can't read. And at the bottom it says mort again, so I'm going to guess it's not me,' Scarlet said, pointing to the words on the page.

'No wait it says something here on the opposite page separated from all the writing; look down across the spine,' Lux said, pointing to the page. 'The family you never knew.'

Scarlet looked at the drawing of the woman more curiously seeing the slight resemblance to herself. It was only Flynn's memory of the woman who could be their mother. A pencil sketch could have never looked so real, like Scarlet could reach out into the page. He had always said she had looked so like their mother, looking at the woman in front of her, she put her hand to her cheek smudging some of the page. Nothing about her was anything near as enchanting as the woman in that picture. She was not that pretty.

Lux turned to the next page, this was not the face of her father as Scarlet half expected, but that of a boy. His hair much sharper, shorter than Flynn's had ever been but with wild eyes much like the woman's, their mothers. There was a gentleness about him, in the softness of his smile. She felt an instant connection to the young face she didn't remember. Looking to the next page of the book Scarlet saw another girl, her eyes darker but just as similar to the woman that could be her mother. Flynn had spoken of a sister; this girl was her. A warmth filled her towards the image as Scarlet peered down. She gazed briefly at the speckled sparks Flynn had drawn in the girl's eyes before Dawson picked it up, casually looking at the pages and flicking through.

'He'd always been a talented drawer, your brother. One of his many talents. Do you mind if I hold onto this for a little bit Scarlet? I have a feeling I might know some of the language and codes Flynn's used, I can see if there's anything I can make sense of, hopefully finding out where he's gone.'

Scarlet nodded. Before saying 'that first woman, was she my mother? And are the other two my brother and sister? What where their names? Did you know them?' Scarlet asked. All of them listened in for Dawson's answer as he now looked at the page beneath his nose.

'Elsie was her name. We called her El. She was your mother,' Dawson said simply, his eyes still on the page beneath him.

'You do look a lot like her, every time you smile, I think that's when it's most noticeable. Her kindness runs through you, a kindness many people have forgotten. As wild as she was, not that many knew that side of her, you Scarlet may just be as untameable,' Dawson said, laughing. 'A handful, that's for sure. The boy, your brother. His name was Hugo – strapping lad he was growing into as well. Impressively charming, your oldest brother, and he resembled your father, especially the way he was incredibly stubborn. And as handsome a young man he was growing to be, it was his heart and love of others that couldn't be faulted. He believed in love more than he believed in getting into mischief. Most of all he loved you, he loved all your family, he would have done anything for you.

'Your eldest sister, we called her Tilda, she glowed with life. She had to know everything, she was strong and proud, and... Now, I think this is all a bit much for just one night, it is for me at least; after all I'm the one left who's supposed to be looking after the four of you. So best you head to bed, go on,' Dawson said, appearing exhausted himself; more so than the rest of them.

'You knew them really well?' Scarlet asked.

'I had a life before the Amari village too, you know,' Dawson said.

Scarlet didn't push him further. There were already so many facts running through her mind.

She did nothing but stare at the photograph of her parents all night while lying in her bed. Not until the early morning, right before dawn did Scarlet go downstairs to find Dawson asleep on the couch with Flynn's notebook clenched tightly in his hand, and a bottle of rum half-drunk sitting on the ground next to him.

She put on the kettle. He rustled awake from the noise.

'What are you doing up kiddo?' he said, yawning loudly.

It took Scarlet a minute before she replied, 'Couldn't sleep.'

232

'Come here,' he said, motioning her to the couch. She left the kettle to boil and sat by Dawson, looking at the empty glass on the table, wondering why he had drunk himself to sleep. It was the first time under his care that he'd really got into a bottle.

'I'm sorry about last night. Everything I told you I should have told you a long time ago,' Dawson said, barely able to look at Scarlet. A deep sigh left him, and he turned to face Scarlet.

'I've gotten use to people keeping things from me,' Scarlet replied, though her breath caught; she hadn't realised how much it had affected her not knowing all these years. Her mind was back up with the photograph of her parents on her bed.

'You've probably told me more than anyone,' Scarlet said vaguely.

Dawson handed her the notebook from Flynn, 'You should look at some of the other pictures.' He opened it up to the page of Hugo and Tilda, the brother and sister she couldn't remember.

Scarlet turned the aging page, the sharpness of the paper's edge crossing over her fingertips. Looking at a young girl with hair twice as long as hers, Flynn had drawn her sitting on a windowsill with her braids flowing over her shoulders and a pencil behind her ear.

In the same picture was a boy who looked so much like Flynn, from his striking eyes, and dimpled grin. Even in pencil Scarlet would have sworn it was him jumping off the page in front of her. He'd drawn the boy sitting on the ground, leaning on a large scruffy looking dog. Again, Scarlet saw below the picture the word mort.

'Looks like Flynn doesn't he. They could have been twins themselves the two of them; Charlie and Flynn. Ambitious and resourceful, a wicked mind too. What a character Charlie was. His mischief sometimes got the better of him, a true rouge. Your sister, Charlie's twin was the only one able to talk any sense into him when he thought up a wacky idea, that usually ended him up in trouble. Don't think he didn't try and take you on his wacky adventures too. Lucky even as a little one you enjoyed getting up to trouble.

Your sister was on her way to becoming just as beautiful and strong willed as your mother. Said the first thing that came to her Avalynne did, it was her mouth that got her in the most pickles,' Dawson said, looking at the last of the pages.

'The last page is you,' he said quietly.

She flipped the page over and looked into her own eyes. He drew her sitting at the dining table, the half grin she used to give when he had tried to make her smile after she'd found out he was going off to training without her. Her curls were messy, and there was a plain piece of toast in front of her. He drew this; Flynn remembered her exactly like this. He was out there. She knew it.

'How do you know so much about me, about my family? There are what, four other siblings in here that no one ever told me about in these pictures. I heard of a sister before, but all I knew is that she's dead, just like my parents. But she wasn't the only one, he knew them all, all along and he didn't tell me. You didn't tell me, not until now. Why didn't you?' Scarlet asked, turning to Dawson. She didn't know if all these tales could be told by someone who didn't know them well.

'You know I pulled you from the wreckage all those years ago. Any more than that, I can't explain to you, not yet. I'm not ready. Understand that I've only ever done what is right for you. There were six of you all together, and not one day goes by that I hate myself for not getting to your home sooner, to rescue more of you. I failed them, but I won't fail you,' Dawson promised. A heaviness in his eyes told Scarlet not to push it.

'Why are you telling me these things now, if you're not ready?' Scarlet said, ignoring her own instinct.

'Because, you may have lost your memories of them, but these people belong to you; and everyone deserves to know where they come from. Hold onto what you can of them. The wind changes so easily, and I don't want you to be left with nothing, not even an idea of what they were like,' Dawson confided in her.

Scarlet stared into his eyes. It was clear he was scared and sad all at once. There wasn't any need for him to say anything else, because she felt his fear. The uncertainty of what the future held for them all loomed, so much of her future was destined by her past. For now, all they could do was live.

Afterglow

Bastian no longer looked in the mirror at a young boy, he barely recognised the man staring back. He'd been a Raven for nearly four years now, and the way the Guardians worked and shaped him, he had grown into a force to be reckoned with, and each of the others were the same.

However, it was only when he caught a glimpse of himself as he washed his face that he was reminded that he was truly becoming what his mother wanted of him. On his bedside table lay her most recent letter.

Bastian,

My boy, I hope you are well. The summer's gone here, and I hope where you are you keep this blanket by you as the winter comes. I miss you each day. I can't imagine the world you live in now; it must be so thrilling compared to our little town. But as always, no news is good. The guards have remained clear of here as always; however a little bird told me that your friend Sticks has been sent out on Winslow's orders to watch a team of Guards scouting closely south of us. I'm sure all is well, and he'll be back soon. I am happy knowing that you are far away from all this, but sometimes I wonder what my father has you up to. You never let on to too much, so if anything, remember to be the sweet boy that I remember. And try not to get yourself into any fights, Please!

My love,

Mum

He remembered when he saw her letters how she had always said that kindness doesn't take much, yet it takes more courage than pulling out a weapon. However, back home he would never have been formed with the strength and mind that had shaped him here.

Holding true to being the man she wanted him to be, even when he felt far from who he used to be – a small outcast; a witches' son – he never missed a chance to try and make others smile. Still, being a part of the Guardians, he needed to concentrate. There were so many things to understand, he soon found that his own mind was fixed for learning the way things worked, which helped when it came to their weapons training. Bastian was one of the few who could handle the multiple weapons in the armoury, taking apart and putting together many of the guns they had. That wasn't the only thing, it came in handy when they learned about mechanics; about machines and movers, as he had little experience with them. There weren't that many movers in Grinnwick readily available to them to tinker with but from what they had at the Guardians Bastian took to it with ease. It was with a steady hand that he was able to pour the liquid Cor-Marinium into the machine's canisters.

The thick wooden panelled walls that surrounded the Ravens' bedroom quarters were now covered in decoration from the handywork of Russ, Mandy, and Verne with white Ravens letters stitched into a black fabric.

His days included getting up before anyone else to get the first bit of hot water; the busy dining hall that bustled through the morning, noon and night; the endlessly tiring tasks in the practice field; Professor Harker's, Sir Dash's, and Ms Madlyn's many lessons, from creating shelters to learning about the foundations of chemicals, medicines and then there was the daily faces of each of the Ravens. Each of them had grown to be family to one another.

While he hadn't yet been beaten by anyone in Raven Squad in their fighting training, he had been placed against a rather large boy named Alaric in Serpent squad who was nearly two years older than him, who also happened to be Rudi's brother. Since their placement Bastian was usually already bloodied before they even entered the practice fields. Verne could be counted on to help him up and say, 'You'll get him next time,' when Bastian inevitably lost.

Bastian knew he'd never beat Alaric, so instead of taking his fights too seriously, he always prodded and poked him, forcing him to be rattled up and making the fight end much quicker with one bigger punch, rather than a dozen smaller ones.

'I just don't know how you do it every day,' Felix said.

'Yeah well, I bet you could handle it. If you had to.'

'Yeah, well I've faced Rudi, and I tell you he's pretty hard to take on already, and he's on our team,' Felix said, but they both looked over at Rudi who was already sitting down at the dining hall talking with his brother, Alaric. They were both as tall as each other, yet Rudi still wasn't the same size in muscle as Alaric.

'No, Rudi is a fair fight I'll give you that,' Bastian said eventually, 'he's tough.'

'Hey guys, the new kids are arriving,' Gertie called out to them, getting them to follow her to the bedroom corridor.

This was the second squad to start since they arrived over four years ago. There were only five in the last one, one of them had already freaked out and left the Guardians. This group seemed even smaller as they walked down the corridor to their new bedroom quarters after completing their first task.

Most of them looked just as nervous as the others, a couple of them bandaged and bruised. None of them looked over at them, one of the girls at the end tripped up and fell over as she walked while the rest of her new squad walked on.

Bastian quickly ran over to help the little girl. She was so small, could they have ever been that small? He pulled her up easily, helping her to her feet.

'You okay?' he asked, pushing his brown hair out of his face and smiling, mostly just not wanting to scare her. 'Got to watch the floor, can be a bit uneven.'

She said nothing, frozen in her tracks. She kept looking up at him then away.

'Don't worry. I know this place is different, and a long way from where home is. But it's just another adventure, okay? Come on,' he said, helping her along to her room.

Standing in the doorway opening it up for her, he looked at the three new boys, none of whom looked like they had time for a girl's tears.

'Oi, you three. You don't leave a part of your squad behind. That's the first rule. Get it?' Bastian said, hoping he was being intimidating enough.

'Look after each other,' he said before leaving the room.

'Well, if they weren't scared already, they are now,' Felix said as he made his way down to where he'd left the others.

'Don't listen to him, that was sweet,' Gertie said.

'Yeah well, they're a team, they've got to look out for one another. They'll soon learn. I'm sure Dash will get them up to speed,' Bastian said.

'Come on you big softy,' Felix said, heading back to the dining room. 'let's eat.'

Bastian had made friends with most of the other squads and Guardian members, even Alaric always had a water waiting for him when they got back for dinner, clearly a gesture of good faith after giving him a beating every day.

The past four years were tougher than any of them expected. It was a constant battle of learning and shaping themselves. Still, he did as he once promised his grandfather and kept his head down. He knew his grandfather believed that that Guardians might be infiltrated, so Bastian usually did his best listening at mealtimes, but in all these years he was yet to hear of anything that sounded suspicious, truth be told he had grown complacent, he had found trust in those around him.

Over the past few years Bastian felt his head overwhelmed and his body exhausted, no matter how strong it had gotten. And as much as he tried, he knew anything could have been happening in the compound; his home. The home he had come to know. Its vast size always surprised him as he always found more rooms that he hadn't explored over the years. Preferably he spent the majority of his time above ground, above the maze of rooms and halls where their studies began. Either in the fields or just out walking on the land, which for the most part, between the entrance to the compound and the cliffs of the deep – as he had come to know the nearby mountains – was not much more than bare land, and a rather large lake that contrasted starkly with the dry land.

Still, as strong as he'd become, his mind was just as sharp, gaining knowledge he could never have imagined. He'd learnt the best type of plants to eat when stranded in different parts of Grinnwick, as well as the ones to watch out for; some plants that even had a mind of their own. Then he learnt the about the many creatures of their land, their names, and abilities. Animals that were thought to be myths, and ones that were concealed by the Guardians for their own protection. He knew how to penetrate technology systems, communications ones that were specifically formed by the power of Cor-Marinium that the Grinnwick Guard used – well to a degree. He had never quite grasped that area as well as Russ and Gertie had. Together they had also learnt how to fix engines and weapons as well as wield as many as they could. Fighting was something that came easy to him, so he found that gaining knowledge on medicines and the treatment of wounds a great necessity. Ms Madlyn, the head doctor had once said, if he hadn't needed to be mended so much, he'd have time to become a proper doctor. She gave him a fair bit of leniency whenever he pulled out a bit of charm with whatever injuries he walked in with.

That same charm had started getting him noticed by some of the girls in the Guardians. But one in particular, had always caught his eye.

***

'Get off me,' Gertie yelled, as Russ landed right on top of her.

'Sorry' Russ said, embarrassed. As he'd fallen his hand had landed on a rather inappropriate spot on-top of Gertie. She gasped at him, less than pleased. They were halfway through the fourth field task, attempting to make their way up the rope climb.

'You alright there, handsy?' Verne said, helping Russ up. 'Let's finish this leg of the field eh. I'm hungry and tonight is lamb roast. I want to get out of here before all the good meat's gone.'

Bastian helped Gertie up, 'You okay?' he asked, slightly smirking at Verne.

'Yes. It's just the end of the week, and I need a day off, you know,' she said, the near defeat in her voice was evident.

'Look. We have tomorrow off, why don't I take you down to the lake, just us,' Bastian said, letting her go first up the climbing rope.

'Sure,' she said, her spirit slightly warmer just from those words. As he said it, he felt a slight surprise of confidence in himself, not wanting to look at the other guys knowing they'd be gobsmacked by his casual initiation of a date.

Waiting until she was up the top before he started up the rope, Bastian was left at the bottom just him and Felix. 'I thought I was supposed to be the smooth one out of us,' Felix mocked, unable to help but make fun of Bastian.

'Shut up,' Bastian pushed him to the side, 'or do you need me to help you climb up this wall as well?' Bastian chuckled. They might have been on level 5 now, but they would have been on a higher level if Felix had managed to get up the rock wall without any help sooner.

They spent their dinner with the Serpent squad students, Mandy and Gertie sat with the girls on their squad Mila, Jessa and Harmony. Bastian hated it when they gossiped, he and Verne always felt under the spotlight whenever they stared over and laughed at them, no matter how many times Felix tried to tell them it was a good thing, he didn't believe it.

'You had enough there Verne,' Bastian asked, half laughing, while Verne's face was covered in meat.

'Man, I dunno. Think I could go for seconds,' Verne replied.

'Here have mine,' Felix said moving half of his lamb onto Verne's plate. 'I'm sick of this food anyway,' he took his plate over to the kitchen before leaving them all.

'You think he's okay?' Bastian asked Verne who was already digging into the extra food.

'Who, Felix?' he asked, looking up at Bastian and to the empty doorway. 'Not sure, been a bit off lately. I mean the rest of us all sort of have things keeping us here, you know. Like we both want to keep our families safe; Gertie and Russ are already tech wizzes, Gertie wants to be here more than any of us, loves to learn that girl does; Russ too really, I mean he's smart, smarter than either of us. Mandy's the same, she wouldn't learn skills like she has here anywhere else; she'll end up being the best medic any squads had in ages, Mrs Swan said so herself. And Rudi, well who really knows that kid's story, but think he wants to be like his brother Alaric… So, I'd say he's a legacy like you, it's in his blood to be here. But Felix, he grew up in the city. He's accustomed to certain things; he probably thought this place was a stepping-stone to his old life, before his parents were found out. Seems he's itching for something bigger. And, since he and Harmony broke things off the other month he probably wants to get away from it all.'

'Yeah. I guess,' Bastian said, a little shocked at how intuitive Verne was.

'On another note, you and Gertie. I heard you asked her out to the lake tomorrow,' Verne smirked.

'Yeah, well it's nothing, we are just mates. I just thought that she's been having a rough time lately with the last tasks in the field, she keeps getting tripped up by the Veridian Tree Roots, they have a knack for finding her every time,' Bastian replied, more than a little abashed.

'Whatever you say,' Verne said. 'What do you think of Mandy though, do you think she would say yes to me if I asked her out?'

'Well, you better ask before one of the snakes asks,' Bastian replied, nodding towards one of the Serpent's, Finlay. He was currently distracting Mandy away from the girls; Bastian didn't mean to deter Verne, but he could see him already look defeated.

***

The morning was crisp up on the top above the Guardians' compound. The pinkish colour of the sky spread overhead, and he watched as the sunrise reflected orange on the low clouds moving above. It subtly turned blue with the blackness of night beginning to fade. He wore a blue knit he'd had since arriving, which was clearly too small as it had been stretched so much to fit over his brown body, but still the warmest and nicest thing he owned. And his ravens jacket casually undone over the top. He smiled as he saw Gertie come down the valley, her red hair covered by a beanie and her cheeks red from the cold.

'You ready?' he asked, taking her hand in his.

'As ever,' she beamed, and they started walking down to the lake on the far side of the fields.

Bastian couldn't help but look at the side of her face as they walked. The way the light shined against the softness of her cheek and the flicker of her brown eyes – he wanted to pull her closer into him.

'Bastian, Gertie,' Russ called.

'Harker, he wants to see us all in his office. Now,' Russ said, eyeing the two of them still holding hands. Bastian let go of Gertie, moving closer to Russ, asking him what had happened.

'I don't know, I was sent to get you both,' Russ noted, as they both started following him.

Their room was frantic; they usually slept in on a day off. Bastian tried to get an answer out of someone. Gertie put her beanie and gloves away while the other Ravens who were still waking up slowly got dressed.

'We know what you do, mate. Sidney was the one who came and told us to go see your gramps,' said Verne.

'It's okay Bass. It's probably just some sort of announcement. We had that one last year remember, about the change in timetable,' Gertie assured him.

'Yeah, that's what I tried to tell them all,' Felix said, acting like getting ready was the biggest task he'd been given all week.

***

The round room of his grandfather's quarters was brightly lit when they all walked in, and a chalkboard was set up next to his desk.

'Welcome Ravens,' his grandfather began. He was not in a fine suit but looking worn in a cardigan, no tie to be seen, and hair a mess.

Emmett stood next to him, rummaging through piles of paper, pushing his glasses up his nose.

'You have been called here for a mission. Sir Dash is currently taking the Phoenix Squad through the details of the mission. The Serpent Squad were sent out late last night along with the Black Widows.'

Bastian held his attention to his grandfather, while Russ, Rudi, and Mandy each turned to each other, a peak of interest and excitement in them.

'I need you all to pay attention,' his grandfather continued.

'A tech specialist, Katika Weiss has a deal set up with Grinnwick Guard. She has designed and manufactured weapons and tech that are being shipped to an outpost onto an island off the coast of Astoria for the Guard.

'The Serpents and Black Widow Squads will be intercepting Katika's transports to prevent the Guard from gaining control of such weapons. An outside squad, the Hounds have also returned to help. They'll make sure the road home is clear for you.'

-'Sir?' Gertie noted.

'If we intercept this delivery, won't they just make another? What so special about this one?' she asked.

'Good question, in truth it's more than just a taking aim at their weapons, it's an opening to gain access into their systems communications,' his grandfather explained, 'What I need from you Ravens, well specifically Gertie, Russ, Mandy, and Rudi is while the other squads are intercepting the delivery, you guys connect into the motherboard at the Port Abel in Astoria. You will manipulate their systems so that our teams go unseen. While doing this, take this chance to imbed their system with this device that we have for you so that we can have access to the Grinnwick Guards shipment communications, and possibly these will link to their other systems.

'Now we need to make them think everything is fine at both ends. Understand? We need both the Guard, and Katika and her team to think that their transaction is running smoothly through the whole duration.

'So, our teams will wait until you give the go-ahead that you have breached their systems allowing for them to go ahead with the switch of the gear into our hands.'

'Sir, why don't we create a power outage for Astoria and the surrounds,' Rudi said.

'No lad, that will only cause a stir, and they will send more soldiers out to check what's happening. Especially when they're expecting a shipment,' his grandfather replied. 'I have an insider at the tech lab, that's how we got these details. He's provided the receiving number that's to be submitted once the "shipments" arrive. So as not to alert anyone that anything's off, and to allow the Serpents and Black Widows time to get away. You will need to send the number off at the appropriate time; this will be once the ship has docked, and after they infiltrate the onboard crew of the transport boat and have unloaded it onto our own transport. Our squads won't be able to exit the port undetected without your help either; you will also need to open the doors from their main systems location. Then when advised by their transmitter you can send the receiving number through to Katika's end.

'Be careful not to alert the system too early. We want to make sure our Squads are well out of there before anyone even knows anything's missing. Even the people on board the ship won't know it was us who were there.

'Ravens, your squad has excelled in the tech side of things, especially you, Gertie and Russ. I understand it's last minute, but you've picked up an understanding of the systems far better than anyone before you. That is why your squad has been chosen for this mission. This mission has come up by chance, as such you will be leaving today, so you'll need to know how to get into the right part of the building too. We have a set of building plans for you all with Sir Dash, I suggest you all use the time in transit to go over every detail. Sidney will be leading you. Remember the mission detailing that we've done before in class, so you should be aware of what to look out for on the building plans, to infiltrate yourselves into the right spots and take control of the systems unit. Most importantly, listen to Sir Dash and listen to Sidney, they know what they're doing.

'We will give you every bit of equipment we can to assist, and Emmett will be at the ready here with a transmitter for you to contact if you need anything to be looked up from here. I also know that none of you have had much training with discs, not since your original tracker discs were implanted on arrival, but it is best to have booster upgrades downloaded. This is usually done at the end of your fifth year however, we need you at the ready, and these boosters will have you on full alert. They are beyond any hack system discs some of you may have encountered in the streets.

'They are high grade, we get them from the same supplier as the Guard, regularly updated too so we can match their skills if need be. Ours are enhanced where possible too by Emmett here. Be warned it does take some time for you to adjust, there can be an afterglow effect that can confuse your mind for some time. My best bit of advice is to roll with the wave of adjustments your mind and body will go through. Got it?

'Phoenix squad will be with you as I said, they have been advised to back up Russ and Gertie who are the prime systems specialists on this mission.

'So, the two of you, I have every bit of faith in you. And Rudi, Mandy, you will be every bit as important in supporting them in getting there.

'Head down with Emmett now and he'll start getting you ready. Go over all the documents, and Russ and Gertie listen to what Emmet has to say about the systems that you will be faced with.'

The four of them left, following Emmett.

Bastian stood awkwardly with Felix and Verne beside him, his grandfather had gone back to his desk, pottering through his paperwork.

'How can we be of help to the mission sir?' Felix added.

This time he found his grandfather's presence high strung even as he was distracted in the moment, especially in comparison to the most recent time Bastian had found himself placed in front of his grandfather.

It was nearly six months ago after playing a trick on the Phoenix squad; his grandfather could barely contain his laughter. Bastian kind of wished for that same reaction at this moment, he felt uneasy watching him seriously look through his desk.

Bastian remembered when he made Russ make Sidney and the other Phoenix squad all think they were being called out for a mission leaving them all caught outside after hours while he filled their dorm with a bubble solution. The sight of them opening their door with a wall of bubbles engulfing them was as hilarious as it was stupid.

Phoenix Squad had attempted to get them back several times but had failed. Bastian was always a step ahead.

When they tried to steal all their clothes while he and the other Ravens were at the showers, he worked out with Mandy who was quite handy in chemistry class how to place a trigger only his squad knew about that poured a slime on any intruders. This backfired when Ms Madlyn came to speak to them in their dorm and unaware of the slime found herself covered head to toe in bright yellow goo and sent them both straight to his grandfather who called the idea 'ingenious.'

At this moment his light-hearted grandfather wasn't present.

'Boys, I need you for something else.'

'You're separating us from the others?' Bastian asked, confusion setting in. It was the first time being separated from any member of their squad for an extended period of time, and being their first proper mission, this didn't seem like the first place to start.

'That's why I have Phoenix squad going with the others. You will be needed to for a separate mission, and you'll be on your own. Entirely.

'The others will be fine; I promise they have a much larger team to work with. You three have been on intel missions before, gathering information with the rest of your squad. It is not gone by unnoticed that you three are quite skilled at integrating yourself into an environment, adapting to what is before you. While you are all skilled fighters and seeing each of you grow over the years has been impressive, it is my trust within you that leads me to recruit you for this task.

'It is sensitive information, and I do not want our knowledge and plan to fall into the wrong hands, that's why I'm choosing you three. You are quite the team, a unit together, and with Felix's background knowledge of Astoria you will slip into life in the city better than most.'

Bastian, Felix and Verne all stood patiently waiting to hear what was so important. Bastian knew that his grandfather had growing concerns about other members within the Guardians that he couldn't trust, and perhaps it was his trust in family that had roped him and the others into this task.

'Look I know it seems strange to be sending you three. But I'm putting my faith in you, okay? There is word that the princess is still alive.'

They each looked to each other, Felix broke his posture first.

'That's not possible. I mean if she was alive the Guard would have her on display, they'd be showboating her and using her as part of all their propaganda. The people of Astoria would pay highly to be within an arm's reach of such a figure. Then again, so would many,' Felix said.

'Look, I get that it seems unlikely, that it was recorded that she passed away. And the same rumours have passed throughout Grinnwick many times of the past centuries. Rumours are often wrong it seems. From the intel we've received her passing was in whole only recorded on the word of the Guard and the Commander Van Helm.

'The fact that she is alive has been speculated for quite some time, but a friend of mine has gotten word to fact to me that it's true, an eyewitness. Now, the facts are that the Guard has held her possession for some time. We are unsure how this happened, as she was said to be in hiding from the time of her family's death. Yet the Grinnwick Guard now control her, and they're making movements to bring her into Astoria.

'Her name is Ava, and as you know she is a sign of hope and power to a lot of people. Although the royals haven't reigned for nearly a millennium, they still hold faith with so many people in Grinnwick. Bastian knew this, people often used their name in praise. He had heard Sir Dash do it countless times, even his mother used to make sure he would say thanks to the old king and queen when they had a special meal.

'Stop for a moment and just imagine what it must be like to spend so much time with no say in your fate, consistently moving though the hands of those in power. All those years, everything she has witnessed. However it has been possible that her life has extended, whatever force is behind it; the fact that she is still here is incredible, and we need to act.

'What I need from the three of you is to travel with the others and separate from them when you arrive at the border of Astoria. You need to go under the guise of the Grinnwick Guards and work your way to the

Fortress du Monde. This is where she is supposed to be locked up, or so my scout has said. We received word that she will be moved there.

'Even though she is ancient, she will appear youthful; it is said that Commander Van Helm has managed to manipulate her appearance, or so the rumours go. Some even say a curse from the extinct faes who once loved her family so, binding her to live everlasting. The answers to these questions we may never truly know. She remains visually the same youthful girl lost her family nearly ten centuries ago. Just know she is not the girl you may see before you, but a woman of many years who has witnessed horrors none of us can imagine.

'Years ago, before her rumoured death we have reports where our squads tried countless times to retrieve her. This was before she fell into the hands of the Grinnwick Guard – this was when the so-called rebels at that time stormed the castle and kept her locked away in the depths of the shadows. Each time those teams failed.

The world thinks she's dead now, so our hopes are they won't have her on show, or as guarded as they once did, and with this opportunity having the Guards focus on the transport it seems like we have an opening to retrieve her.

'Now is the time to get her back. Position yourselves close as possible to her position, and get her out.

None of you have ever gone this deep before, but I've seen your tricks and your charms. I'm believing in you.

'Do any of you have any questions?' Bastian's grandfather finally asked.

'Umm... I do,' Verne said. 'Why me? I mean I get that you chose Bass... he's a great leader, sharp and talented, but he's your family and you trust him with private information. And Felix's family were undercover in the Grinnwick Guard living in Astoria, it's pretty much in his blood. And after living off the streets too he has seen both sides and knows the city better than most. But I'm a farmer, I don't know the city, and I don't know you well enough to truly hold your trust,' Verne questioned, serious as much as he was confused.

His grandfather sighed, and looked at Verne.

'You're right. And I did think about sending you with the others, after all, you are just as good a leader as Bastian, and the other Ravens would have valued having you. Instead, I chose you for a mission well above your skill level, above the skill level of all of you really. But, I chose you because of your friendship that you have formed. Sometimes our squads don't always mesh well, sometimes they do. The fact is you three have shown such joy in your friendship that I trust you to look out for each other in the task at hand. I fear it's going to be tougher than any of us realise, and having your friends with you is what you'll need. Do you understand?'

'Yes,' Verne replied, still clearly a little uncertain.

'Well then boys, I advise you go get ready with the others. They have since been advised you three will be on a separate mission, the true task has been kept from them, and is to remain that way until you return. Also remember, you are Guardians and are to keep your true self hidden. Don't trust anyone, just trust in each other.'

'What about this princess, where are we supposed to get her when she's safe?' Bastian added.

'Bring her here if you can, try and help her to blend in so she doesn't stand out,' his grandfather answered.

Bastian left the room, a hot rush underneath his skin; an acceleration of alertness. None of them looked at each other until they reached the Armory.

'What's going on?' Rudi said. 'Emmett told us you three had to go on another mission?'

'Yeah, doubt ours will work. Seems like just more intel work that they need to be done while they'll be distracted with the shipment,' Felix said.

'Well, at least you're still getting out of here for a bit,' Russ said, encouragingly. Bastian smiled, patting him on the back. He could see the nerves all over Russ. The unsteadiness in his stance. During any intel-gathering missions he was good at being quiet and listening in, this time the skill required by him was more than he was used to. Bastian knew he was more than capable of doing it, he just hoped that Russ believed it himself. That the pressure wouldn't confuse him from his task ahead, especially with the rest of the team in his hands.

'You got this Russ; you can hack a whole ship remember. I bet that you could hack half the systems in this place too, if you wanted. This will be a walk in the park for you and Gertie,' Bass said pumping him up, relieving the nervous look from his face.

Phoenix Squad and Sir Dash helped them all gear up. Bastian was handed a knife to strap to his leg and a gun that he holstered underneath his clothes. They'd each been given Grinnwick Guard uniforms that were a unique combination of heavy and breathable, with a leather jacket to match, each with the Grinnwick Guard crest on each side (a rounded circle of leaves, and the black sword separating the two G's.) The pockets on the front each had their own specific number. Sir Dash came as they dressed entering the numbers into a system that he had linked to the Guard's soldier database.

Bastion buttoned up his shirt, thinking of what was ahead of him. Looking at his friends around him his thoughts of himself drifted, and he focused on them, nervous with worry that he wasn't going to be with them. If something happened to them, he wouldn't know; he wouldn't be able to help them.

'Do you think the guard knows what they're in for?' Mandy pondered.

'We are just going to swoop in, and they're going to be left scratching their heads. They won't even have any rebels to chase after,' she mused.

'Well, I wouldn't want to be any one of the Guards if they come across you Mandy, I've seen that right hook of yours. Just make sure you stay one step ahead, remember,' Verne said, stepping closer to her, fixing her black cross tie so that it was straight, seemingly unaware that everyone was staring at them both.

'That's enough you two. I might just vomit,' Sir Dash rasped, inspecting every Raven squad and Phoenix squad member before Emmett came around.

'Arms out everyone. Emmett is coming around with your updates,' Sir Dash called, following Emmett who held the scanner.

Bastian hesitated; this was the part he was most concerned with.

He had grown use to Emmett over the years, and with his grandfather concerns originally thought that Emmett was a curious character but had learnt over time his social skills made him withdrawn, robotic, and brash in his ways of communication. But he was not questionable in his character and really was quite brilliant, and always readily available whenever they had

had questions about such technologies. These disc's were clearly an area he had found solace in perfecting.

'Grinnwick Guard members have these; we have advanced it so you will be ahead of the game. The chip you got when you first arrived – now, feel it under your skin, most of you would have forgotten it was even there. It was a locater, it remained embedded ever since you arrived, and will always be in there unless removed. This here is an update to the same chip. It will send the update to you through your central nervous system. This booster will increase your endurance, strength, patience, and awareness. Once I've updated the chip, the chip itself isn't required, so in the case you feel you may be caught, remove it so they can't trace where it came from; otherwise keep it in for future updates.'

The Armoury was quiet while they all took in turns getting their updates. Bastian felt nervous as Emmett took his arm and pressed the scanner that was connected to a computer on his arm. It clicked across once, twice and finally a third time.

Bastian waited a moment, staring at his arm trying to see if he felt different.

He felt nothing, at least for a moment.

A movement through him like a warm bust of liquid had been inject through him suddenly gave him a shiver. Slowly a glow of clarity to the room around him brought the smallest things into focus, things that he might not have noticed; the dirt on Sir Dash's shoes, or the names of the weapons on the walls. It was like he was assessing all the details with an intense perception.

He could also hear Russ's heavy breaths from across the room and noticed the smell of one of the Phoenix guys who looked rather repulsive as he itched underneath his arms.

'How do you feel?' Emmett asked them all.

Bastian wasn't too sure what to answer, the nerves that he had suddenly vanished with a wave of calmness that he could only predict was coming from the disc.

'Okay…' he answered, unsure of himself, but noticing he wasn't the only one. Both Rudi and Gertie were sitting down with looks of confusion on their faces.

'Take your time, like August said, it gives an afterglow feeling for some time before you adjust. You'll have the trip into Astoria to gather yourselves and the update should be settled in by then. The main thing you'll notice instantly is the calmness, this goes along with patience. These updates are important to ensure success for your mission, to leave you confident in your decisions.

'We will have all the details on your mission in the truck ready for you to read and take on. The updates will help you pinpoint any of the smallest details. Take your time adjusting, but not too long, your truck will leave in twenty minutes,' Emmett finished, packing down his computer, while Sir Dash started talking.

'Eyes here you lot,' he barked at them. Bastians focus instantly drew to him, robotic like even. It felt like a form of control, as though he had no other choice. If the Grinnwick Guard had an increased manipulation of this, he could only imagine how easy it was to control their perception of the world. Bastian drew away from Sir Dash, intent on having his own control, proving to himself that he did. He focused to his side, to something he cared about, someone. Her focus was on Sir Dash, but he could see the peachiness in her cheek, still flush from the coolness of the morning.

'Now, Rudi you are going to oversee the Ravens on the transport mission. You are to work with Sidney here. He is your head Guardian,' Dash said, patting Sidney on the shoulder, who held a half-smile awkwardly, clearly hating the attention.

'Sidney as you know is the Leader for the Phoenix squad. Work together to understand your plan. Infiltrate, and get the job done. Phoenix has been undercover for the Grinnwick Guard before so Ravens make sure you listen to them when they say something, it might just save your neck,' Sir Dash said before turning to Verne, Bastian, and Felix.

'For you three there isn't much paperwork for you to follow. What I have here are details and supplies to organise yourself a base. August didn't go into too many details to me about what he was getting you to do, but he did go on about the seriousness and urgency of it. All I can tell you is, listen to each other, and don't take this task lightly. You'll have no back up out there; this isn't one of the petty intel missions you've done at a bar or party. That is nothing compared to getting yourselves this deep undercover with the Guard. Truth is I'm not too sure why August picked you lot over any other more experienced squad members, but he thinks you can do it. So, let's see what you've got,' Sir Dash said, eyeing the three of them directly before turning to the group.

'Remember take an alias name. You don't want to be caught out and have the Guard led back to your families,' Sir Dash finished, before leading them to the white truck waiting up topside.

Bastian jumped in the truck next to Russ and Gertie, the whole of the Ravens had only ever been on two intel mission before, in comparison this was going to be huge.

The excitement had been electric on the way out to their first mission; it was to a busy bar on the city limits of Astoria. They were tasked with joining in on the festivities of a wedding, and they used the event to keep an ear out for the connections the party held with Guard soldiers. Remembering how on their way there every one of them had been chatting away with nervous, yet all completely exhilarated, mostly just for the chance to get out of the Guardian's compound, and for a party no less. This time however the excitement was gone, and even with the calmness that swept over them with the help of their updates, the nerves about what they were walking into crept up on them.

Turning to Gertie, Bastion felt her grabbing hold of his hand. He looked down at her hand on his, and felt the uneasiness of it.

A few moments ago, all he wanted was to be close to her. Now, he cared enough about her to know he wouldn't be there to help this time around, and emotions like this wouldn't do well while they were out on separate missions, it would only be a distraction. Already fearing the worst for not only her but all of them, he pulled his hand back and tried his best to ignore her look of confusion.

Fortress Du Monde

Fear was the only thing that consumed Bastian the night of the transport mission, even though it was all happening what seemed like a world away from him, and the other Ravens were somewhere else in Astoria playing their part. He wished he could have been there by their side. Instead, he was faced with their own task.

Bastion walked into The Top Cat, passing a brunette dancer who tried to brush her red lips against his cheeks.

'Every night you walk in this door. And every night you walk right past me, but a girl can tell when a boy or should I say a man will enjoy her company,' she whispered with a grin.

'Not in the mood for any company this evening miss,' Bastian replied, yet finding the urge to pull himself away a task in itself; tempted by her soft skin, enticing smile and the way she moved her hands on him.

'Don't you think I'm pretty?' she said swiping away her brown locks and closing up against him once more with her doe eyes pulling him in, then pulling his hand towards her. His eyes glared away from her as a haze of smoke that gleamed with from the dimly lit made him wince.

'You are more than pretty; you're stunning. Still, I'm here to talk to friends and I don't need a sweet distraction like yourself. Maybe another time,' he enchanted her, softly loosening his hand away from her touch. His instincts told him otherwise, but his mind knew it wasn't the job.

'You're a heart breaker, I see. Well, I hope another time comes soon enough; I'll keep a look out, I couldn't forget this face, those blue eyes,' she said back to him. He watched as she turned back to a slow mesmerising dance, and wondered how many men she had said those same words to.

Her beauty was priceless after all, and it didn't take long for another man to be lured to her.

He pulled his thoughts away from the mesmerising woman as he reached the booth that they had come to call their own, the music played by a bopping jazz band in the middle of the bar. The saxophones and trumpets were currently playing swiftly in beat that seemed to repeat itself over, with a whimsical piano player chiming in bringing the room to life.

A light buzz to the air, a weird haze in the large dimly lit space.

The Top Cat. One of their frequently visited clubs over the past few nights. The Top Cat was a lavish spectacle, where the guards succumbed to many of their desires. To Bastian it was a circus, while it was dimly lit, there were glaring lights spread throughout of multiple colours, nearly tacky as it was supposed to be seducing. But the Grinnwick Guards indulged in everything in front of them; from the women dancing in their undergarments that glimmered, while moving in their gentle, yet intimidating flow; the drinks that never stopped flowing, and the rich meats that fell off the bone laid out on trays all around them.

Like the nights before Bastian's heightened senses made him notice every single detail in a whirlwind. He saw the women, the smoky haze, and the laughter of the men, as well as the guards giving into the women around them all at once. Felix got caught up in the excitement of it all, Bastian was shocked how easily he looked passed the vulgarness of it all, as lavish as it was – still Felix laughing along with the guards like he was one of them.

Bastian and Verne were much more like fish out of water, each doing their best to concentrate on their stories to ensure they weren't caught out;

nearly overthinking every single word they said. Anything that could help them.

The tales he'd heard from the guards he's spoken to so far already turned his stomach. The people they had dragged away from towns that they'd already devastated, talking about how easy it was. How the factories, where those people were taken to were getting too full, that they needed to be thinned out. Mocking their own people, saying that they wouldn't understand the complexities of the world around them, blinded by the life of pleasures while they kept the filth outside in line.

Bastian soon learnt how to talk in the same coarse and vulgar way yet completely refined as the guards did. He imitated them with his added natural charm in the mix, making up stories of teaching those in the lower western sector of Astoria a lesson, resulting in cheers from his table.

He'd caught on that many guards responded to confidence, that the most confident around them were those men who were in higher positions with the Guard, and he wanted to be seen exactly as such.

The one lead they had made out so far in the past few nights was the Fortress du Monde, just as his grandfather had predicted. On the northern hill, the fortress sat, and it was only ever mentioned by a couple of guards, but never much about it was told.

The previous night Verne had heard a red-headed guard mention the fortress to another guard, who too seemed interested in it. Verne couldn't get close enough to hear them that night, but they were all sure to try and find them again tonight, and anything that they could find out to help them sneak through undetected was all that they needed.

Bastian drank with Felix and Verne giving the appearance that they were enjoying themselves, right up until Verne spotted the red-head. Felix had paid one of the dancers to bring them all a round of fire shots and included an extra for their soon to be new friend.

'Hello, we over ordered. Care to join?' Felix tapped the shoulder and asked the red-haired man, as they all stood up around the dancer who held the tray of shots for them.

'Why not,' he replied, already in good spirits.

Bastian hadn't had a shot before this, but every sense with his update told him he wouldn't be the better for it. Still, he pressed it to his mouth and tried to hold back from smelling it, shooting it straight down.

'Wow, they're good. How's about another round, you too Phil,' the red-haired man said, grabbing in his comrade, who looked every bit as nervous as Bastian felt.

'Names Eli. We're celebrating. Phil here's got himself a new posting. Just found out,' Eli said enthusiastically.

'Yeah, I just hope it all goes smoothly,' Phil said uncomfortably.

'Don't be a fool, you'll be fine. Apart from all the kafuffle it's both one of the most important postings, and the easiest. Trust me it'll look good on your record.'

'New posting?' Bastian added, trying to think on the spot. 'Say, we are out celebrating the same thing,' he sounded surer of himself than he felt.

'Well done. All three of you?' Eli asked his excitement only increasing.

'Yes, well that's why we all came together. It's been a long time in the making you know,' Bastian said.

'Where's the posting then boys?' Eli asked, an eager grin on his face as a brightly red dressed waitress brought them their next round of shots.

Caught for a moment, 'Can't say sir. Need to know. You know?' Bastian said, finding exactly the right moment to find his voice.

'Too right, you three. Keep your lips sealed, you never know when there are spies at hand. But you can tell me, I'm a captain; my knowledge will only help in your position at hand,' he said brightly.

'Of course, Captain, our apologies, we didn't mean to offend you. It's just you never know who you can trust, even amongst friends,' Bastian said, acting taken aback and changing his tone to one of respect as a low-level soldier, 'We will be located at the Fortress,' Felix added at a whisper that only Eli could hear.

'Don't be daft, out of all the captains out there I'm one of the least likely ones any experienced guard would recognise. After tomorrow I'm sure you will though, that's my posting. And Phil's starting up there too,' Eli cheered.

***

Bastian drank as much as he could handle while still engaging in high intel conversation. He soon found they weren't getting any more vital information out of the captain, so quietly retired from The Top Cat.

'You can't go now, the night's still young boys,' cried Eli, clearly needing the relief of a big night.

'Sorry Cap, we really need our rest. But looks like you've got Felix a little longer,' Bastian said, nodding towards Felix who had his arm over a woman on the way to their booth.

'Yes, well I'll make sure he isn't home too late. Big day tomorrow,' the captain smirked, leaving Bastian and Verne to take their leave from the madness that was escalating into the night underneath the Top Cat's roof. Still, neither of them had been able to get another word about the fortress out of the captain. They had been sure that the fortress held the princess, no other facility within Grinnwick had the same sort of security set up with such secrecy within the ranks, and every other area the guards were more than willing to tell you exactly what was going on inside. They only needed confirmation of their hunches that the princess remained inside to ease their minds. And as much as it made sense that they would hide her in the fortress, their plans laid only on a hunch.

Leaving behind the noise of the Top Cat they found their way towards the darker streets where their apartment was in the western district. Bastian noticed something odd. Phil, the captain's comrade had left right before them. He now saw him up ahead, skulking down an alley nearby. It was an odd way for an actual guard to be walking on this own. Bastian thought to follow him but was too tired to pursue such curiosities as he followed Verne back to their apartment, to an unrestful sleep.

Sunlight broke through the window waking them all up, including a weary Felix who'd managed to roll in at the early hours of the morning.

'Well, anyone ready to turn back now?' Bastian asked his friends, half joking but also completely serious.

'We've got this,' Felix replied, buttoning up his own Guards uniform, washing the muck from the night before off his face.

The streets of west Astoria in daylight in their Guard uniform was an experience none of them thought they'd ever get used to. Head high as other guards did, careful not to disrupt the characters that they took on. Still, there was an uneasy feeling that took over Bastian as he noticed some small kids hiding when they first saw them. Bastian wanted so much to tell them that it was okay, he was a friend. But the reality was today he was someone completely different.

Breaching their small alleyway streets, he broke out into the central part of Astoria where the wealth of their city really started to shine.

Each of their eyes lit up, looking around at the marvel that Astoria truly was; golden light poles and a white marble fence along the Rubicon River. Women walking down the river chatting in their fine dresses, looking like swans unlike the night creatures they had seen at the Top Cat the night before. Their beauty was elegant, each of them wore large hats to protect their gentle skin from the sun. An echoing ring drew Bastian's eyes behind him, towards the Astoria Cathedral. The old building was one of the last relics from a lifetime ago. The bells rang in the cathedral's towers, calling out to all the finer citizens of Astoria. More people began filling the streets as the bells echoed, they too heading in that direction, every one of them dressed to impress. Bastian looked to Felix to see if he knew where they were going, he hadn't heard of people gathering like this before.

'It happens with every new moon,' Felix stated.

'The people go to the old cathedral and celebrate Van Helm, it's kind of weird like a very large tea party. The Cathedral from memory had beautiful gardens inside. It's one of those silly occasions that these people use as an excuse to get dolled up.'

Bastian rolled his eyes, because how could he expect anything more than that. The people around him looked like they had not a care in the world.

'I hear back in the day the old cathedral was used for ceremonies of love, that when two people tied themselves to one another they did it there,

266

that it connected their love to the love of the Old King and Queen, and in doing so would grant them a blossoming life together,' Verne added.

'Ah nonsense, that's the stuff of fairy tales,' Felix retorted.

'Well seems like a nicer thought that these fools celebrating for no other reason than to impress a crazed leader,' Bastian noted.

'You're not wrong there,' Felix replied.

Walking in the opposite direction of the crowd the three of them managed to make their way over the bridge, and across to another street full of dozens of shops. Many of them were filled with fancy clothes made from the finest materials he'd ever seen; dresses of silk; thick, tailored jackets and suits, and vests in a dozen colours. Other stores had jewellery that had anything one could desire, a blue peacock broach took his eye thinking that maybe he could send it home to his mother, he hadn't sent her even a letter for such a long time, but he knew he hadn't the time or the money to shop. Verne and Felix each found themselves in the same predicament, catching themselves staring into another window covered in lacy underwear.

'We don't have the time for this,' Bastian persisted, dragging them away.

'We never have time for anything fun,' Felix replied.

'Oh yeah, says the guy who was out all hours last night,' Verne replied.

'I was just making sure we didn't miss any valuable intel. Shouldn't you be keeping your mouth shut out here anyways, you're supposed to be a mute remember,' Felix said, smirking, not noticing Verne rolling his eyes.

Ignoring them both Bastian pushed forward. Finding that the wealthy Astorians also tried to distract him from his task with meaningless pleasantries by catching his eye in a show of respect for them as Guard officers. Playing along Bastian did his best to move by them quickly, sweeping through streets making his way up the hill to the south where Fortress du Monde waited.

On the outside of the cobblestone wall, near the gate of the fortress the three of them waited; they had observed the patterns of Guards entering inside the days before and knew that soon enough the morning shift would arrive, and they too would join them through the gate.

'Oi, what you three doing?' Came a voice. 'Can't be hanging near the gate can you now.'

Bastian froze, he knew he had set himself up for this. But the reality of it all still made him jump.

'Sorry, first day on the post, we weren't too sure where to wait,' Bastian answered turning around to the guard behind him, standing as tall as he could, with his most formal greeting. Only to be met by a broad freckled smile.

'Just messing with you three,' said Eli. 'Welcome to the fortress, she's pretty intimidating isn't she.'

'You can say that again,' Verne said under his breath, so that only Bastian and Felix could hear him. And he wasn't wrong, Bastians neck arched so far back as he looked up at the height of the cobblestone wall. The idea of getting the princess out of here, and how hard that would be, was starting to dawn on them. They had briefly spoken about it with each other, but the biggest part of their plan was having her disguise herself on the way out.

'Captain Livingston,' a harsh voice spoke rather demandingly, and rather loudly, bringing Bastians attention back.

The four of them turned to face another guard who was tall and slender with a rather crooked nose and eyes ready to attack like that of a rabid dog.

'Yes, Captain Archbank, how can we help you this morning?' Eli said, in a tone that was not daring to challenge the man who was another head taller than him.

'I expected you here an hour ago. You will come with me to the commander's meeting this afternoon,' Archbank ordered.

'Of course. While you're here Captain, have you met Smith, Harker & Grover?' Eli said announcing them to the captain's attention.

Archbank turned his gaze to the three of them, like a bird staring down pray, Bastian felt like he was under the microscope – but still maintained his eye-contact, not wanting to turn down. Archbank barking out judgement which unnerved each of them, yelling at Verne for not standing straight, forcing his shoulders back, and at Felix and Bastian for both needing a haircut.

'These aren't soldiers Livingston, see to it they are fit for such a position, or it'll be straight to reform for them,' Archbank noted to Eli before he left them.

'Come on boys don't mind old Archy. Reckon he's got a heart of gold in there... somewhere, Eli half-heartedly mused, but Bastian could tell he was still looking down the path that Captain Archbank walked away, possibly nervous to say such a remark when it could be heard by the captain.

'Anyways, we better wait up by the gate. Phil said he'd meet me up there,' Eli said, grabbing Felix's shoulder and pulling him onwards towards the gate.

'How are you feeling kid?' he asked Felix, his joyful humour back now that Captain Archbank had walked off.

'Don't think I've woken up this worse for wear in a while,' Felix laughed.

'Well, you tried to keep up with the likes of me that's why,' Eli said, laughing. 'Ahh, here he is,' Eli welcomed Phil as they arrived at the gate. 'You look even worse than Grover here.'

He wasn't wrong. Phil didn't look well at all, his face looked sweaty and pasty at the same time. Whatever he drank the night before clearly hadn't sat well with him. Bastian remembered him leaving the Top Cat around the same time as he did, maybe he headed to another bar afterwards. The alleyways of Astoria could have led him to all sorts of nightlife within the city.

'Yeah, I guess I had one too many last night,' Phil said, trying to wipe the sweat off his head.

'Don't worry, you'll be fine,' Eli patted his back. 'Why don't you come and meet the other guards on this morning. Boys, this is Adam, Sven, Manny and Neil,' Eli said, introducing them to four other guards who Bastian politely nodded to, his attention on the gates, as they made their way to the entrance of the fortress.

Eli spoke to the man on the gate, a balding man with an automatic gun that laid on the table next to him, who had a constant look of distaste on his face. He had a glass screen in his office, that had images of different sectors of the fortress.

'Ay Bern, looks like we got a few more guards added to the list, I'd say because of you know who.

'Anyways, not too sure if they're on the manifest yet, but I've got Phil, Grover, Harker, and Smith. Oi, boys write down your tag numbers and bring them up here will you, Bern will put it through the system for you.'

Each of them wrote their own number that was written across their pockets onto the sheet for Bern, enduring a curious glare from him as they came up to his counter. Bastian was sure for a moment he was about to pull the three of them up. But with a click their numbers went through.

Passing through the wooden gate and being inside the giant cobblestone walls was a massive relief if only for a moment.

Inside the walls brought chills to his bones, there was an eeriness surrounding them as they faced what seemed like never ending outside walkway, that circled around this lower level of the fortress. It was every bit as overwhelming as the walls from outside. Every inch of the stone fortress looked even more impenetrable. The tiny windows leading up walls of the main tower were covered in stained glass and iron, and the crashing sound of waves from the other side of the fortress echoed around the corridors.

Bastian looked up the intimidating walls of his surrounds, their situation now all too real. Looking over at Verne, his eyes wide, the reality settled in for them all even if they already knew the intense difficulty that their task brought on. Still, they kept quiet while Eli allocated them into pairs to secure certain areas of the fortress.

Felix and Verne were paired together, and Bastian was placed with Phil who stood so still he was like a statue, remaining just as steady and certain as some of the fiercest guard officers Bastian had seen, he had a warriors build too. No doubt he had been shaped from a young age to be one of the best guards, had he not looked like he had a stick up his ass as he pompously walked along, and surely the warped mind of a Grinnwick Guard, Bastian may have tried to warm up to him. But Phil didn't seem one bit interested in trying at all.

271

'You two will be in the northern tower,' Eli said to them. 'Now I know you don't know where it is, so I will take the four of you with me and drop you off at your detail areas.'

Eli called them to follow him along with his fellow guard, Manny. Manny was a giant of a man; he could have squashed the life out of any of them with one hand. Strong silent type too, not a peacock like the other soldiers, Bastian recognised him from before, at the Top Cat; his eyes blankly looking out a few nights back, surrounded by a dozen of others, having no interest in anything besides a drink. Right now, he was fully alert, and a deadly foe, if they were forced to go against him Manny would easily take them out.

Walking around the outside of the fortress would have taken them at least an hour if not longer if they went the whole way past the cliffs edge. Walking for about ten minutes, which already felt like twice that, considering Manny didn't speak, left plenty of awkward silences even with Eli who spoke nearly enough to make up for his lack of conversation. Thankfully Felix was more than happy to chat back, while Bastian settled back to listen to what was said. Verne on the other hand seemed to be taken by the vast size of Manny. Verne has grown into quite the sizable man himself, but compared to Manny he really looked just about regular.

'You'd think a place like this would have a hundred guards,' Felix said, completely in his role.

'Not anymore, not since the commander made us move all the petty criminals to that place in the country. Didn't like having the people of Astoria so close to the low lives. Only the high security ones are held here nowadays. Doesn't take too much work for us, which is good,' Eli said. It made Bastian wonder if they'd be caught, would they be considered high

272

enough of a threat to end up here, or would they be sent to the desolate fields with the other criminals? His thoughts took a back step as Eli continued.

'The further our forces move across Grinnwick, the crazier the things we find, and the more Commander Van Helm realised he couldn't lock up everyone who rallied against him. He only captures the things that interest him, his little treasures. Say where were you boys posted before here? Don't remember much of our conversation last night, I'm sure you told me though,' Eli asked, looking to Verne.

'Ahhh, poor Jones is a mute. The three of us where up on the frontlines near the eastern woods keeping control,' Bastian said.

'Ah yes of course, sorry about that Jones. Forgetting my own mind.'

'Wow, well you would have seen some action up there. Few unruly natives I hear, a bit of sense's what they need,' Eli said.

'Where were you posted Phil?' Felix asked.

'Tell them Phil,' Eli said encouragingly, but Phil didn't seem to be interested in sharing.

'Ah, he's modest, he's come from the outskirts, laying some pretty solid groundwork with our team up there, sussing out what areas are weak and ready for the Guard to set up structures. Van Helm will be mighty pleased he's got someone of Phil's calibre here at the Fortress.'

Bastian couldn't help thinking the Van Helm sounded like a loon, of course he had always heard of the Commander's thirst for power, it was just different hearing it from someone closer to the man; someone who possibly idolised him.

Standing on the eastern side viewpoint of the fortress now, they looked out at all of Astoria to the north and the Squall Seas to the south.

Eli told Verne and Felix to remain at the viewpoint, to make sure there was a lookout at this point of the wall.

'Someone will come take your place and tell you to come to the entrance hall soon,' Eli said, before leaving them there with two large jackets to keep them protected from the sea breeze.

'Follow me you two,' Eli smiled to Phil and Bastian.

Making their way into the central rooms of the stronghold of the fortress, past the lower entrance hall where two guards already stood, they walked up a corridor that circled around.

'This is where I want you both to patrol,' Eli said to Bastian and Phil.

'We should be down in a bit, follow us once we walk back through. Keep a steady eye out,' Eli warned.

Bastian looked around at the dark hallways as Eli and Manny left up the one set of stairs from the circular corridor that they were in. There was nothing on the walls, no seats, nothing but the two of them.

'Well, this place is dull,' Phil said, who seemed to be looking a bit better than earlier.

'Tell me about it. Let's do a circle around, see if we come across anything,' Bastian said.

'Sure,' Phil agreed, following in suit as they started walking around the corridor.

'How long have you been a guard for?' Phil asked him.

'A couple of years,' Bastian answered. Having no idea what the usual age guard soldiers started out at.

'I've been about five,' Phil replied.

'So, you've always been in the city, I mean apart from your trips to the outskirts?' Bastian asked.

'Yeah, last couple of years. You?' Phil replied.

'No, I'm from the beach, just came to Astoria to join the Guard,' Bastian said, he'd nearly forgotten himself, wanting to kick himself for even mentioning the beach, his home.

'The name Harker rings a bell,' Phil noted. 'Can't remember where from, but still familiar,', but before Bastian even had the chance to pry into where Phil's had heard his grandfather's name, a smash echoed from above.

It left them both quiet and quickly returning to the stairs that Captain Eli and Manny had disappeared up to.

'I don't think anyone is coming, it's okay,' Bastian said, his tense body relaxing. But at that moment, Manny, still sour faced as ever walked down the stairs with Archbank who must have arrived before they even entered the circular corridor.

Following them was Eli, accompanied by what was surely the brightest thing to ever cross these corridors.

'If you don't mind Princess, Commander Van Helm is waiting for you. You know he doesn't like waiting,' Archbank said speaking exhaustedly, now waiting at the bottom of the stairs like every word took up a precious moment of his time.

Both Bastian and Phil drew back allowing them to pass, they were nothing but a part of the dark corridor to the princess as she passed.

Bastian remembered what Captain Eli had said and followed them.

Jumping behind them with Phil, who walked just as nervously as Bastian felt, his warrior stance now seemed ridged. The fierce Guard that Bastian thought Phil was, was suddenly all over the place. Needing to remain in character he didn't say a word, still following behind what looked like a long blue silk dressing gown. The brown long wavy hair barely moved across her shoulders, as she gracefully walked the down the corridor. Continuing out into the entrance hall of the fortress, Verne and Felix waited with two other guards ready to join the line.

They walked along another corridor that stemmed off the entrance hall before they came to a halt.

Bern, the bald man from the gate had come inside, whispering intently to Captain Archbank. His face went as red as Eli's hair.

Bastian couldn't think, his insides where stiff. He nervously looked back at Verne and Felix, but Archbank wasn't sent for them.

'What's the meaning of this Archbank, like you said the Commander hates waiting,' the princess said, her voice light, amused.

'Princess Ava, the Commander can wait for this. Bern said this Guard's numbers don't match up,' Archbank steamed. Bastians heart fluttered, had they found him out, surely not. The Guardians had been entering code numbers into the Guards ranks for ages. But Archbank wasn't looking at him, he was eyeing down Phil like a dog looking at its next meal.

Phil didn't shy away, he stood tall in the face of Archbank's accusation, but the sweat from his brow and his heavy breathes only increased how guilty he appeared. Two other guards swept from behind Bern and grabbed him.

'He's alright, I promise you. What more do you need?' Eli said, trying to pull Archbank's hand back from hitting Phil.

Phil didn't wince, he stood tall and opened his eyes. Bastian noticed his eyes weren't looking at Archbank, but at the princess.

She was covered in shock. A true sadness behind her falsely young face was all too easy to see, she couldn't hide it if she tried in that one moment.

'I'm sorry,' Phil said to Archbank, but it was clear to Bastian it was meant for her, the princess.

'You should be sorry. I don't know what you'd think you'd accomplish. Did you plan to attack us? Plan to attack the Commander Van Helm, knowing he was here? You think you wouldn't be caught, scum?' his rant, building up until he could no longer face Phil.

'Boy, what's your name… get this criminal out of here,' Archbank said to Bastian.

'Harker sir. Yes, sir,' Bastian answered quickly, a sigh of relief as he grabbed Phil's arm, knowing that he was no longer under scrutiny. Still his chance to grab the princess would not be taken today.

'Captain Archbank, he's just a boy. Must you really,' said the princess, not hiding her emotions well.

'This is a secure fortress Princess, you have as much leniency as you could possibly have, but I will not allow you to choose the punishments for a crime such as impersonating a Grinnwick Guard soldier. Harker make sure you deal with him properly,' Archbank said.

Bastian took Phil by the arm with force and led him out of the fortress, the eyes of everyone on them as they exited the gate. He didn't know where he was supposed to go to deal with Phil, handing him over to an actual Guard member wasn't going to happen. Whatever would happen to him under their care wouldn't be fair.

Walking down along the outside of the fortress with Phil, he did his best to keep his face serious and to not say anything, before taking a quick left down an alley and into the busy streets of Astoria.

'Where are you going to take me?' Phil said steadily.

'Shut it,' Bastian said, his grip tightening, anger firing in him, mostly annoyance from this fool only making their chances at getting to the princess even lower.

He walked for minutes, through the fancy streets of Astoria, having people stare at him dragging Phil through the streets like a common criminal. If only they knew the real evil their city was a part of. The worst part was they probably did. Ignoring their gazes, he turned off towards the outer streets, taking the quieter route towards the calmer western alleys where no one paid attention to any mishaps going on. Taking a chance Bastian pushed Phil into a dark alleyway, away from prying eyes and pinned him to the wall, close enough so that just Phil could hear him.

'I don't know who you think you are, all I can tell you is that was utterly stupid. Run now, and don't ever look back,' Bastian said.

'What, but the captain said for you to deal with me,' Phil questioned.

'He's not my captain. And, from what I can tell you were there for the princess, but you messed up big time going in there yourself, whoever you are, you are way too close to this. Leave it to guys like me to get the job done,' Bastian grunted.

'You were there for her?' Phil asked. 'I thought everyone thought she was dead. I thought they'd forgotten about her.'

'Not everyone forgets, just get out of here. Go,' Bastian said, moving to turn away.

'Wait, she'll want to see me. I've tried for so long to find her, for that chance to get to her. And you just walk in off the street, how?' Phil pleaded, grabbing hold of Bastian's shirt tightly.

'If you get out of here now, you're safe. I have my way. Let me do what I came here for and maybe one day she will see you again.' Bastian left Phil alone in the alleyway. He wanted to help him, to take him back to their apartment and tell him to wait there until they helped her escape. But guardians were shadows, they weren't seen. Phil's desire wasn't his mission, and he wasn't a guardian, so keeping him safe and out of harm's way was all he could do.

Returning to the fortress gate where Captain Eli and Archbank were still bickering with each other Bastian stood with ease, waiting for them to direct him.

'Ah Harker, you've dealt with the situation?' Captain Archbank barked at him as he arrived up to the gate.

'I dropped him off to the Astoria border for transfer to the country cells,' Bastian replied, he'd heard one of the guards talk about the country cells at the Top Cat and was glad he'd been able to recall such information readily.

'Good, the liar won't last long out there. They never do,' said Captain Archbank, an evil smile piercing his hollow face.

'Look, why don't you head home for the day Harker, we'll see you nice and early tomorrow,' Eli said to Bastian, relieving him for the day.

Hope at Hand

'We could go out a window, to the cliffs on sea,' Bastian suggest, knowing perfectly well it was ridiculous.

'To our death. Great idea,' Felix said, rolling his eyes.

'Well don't see you offering any ideas,' Bastian piped back at him, 'Look, going out the window is kind of our only shot if we can't get her through the front gate. Which is highly unlikely. We really need to find out what door she's in and work from there. It would be preferable if we could get her out of one that you two were on patrol of,' Bastian said, trying to explain. 'We only need to get her down to that outdoor pathway corridor.'

'And then what, jump off the ledge of the fortress. What's that, over a hundred-metre drop into the sea…,' Felix said, not helping.

'No, I don't know. Maybe, we could climb. That doesn't matter right now. We'll have a look tomorrow, and try and see what we can make happen okay?' Bastian tried to think, giving in to Felix's stubborn attitude.

The events of the day had gotten to them all, and Bastian had decided to call it quits on brainstorming for the afternoon while the others went out in search of food. Verne not long after came back alone with a loaf bread to tide them over.

'You think it's a stupid plan?' Bastian asked Verne, while they both sat on the wooden floor picking at the loaf of bread between them.

'No,' Verne replied unconvincingly. 'It's just that it's half a plan. And it is already farfetched you know. I just think, maybe you're making it too difficult for yourself. Instead, what about what you said about walking her out of the front door. I mean I know you were joking, but perhaps there's a way. Let's try think of a way it could work. What I'm saying is we need to insert ourselves a bit longer before we are trusted enough to do something like move her to another location, giving us opportunity to get her into our own mover.'

Bastian nearly hated how much sense Verne made. As much as he wanted to storm the castle it wasn't the right move here.

'Okay Verne, let's do the impossible,' Bastian said, 'we'll go tomorrow and work out a way to make it happen.'

***

The following morning ran with ease as they arrived back at the fortress. Even though they had settled on forged paperwork through the old and grungy guard who oversaw the entrance to the fortress way to walk the princess out the front door Felix kept himself distant from Bastian and Verne.

Neither of them said anything when he arrived home late ; ignoring his chummy smiles in the morning, he had clearly gotten up to something devious to put it there.

'Boys, I want apologise again for yesterday, I had no idea about Phil, can't believe I thought I knew him,' Eli said, as they entered the gates into the fortress. 'I'll never make that mistake again.'

Bastian almost felt bad for the guy, he obviously could tell that they were nice people, but in a world full of Grinnwick Guards that wasn't exactly a good thing. The exact same thing that should have tipped him off with Phil.

'Anyways, after all the commotion yesterday, I've had a request for you to guard the second level prisoner today Bastian. Peculiar to have such a request, but orders are orders. So, you'll head up there with Manny today. Got it?' Eli noted to Bastian, then turned to Verne and Felix. 'You two, you will come with me, we need to make sure the Commander's quarters are secure for him before he arrives.'

Bastian smiled at the others as they followed Captain Eli down the corridor around the bend.

The extreme size of Manny's shadow made it evident that he was right beside Bastian; he could even feel the hot breath flutter atop of his own head, the idea of personal space apparently not exactly a thing to Manny.

Walking as quickly as possible to keep up with Manny's large steps Bastian thought to start a conversation but wasn't exactly sure what to say. Instead, he stayed quiet and followed Manny all the way through to the entrance foyer and the circular corridor that led up the tower.

Reaching the first level there was a door that rattled with aching screams that only increased they got closer. Bastian lingered, but Manny did not have time for others. He pushed Bastian ahead of him and they continued up to the second floor. Bastian saw the large double door of heavy metal beneath an archway. It was cold, and unassuming that anything of importance should and was hidden behind it.

'Do we just stand out the front?' Bastian asked.

'Wait, don't speak unless you're spoken to,' Manny said.

He knocked on the door and unlocked it with a code. Inside was a fourposter bed and a lavish bedspread, with a silky array of cushions; a vanity full of make-up and an open closet showing dozens of dresses. A small side-door within the chambers opened up, and Bastian felt lost for words. She walked out of what appeared to be a bathroom in a casual, yet elegant manner, dressed in a blue slip dress that went to her ankles, a towel around her head, unwrapping it to let her damp brown hair flow.

'Morning boys,' she said a little sprightly.

'Princess, your requested guard has joined us today,' Manny said, standing tall still at the doorway entrance.

'Tell him to enter. Then leave us please Manny,' she said, eying Bastian most curiously.

Manny stared at Bastian, who looked from him to the inside of the princess's room. He was unsure if this was a trap, but Manny's face didn't look any different.

'Go on boy, I don't have all day. I'll be right outside,' he said, a warning to Bastian and a reassurance to the princess.

Bastian walked through the door, taking a small step in as Manny closed the heavy doors behind him, leaving him alone with the princess. Was this whole plan turning out to be easier than he could have ever hoped?

'What's your name boy?' she asked.

'Harker,' he said, unsure if he should be lying to her, after all she was the one he wanted to help.

'Well, proper introduction then. I am Princess Ava Dae Thorn. It's a pleasure to meet you Harker.'

Everything about her was stunning, from the light freckles on her cheeks, to the glimmer in her eye that reflected her dress. Taking her vision in left Bastian dazed for a few moments. In person she didn't seem as old at heart as his grandfather said she would be, nothing about her suggested her true age. She seemed so young and real, with a gentle grace that he just had to have.

'Sit down boy,' she said, pouring them both a tea. 'Here' she handed him the cup, a spiral vine tattoo noticeable around her wrist, twisting around her smallest finger.

'I heard you're new to the fortress. Well let me explain something to you; I may be a prisoner, but that doesn't mean I don't get certain things I want. And do you know what I want right now?' she said, her luring voice had Bastian flustered. His head spinning and as much as he wanted to tell her there was no time for this, that this was his chance to help make a plan for their escape. There was a whole other part of him however that she now controlled, holding his full attention. Bits of him sprung to life, and he felt engaged in her entirety. Shaking his head, he had no clue what this beautiful creature before him wanted. He sipped the cup of tea and took a seat.

'I want to know what you know about that man yesterday, who was he? Do you know him well?' she asked.

'Phil?... He said he'd been a guard for five years. But I'm guessing that was a lie considering he got caught for impersonating a guard. I'm also guessing Phil's not his real name either. I do know that he came here for you, he said he had to speak to you,' Bastian said, hating himself for not helping Phil. He could see the worry in the princess's eyes; she wished he was Phil. That she was with him right now instead of Bastian.

'He's okay. I didn't do what that captain, what Archbank said. I took him to an alleyway and told him to run and never look back. I said if he wanted to help you that would be the best thing to do,' Bastian said. The princess pondered, intently looking into Bastian so much so that he felt as though she was looking inside of him, breaking down the boundaries of his mind to see what was inside; she sighed, a relief drifting from her shoulders as he told her he had spared Phil's life.

284

'Thank you for that,' Ava said.

'I saw your face yesterday, you didn't expect to see him there,' Bastian said.

'No, I thought I'd lost him a long time ago. I guess you probably think that I've lost a lot of things, why did I let him get to me, especially in front all those guards.'

'Well yeah, but in saying that he must have been someone important to rattle you so,' Bastian said, feeling foolish for not letting Phil speak, to hear him out fully. If she cared so much about him maybe he would have been an asset to have on their team.

'You have a great deal of thought behind those handsome eyes,' Ava wistfully noted.

'And yes, he was important to me. You see Harker, I'm guessing you've heard what a long life I've had. Not a pleasant one, being Astoria's, and the Guard's puppet, but at least when I was portrayed as alive to the people I got to get out and about, now I'm a trinket they keep closed off, practically forgotten; something that you keep at the bottom of their luggage, carting me around like an old toy. You see all those years ago, you may not believe this, but it was a magic that made me stay so young, family magic of sorts. I've been told of rumours that it was Vander; Van Helm who did this to me. But no, it is my curse, a curse that he has gained so much from. Still, I chose this path, a weight that I alone can bare. My light may not be bright, it is not but a flicker, yet even the smallest spark is enough to light this world.

But yesterday, that man called Phil…,' Ava started, there was a look in her eye of heartbreak.

'Who was he?' Bastian asked.

'My brother. He was a boy the last time I saw him. He'd aged, but not by much. Not frozen like me,' Ava said, more than a little lost in thought. 'Don't,' Bastian said, seeing her start to get upset, he put his hand to her face, 'you don't have to fight any more, I'm going to get you out of here. I'm a guardian, it's my mission to free you. That's why I let him go, that's why I'm here,' Bastian realised he had a hint of desperation in his voice.

'Oh, my dear Harker, I may not look it, but my heart is tired, it's worn.

Whether they've kept me locked away like a dusty old coat or had me behind bars on display for their parties, even tested me to see if rumours and myths about my family's magic are true, I have held onto hope that one day I'll be at peace. I deserve that, don't I?

'Yet, escaping is something I cannot manage.

'You are full of courage, and have a true heart… everything a guardian is supposed to be.

'Meeting you, that is not all I sense, there is something else about you too, you have a strength that not many others hold, your future is filled with light, a light that I believe is waiting out there for you. Do not dwell on the here and now… follow the joy in your life dear boy, leave behind the darkness. You're an adventurer at heart I can see, so find that light… and perhaps knowing that it is out there in your future, my time of peace can come,' Ava said in a soft voice, touching his chest as she spoke, leaving Bastian almost breathless.

'Princess,' he whispered, not wanting to disturb her, not wanting her to let go.

'Please let me help you.'

'You already have. Knowing my brother is alive, it brings a glow that I have not felt in centuries. Hope for the future. You too should be careful, the Guard is not to be taken lightly, they will not be fooled by you for much longer. Go now,' Ava said, holding her head close to his chest, then looking up, her eyes focussed on his before pulling back, and with one of the saddest smiles he had ever seen. She looked happy, but her tears said otherwise.

'Manny, that will be all,' she called out, stepping back from Bastian and returning to her vanity mirror.

Manny forced the door open, waiting for a lingering Bastian to depart the room. 'Stay by the door,' he said. Bastian noticed the giant of the man didn't seem so big, his face softened as he looked in at the princess, his hardness melted away and a younger man came out.

'Come in,' the princess said.

Manny stepped inside, leaving Bastian alone in the entrance. The door closed in front of him, and he was left with his thoughts, mainly one; why didn't he do all he could to get her out, why did he feel like he was weak in her presence. That her enchanting demeanour kept him from getting the mission underway. What was he thinking leaving her there, stupidly just standing here outside of the door like a hopeless fool? He kicked himself for the entire meeting, he had failed. He wouldn't tomorrow.

***

On their way home Felix and Verne told them everything they'd learned from Captain Eli; there was an underground tunnel system, that could be their way out, instead of finding a way through the front gate. Apparently it ran through the whole city. Bastian let them talk about every detail of information before he informed them about being unable to free the princess himself.

'That sounds like a great plan, I can get her there. I worked out how to get to her, well not so much worked it out as she invited me to her quarters,' Bastian said, dropping the events of the day on them both.

'What,' Verne blurted out, causing the street to stare at them.

'You're kidding. What happened?' Felix asked.

'She was the prisoner we were sent to guard on level two, and Manny surprisingly was pretty lenient with it all. Left me with her all on my own – think he might be an actual good guy. She was waiting, she wanted to know about Phil,' Bastian said.

'Really, wouldn't have expected him to be so friendly. What did she want to know about him for?' Felix asked.

'Did you tell her we are going to help her?' Verne added.

'He was her brother. She thought he was dead,' Bastian stated, waiting for the look of shock on their faces. 'Yeah, I told her we would help. She didn't exactly take to the idea of an escape, she said she was too old. I tell you right now, she didn't look old one little bit,' Bastian said, his mind confused as ever. He wanted to go back right now and get her out, he knew he had to wait again until morning, until their next shift.

'I bet she was a stunner,' Felix gushed, cheekily raising his eyebrows.

'Yeah! I couldn't think straight, just from being in her presence. I mean I've heard tales of the old royals being enchanting, but that was like a force that I couldn't escape, once she locked in on my eyes, I was pretty much there for anything she needed. I can't even imagine a whole family like that... no wonder they're family ruled all of Grinnwick. People would have loved them all.

'Seeing Phil, it was like she had hope for the first time; and she deserves it after all these years being their plaything. We have to get her out of there,' Bastian said.

Not able to take his mind off her all night, he fell into his own thoughts of what she said. That there was light in his future, that he had a strong true heart. He had wondered that the past few years, after being away from his mum and friends if he had held onto the boy that he was. She saw something in him, something he forgot about himself, the fun he used to love having. Things had gotten so serious here and now, he missed the days where he'd sit around getting up to mischief with Sticks.

'You all good?' Felix asked, as he finally lay down for the evening too.

'Yeah, just thinking about home,' Bastian said. 'The smell of the sea reminds me of it.'

'Yeah, being out like this. Not following proper rules kind of makes you wish we never had to go back,' Felix said.

'I think after this, I might ask to go home for a break. Do you think we'll be allowed?' Verne pondered.

'Who knows, I've got no home to go to anymore anyways,' Felix said.

'You're welcome to come with me,' Verne offered.

'Me too,' Bastian said, 'Let's do it anyway okay? We deserve a break.'

After agreeing that they'd make sure they'd visit their homes, they each slowly fell asleep, none of them prepared for what the following day would bring.

Goosebumps across Bastian's neck woke him up, waiting for Verne and Felix to get ready that morning seemed like forever. He wanted so badly to get back to his post and see the princess; to start working on getting her out. He would work out something with Manny he was sure of it, convinced that he cared for her.

Clearing through the gate, he went his separate way looking for Manny, who was nowhere to be seen.

Captain Eli himself was already in the fortress and had come running out of the entrance hall.

'Bastian, you're here. I realise we didn't have any details for which guard quarters you're living in. I've been trying to find you all morning, been sending people all over town. Come with me,' Eli said flushed.

'Oh Verne, Felix you boys stay down here, go to your northern post and keep an eye out okay,' Eli added to the other two.

'The rest of you, please go to your usual stations,' Eli barked at a few other dumbstruck guards.

Bastian looked back at the others; he felt the confusion all over his face.

'Captain, what's happening. Where's Manny?' Bastian asked.

'Manny asked you to be brought up stairs. I just never thought, you know,' his face was shocked.

Bastian followed him has quick as he could to the first floor, which was incredibly quiet this time around. Making their way up to the second floor suddenly seemed like slow motion as there were a half a dozen people around who Bastian hadn't seen before.

Two women, who could have only been maids that serviced the room held each other outside in the entrance before the doors. Feeling his heartrate increase Bastian pushed his thick, messy hair out of his face and moved closer to the door. The small room inside of Princess Ava's quarters was open to reveal the bathroom, flooded.

The water red.

Towels on the floor stained and bundled up on the ground. A wrapped-up body laying across the bed, nothing but a delicate hand laying out in his view, the tattoo of spiralling vines in view. There was a hint of bitter rust in the air, enough that Bastian felt he could taste the scent of metallic in his own mouth. This must have been some fort of effect from the chip upgrade inside of him, forcing him to notice these small details.

Manny, the giant of a man, looked completely defeated on the chair that Bastian was only sitting at yesterday.

Shook, confused. This wasn't supposed to happen.

He was supposed to help her; he said he'd helped her.

This didn't look like he had helped her one little bit, getting her out of here could have stopped all of this. Why didn't he do it yesterday? Why didn't he force her to come with him, why didn't he risk it then instead of waiting?

She could have really lived.

Manny stood up, came to his side. 'You're here. She will be happy you saw her one last time.'

'I barely knew her, why me? Why did you request me to come to see this?' Bastian stammered, looking at Manny who it seemed shed real tears for the woman he'd held prisoner.

'You thought I was a monster because I guarded her, but I protected her as best I could,' Manny murmured so that only Bastian could hear, defeat the tone in his voice. 'Even though I knew deep down that she wasn't capable of love after losing so much.'

Bowing his head Bastian reached to put his arm on his shoulder. 'I'm sorry, I thought I could have helped her too.'

'I know, she told me. Even for a moment, I had hope, so much that I ignored the tears in her eyes when she said her last goodbye to me yesterday. But you, you needed to see, to understand that she was truly gone, that the fight for her is now over, you can tell the others,' Manny whispered, then stood tall and pulled in the softness he'd just shown Bastian.

'Commander Van Helm is on his way boys, you best get out of here,' Captain Eli said, nodding at them both. 'You should take the day off, both of you, it's hard to see someone do such a thing.'

Bastian looked over again at her lifeless body, wanting to stop it from being real, to pull her back into life. He couldn't, there was nothing left; no words, no way to go back, no light. His mission was over.

Standing at the gate, Bastian was frozen. Manny looked down at him.

'You best get out of here. You're not one of us, and what you were sent to do can no longer be done' Manny warned.

Looking into Manny's red eyes, Bastian held his ground.

'Don't worry, I'm not going to say anything. Doubt I'll be around much longer myself. Just a heads up is all,' Manny assured him.

'Thanks,' Bastian replied awkwardly. He was unsure of what to do, Verne and Felix were still inside.

'Look, come with me. I know a place away from all this that might be your scene,' Manny said.

Bastian followed him down the streets of Astoria, not paying one bit of attention to where they were going. The image of her delicate hand slipping out of the wrapped covers still captured in his mind, the shock was one thing but the tear that dropped down his cheek made it too real.

'You got a shirt on under there?' Manny asked.

'Yeah,' Bastian said, pulling off his Grinnwick Guard uniform shirt. He was wearing a black tee-shirt underneath.

'Good,' Manny said, taking off his own as they walked along revealing a grey shirt. 'Place is a few minutes away.'

They were deep in the western streets of Astoria. They'd passed Bastian's apartment and were moving closer towards the border where the streets became busier.

The Half Hound was a pub completely different to the ones the guards frequented. It didn't have the same lavish outside, nor alluring setup. It was simple; the windows were stained green, and you couldn't see in. Inside the booths and tables were old and worn. And the man behind the bar looked just as worn. But the customers were relaxed, at ease. No one was one edge, and everyone spoke freely. Bastian could see a sign for lodgings upstairs. A few sailors were making their way down to a table, and a group of men was talking away over a hand of cards.

Taking a seat, Bastian didn't say anything while the bar keeper came to bring them their beers.

'Who you got here Manny?' the Inn keeper asked.

'Calls himself Harker. Boy, this is Wilbur. Good Man,' Manny said, paying Wilbur for their drinks.

'Not a talker I see,' Wilbur noted.

'Yeah, we've had a rough day. Lost a friend,' Manny said.

'Ahh, I see. How about I bring something stronger around,' Wilbur offered, walking off back to the bar.

'I didn't think guards drank at places like this?' Bastian observed.

'Thought you were smarter than that. I'm no guard. Not really, not anymore. Wilbur here is my ticket out of here. He can be yours too, if you want,' Manny said, shifting his large back side in his seat, his face still dead serious.

'Look, I don't know exactly where you've come from, or why you tried to help Ava. But don't dwell on it, she was sad for such a long time, in truth I'm surprised she lasted that long. She always made it out like she couldn't leave, like she had to stay, she seemed to have the world on her shoulders the poor girl. But since yesterday, a weight had lifted from her, a peace took over her. What she did was no one's fault. No one could have stopped her; the light had been drained too much from her.

'You can go back to whoever sent you here, tell them what happened, what you saw. And tell them, the guard is stronger than anyone wants to admit. They want all of Grinnwick to fall to its feet, and it will if no one stands up against them. But, if you want to escape the politics, the bloodshed, you can join me,' Manny finished his beer in one steady swig.

It was not an offer he expected to receive when waking up this morning, but after what he'd seen, he wanted to escape everything as quick as possible. He felt stupid; ignorant that the world around him caused so much horror to people. In truth it was his first time seeing the effects of the Grinnwick Guard firsthand.

'Thank you, but I do have to go back,' Bastian said softly, when Wilbur came back with a glass of whiskey for them each.

'Who was it?' Wilbur asked, restarting his conversation.

'The princess,' Manny replied.

'Really?' Wilbur stuttered, confusion and a duller tone taking hold of him, 'you told me to send word out that she was alive. I thought there was a rescue mission under way,' Wilbur noted.

'Seems it failed,' Manny said. Bastian could tell he was looking right at him.

'You were in there undercover?' Bastian said, changing the subject.

'Boy, Manny here is one of the best. Just look at the size of him; not one of 'em would have questioned his desire to join 'em,' Wilbur said. It was undoubtedly true. Manny had stayed quiet around most of the guards while Bastian had been there, his dead straight face put an uneasiness in any man as strong as him. Here and now, sitting comfortably in the booth, relaxed talking to Wilbur was like watching a whole new person.

'Yeah, well Wilbur, they might be a bit curious about me after I take to the hills,' Manny said, polishing off his whisky. 'Can you load me up, before I head off? And grab the kid something too will you, seems he's got a bit of a trip ahead of him.'

'No worries. Give me a moment and I'll get you both sorted,' Wilbur said strolling back to the kitchens.

'Look Harker, I get that you're sad. In a perfect world, you would have done it, you would have gotten her out. In an even more perfect world, I would have gotten to it earlier. Don't get me wrong what we just saw was unspeakable. But the fact that the Guard had control of her, only added to their strengths, in more ways than even they'll know.

'Her being at peace has not only released her from them, but maybe it'll stop Van Helm from having control over everything now that he doesn't have her under is control.

Just make sure... don't hold onto the sadness, it will only add to the dark inside of you. Your young, there's a whole world that you can still help, even if this one time you couldn't do what you wanted,' Manny tried to reassure him, before getting up to take Wilbur's bag of goods, passing one along to Bastian and then walking out of The Half Hound for good.

Bastian sat by himself, looking at the empty seat across from him. The image of the lifeless hand stuck in his head, the bloodied water spread out across floor, and crying women… and the eerie feeling in his gut that no matter what Manny said it was all on him. That he had failed her; that this day could have been so different.

Parting of Ways

Verne and Felix both said nothing when Bastian entered their apartment door. They stood looking at him, waiting for him to say something, both of their bags already packed.

'Guess it's time to get out of here,' Bastian advised the others.

'You okay? Did you see…,' Verne asked.

'Yeah I did… No. I don't know. This wasn't supposed to happen,' Bastian said, putting the bag Wilbur had given him into his bag.

'No one thought it would have happened,' Verne said. 'I mean part of me expected us to fail, but not like that, I thought maybe we'd go down fighting or something. I honestly thought we'd all be dead.'

'Yeah well, how were we supposed to predict she was going to do that?' Felix commented. 'It's not like she said anything yesterday did she Bass?'

Bastian stood frozen, 'I, I don't know; I should know. She kept on refusing my help, maybe that should have been a clue.'

'Don't be stupid. Never in your right mind could you have jumped to that thought. She's been held prisoner for multiple lifetimes, I'm sure that's bound to drive anyone over the edge,' Verne said, patting him on the back. 'Let's just get out of here, we need to get back and tell everyone what's happened.'

Grabbing his things and following Verne to the door, he felt Felix behind him, standing still and maybe a little awkward.

'What is it?' Bastian asked.

'I'm not going back,' Felix said simply.

'Of course you are, don't be stupid,' Verne said, his own patience waning.

'Look, it's not like I'm staying to join the Guard. I just don't want to be a guardian. I want to be a part of the world, I'm going to catch a ride out to the country, maybe find a job out there,' Felix said. His face was serious, and Bastian saw the desperation clear in his eyes.

'This is ridiculous. How are you going to survive?' Verne questioned, 'this is a stupid joke Felix.

'I won some extra money the other night at the bar. That'll keep me going until I find something,' Felix noted.

'You can't, you're a Raven, we are a team,' Verne hesitated, clearly unsteady with Felix's choice.

'Here, take this,' Bastian passed him the bag Wilbur had made him full of apples, bread and water.

'What are you doing?' Verne asked, stammering at Bastian, shocked by his acceptance of Felix's choice.

'Verne, we just lost the person we were meant to save. She said something about following the things that give us joy in our life. Felix is Grover now, and he should have the choice to find a place that makes him happy, how can we deny him that? He has his own life to live, that doesn't mean we won't always be friends,' Bastian said, hugging Felix one last time, patting him on the back as he got ready to leave.

***

'Stay out of trouble, you won't have me there to save your skin,' Bastian said as his parting words. They left Felix inside of the northern gate of Astoria; it was quick the way that he vanished into the bustling market, like a swarm of bees Felix nestled too quickly amongst them, leaving Verne and Bastian alone.

'Come on. Let's get out of here,' Bastian said.

'I can't believe you just let that happen, I don't even know what to say,' Verne said, more than a little gobsmacked.

Finding their way back to the meeting point to get back was at least a two day's drive away. Verne, exhausted and grumpy from Felix's departure stole a mover from the back of the markets. It was an old van, that looked like it had driven longer than most.

Verne drove straight through the night; he'd hardly said a word to Bastian by the time morning came around.

Bastian took the wheel, letting him sleep, knowing that he had every right to be upset. Bastian let Felix walk away too easily, he just didn't have it in him to stop him, not then, not after what he'd seen. It didn't mean that he didn't miss him being there. Felix would have broken the silence and the sadness from what he'd seen. He would have found something to talk about, and the car would have been filled with something other than Verne's constant snoring.

After a sleep Verne was in a slightly better mood, he snacked on some apples Bastian kept for them.

'You know what. He probably would have hated visiting the farm with me,' Verne muttered. 'I don't think he'd do any good milking the cows either.'

'Don't think you're wrong, probably left just so he didn't have to face everyone when we tell them we've failed,' Bastian murmured, the hint of uneasiness at how everyone would react to their news scared him.

'Oh yeah. Forgot we had to tell them that. Still, we don't know if the others succeeded either. But I sure hope they did,' Verne said.

Bastian lost concentration from the road for a minute, slightly swerving; he had forgotten in the commotion of their mission about the others, and now his fear turned entirely towards the rest of the Ravens.

'You okay?' Verne asked.

'Yeah, I just hope they're okay too,' Bastian replied.

A small shack in the middle of the plains of a small, deserted town known as the Brim Lee Crossing was their meeting point. It had a pin coded box full of supplies for them inside, and it alerted the Guardians once it had been opened that someone was waiting for them.

They waited in the van drinking some of the water they'd found in the supply box when the car that had dropped them off arrived.

***

Sir Dash, Emmett, his grandfather August Harker, as well as a stranger; a man hidden in the shadows of the corner playing with a small knife waited as they entered his Grandfather quarters, the echo of the closing doors behind them from the moving trolley like cupboard that lifted up to his floor were all that where heard, the silence waiting to be broken.

'Boys, welcome home,' his grandfather greeted finally looking up from his desk. Coming in to hug Bastian and Verne. Both looked very uncomfortable at the audience they had to inform of their failure.

'How do you feel?' Emmett asked.

Both Bastian and Verne looked at each other; did they already know what had happened? They couldn't possibly.

'Emmett is talking about your chips – it's a big step. Just making sure you're adjusting alright,' his grandfather said, settling their nerves.

Bastian had honestly forgotten all about his chip settings, he had gotten so used to the heightened hearing and senses, he had barely noticed any change as his focus so entirely on the mission. Now thinking that the structure of the chip was to help focus and that probably would explain why he was so intent on his mission.

'Weren't there three of you?' Sir Dash commented. 'Where's Felix?'

'Yes, about that,' Bastian began, trying to find the right words. 'Felix… well, he decided he didn't want to come back. The life outside of these walls was something he couldn't refuse.'

'Ah, I see,' his grandfather remarked calmly. It is understandable, especially with your chips that you would feel the smallest emotions heightened. He followed the choice that he needed to it seems. I'm sure you are both saddened by his departure, just remember that freedom is each of your rights, and that it is our freedom to choose that set us on our paths in this life,' he said trying to ease them both.

'That's not all Sir,' Verne began.

'Yes, what is it Mr. Greenleaf?' Harker added.

'About our mission, we failed sir,' Verne admitted.

'Well, obviously. Would you not have had the princess with you if you succeeded? What happened, were you found out? Could you not get in?' said Sir Dash. He reminded Bastian of Manny's uneasy attitude.

'Sir, it was my fault really,' Bastian said, stepping forward. 'Part of me hoped the news had reached you all. The princess, she took her own life.

'We did make contact; I spoke to her. We were working on a plan to get her out, but she wasn't willing. When I returned the next day, she was… Well, she was gone,' Bastian trailed off, trying to keep his voice from wavering.

None of them said anything. The man hidden in the corner of the room stepped forward, he was younger than any of Bastian's teachers, possibly in the later of his thirties. His deep green eyes stared into Bastian, just as the princess did, but this was no where near as comforting.

'Are you sure it was her?' he said, and angry fearsome look covering every inch of his face.

'Yes Sir. I saw her body myself,' Bastian said.

None of the others said anything. The man without a name sat in his grandfather's seat, looking defeated.

'Dawson, you thought she was lost to you before. It will be okay,' his grandfather said to the man who was in his seat, small tears falling from his face.

'August don't test me. You haven't seen the things I've seen. Compared to mine your life so far has been a joy. You haven't had to come back and find thousands of lives destroyed. My own being one of them. Trying to put the tiniest pieces back together is tearing me apart.'

'Yet, you've not since shared how that happened. How you survived. What of that, what else are you keeping from us?' his grandfather snarled back.

'August, you don't know the half of things. Then again neither do I, I wasn't there, and I haven't been the same since. But you, you've sent boys to do a man's job. How could they know, how could any of you know or understand?

'I saw it all before any of you guardians stepped in. They may have been men before your time, but you are all one and the same. Gutless. I watched those soldiers slaughter what was left of the survivors of my homeland. What did your people do, come in after the havoc was reckoned, after the palace was burned, and the cries were stopped. Your people didn't act, although they pledged their entire allegiance to ours, they waited too long, not thinking how quickly the darkness is able to spread. The few that you all found could barely fill a tent, with nothing but a sticker to identify them. I managed to find two of mine hidden, still in the ruins of home, if only Ava had been hidden as well. I couldn't protect her or the others then, and I haven't now,' Dawson fumed.

The man in front of him wasn't an old man. Yet he spoke of the War of Darkness like it was fresh in his mind, as though he was there, when it happened a thousand years ago. He should be long dead and forgotten, not standing in front of them now barking orders. Bastian went to ask how he could possibly know so much but was interrupted by his grandfather.

'Look, I'm sorry. But I can't be held responsible for the men of the past, all I can do is work towards a better future. I know it never should have happened; she should have been rescued centuries ago,' his grandfather said.

'Her brother...' Dawson said, ignoring August's words, his mind clearly lost in his own thoughts. 'He went to get her as well. From the moment we knew he's been ready to jump into action, to find her. He's had years out in this world, what has he been doing, he should have made it to her, to help her.' Dawson said standing up and knocking the chair over.

'Sir, he did find her, I saw him,' Bastian butted in. 'I had to pretend to arrest him, then I told him to run. He told me the princess would want to see him. That he thought people had forgotten about her. Said that he was there to help. The princess saw him, she knew he was there. She didn't know he was even alive before that,' Bastian said.

'You saw him? Was he okay?' Dawson asked, walking right up to Bastian and Verne, breaching their personal space.

'Yeah, said his name was Phil. He'd done what we had, working his way into their lives. Probably took him ages tracking down where they'd hidden her, didn't have the help of the Guardians to get him in the ranks like we did. Sounds like they had her on the move quite a bit, keeping her out of the public view. But his paperwork with the Guard didn't check out. He got caught, and I was sent to take him away. Well obviously, I let him go. I don't know where he went. But him being there, I think he just made things worse for the princess,' Bastian said.

Dawson took Bastian's words, easing back off the two of them. Clearly still upset he lent up against the edge of the desk.

'Sir Dash, Emmett, will you give us a moment?' his grandfather said. 'I will send the boys to you and Ms Madlyn soon to make sure they're in good health. If I could ask you both first not to mention Princess Ava's demise to anyone else just yet,' he asked the two who agreed.

After the other men left the room Verne turned to take a seat himself.

'Sir, I wondered if the other mission was a success,' Verne asked.

'What?' Dawson snapped.

'The mission, the rest of their squad,' his grandfather added, keeping his own voice calm.

'Yes, they were quite successful all of them. The rest of the Ravens are fine. I believe Russ got into a bit of a predicament; however, the rest of the team were able to keep him from too much harm,' Harker said to the two of them. 'I'm sure even without Felix, they will be extremely excited at your return.'

'Sir, we also wanted to know,' Verne started, but hesitated in the moment, turning to Bastian.

'Grandfather. We would both like a break, we want to go home,' Bastian asked.

'Hmm,' he pondered.

'Just let them go August, you may as well,' Dawson said carelessly with the flick of his hand.

'Well, I shall think about it. I'll let you both know,' he said. 'Firstly, I did want to speak to you. If you heard of anything while you were in the city, anything that might connect to someone back here?' his grandfather asked curiously.

'No sir, I heard nothing,' Verne said.

'Me either,' Bastian said. 'Nothing connecting anyone to us. No word of the Guardians, nothing. I did come across a man who was undercover himself, but I think he was just working alone. He took me to an old rebel bar in the outer quarter of Astoria, asked me to go with him.'

'Yes, well you've got too much sense to be following a lone rebel,' his grandfather advised.

Bastian wasn't convinced entirely on this. Part of him wished he followed Manny, not constricted by the rules of the Guardians. His education and knowledge that he gained never outweighed his feelings that this life was a half-life. He wouldn't have wanted to go in the same steps of Felix, still inside he held a feeling that there was something more meant for him.

'We should go see them,' Verne said.

'Yes, you should. Before you go. I'm sorry for what you had to see Bastian,' his grandfather noted, putting a hand on his shoulder, before embracing him again. Bastian returned the hug, release of emotions in the moment nearly overwhelmed him.

Bastian, unsure of himself as he pulled away forced a smile. 'I'll be okay,' he answered.

'Did she say anything to you?' Dawson asked looking at Bastian.

'She said,' Bastian hesitated. 'That my future would be full of light, that she saw it. She spoke of magic, and how she felt older than she looked. It all seems a bit ridiculous now.'

'I wouldn't say that. She always had a way of seeing the truth of someone,' Dawson looked at him curiously as though suddenly he, Bastian was now slightly more a person of interest.

'How did she look?' Dawson asked. 'Before?'

'She looked stunning, like a blooming petal with deep rose lips and cheeks. I could barely speak when I saw her, she took my breath away. She didn't just walk, she floated with a delicate grace, and strength. But up close you could see in her grey eyes there was a heaviness to them. I ignored it then, mesmerised by her presence,' Bastian said, starting to feel his anger burning at himself for not saving her.

'How exactly do you know her?' he asked, confused at how Dawson was related to one of the most stunning and complex women he'd ever met, who also had to be at least a thousand years old.

'Don't blame yourself boy, this was a task meant for more than three of you. People have tried before and failed. It was idealist for me to expect another outcome.

'As for me, that's a harder one to explain than you could probably understand. It'd be hard for anyone to understand really, the complexities of this world are stranger than you could imagine, magic stretches further than just what is written in these silly old books. Like her brother said most people have forgotten the truth of it all. And after all August here doesn't teach you everything. Even if he likes to think he does.

'And Ava, well how I know her may be harder for you to understand. You call her a princess, but she was once family to me. I've been kept from her for some time, without word that she even survived. So long has passed, unable to do what I should have. The last I saw her she waved to me, her youthful pout still glowering at me, upset that I was leaving,' Dawson said.

'But I've read the books, High King Geoffrey was her father. He died, along with the others,' Bastian said.

'That he did. He was a great man, and I was his closest confidant, like a brother. What was written is what we wanted the world to know. A lot of people died that night. There's a whole world out there that can't be seen anymore because my family was killed, because without them it wasn't safe for magic to thrive. Little did the people then understand how important our family was, and how without them their world would be thrown into turmoil,' Dawson said, the green in his eyes had a hint of grey, with a heaviness that Bastian remembered in Ava's. This man before him was her family. Bastian felt heartbroken for him, he had only seen the death of one girl, but Ava's uncle must have seen so much worse.

'I'm sorry,' Bastian said. 'If only I got to her sooner, if I took the chance when it first came instead of planning. Instead of waiting. She wouldn't have; she would be here now,' Bastian's breaths quickened with every sentence.

'Bastian, Verne why don't you head off and get yourself checked out by Ms Madlyn?' his grandfather insisted, putting his arm around Bastian's shoulder and turning him towards the door.

He wished he could have done more for Dawson, but there was nothing he could do. The confession that the High King may not have been the true father was intriguing to say the least, but the truths from a lifetime ago nearly meant nothing to the world they lived in now. Nothing but a memory, a reminder of how things were.

***

Their entrance back into their quarters after being checked over by Ms Madlyn was met with a large welcome. No one expected them so late at night; Bastian felt cold even as Gertie and Russ both jumped and hugged him tight. Rudi even hugged him. Mandy too. She then surprisingly kissed Verne, who looked just as shocked as much as he enjoyed it.

All of them stared, feeling like they were intruding on their moment.

'Wait, where's Felix?' Russ interrupted. This forced Verne to pull away from Mandy.

'He stayed behind. He didn't want to come back,' Bastian said.

'No. What?' Gertie stammered.

'He just left us? He wouldn't do that,' Russ said.

'He would. Couldn't you tell, he was getting toey being cooped up here,' Rudi added.

'Yeah, well he loved it out there. Think he's just meant to be a part of the world, rather than cooped up here.' Verne took a seat on his bed, and each of them all followed suit. Bastian couldn't look any of them in the eye.

'Well,' Russ said.

'Well, what?' Bastian lay down trying to get comfy on his bed.

'We want to know what happened…,' Rudi said, kicking Bastian's bed, trying to get his attention.

'We failed,' Verne said, not going further into detail, leaving them all in silence.

'Well, you're back. That's the main thing. Hopefully, on our next mission they'll keep us together. I don't know what that was all about, why separate us. If you had all of us maybe you would have succeeded,' Mandy said, and Gertie agreed.

'We did alright. We infiltrated their system easy enough but getting out of there would have been a disaster if we didn't have the Phoenix squad there with us. I guess they had to make up for us not having three of our team,' Gertie said.

'Good, I'm glad you had them,' Bastian sighed and got up; he did want to hear about their mission. He was happy they were all safe, but his mind was exhausted, and in honestly all he wanted was to be alone.

'Bass,' Gertie called after him as he grabbed his towel and headed for the showers.

He waited outside of their room for a moment as some of the younger squads were hanging out down the hall. He could hear Verne tell Gertie to leave him be.

He paused, listening in.

'He seems a bit out of it,' Verne added.

'What happened?' Gertie asked.

'Our mission was to rescue the princess. She was alive. Well, we lost her, I didn't see anything. But I heard one of the guards say that she took her own life. According to them her suite's bathroom was a mess with blood. Bastian was on her patrol, he saw it. I think he's taking it harder than he'll let on,' Verne said.

Even from outside of the room the silence echoed into the hallways and into Bastian's bones. Princesses Ava's tired smile, and intoxicating. He finally continued down the hall to the bathrooms, leaving the silence behind.

***

Bastian felt a shifting distance grow between him and his friends, and nothing but the desire to go home crossed his mind. Every moment was spent waiting for his grandfather to just give the go ahead, to let them leave. Gertie had tried to get through to him multiple times over the past few weeks, but every time she reached for him, Bastian couldn't help but pull away. Verne did his best to make him laugh, and pulled up the slack at the practice fields, by making sure everyone got through together when Bastian spaced out.

Even on their day off Bastian lay in bed while the rest of them went out for a swim to the lake on a burning forty-degree day. Bastian didn't have it in him to go outside, though he knew he should. That it'd be good for him, that like Princess Ava said he should follow in joy, but a sadness covered him as he lay on his bed. All he could do was feel like a light inside of him had gone out, so much so that it weighed on him, burying all his thoughts in darkness. Ava had been such a rare glimpse at true magic in this world, her light was meant for so much more than being strung up by Van Helm, if she was free and others felt her power they would be overwhelmed with possibilities, with a brighter future. But without her, that future, that chance for peace amongst all the people, was gone.

The thoughts that continued to weigh on him swirled and tangled from his mind to his heart, the pain of it all pulling at his already weakened spirit. He thought about the Guardians, the place that had become his home.

These people were his family. But all he wanted right now was his real home, his old friends, his mother.

Was Felix right? Was being a part of the world a better choice, a better way to live.

Living in the shadows, making waves under someone else's orders seemed stupid. Who chose the orders, he still didn't truly know. A combined effort on people like his grandfather, but surely there were others. Faceless others. But how could he trust in people he didn't know. Part of him hated the Guardians, his mind fixed that if he had known about the princess earlier, he would have gone sooner. Perhaps he could have actually had made a difference. Where were the eyes of Guardians in the world while Ava was left to struggle in silence, why did they forget about her, for nearly a thousand years how had she not been saved.

He felt constricted, like he was spiralling. As he fell deeper into his own despair, Bastian completely ignored a knock at his door.

'Why aren't you with the others?' Rudi's brother Alaric asked Bastian who lay in bed with the lights on at midday.

'Didn't feel like it,' Bastian moaned, turning over.

'Okay, well I was going to leave you a note. Professor Harker wants to see you,' Alaric said, and left Bastian alone once more.

Bastian pulled himself out of his bed, dragged his shirt on and searched under his bed for some shoes.

The halls where empty, everyone must have been given the day off and been down at the lake. Strange, yet nice to have so much space to himself. Although, it was weird that Alaric was hanging around the compound too, he wondered what kept him back. Bastian felt guilty as he walked the halls that he hadn't joined his friends, the past few days he had been so low, but part of him hated facing them, hated seeing the looks in their eyes; their puppy dog faces, it nearly broke him.

'Ah, Bastian. You don't look so good boy, take a seat,' his grandfather said. 'Have some water.'

Bastian drank the water; he felt the dryness in his mouth softly diminish.

'Now, son. I have called you here for a number of reasons.' His grandfather did not seem like the professor anymore, he was on edge more than usual, but more in tune with Bastian at the same time, projecting a cautious look towards him, talking to him as his grandson.

'I had Verne and Gertie come and see me. They are both worried about you, Miss Bell was practically distraught, and I finally see what they mean,' his grandfather said, taking the seat right next to Bastian, facing him quite closely.

'I understand the mission to Astoria has gotten to you more than we, than I could have foreseen. I am sorry for that, but I understand meeting the princess is something very few can describe. Dawson may be from her time, a time of great rulers, of magic, and while some say he has a similar presence, his seems to have faded since the passing of his wife. I believe they say that the princess was still a sight to see,' his grandfather said.

'That's an understatement. Van Helm must be stronger than most men, because she had a way about her that most would give into,' Bastian noted.

'You aren't wrong. Van Helm holds his own powers, after all he has lived for centuries himself. Some say he was once a nice young man, his heart pure; but he was twisted by power. His life was tied to the princess, that's how he lives so long. But that is all rumour too… it's also said that whatever way her life was managed to extend he used the same magics on himself, and it cost him a high price… who is to say what the real truth is. But with her gone, perhaps this leaves him weak, only time will tell.

'But you boy, seeing her, understanding how pure and powerful the princess and those like her were, how drawn to them one can be. It is hard to fathom that they are gone from this world. Even now I am an old man, I've grown up on myths and tales of their beings, on the supposed power of the royals. The notion that without their bloodlines there is an emptiness left on Grinnwick of what could have been, it's heartbreaking. What once was can never be again.

'I can't even begin to understand the awful manipulative things that she has been subjected too first in the wake of her families demise, but then to be swept up in the rise of the Grinnwick Guard, and be one of their chess pieces, only to be thrown and away like an old trinket when they were done playing with her. What, the Guard did to drive that poor girl to end her life… I don't think I could ever fathom. But that was her choice. Understand that Bastian, it is not on your shoulders my boy. You said she spoke to you; it sounded like she said you would have a good future. Hold on to that. There's a whole life ahead of you.

'Do me a favour and don't push your friends away, they are the ones who are there for you in the dark times so you can enjoy the good ones.'

'Yes Grandfather, I promise I will try harder,' Bastian said.

'Just let them in, talk to them. They're your friends,' his grandfather advised.

Bastian nodded.

'Now that isn't the only reason I needed you here. As you noticed, it's extremely sparse around here today. I have orchestrated it that way. I have my eyes on a couple of people who are leaking our movements to the Guard.'

'Our movements?' Bastian asked, he was now concerned for his grandfather who seemed fixed on the notion of spies infiltrating their compound.

'Yes, well sometimes older squads are sent out on smaller details,' he started, before noticing Bastian's peak in interest.

'It always quite amazed me how none of you ever seem to take notice of anything else than what is immediately around you when studying here. Older Squads are sent out every now and then. You students always seem swept up with yourselves.

'Anyway, it seems our last two missions were intercepted by taskforces already in place of our set location,' his grandfather noted.

'Okay, what can I do?' Bastian asked.

'Well, I need you to make sure you trust the Ravens first. You need to become a proper team member again.

'There is nothing else you may be able to do if our Guardians compound is truly compromised. All I can do is let you know what I do. And I feel like there are spies in our walls that are planning an attack, and I don't know how safe it will be here for you anymore. For anyone. That holiday you wanted may be upon you sooner than you think. I know your mother will not like it if I kept you here knowing that something was awry. Until I give you the go-ahead, keep your friends close, they'll have your back for when you need them most.

314

'Do you understand Bastian? These days the Guardians are not like the ones we read about in my classes; we no longer hold the Heart of Grinnwick. A myth, a motto, whatever it was or may be… the purpose of our beliefs is getting lost. It has not been a part of our stronghold since before even I was born. We were banded together to protect the so-called Heart, the spirit of this world, and by doing so protecting Grinnwick.

'We don't have the Heart, we don't even know exactly what or where it is, if its real. As much as we try to protect Grinnwick, to look out for the people, it seems we aren't as subtle as I'd like. And either there are insiders in our midst, or our tricks are no longer going unseen, we are seen as a threat to those in power. Not just the Guard either, there are those further beyond who believe something has awakened and see putting down any Guardian to ensure the darkness of this world succeeds. I don't know how much longer this foundation will hold together. I am preparing everyone I have, that includes you,' his grandfather warned.

Alarmed, Bastian instinctively wanted to stay and defend the Guardians if an attack came from the Grinnwick Guard. But, if they could attack here, they could no doubt be ready to attack places like his home, and perhaps they were already there. He had a strength and skillset now that he hadn't had when he arrived. And this might be his chance to escape the formalities of the Guardians, to do what he wants, what he can do to help those just like the princess, instead of waiting for a course of action. This may be the time for him to put everything he'd learned towards protecting his home, and his mum.

***

Bastian waited at the top entrance as the rest of the Ravens arrived home. A few of the other squads had already passed him on their way back through for dinner.

'Well, look who it is,' Rudi said. 'Thought you'd join the living?' It reminded Bastian of something Felix would have said.

'If I was, it wouldn't be with you. How are you still that pale after a day out in the sun?' Bastian said, causing the rest of the squad to laugh.

'Ahh, you missed a good day at the lake mate. But I hear tomorrow's going to be just as nice, and we just got the word that we all have another day off, so looks like we'll be back there again. You might actually have to join us,' Verne said, grabbing his shoulder and walking them both back inside.

Bastian ignored the heaviness that had been on him for the past few weeks and tried enjoying the moment.

'If we go tomorrow, can we take extra snacks? Russ got into all the good sandwiches early,' Rudi said.

'Oi, I offered them to you first remember,' Russ challenged. 'Not my fault you didn't take me up on it. A full Guardian is a happy one,' Russ said gleefully.

'I don't know if it's as hot as today, I'll just want fruit and water. I could barely do anything but swim, that heat was exhausting,' Mandy said, still wearing a large, brimmed hat and her face flush from the heat.

'You had enough energy to push me off the dock, fully clothed,' Verne replied, half laughing, swishing his hair about with a sly grin her way.

Bastian had missed their relationship grow over the past few weeks. The distance he'd kept them at, he hadn't even noticed how obviously they both cared for each other.

'Guys, I do actually feel like eating tonight, can you stop it?' Russ rolled his eyes making Bastian laugh.

'Don't think they know how to stop,' Bastian joked.

'What a sight, Bastian actually making jokes,' Gertie said. Bastian could tell she was smiling at him, but knew she was the most hurt by his distance.

Stepping back to where she stood, he slowed down with her and apologised. Gertie stopped dead.

'What makes you think I'm going to accept it. You've barely spoken a word to me in weeks. I thought we were friends, at least,' Gertie said.

Bastian could feel the others continue walking downstairs, awkwardly looking back at them as they left them alone.

'I know. I can't say how sorry I am for pulling away, I just haven't been myself. I'm still not really. But I am sorry, you all are my friends, and I shouldn't shut you out. I just forgot, I forgot we weren't just a team,' Bastian said. He could feel his words mixing up. He could see the longing in her eyes – he wished he could embrace her – his truth was that he wasn't sure he had the same feelings towards her as he once did before his mission.

This didn't stop her, she leaned in to him quickly, kissing him.

Taken aback, he stopped before kissing her back. Putting his arms around her and embracing her, forgetting his own feelings and going with the feelings of having her in his arms. Her lips were soft on his, and he could feel her soft skin brush across his hands. He pulled apart from her if only for a moment, as she guided him into the empty armoury. There Bastian continued to draw her in, pulling her closer. Pushing her up against the cold stone wall he felt her deep breaths as he began to kiss her neck. For a moment he stopped. Stepping back, looking at her.

'What is it?' Gertie said, confused.

'Nothing,' Bastian said, he held her face in his hand for a moment. 'We should go,' he said quietly.

'Now? We don't have to, no one is up here,' she said, pulling his face towards hers gently. He kissed her once more, holding her face in his hands as well before pulling back one last time.

'Come on, not here,' he said softly, smiling at her and grabbing her hand, leading her down to the dining hall where everyone was.

'Looks like you two have been up to a bit of fun,' Russ said as they sat down next to the rest of the Ravens looking dishevelled. Bastian patted down Gertie's hair, so it wasn't as messy, who blushed as he touched her.

'You're going to break all the other girls' hearts here if you're officially off the market mate,' Rudi assured him.

'I'm just glad you're talking to us all again. Told you all he just needed some time. Me mum always says you can't go rushing these things,' Verne said as he stuffed his face.

'Yeah… bit of time,' Bastian said a little aloof, he wasn't sure it was enough time. Like his grandfather said, he had to make an effort, he had to try and pull himself back into his own life. The warmth of Gertie by his side gave him a spark of excitement, a piece to grab hold of.

'Well everything seems the same. You're still stuffing your face every meal,' Bastian laughed.

As distant as he had been, it hadn't mattered to his friends. He lay in his bed that night, more peaceful than he had been for weeks. Even the surprising touch of Gertie who lay next to him, grabbing his hand was a sweet reminder that he wasn't alone. His grandfather had told him to look out for them, to rely on them. Bastian wished he'd done this sooner, the comfort not only from Gertie but from them all was everything he had nearly forgotten.

Gertie woke before Bastian; he felt her head on his shoulder leave his side. He didn't move, it was too early to wake up. She sat back by him only to wake him.

'Professor Harker was at the door for you,' she whispered.

They were the only ones awake in their room.

'What do you mean, why is he here?' Bastian asked, struggling to get up.

'He didn't say. He just said to tell you to meet him in the kitchens,' Gertie yawned.

Bastian sat up, he still felt half asleep but dragged himself up putting on a jumper and long pants before he made his way up to the dining hall.

The double-wide entrance to the kitchens was open, it was usually locked up at night even though he and Felix used to sneak in there at least once a week to fill up on snacks for the week ahead.

There were usually three elderly women who did all the cooking, None spoke, and they each wore the same grey uniform. He didn't know if they had once been Guardians or how long they had belonged to the compound, but they always smiled whenever they came out of the doors to greet them. They were sweet and gentle; motherly. He felt bad for taking extras, he never wanted to get them in trouble, but they seemed happy to give away food.

Bastian stared around the dark kitchen now, none of the women were here, without the warmth of those women the kitchen was left cold. His grandfather was at the far end taking fruit out of a large bowl.

'Grandfather?' Bastian said.

'Ah Bastian. Yes, you're here. Wonderful.

'I'll be with you in a moment. I just need... ah, here we go,' his grandfather said, finding a loaf of bread in the pantry, putting it into a bag along with the fruit he'd put onto the table in front of him.

'That'll do,' he said, zipping up the bag. Making his way to Bastian.

'Sorry to wake you. Take this.' He handed him an envelope, but his attention still seemed a million miles away. The front of the envelope read *Bastian Conway*. He opened it up to see his grandfather's writing, and a folded map enclosed.

Bastian looked up at his grandfather.

'What is this?' he asked.

'Bastian my boy. I understand our meeting was a tad confusing. I told you to keep an eye out for the Guardians. However, little did I know the time for that has passed,' his grandfather said, more than a little scattered.

'I'm leaving tonight,' he said, leaving Bastian shocked.

'What. Why?' Bastian asked.

'News has reached me, and I can't stay any longer. The Guardians are vulnerable, this compound is being watched by the Grinnwick Guard. Who knows how long it'll be before they make their move on us; if I stay and we're overwhelmed, if they get their hands on me the Guard will know too much. If they got me, who knows what measures they'd go to, to get information out of me. If they'd use the other students, I couldn't put them in harm's way like that,' his grandfather spoke frantically, and his stance was uneasy.

'What will you do? Where are you gonna go? You're just going to leave them to defend themselves?' Bastian asked.

'No. No. No… Emmett is going to slowly distribute them out to safe houses over the next couple of days. He will start first thing in the morning and remain until everyone is gone. I'll be safe, I have an old steading far away from here that has been in our family since before I was born. I have written the address in the letter in case you need to find me,' he said.

'Am I supposed to stay here? How long will you be gone for?' Bastian asked.

'I'm not coming back boy. Sir Dash has already gone. I have destroyed all articles that may be of value and put volumes from our library in a truck with the help of Emmett to keep safe.

'I have organised the safe houses, so all Emmett and Ms Madlyn need to do is organise the children, and advise the other teachers when necessary. You won't stay either.'

'But you brought me here to be a Guardian. I haven't even graduated yet,' Bastian stated.

'You are a Guardian. Every one of you is. There's no point waiting another half a year to graduate when this place might be gone by then. The Guardians compound; this facility will no longer remain. Besides, I have my own mission for you, one that is more important to the Guardians cause.'

Bastian's mind raced; he half thought his grandfather had gone mad.

'What do you want me to do?' Bastian asked.

'Find the Heart of Grinnwick.'

Bastian wasn't sure he was serious. He even let out a gruff sort of laugh in reaction.

'I understand that it's hard to believe, especially after I encourage the notion that The Heart is only a myth, that it was a basis of why we hide in the shadows, for its protection.'

'But it's possibility has come to light. Somehow, there are signs no one has seen or heard of that are only relevant to the Heart. This magic, it's real. The books, the creatures and beings that we have taught you all about are real, whether you believe in them or not. Magic is out there, it is a part of our world, only it's retreated so deep into our world that iy has become that of make believe. Yet, you yourself have witnessed some remnants of it; in princess Ava, the power around her, I saw it in the way you spoke of her to Dawson, that force that she held there was something undoubtedly mystical about it... wasn't there? And the Heart of Grinnwick is the drive that formed all these magics, from the start of creation. I know you've read the myths—'

'Yeah myths,' Bastian butted in.

'You don't see it yet, but I have faith in it's light, in its power. The connections since the princess's death have been undeniably lighting up, and all my sources seem to be leading me to the Isles of Perdita.'

'Look here,' he moved to the map pointing to the north, above the out-skirting districts. Bastian saw an outline of the cluster of islands on a piece of stencil paper that lay above the map.

'Perdita's made up of a cluster of isles. Although it main island is believed to be a larger island at the centre of the cluster. It's not on any maps, as it's a folk tale, a thing of storybooks, something people I believe the source seems to be coming from those northern isles. The isles are on no other maps in Grinnwick, so hold on tightly to the one enclosed in that envelope.

'What source? how can you know there's power coming from there?' Bastian asked.

His grandfather almost childishly smiled at him, beaming with positivity at Bastians question, 'See now, such power in terms of magic can only be seen through changes to the environment, like force that attracting events, whether they are positive or negative is dependent on the phase of the power source. Western towns, much like your own little hometown has been dealt a years of prosper for their crops, such perfect conditions have even put them on the map of the Grinnwick Guards interest. There have been flourishes of growth beginning from the very place you call home. That flourish of harvests through to the north, up in the outer districts, places that have been deserted landscapes for centuries, are now starting to grow… and beyond the outer districts, as north as you can possibly imagine, is the isles of Perdita. A place no man has visited before.'

-'than how do they know it's there? And what of Bellevue, what exactly is it that you know grandfather?' Bastian butted in. Alarm bells sent his head into a spin, but still wanting to know every piece of information.

'Your mother is fine; your home is fine. I do not believe the Grinnwick Guard are looking into as closely as I. However, their good fortune has put them on the radar – I have been in communication with your mother for some time to ensure she is prepared, and ready to flee should the time come.' These words alone weren't enough to calm Bastian. Who felt himself completely distracted.

'You can't know that, how could you? They could be there now, she could be there alone, defenceless.' Bastian blared, feeling the anger build inside of him.

'Look at me boy,' his grandfather pulled his face towards him, breaking through the manic of Bastians own mind.

'She is safe, your mother is strong, she has been keeping an eye out for signs of them, and there has yet to be one in your town, or close by village.

'You can't leave her there alone, I can't,' Bastian warned, a madness in him had stirred out of nowhere.

'I won't, I never have. I have an inside man at Bellevue Point, and he is as skilled as any of us, names Joesph Monroe. He has always been there since the day she arrived, and will remain as a sleeper at her location in case of any emergency. He is one of us, you can trust it is Monroe who will guide her to safety if needed, that I promise you.

'If that rightly satisfies you, let's get back to the signs from the Heart of Grinnwick,' his grandfather began. Bastian listened intently, but his mind practically bled hatred. His mind felt fixed like that of a bull. His grandfather had once again become the man who cared not for his family, who abandoned his mother all those years ago, with his fixation entirely on work. Bastian was just a tool for his grandfather to continue.

'…Sailors who've survived the turbulent waters of the north, not that there have been many, but a few saw the outline of the isles before they were washed up back on the shores of the mainland.

'I need you to go and find these isles. You must search the lands that most men wouldn't dare go to. Nothing about getting there is set to be easy; the seas are rough, and no sailor would go through them in their right mind. You must find one though, you have to find it before the rumours that reached me, reach the wrong people.

'If I'm right, and you come across the Heart, protect it at all costs. From what I have read, it is not what it seems; some kind of trinket, or stone I presume, with magic to protect itself. As much as I'd like to go myself I can't.

'I'm too old to take this journey, the journey alone may be the end of me. I don't have the strength like you to push through whatever this world throws at you. In truth you are the only one I can entrust with this,' he claimed, almost manic.

'Grandfather, I still don't understand. What have you found? What makes you think it's there? The Heart of Grinnwick could still be just a myth, this could be a wild goose chase,' Bastian said, he could tell his grandfather believed so strongly. His mind so fixated on the Heart of Grinnwick, yet Bastian couldn't get a handle on why it was so important.

'Son.' His grandfather sighed. 'look, I know this is a stretch for you to believe me on. But the land we know has been stirring, things that have long been dead, have awoken. My contacts in the outer districts have each spoken of signs. Creatures that people have not seen before are reappearing... one man sent word that he saw mermaids return to the Emerald Harbour only two full moons ago. There's more rain, more crops in the outer districts. I've contacted multiple people, a couple of them being in some of the furthest reaches we could find. Many said things I couldn't quite make sense of.

One said that it has been a long time since the sea had been so at ease. A small sign indeed, but the seas have been at unease for such a long time, and there are paths that not even the most daring man would navigate that are now free of worry.

As I reached out further, I got a reply from an old friend that said, "Perdita holds the key". Strange a place as any, on the far side of the outer districts, practically unreachable by man. Why would anyone think of it as the home of a most precious power source? Of what the Guardians originally devoted to protecting.

However, he sent the map that supposedly held the precise location of Perdita. His message said history holds tales that connect it to old stories of magic of how Grinnwick came to be, and perhaps these stories hold some truth.

'Another friend messaged me telling me something unknown to many: that the Heart was originally found in the sea. Which would explain why Perdita, being an island, is a likely location for the Heart of Grinnwick.

'Finally, I got a warning; "It is what keeps this world balanced. Do not search for such treasures, for they are as tempting and treacherous as they are magnificent."

'I know I told you that you could go home soon to be with your mother, and I wish I could tell you too. But right now Grinnwick needs someone, and perhaps that someone is you?

If others have read these signs and believe like I do that Perdita will again be the place where the Heart can be found, then they will too be searching. And they may not be as good as you are my boy. They may not have pure intentions when it comes to using it to draw Grinnwick back into a golden age.'

Bastian looked at his grandfather; as much as it was to take in, it seemed that his grandfather truly believed in the Heart of Grinnwick. That it was possibly more than a myth, a legend. The idea seemed wild. It was the largest adventure the small boy inside of him could have ever hoped for, a true quest. Yet, he wasn't sure he was ready for another mission. Not yet. He was still reeling from the last one. But the heat inside him filled of anger was extinguished, he wasn't mad, he'd calmed down to realise that his grandfather was entrusting this to him. His mother was in safe hands until the day he'd return to her, and perhaps this power, this Heart of Grinnwick was the key to keeping her and all of his friends safe.

'It's okay, I'll go grab the others. I'll have the Ravens ready to go before sun—'

'No,' interrupted his grandfather.
'You must go alone.'

'I can't. I need them, they're my team, my friends. They will hate me for going alone.' Bastian said.

'I know you trust the Ravens. This task though will be a burden on anyone who takes it. The time it may take, the type of life you may have to live until the time comes, until you can find your way to The Heart. It is one you can't coordinate amongst others. It will be hard enough getting yourself to the Heart, let alone a whole squad. If only for their sakes, knowing that the more that are with you, perhaps the less will return. In your case, much like your mother I know you'd want them somewhere safe.

Bastian took a moment, nodding. Of course that's what he wanted, he wanted everyone safe.

'You must make haste son, leave as soon as you can. This is the last mission I give to you son. You alone, and you are a fine guardian, but an even better man. You will have strength when it comes to protecting the secrets of this world, you need to find them and keep them close my boy. And if you find the Heart, you must protect it from the world.

'I have sent word to a Guardian amongst the men of Sildor, the mountain miners, that you will be joining them. It is the closest town on the edge of Grinnwick in the outer districts to the Isles of Perdita. Getting passage across the sea will be far more difficult than it looks, it is made to protect itself from man, but you my boy must find a way.

'While you search lay low within the miners. They are tough, and gruesomely rough, but they look after their own. Listen out, because you may just hear of a way across. The universe will find you a way, make sure you listen out for the signs, and you will get there. Don't fret it may take more time than you realise.'

'But I can't leave the others here, not if the compound could be ambushed soon,' Bastian said, he hated himself for even thinking of leaving them.

'You must. You don't want to alert anyone that we are onto the Guard infiltrating us so tell them, I said for them all to take a holiday – each of them should head home. Don't talk of my concerns for the Guardians, after all you can't ever be a hundred percent certain when there are spies in our midst. Don't tell them of your mission either, just in case.

'All of you leave at first light. Do you understand? There's a transport for you all to get to the nearest town, just head south of here. Leave on your mission from there,' his grandfather advised, handing Bastian a bag of gold.

Bastian looked at the bag he was now holding and then up at his grandfather, scared after these past few years that this might be the last time he saw him.

'Grab some food and go,' he said before quickly hugging Bastian. 'I fear that stranger times fall ahead of us all,' he said, before dashing out of the kitchen.

Bastian stood frozen for a moment. He pulled out the letter; it had the address on it, and below was a passage.

Fidelis Estate, Montgomery

Bastian, stay true to the boy you were and the man you have become. Remember there is a world of unimaginable possibilities that you have yet scratched the surface of.

You are so much more than a guardian. Use this map well, and find out the mysteries of our world, one Harker should be taking this trip, and I'm happy it'll be you. Good Luck.

Your Grandfather, August.

***

Waking everyone up and handing them bags of food while telling them that they were all finally lucky enough to go on holiday wasn't as easy as it sounded. It was lying to each of them, especially when he didn't want to pain them. He hated that he couldn't let them in on where he was really going, or why they really had to leave. Gertie and Verne especially would have hated him if they knew. He pushed their future hatred aside from his mind. He not only had them in his thoughts, but he was also leaving behind the other squads, Guardians who were much smaller than he was, none of them knowing a potential downfall was heading to them. Their fates lay with Emmett, and Ms Madlyn. They would hopefully all be dispersed back to their homes in the coming days.

Gertie turned to him.

'Bastian, this is great. But where exactly am I supposed to take this trip 'home'? And not just me, but Russ too. He doesn't even know where his dad's ship is, and Mandy's father could be anywhere. Are we supposed to go sit somewhere for a couple of weeks and drink wine?' she said mockingly.

Bastian nearly forgot, before Verne jumped in.

'Don't be silly. You're all more than welcome to come with me. It'll be great having everyone at the farm, well if you want to that is,' Verne said, putting his arm around Mandy and kissing her on the cheek. He didn't question the news of leaving at such short notice. The idea of home on his blissful farm got him up and about in just a couple of moments. A few of the others definitely questioned the spontaneity of Bastian's news, but none of them did much to go against the chance at a break.

Gertie looked at Bastian as if he would say something.

'Yes, you should all go with Verne, that would be great. I'm off to see my mum, can't wait to see how surprised she'll be when I turn up home,' he added, slightly distracted, noticing he sounded a little neurotic. He tried not to take notice of Gertie's disappointment in him not wanting to spend the holiday with her.

'Yeh, I think I'll go home too; my mother would be over the moon to see me. Best you guys go to Verne's. Too many guards down my way,' Rudi added.

'Easy, well we'll all get to the closest town, I've been told it's just south of here. And we can all find our own ways from there.'

'Umm, how long do we get to take, did your gramps say?' Russ asked.

'Oh. He said they will send word when we are needed back, you know him, talks in circles that man. He's gone away as well so we get to enjoy our break,' Bastian said, feeling as scattered as his grandfather was before.

'What about the other squads?' Rudi asked. 'Is my brother going home?' he asked.

'No. Just us, I think everyone other squad gets time off like this after a while. And this is our turn,' Bastian said, he wondered just how many lies he could get away with. But mostly he tried not to look at Gertie because she was the one who would get the truth out, with just one of her looks.

'I didn't think we got that time until after we graduate,' Gertie questioned.

'Yes, well things got moved up it seems. Truth is, it's because of me. Because I struggled so much with our last mission, he wanted me to get some time, said I needed it to be a Guardian again,' Bastian replied, trying to act as convincing as possible.

He passed out the food and drinks he'd taken from the kitchen, and raced them all upstairs, making sure not to be seen by any other prying guardians who might be up early. They found the mover waiting topside, the keys in it ready to go, making the fact that they were indeed leaving real for them all.

The excitement built up as they left the Guardian's compound behind them. He knew a lot of them trusted in him enough to follow him, but didn't know if they really believed his story.

Bastian wished he could tell them everything. Not to go back once he was gone, without giving away anything. He sat there quietly as Verne drove down the dirt track, the wind blowing in his hair.

There was a calm, relaxed side to him compared to their drive back from Astoria. Sitting back, Bastian decided to relax with Gertie asleep on his shoulder and Russ explaining to him the mechanics of his hand-made gun that he decided to bring along. As Gertie slept, he pushed a note into her jacket, one that read, *Don't return, the compound is compromised, look after yourselves. Bass.*

Knowing that he had at least left a message, Bastian enjoyed the last few hours with his friends as the sun rose across the horizon beside them, wishing beyond anything that he could be joining them on Verne's farm, or taking them all back to his small home in Bellevue Point.

Pondering the path ahead, his fear mixed with anxious excitement at what would await him. The Guardian's compound was no longer his home, and the people who had become his family he was leaving behind, perhaps forever. He had done this once before, and the feeling was the same, though this time he did it for a mission. Not ordered by the Guardians but by his grandfather alone. The question he posed to himself; did he really believe the myths of The Heart of Grinnwick were true?

The End of the Beginning.

It was only one wobbling book that sent the piles around Scarlet tumbling down, and a whirlwind of dust breaking out in her wake. Leaving Scarlet shocked, coughing and squinting her eyes from the dust, surrounded by the multiple book piles that had fallen around her. Monroe could be heard groaning as he made his way closer to her.

'What have you done now?' he asked; she hated his tone of annoyance.

Scarlet had been deep in organising some of the older book collections in the store when the piles had consumed her. Now, all she could think of with the mess around her was that she would have to start her organising the whole section again.

Lux swooped in and pulled her out of the books that surrounded her.

Both ignoring Monroe who sounded as though he was muttering his frustrations under his breath while frantically picking up the books all on the floor.

Scarlet dusted herself off and shook the dust from her hair. Which was already in a messy bun atop of her head.

'I hate it when that happens,' she coughed and laughed at the same time, 'don't get your nice dress covered in filth,' Scarlet warned Lux, who was dressed in a beautifully wrapped lavender satin dress that had a hem of ruffles at the bottom.

'Well, if you weren't so clumsy, I wouldn't have too!' Lux mocked.

Scarlet looked down at the mess around her, she'd been filtering through the titles while organising the books into their categories, a task that Monroe himself was never fond of doing.

'Alright, turn around – let's make sure there's no marks on the dress,' Scarlet insisted to Lux, partly teasing, but still wanted to check – she knew how nervous Lux was. Out of the two of them Lux had certainly moved away from her desire to adventure outdoors, becoming quite relaxed toward continuing her fighting skills; she'd become more intwined in the town's societal scene. Her confidence had built over the years, all from being a part of the dazzling mayors parties and mingling with the young members of the high-standing families, she was very much a part of the clique. She had managed to charm herself into their circles; Scarlet often thought some of them saw her as a token outsider, to make them seem more accepting over others outside of their family groups. Perhaps that's why whenever Lux had invited Scarlet into their group outings she never accepted, part of her thought they seemed a little surface level. But to Lux, being accepted was all she wanted – and as she turned the green and white stripes skirt that slightly blew up towards her knee as she did, she seemed pleasantly happy. The outfit itself gave her an elegance of style and highlighted how stunning a young woman she'd become. Her brown skin glowed and had grown even more radiant with the years that had passed. Small dark freckles now covered her nose and cheeks, and she had her hair cut just above her shoulders. Lux really had become the bell of any occasions; her days of practice fighting were now long behind her. Scarlet wasn't usually the sort for dresses and parties; Lux often called her the earthy one, which irked her in the sense that there was so much more to her than just a love of nature. The truth being she only wished she had the confidence that Lux had when it came to integrating with the towns people, sometimes she thought that perhaps her differences made her feel the need to keep out of the spotlight. The desire to put on a dress was inside of her, to feel beautiful, to stand out. But in truth the years had passed, and she still had zero understanding of the power inside of her, it has presented randomly through her enacting small forces of nature, or visions that she saw. Although they had become more frequent, but most of the time they were such small events that she never even mentioned them. The latest being a few days ago when she accidently felt the burst of energy rush through her, but it didn't escape her, and for a split second she felt as if she was surrounded by fire, the markets around her in ruins. A weight held down on her chest in that scene, before she returned to where she was. A memory, a flicker of the future, the dark ones she didn't like to hold onto, some of the ones that had been brought into her vision since leaving the Amari had been terrorising, so she liked to separate them from reality as much as possibly constantly reminding herself that they weren't real. However, it left her spacey at times, and not conducive to making outside friendships as well as Lux had.

While it wasn't unusual for Lux to prepare herself at Monroes for an outing, tonight was a first date. And Scarlet could tell from her fidgeting all day that it meant a lot.

'Would you hate if I left early? I'd love to stop by Nora's and see if she has any earrings for me before the date,' Lux asked her.

'Of course not, do you think Monroe wants either of us here anyway?' Scarlet assured her, enjoying the beam smile she got in return.

'Thanks,' Lux hugged her.

'Lux's is headed out' Scarlet called back to Monroe, who nodded and waved her off barely paying attention. Scarlet turned back to her shaking her head at his rudeness.

'Don't worry about him. Go, have fun.' Scarlet said, walking to grab her a coat, helping it on, and pulled the hood over her head.

'We'll be fine,' Scarlet promised her, 'Go!' she said opening the door, and watched Lux go out into the gloomy looking rain. It was so eerie sort of day today with a low laying fog on drizzling rain, like the sky was sad, so much so that it gave her chills. Ignoring the feeling of unease as Lux ran out into dreary weather Scarlet closed the door and returned to restack the fallen books on the ground. Thankfully many of the piles had landed together so she separated each of the groups she'd made. One on herbal cooking, another on ailments and the body, and another on history.

Scarlet noted these categories to Monroe so he could help find them a correct home amongst the shelves.

'You know, you should be going out with Miss Watts. With all the books on adventures you read, why not head out and have one yourself; you might actually enjoy it.' Monroe said.

Scarlet couldn't even look at him, she'd heard the same thing from him time and time before. Ignoring him she just kept her head down taking to books from their piles and making them a home.

'You hide behind these books, your family, tucking yourself away in that cottage, only stepping out on your once weekly visits here, or when visiting Nora and the boys,' Monroe stated.

'I get out,' Scarlet said, mostly trying to convince herself.

'You get out and explore the forest, the beaches, but how much do you interact with others,' he asked her.

Scarlet still didn't reply.

'Look, all I'm saying is Dawsons gone again, right? He took the other boy with him. Their out, whatever it is that they're up to, but my point being they're not stuck here, living the same life as usual.

'Look at you - hair up in a messy bun, dust and dirt all over you from head to toe, and don't say you don't usually look like that, you are a mess every time I see you, that's no way for a lady like yourself to be enjoying her youth. You should be out, having fun. Being cooped up in here won't get you far in life.'

Scarlet looked to him, 'Maybe I'm just happy just here. I don't need all that… excitement,' she noted, trying to convince herself more than anything.

Seeing Monroe look completely unconvinced, 'I promise, I'm not made for that sort of lifestyle. Besides, I don't won't to stick out like a toad amongst all those fancy pants townies.'

It was the truth. Monroe may not know about her abilities, he but he knew that she wasn't exactly comfortable in group situations. He knew that as a family they feared exposure, that Dawson wanted a simple easy life for each of them.

That wasn't all either, the fear of the Grinnwick Guard had grown amongst them over the years the threats to surrounding villages of Bellevue Point had been increasing drastically of late. With no warning of their presence, just the dramatic outreach of violence; the guard did not care for keeping survivors, their interest in the land wasn't in controlling the people, but in acquiring the land for themselves. The soldiers themselves practically mindless from what Scarlet had heard. In the months that had recently passed Monroe had warned them since Dawson left to have themselves prepared in case Bellevue Point came onto their radar. And from his tone, Scarlet was sure he knew something he wasn't letting on. He had become fidgeting, packing away into his personal collection some of the oldest books he had. So, the truth for Scarlet was that reaching out to others, and socialising was the last thing she felt she should do - in this world completely void of magic, where it had long ago been shunned so far inward that it was practically forgotten. It wasn't a place where she could flourish or understand what she was. Archer had that at least, being an Amari, growing up there he understood his capabilities, he knew exactly how he differed and how to hide it in this world. Whatever capabilities she had, it was the lack of trust in herself to draw attention, and her fear mounted and possibility of someone outside of their circle would notice her differences only then to manipulate her, and the what ifs from there often overwhelmed her like a heavy wall of anxiety.

'Fear is everywhere, but I promise you. Life was meant for more than just existing,' Monroe noted.

Scarlet thought of what Dawson would say to that, he was always full of warning, most notoriously towards Scarlet, but Archer as well. *'Best just come straight home;' 'you can't let anyone get too close or they might sense your difference;' 'don't force your powers;' 'try to keep your emotions levelled in public, you don't want to cause a commotion.'*

It was comments like these that had undoubtedly consumed Scarlet's mind against pursuing more of a life beyond that of her family, as well as Nora and Monroe, plus a few older stallholders that she'd come to like down near Winslow's hall.

Scarlet couldn't deny it that with Dawson away, and this being for a third time this was a chance to explore without feeling remorse for acting outside of his guidelines.

Shaking off the feeling, there was no need to rebel against his wishes, the thought was entirely ridiculous. What would she do, go out with Lux, get dressed up just to hang out with the so-called fancy folk. No.

She wasn't against Dawsons plan to have her stay out of harm's way, he only wanted her safe, that's all she wanted too.

Yet the unknown of when he would return, and in truth the possibility of if he would; as every passing day made his departure longer and longer than the last time; that was something she certainly didn't like to think about.

His absence took its toll on her most of all, while Lux and Hudson continued to thrive even when he was away.

Dawson's first trip two years ago. From the night he told them he was going to set out, that he wanted to find his old home; that he needed to come to terms with the fact that it was truly gone. They'd been in their cottage at that point for six years all together, they understood his need to find answers, and encouraged him. Scarlet could tell he'd been stuck in a time lost to him. He spent countless nights looking at the book that Flynn had made, like he wished it into reality, and unless is was to be by their side he'd barely go out, never socialising (not that she could talk- but she made small efforts to go to Monroe's shop, to head to the market when she could). But she wanted him to be present in this world, in the life that was ahead of him. Her memory loss to not be held back by the past, something she had come to truly appreciate. The past for her was what drove her brother away; a life and time that would be nothing more than a story. But for Dawson the journey was something he had needed for years, to finally see what relics remained from his past. To put together the pieces of what came after he left.

When he came home to them, a light within him opened up to them, eager to share bits of his past. He brought home a large piece of material that had a stitched image of an old stone castle nestled amongst greenery of a forest valley.

The picture now hung across the wall of their cottage. Since it did Scarlet thought he seemed much more settled in his surrounds, he had even attended the wedding of Nora a year ago. Nora still held a sweet spot for him - the way she blushed when he was around always made Scarlet and Lux giggle. But there were always things about Dawson that they would never know, a past that he withheld from them. She wondered at times how much it had to do with her own lost family, how he fit into that picture. But with the passing years she had tried to let those thoughts go, the fact was he was here now, he along with Lux, Hudson and Archer were her family. Yet she was sure he held onto the love of another, she saw it in his eyes when he had quiet moments to himself, she hoped that perhaps his journey home would have put whoever it was in the past – but love like that was something she didn't quite understand.

The second time he set out he didn't divulge much information, and no matter how much they prodded or poked he could not be broken – that is except for a small insight he did tell Scarlet before he left – that if that trip went well, he may have word of Flynn. Something that she hadn't had hope for in a long time. Their search in Bellevue had reached nothing but dead ends since the first retrieval of his belongings from Monroe, which now felt like a lifetime ago. The promise Dawson had made to her to help find her brother had bound them both, and Dawson had held onto hope just as much as she did with reuniting with him.

On his return he brought no answers, not words of sighting, only a solemn warning about Van Helm and the Grinnwick Guard. He didn't make too much of it, but had spent quite a bit of time down at Winslow's after – Scarlet suspected working with him on his rebel plans.

On his most recent departure Dawson had requested Archer join on his trip to the far side of Grinnwick, a trip that he had no knowledge of how long it would take. Only noting that Archer's senses as an Amari fae would be of assistance to him in his journey.

So now she was without her best friend, without her protector, her everyday life starting to feel quieter in their absence.

The door chimed, and Scarlet's attention was drawn to a very damp and dirty, and bloody Hudson.

'What happened?' She asked, taken aback and shocked.

Monroe dropped the books this time, with a large sigh – 'do you kids ever let an old man have a quiet moment.'

Scarlet ignored him, rushing over to Hudson's side as he sat in the chair next to the counter and wiped his shirt across his bloodied head. It was a large gash across its side. Scarlet went to the back room of the shop and poured some water from Monroes private kitchen onto a clean cloth.

Dashing back out to Hudson she pushed his hand aside, and placed the clean cloth a top of the gash applying pressure.

'Well?' she asked again.

'Well, what!' he barked backed.

'Don't bite my head off, just tell me what happened to you.' Scarlet demanded.

'Sorry,' he replied,

'Well, the rain is notably the reason you're looking like a wet mop,' Scarlet comment, 'but that has nothing to do with the blood on your head, and the dirt all over you. Did you fall somewhere on your way into town?' she asked. Hudson wasn't clumsy at all, so it was a slightly sarcastic, but she knew it would make him bite. To her delight she wasn't wrong, as the look of annoyance covered his face at the mere mention of him having such a trivial accident.

'So… what happened?' she demanded.

'That brute Amos, I swear his ego is bigger than his brain cells,' Hudson said.

'He did this?' Scarlet interrupted.

'Yeah… I was down at Winslow's Hall,' he started.

'What were you doing down there?' Scarlet asked. She hated when he went down there, most of them thought themselves to be rebels against the Grinnwick Guard, but whenever she went into the hall it only ever seemed like a place for drunken travellers who were sad and lonely – noting to herself it was never a place for a lady to go alone.

'What do you think, I was checking with Winslow for any updates… someone's got to with Dawon still off gallivanting.'

'Jealous, much?' Scarlet mocked.

'Don't pretend you're not,' Hudson noted back, 'Anyway, I was down there, and this traveller was loitering out the front. He looked a bit beaten, but mostly exhausted, so I tried to help him inside. But Amos blocked me

– '*we don't want his kind in ere,*' he said. Hudson rolled his eyes. - '*he's one of them,*' he added.

'I have no idea what he was on about – I had one arm helping the guy up and tried to get past him. But he pushed us both back, and the poor man just fell to the ground… So-,' Hudson went to continue.

'So, you got up in his face, and ended up like this…' Scarlet added, a little smile on her face for Dawsons predictability.

'Basically, but he's much worse off than I am.'

'Who was the man?' Monroe pipped in.

'Don't know, once we we're separated someone said they'd already taken him inside. Winslow would have had enough on his hand without dealing with me – seeing me fight with one of his men would have set the meeting off to a bad start anyway – so I never even went in, besides thought I'd better get this head seen to by the likes of you lot.'

'Strange,' muttered Monroe.

'What?' Hudson asked.

'Strange why Amos thought the man to be so different – after all that's what Winslow does, take in stragglers from the road, helping them find means of a better life.

'So, what was it about that man that Amos deemed unworthy of that help,' Monroe questioned.

'I – I don't know,' Hudson added plainly, 'he looked just like any other traveller, and he wasn't different in any way I could tell, no noticeable difference, he was just like any other man.'

Scarlet turned to look at Monroe, what was he thinking, did he know something about Amos objections to the man.

She wondered perhaps if the man was some sort of creature, or being like the ones who were supposedly hidden in the depths of the world, much like the Amari fae – after all Archer was now a pivotal part of Grinnwick; he, a being unlike the world had truly had in their presence for centuries… or perhaps he was not the only one.

'Just thoughts of an old man,' Monroe added, 'why don't you two head to Nora's, she'll have some ointment to put on that head of yours, and I'm sure she'll have dinner on for you too.'

***

Against the darkness of the growing evening the windows outside of Noras townhouse in the northern side of town, inside sparked brightly of warm colours. As they entered, dozens of family photos hung along the hallway, generations of Monroes beamed at them. Scarlet loved to visit Nora's; it was everything she could have dreamed of in a home. Full of love, cheer, and cosy like a big blanket on a cold day. She wished that theirs could be as bright and welcoming, but without Dawson and Archer it seemed drearier than usual.

Screams of joy came from the far end of the home. Walter came running down the hallway, reaching Scarlet first and jumping straight into her arms.

'Aunty Scar,' Walter cried for joy with his deep brown eyes and the same curls at the end of his hair that Nora had.

'You've grown, little man. I don't think I can carry you anymore,' Scarlet laughed, his smile always made the worries of the world slip away.

'I grew a whole two metres since you last saw me,' Walter said proudly.

'I think you'll find that's centimetres, my love,' Nora added, welcoming Scarlet and Hudson.

Her husband, Nicholas waved from in the kitchen stirring whatever was in the pot for their dinner. A pleasant man, polite and sweet, who's abilities in the kitchen were always exceeding any expectations.

Walter jumped onto Hudson as soon as Scarlet put him back down.

'She's not lying Wally. It felt like only a week ago it was much easier to pick you up. Surely you can't be four, can you? This is the size of a five-year-old,' Hudson said, winding up little Walter who reassured him he was only four.

'How are you both?' Nora said, bringing them both in towards the kitchen table. Scarlet saw a picture on their wall of herself with Dawson, Lux, Archer and Hudson that they'd taken years ago a few months after they'd first arrived. Photographs were something none of them had been familiar with – Archer wasn't the only once intrigued by the contraption; that first photo captured their curiosities more than anything as not one of them understood they had to smile.

'Well, you can see Hudson needs a bit of tending too – run in with Amos. Classic. And Lux is off on her big date, but apart from that we are doing well,' Scarlet said.

Nora shook her head at Hudson, pulling the wound closer for her to inspect before running off getting some cream and bandages for it.

Hudson had Walter up in his arms spinning and laughing together, Scarlet joined in tickling little Walter as he turned and turned.

'Stop that you three, or you'll turn your tummies before dinner,' Nicholas noted to them, 'I presume your both staying to eat?'

'If you don't mind, we'd love to,' Scarlet replied, while Hudson put Walter down.

'Of course, please do! There's always extra here for you; you both know that,' Nora chimed in, then forced Hudson to sit so she could tend to Scarlet's head.

'How have you been feeling?', she asked Scarlet while she cleared the gash on Hudson's head.

Scarlet wasn't too sure what to say. It had been a couple of weeks since she had collapsed now. She still felt embarrassed from the whole ordeal, and part of her didn't like to think about it. Usually, her health of all things was never a problem. Her happiness – that had been all over the shop in the last couple of years; in truth, she felt stuck; stuck in this small town, feeling like the days were on repeat. It was exhaustingly boring. But inside she was unsure of how she felt – not sick, only an eerie sensation in her gut that things weren't right. The whole situation had only made her worry about Dawson and Archer's absence more.

Not only that, it was since they'd left that unexplainable things started happening around her; like the fog that surrounded their home, or holding the kettle and the water spontaneously boiling while in her hand with no source of heat – undoubtedly a part of her mysterious power, but usually it wasn't so dangerous in the sense of nearly spilling boiling water on herself.

The day Scarlet fell ill was like any other; running through their daily activity – she was with Nora and the girls from St. Augustine's that Nora taught. They were going out to help plant crops for a farmer. She was halfway through telling the girls to go fill up their water bottles and grab hats when her breath caught, her head felt light, and her skin shivered. The sensation brought her falling to the ground out cold.

Since that day she had been left feeling cool and empty like a rain cloud was constantly surrounding her. From that afternoon a mist set in at their cottage, it was as though her surrounds were matching her insides – cloudy and lost. Spending time up on the cliffside was the only place in all of Bellevue Point that she managed to feel at ease again, breathing in the salt from the sea and the sprinkle of ocean helping her to breathe.

Forgetting that she still hadn't replied to Nora, Scarlet realised that nearly everyone's eyes were on her.

'You okay?' Hudson asked.

'Yes…' Scarlet began but the words were lost.

Blasts from an explosion rocked them all, knocking Scarlet to the ground. The glass from the front windows was shattered, and the power cut. Walter screamed echoed in her head, along with the screams bellowed from outside. Hudson and Nicholas ran to the window. Nora picked up Walter in her arms.

A thundering vibration set-in beneath them… a light of urgency swept through them all.

Scarlet looked up at the others around her.

She felt frozen, like she wasn't a part of the scene unveiling before her.

The blast knocked her, her vision was blurred; everything spinning. The warm tones of the room began to wash away before her, her mind lost in a haze of screaming and yelling. Swept off from the space before her to a distant void of darkness. Voices could be heard echoing down what she could only describe as a pitch-black hallway, and outline of it started to make shape. Their voice turned to painful cries, wanting desperately to reach out for them to grab hold of something, someone in this vision, but only felt herself falling.

'Breathe. You are not alone,' she heard a voice speak to her, the voice pulled her in, as if to hold her steady through the vision of the void, drowning out the screams through the blackness of the vision.

It repeated itself over and over...

Breathless, Scarlet's mind slowly returned to the mayhem before her.

Tears dripped down her cheek, but she hadn't remembered crying. Hudson was holding her. Had they all just seen what she had? Heard the voice?

In the corner of her eye Scarlet saw little Walter in Nora's arms looking around the room nervously. Scarlet had seen that look of concern before. This time it was more fear itself in the little boy's eyes. It wasn't because she'd collapsed, there were shots being fired in the distance. And Walter's scared look was mimicked in Nora's eyes as she held onto him tight.

'You okay?' Hudson asked Scarlet.

She nodded, unsure.

Scarlet turned back to the window where the loud noises still echoed, vibrating the walls around them.

'It's the Guard,' Nicholas said fearfully. 'They are making their move. Snuffing out any hope of resistance.'

'I told Winslow... I told him if he kept on making so much noise amongst the rebels that they'd find his hall, and target not only them but the town,' Nicholas cursed.

'I thought this place was protected,' Hudson bellowed at Nicholas and Nora.

'Don't be foolish. We were out of their way, that was all – out of their line of sight. We were never a threat. We kept word about our town to a minimum, held our own storages of Cor-Marinium from private sources. None of that means that it's impossible to find us, spies have been captured before, but we were never worth their time... until now,' Nicholas noted, still looking out the window, 'Surprise is always their best weapon, a show of force for everyone to fall in line.'

'We need to get out of here,' Hudson warned, he was still holding Scarlet up. She hadn't wanted to move just yet. There was so much going on in her mind and outside the front door, she felt frozen as though it was all too much for her to even comprehend.

'I think that might be a good idea. Nick, pack what you can from the cupboard; I'll grab our things,' Nora instructed in a light tone, almost a whisper. 'Wrap up the rest of the food too, we've barely touched it.'

'We can't go with you,' Scarlet said. She didn't know why; it would keep them safe if anything to have her and Hudson by them. But safety probably wasn't the direction they were headed in. Scarlet couldn't explain it, but whatever had been off within her, whatever she'd just witnessed in the vision, she needed answers.

Hudson agreed, 'You two go, head as far North as you can, stay off of the main paths. We've got to find Lux first, and get back to the cottage for some of our things. Hopefully, we'll cross paths with you all again. If not, be safe.

'You too Wally,' Hudson said, hugging both him and Nora.

Scarlet did the same, probably a little more rushed than she would have liked – after all she had no clue when they'd see them next. On top of that she still felt somewhat aloof after her vision, the screams down that dark

349

hallway were hard to forget; echoing in her mind, even with the current cries of commotion going on outside.

Hudson's eyes were still on Scarlet as they opened the door, holding on tightly to a portion of food Nicholas had wrapped up for them.

They could see fire growing atop of the building just a street over, and the noise of yelling and screaming was only getting louder. The street here had dozens of people fleeing before them. Nicholas pulled Hudson back and passed him an old fire weapon, holding it out ahead of them. Scarlet wondered if he even knew how to work the weapon, but he seemed sure in himself as his attentions swiftly diverted to the street ahead.

Together they stepped out into the street and were swept up into the fleeing townspeople, but still were yet to see a soldier. Amongst the mayhem Hudson pulled her to the side of one of the houses, hoping to take a breath.

'You okay?' he asked.

Scarlet nodded, an energy coursing through her as if she was in survival mode- Nora would have called it adrenaline.

'What happened to you in there?' Hudson added, holding Scarlet's hand tightly, trying his best to focus on her as the chaos erupted around them with the rumblings of another explosion going off what must have been a couple of streets over.

'Geez, at this rate their going to flatten the entire town, there'll be nothing left but rubble.' He said, before turning back to Scarlet for an answer.

'...I'm not sure exactly, I saw something, and I could hear something awful happening... and then a voice letting me know it would be okay,' she tried to explain. She wondered hopelessly whose screams were in her mind, and even more so whose voice she'd heard. She tried to hold onto their words.

Hudson quickly pulled her back further as a group of Soldiers ran down the street with guns filled with green Cor-Marinium. The glow of the weapon lighting up each soldier's location.

Taking a breath of release he turned back to her, grabbed out his hanky and wiped her cheeks; she hadn't even realised she'd been crying; she took it from him and continued to wipe them away. Looking down at the hanky she found they were blood red. She thought that maybe she hit her head when she collapsed, and was left with a scrape, but then realised that it was the colour of her tears. She felt her heart drop – what was wrong, what was happening to her.

'Scarlet. Scarlet. Scarlet,' Hudson said to her, trying to gain her attention, he didn't seem so shocked by the blood as her.

'This is serious, are you listening to me?'

(you've got to be kidding me, she thought. She was practically falling to pieces)

He turned her head to face the fires on the far side of town.

'The Guard is here, Scar. We have to move,' Hudson demanded, taking her arm, pulling her along. He didn't say anything else but walked at a steady pace, dodging the people and looking up and back down the street. He kept pausing in the shadows, checking for guards. She couldn't speak – she felt stunned.

She wanted to be at home in their cottage, hiding from everything, but Hudson wasn't leading them that way. Scarlet allowed him to pull her along, ducking when he said to, moving as he did.

351

'Ouch.' Lux cried, picking up her bag and brushing her satin lavender dress down. Their momentum around a corner had knocked her over. She was accompanied by Alwyn; her date, he was one of the Mayor's nephews. He was a handsome man, with a moustache that was thick considering his still younger age – he was dressed in a fine suit that was expected of a young man in his position, and he held a pistol not to unlike the one Hudson held.

'Sorry, didn't mean to. Just trying to get through,' Hudson said, nearly as if he didn't register it was Lux.

She came running straight for them both, as soon as she realised, hugging them. Still stunned Scarlet felt the hug as a sense of release, and felt the tears flowing more down her cheeks.

'What's that on your face?' she gasped.

'Theres no time Lux, I'm glad we found you but we gotta keep moving,' he cautioned.

'Lux,' chimed in Alwynn. 'You can come with me, my uncle he has transport out of here. You all can.'

Lux looked awkwardly to him, 'You're very kind to offer Al, but I need to go with my family. Stay safe okay,' she said, then kissed him on the cheek. He smiled back at her before pulling away into the darkness. Scarlet felt almost bad for the guy, he was sweeter than she thought.

He was just around the bend when they heard shots firing in that direction.

Scarlet's heart sank; surely it hadn't been him – it couldn't be.

The shots continued, Lux pulled to run around and check, but Hudson held her back.

'Don't do it to yourself – we need to find our own way out.'

The fear in his eyes reflected hers.

'Where are we going, this isn't the way out of town?' Scarlet said quietly, it was almost a whisper.

'The bookshop.' he answered.

Pushing past in the opposite direction of the firing, they made their way to the street of the bookshop – eerily the explosions and shots seemed distant, yet there was a dusty haze to the air along and the light from the fires growing on the northern side of town lit the sky with a foreboding glow. They dashed through puddles that were left from the rain earlier. A cool breeze brushed past Scarlet's hair as they cot closer. The sign above squeaked while Hudson knocked heavily on the wooden door.

A concerned Monroe pulled the heavy door slightly ajar. Eying them through the gap, he took in the loud noises from the town around them. His eyes big and darting across the building tops to the north.

'Get yourselves out of here,' he barked.

'Dawson said that if I needed to, I could bring Scarlet here. He said you would be able to help,' Hudson claimed.

Not recalling Dawson saying any of these things to Hudson, her confusion only increased.

Monroe sighed. 'Come in then,' he urged, ushering them both inside, looking out to the street which had started to fill up with people scurrying to get out of town. He had been packing his own backpack full of old clothes and water, all his items laid on the table ready to be put in.

'Were Nora and the boys okay?' he asked curtly.

'They were leaving there just as we did – I told them to stay off the main roads. But there's a lot of commotion out there,' Hudson added.

'Good. Good. I'll be sure to follow suit, just as soon as you three are out of here' Monroe added.

Scarlet sat down by a stack of books. She wanted to catch her breath for a moment as much as she wanted to find out what was actually happening to her, and what they were going to do about the swarm of guards in their mist.

'So… don't waste time boy, what do you need?' Monroe said, putting another jacket over his jumper and packing up some items from his desk as they waited.

'What's happening?' Scarlet asked instead, feeling an urge of desperation take over - feeling like this was the most pressing question. Lux sat next to her, taking her hand.

'You look terrible. How long has she looked this way?' Lux asked Hudson, 'We need to get you to see a doctor,' Lux said, her voice so proper that Scarlet hardly recognised it.

'She doesn't need a doctor. Dawson said this might happen. If he were here, he would've known what to do. 'Said she get flashes of her old memories, and I think she was triggered by the explosion tonight too.'

Monroe moved closer to her, lifting her face up towards him with his hand – looking intently into her eyes.

Ignoring Monroe assessment, Scarlet turned to Hudson, 'So glad you all talk about me without filling me in at all. For crying out loud I've been weeping blood, this is not normal. Not even for our standards!' Scarlet insisted. 'I mean, I know what I saw in that vision. It was all a blur; there was a hallway of sorts, lots of screaming…. and a voice. How is seeing shit like that supposed to help me.'

Hudson turned to Scarlet. 'None of us saw that. That's part of your memories, I'm sure of it. You're getting glimpses to who you were it seems. Drips and drabs are starting to come to you whether it be though powers or through your memories.' Hudson explained.

'- we don't even know what powers I have exactly,' Scarlet added.

'No, I know that. But there's something going within you, you can't deny that. I don't know what's kicked it off, but all I can say from my end is when that first explosion hit, its force sent you to the ground. I mean it sent most of us to the ground. But it was like the noise set you off.

You've done strange, impossible things but I've never seen you go into a trance, and cry blood tears.

'Dawson always insisted we kept it to ourselves if we ever noticed anything different when it came to you. He explained that whatever abilities you'd need to find your own way. He didn't want to make you feel abnormal, especially as we were, and I guess still are at times discovering this world together. Up to this point from our view your powers can be subtle yet extreme all at once. Like you see things we don't at times, and you space out for a moment or two. Or you bring out the beauty in everyday things. I remember on our walks into the woods, you once picked a flower from the bushes and when you put it down it turned into a butterfly. You looked at it like it was always a butterfly, like nothing strange had happened. Then when it flew off, I swear every flower on that bush did the same thing. I had no words then, and I don't have any now. But, like Dawson said, I never mentioned it,' Hudson said.

Scarlet didn't say anything for a moment, she knew. She remembered those flowers too. And it's not like she didn't know things happened because of her ever since they left the Amari, she just never wanted to face up to it. The ghosts she'd seen, the small bits of magic she'd felt within her, the force of nature that built in her at times, its presence had slowly become like a familiar part of her. She just didn't realise how much everyone had noticed. She was glad she's kept herself from being to social now – imagine the townspeople when they realised that magic was indeed still a possibility, would they even accept it.

Lux looked over, chiming in, 'It was unlike any magic the Amari ever held, that I could tell. Where the elders made one flower grow, you've magnified such capabilities to the extreme. For ages, I couldn't grow anything in my garden remember, until you came out and helped me replant all the seedlings that the birds had dug up. You helped me for weeks, setting up the scarecrow, and watering and tending to every seed until they began to sprout. You probably think I just needed a bit of help, but when you patted down the soil and watered the ground, it not only brought my plants to life, but the dead shrubs around them to. I was so thankful to have someone to help me that it took me a long time to realise that it was all because of you, that they came back to life for you. That was just the first of many things I noticed.

'It was like when you went swimming in the sea, you dived deeper than any one of us could. You didn't notice, you thought it was normal. None of us ever made you feel like it was any different to any of us. But like Hudson said, there were so many subtle and extraordinary things,' Lux commented, still holding onto Scarlet's hand. Scarlet look down on it, it still had blood on them that she'd wiped from her cheek.

'Tonight wasn't a small thing. The sounds of the Guard arriving covered most of your reaction, but I still noticed. When the whole house shook from the explosion outside. You turned pale as the moon. Paler than you already were, your face hollow. Nora said that was how the girls described you before you collapsed last time too. They said your eyes bled blood tears too – she insisted that you had had some sort of a bleed in your head which caused it to emerge through your tear ducts – a logical explanation. But I'd say its derived from who, possibly what you truly are,' Hudson suggested.

Scarlet had never thought of herself as a what before. The notion that she was not human seemed odd to her, after all if she was fae, she surely would have been sent to live with her own sort of people, not the Amari all those years ago.

'Tonight you seemed unconscious for a moment, but confusion set on your face like you couldn't lift yourself up, the more fear in your eyes the more warmth was sucked out of that room, then the tears began. When you came back to, the power was cut because of the Guards attack, and the attention of the others was diverted,' Hudson said.

Scarlet squeezed tightly on Lux's hand.

'Did the voice say anything to you?' Monroe asked.

'It told me to breathe, that I wasn't alone…' Scarlet recalled.

'That doesn't seem too bad,' Lux added.

After a time, Monroe spoke. Scarlet had completely forgotten that he wasn't privy to the information and knowledge of magic as they knew it, to him it was surely a thing of storybooks, of the books in his collection.

'Hmm, let me see,' he still looked at her intently, but had stopped assessing her so closely. 'Time is a strange thing. And I know more than any of you think, so don't think you notions of power and magic scare me. Scarlet my dear, you are still something many haven't seen. I think Dawson thought this might happen. Though you could tell he hoped it wouldn't. It almost seems strange that it has taken so long, after all the same sort of presence was last recorded to have died over a year ago.'

'-What, there was someone else like me?' Scarlet noted.

'A bound kin. But you are all but remains, and this power is needed – you are needed. It will continue expelling itself; swiftly it will build – controlling and understanding it is the only answer. Ensuring you are ready to face the world,' Monroe rambled.

Lux, Hudson, and Scarlet looked at each other, none of them really understanding what he was saying. Each of them ducked lower as the lights of fire outside of the storefront blazed past, and the sound of gunshots drew closer.

'Look I'd like to think we had time to ponder, but we don't,' Hudson snapped, impatiently.

'Here,' Monroe said, seeing their confusion. He stood up carefully and moved behind his counter and took out something from below.

'There would be some who might kill for this, if only they knew it existed. To them, they wouldn't check a silly book shop this far out in Grinnwick. Now, you've seen this before. This is the map your brother left for you Miss Rivers. Dawson brought it to me years ago for safekeeping. Said if anyone tracked it, he didn't want it to be anywhere near him, or you.

'Before he left, he said that you may need this. He spoke of you dear girl, and this gift you have. Strangely I sensed the same sort of strength in you long ago when we first met. And of course, the rumours I heard from Winslow, that you descend from the Corazon Forest from the last of what is thought to be fae kind. The good inside you could bend anything and anyone to its will. It is like you didn't see the power you yourself hold,' Monroe said, staring curiously at Scarlet.

'Is she some sort of witch? I mean we would know if she was a fae,' Lux asked.

'A witch? I think I'd know if I was. And I'm not naive as you think,' Scarlet retorted.

'I don't have the answers, only my own speculations. I believe you have something to find, and no, not your brother – as much as I have tried to keep an ear out for him every time you ask. I don't believe your answers solely lay with him. And his path is not the path for you to follow now. You require a journey for an explanation for what you are, and who you once were. You call these two family, but I think your true family holds the answers, and they left this for you to follow.

'Flynn wanted you to follow it if you remember, and it seems now is the right time for you to find the answers. Dawson saw to it that I knew this when he left, he said you might show signs of being ready. Caution should be met though; this map is going to take you places men haven't dared journey before. But maybe there's a reason for that, maybe because it takes someone who is more than a mere man.

'Your life has been so sheltered, keeping you safe. Whatever answers you find keep any gifts you have to yourself, at least for now. This life is not as generous as the one you were born into. Try as hard as you can not to let your feelings overpower you so you can keep your gifts in check Scarlet. The more you leave yourself open to the wrong sort of emotions, the more open you will be to the evil in this world. And Grinnwick is full of hate-filled people who you can't trust, and if they catch wind of you, it won't end well. Go home, pack as much food as you can, and follow the map.'

Scarlet took the map into her hand. It had been years since she'd looked down at it. She remembered to the others it just looked like a map of Grinnwick, with nothing to tell them about the path ahead, but to her the path glowed. There were instructions on the side, and it lit up with white writing showing her where they were now, and where they needed to go. The light glowed on the map and stretched to the far north side of Grinnwick, through the outer districts and towards the sea, and stopping in the sea on a set of islands that she had not ever seen on any other map of Grinnwick.

'I'm not ready to go; Dawson and Archer need to be with us. Dawson promised,' Scarlet said. 'He said we would all go, when I was ready.'

'You don't have a choice. He isn't here – and time is now against you. You can't stay in Bellevue Point with the Grinnwick Guard here, they'll kill you all. There is nowhere that you can hide here where they won't find you, and if they do and they'd notice your difference if they let you live, which will only end in more pain. If you stay, you will end up their prize. Dawson knew this, he knew once you started to grow this was possible. That without full control of yourself that the cottage would be the safest place for yourself and those around you, until you learn what your powers really are. Even now though there's no guarantee that they won't find you there,' Monroe said bluntly.

Hudson cleared his throat. 'Scarlet, we don't have a choice. We've always been different, all of us. Growing up with the Amari, we were stuck in time but protected from the wars of this world. We were safe. We barely know anything about the way the Guard works. It was Dawson who kept us as safe, he cared for us as best as he could. He made sure beyond everything that any sign of difference – especially for you – was hidden to those in Bellevue Point. I know you two had a bond, we all know that. But he wouldn't want you to stay here.

'You've wanted to take this trip since you first found out about it; and think about it, it might just lead you to Flynn and the others too. Please we must go, I won't stay here and watch you fall apart, or watch them pull you away from us,' Hudson said, pleading with her.

Scarlet stared at him; she knew he was right. For years she had wondered about that map. Dawson had always told her she would be ready to take that journey in time.

She was not a child anymore, nearly in her twentieth year, and Scarlet still longed for answers to everything, never having lost the will to find Flynn. She was always getting Dawson to check with wandering travellers through town, but not a whisper of him had been heard of in the past 8 years. To her everything was very much the same, she was still the same girl ready for adventure. Realising now that the way that her friends saw her had changed so much. She wasn't like them at all – not even Archer who was fae born. The truth was that whatever was happening to her felt off, and whatever power she had, she had no control over. Terrified, Scarlet agreed to go.

***

From the moment they opened the front door of Monroe's, any plans they may have formed went out the window. Running down the street Scarlet, Hudson and Lux headed away from the noise, where gunshots echoed towards the alleyways markets. There were still a few people fleeing, the fancy townsfolk in their nightgowns and winter coats ran from their buildings.

Scarlet, Hudson and Lux moved into a side street on their way out of town as Guards made their way into the street, keeping clear of their warning shots. But others weren't so lucky to escape the shots, her glare fixed on the body of the innkeeper on the street, and some other poor souls on the ground, none of whom survived the shots. The soldiers didn't stay around, and as they eventually turned back in another direction Hudson ushered them back out to the street to keep moving – aiming for a small exit out of town. Passing the lifeless bodies was brutal, the look of shock still in their eyes, the pale colour of their skin. Her thoughts were torn away by the echoing speaker telling them all to surrender in the centre of town, anyone running away would be found and shot.

Hudson pulled them both closer, 'We'll be okay,' he whispered.

He guided them forward when it was clear.

Reaching the town wall, where there was already a barrel pushed against it (others must have used this wall as their access to escape too Scarlet presumed). Hudson helped boost both of them up the rough stones to climb up and over, Hudson climbed the barrel and Scarlet who was still at the top grabbed his arms, pulling him over.

Once they were all on the ground, they ran harder than they ever thought they could.

Other people were running too, heading for the pathways out of town towards the roads that led to the outer districts. A family not too different to Nora's; a man and wife with a young baby who was screaming, were running to the left of them, dust-covered their faces.

Shots fired over the wall, some of the young girls from St Augustine's were not far behind them, they were further to their right. Scarlet's heart stopped at the sound of their cries as one of their friends was struck down. With no time to stop and mourn, they cried as they kept moving.

Hudson got them to the trees. Each of them taking a breath.

Scarlet looked back to the valley, with people still fleeing in their wake – she noticed a small house on the outskirts of town, there was a woman out the front screaming and throwing things at oncoming guards. One of them ran at her, pinning her down.

A burning sense of rage engulfed Scarlet; she couldn't stand by anymore. Turning back to valley, leaving Hudson's side, she ran over to the house where the woman thrashed against the man, picking up a large stick on her way. With no clue how her petty stick was going to ward off armed soldiers – but she felt her insides build with a strong force, larger than she'd had before.

She didn't notice at the start, but the dirt from the ground behind her rose like a wave, eventually passing by her and toward the soldiers; forcing dust, rocks and twigs into their faces; making them retreat as far back as they could as the air became thicker, pushing them back, but leaving the woman spared.

Scarlet ran to the woman's side who couldn't get up.

'What happened?' she asked Scarlet.

'Nothing, I got rid of them,' Scarlet told her, knowing full well this was one of the strange occurrences that she shouldn't be sharing with a stranger.

'But the wind,' she stammered.

'Here let me help you,' Scarlet said, ignoring the woman's comment. 'You can't stay here.'

'Scarlet what are you doing?' Hudson yelled as he caught up. 'Do you want to be caught.'

'We have to help her. She can stay at the cabin, until she's better,' Scarlet told him.

Hudson didn't have it in him to fight; he helped up the woman, using his strength to help her walk into the woods.

***

'Thank you,' the woman said as she sipped tea on their couch.

Scarlet sat with her while Hudson and Lux ran around and gathered a bag full of supplies.

'This is our home. We have to go, but it is yours as long as you need until you feel up to travelling. The Guard shouldn't look for you here, at least not for some time. We are going to Winslow's before they're raided too; we need to get his help. When you're ready he would probably help you too,' Scarlet said.

The woman looked at Scarlet intently.

'You are brave child. Not many people would have come back for me,' she smiled, holding Scarlet's hand. 'I will be fine here, you should go. You all need to be far from here,' the woman said.

'We are going. Go grab your things quickly Scarlet,' Hudson ordered.

Scarlet ran upstairs and grabbed her things including her locket with the E & G initial embedded, the picture of her parents and Flynn's notebook along with her clothes.

'Here,' Scarlet said, handing the woman on the couch her blanket from her bed.

'Thank you. Please be safe out there,' she said.

'You too, miss…?' Scarlet asked for her name.

'Call me Liz,' she said.

'I hope you stay safe Liz,' Hudson said, opening the front door and waiting for Scarlet and Lux to exit.

The thick mist still surrounded the house as they journeyed outside like it knew the house needed a blanket of protection from the searching Guards around the area.

The Gauntlet

The rickety upstairs office moved with the movement of the people below. Winslow, aged and intent, stood across the table from them. Flynn's map was spread across the table as he stared down at it and across to them countless times.

'You should have told me when he didn't come back. You come here, now in the thick of things and expect me to drop everything for you,' Winslow grumbled at them all, his frustrations peaking as several men kept on knocking at the door calling for him to help.

Scarlet leaned over the table looking at the map while Hudson tried to explain to Winslow that they didn't mean not to tell him. That it wasn't until now that they had really needed help. They thought Dawson and Archer would have been returning soon. Scarlet could barely look at either of them, she only caught a glimpse of Lux who was just as awkward as she was, knowing all too well that they all felt Winslow was their last resort.

There were countless new and aged maps already posted across his wall, many with markings on them. Something to do with the rebels, but nervously Scarlet kept her face drawn from them; it wasn't her business.

Winslow knew Grinnwick, that was all she cared about, and the fact that Dawson trusted him. His connection with the underworld of rebels and outer districts was valuable no doubt, but none of them really understood him. He spoke in cryptic strings, a way that made sense to only him, while still sounding wise. Monroe knew things; secrets and such, but when it came to the nitty-gritty of experiencing the world Winslow was who Dawson would have wanted them to turn to.

'Look, there's a place on this map. Can you see it? That's where it wants me to go,' Scarlet interrupted his ranting to his men at the door.

Winslow closed the door once his men departed, and eyed Scarlet unsurely, before looking at where she was pointing to on the map.

'There's nothing there,' Winslow said, looking quite rigid at the sight of where she pointed too.

'Well, this map says differently doesn't it; clearly something is there,' Scarlet replied.

'Look my dear, there you'll come upon storms and dangers that sailors are warned of, but as close as I've come to that spot, I assure no land was ever found. A fool's journey if I've ever heard one.'

'Well, you might not have come close enough,' Lux added. 'And if you didn't, who knows what's in there.'

'Exactly, come on. Didn't you promise Dawson you would look out for us, right now this is us asking for your help,' Hudson claimed.

'I don't just mean the storms that are there you three, I mean savage hurricanes that will break any vessel apart, unchartered rocks, and creatures of the deep like monsters from a tale that just may be the last thing you ever see,' Winslow warned.

Scarlet took a breath, thinking for a moment. 'Winslow, you once tried to tell me of your love for the sea, how wonderous and beautiful it is, you also called it a trickster. Just maybe the sea itself is playing a part in protecting the island. You can't see it, but this map wants me to go there, it's drawing me there. I think the island itself has been trying to get me there for some time,' Scarlet told him.

Winslow stared directly at Scarlet across the table; she had seen that look before. It was a look of disbelief... Dawson tried to hide it when she told him about the glowing lights when they first walked through the Corazon Forest.

'Look all we need is help to get there, that's it. I know that you're bombarded with the guard infiltrating town, and I'm sure they'll be here sooner rather than later. I know you're needed here; and so, you need to save as many as you can. So, let us not waste any more time,' Hudson started.

'We know nothing outside of Bellevue Point, we need you. We aren't ready to take this journey on alone. It's the only thing right now that I know should be done. Please,' Hudson said, tearing Winslow away from his intensive glare at Scarlet.

'The winds are ready for change, but I cannot take to the seas; even for you dear girl. A trip will be taken, and for you... there may be one man crazy enough; Armistice Grey, him and his ship the *Gauntlet*. Just show him this. I'll send two of my men with you, to keep you safe. It is the least Dawson would expect of me.' Winslow reached into his desk-drawer and pulled out a chain with a flat rounded stone on the end, the stone had a mark imbedded into it. He handed it to Scarlet, who could see the mark of a bear in front of a burning sun.

He moved towards Scarlet's side, the sense of intimidation overwhelming, yet it only inspired her to act brave.

'Dawson hid things from me too, but not everything. He always conceded that your safety was the most pertinent. I can tell there is more to you my dear whatever that is; however curious it may be... Don't reveal it to anyone. Find what you're searching for. Make sure you're prepared Miss Rivers, this path may only be possible for someone such as yourself,' Winslow said, before looking to Hudson and Lux, 'The risk you two take going on this trip with her may lead to nothing more than death for you both.'

'You are happy to give two of your men to my cause though, to help us even if our path doesn't end well?' Scarlet asked.

'It's a big world out there, and the more protection between you and where you need to go is only wise. The boys will be upset that they can't fight by my side, but in the end, they will be glad to get out of here, just as much as you'll need them.

'In the end you are all hidden pieces of a puzzle; you don't think just anyone is sent to a place like the Amari Village for safekeeping do you? It wouldn't be wise for me not to help those who were once incredibly important,' Winslow said.

Scarlet surprised herself even as she wrapped her arms around him, her gratitude towards him was a glimmer of hope she desperately needed at this moment.

'I don't think we are that important. Still, thank you,' she said.

'It's hard to see parts of ourselves in a true light. You've come so far; your lives were never meant for this small town. Gather the map and your things and I'll have Mason and Sticks meet you out the front,' Winslow said assuring her.

Scarlet almost laughed, their lives weren't meant for the Amari once upon a time, now they weren't meant for Bellevue Point... where exactly were they meant to live out their days?

Outside was drizzling again, making walking out from the heat of Winslow's Hall that much more dismal.

Mason and Sticks, Winslow's two men greeted them, both protected by large travelling jackets. They handed one each to Hudson, Lux, and Scarlet before they headed outside.

Pulling the heavy hood over herself, she looked down at the path ahead of them, while Winslow talked to the boys. Ignoring the commotion of his own people taking in wounded stragglers, his attention was fixed on getting the five them out.

Pulling out her locket from her pack, she placed it around her neck, tucking it underneath her jacket, along with her stone on the chain from Winslow. Then she took out the picture of her parents and placed it tightly into her breast pocket, making sure the pack was tight shut so the rain wouldn't get in and wreck anything else.

Treading through puddles as they walked down the track, Scarlet was distracted by the forest around her; the strange echoes of people she knew were only in her mind – these people did not seem affected or even acknowledging the chaos that had been around them, perhaps they were ghosts of her past, she couldn't say. There were voices from nearly every direction. She looked to the others, but as usual with her ghostly figures, they seemed not to hear it, and she ignored it as best she could. Between the trees Scarlet saw a distinct figure, glowing like a guiding light. It felt like a farewell and that the ghosts of her mind had come to wish her well. She walked on ignoring them; they weren't real.

It had been years since she'd seen one; a memory or ghost of a person. She once described them to Dawson thinking that it was ghosts of the forest. Ghosts that only she could see. Dawson called them protectors, a form of angelic creatures he couldn't quite recall. Shadows were all they were to her, they didn't often speak, and usually their sounds weren't coherent; like a background noise. They were spirit guides, he had explained. They confused her mostly when they decided to take the form of Flynn, distorting her memory of him; knowing that it wasn't really him. Dawson said that they would look out for her, appearing as people she knew, memories of her forgotten past. Scarlet wouldn't look at the one in the trees properly, though she thought there was a woman there. She heard the echoes of children around it too. A joyous sound, but this wasn't the time to indulge in such lost memories.

Mason and Hudson took the lead, setting the pace. They headed south, via the coastline. Scarlet hadn't trekked further than the woods around their cabin which was north of Bellevue Point. The further on they went the less familiar she became with the territory, and it was even harder in the dark to get a gage of the path ahead, but she still smelt and felt the salty sea breeze cross her face. Mason was a quiet guy, his shaved round head, and shark-like intent eyes were fixed on the goal to get them on their way. Sticks, on the other hand, was much more relaxed; he spoke constantly as though the sound of his voice was a joy to entertain those around him.

'Weren't there four of you guys?' Sticks asked, his voice loud so they could hear him over the rain. 'What's his name Arrow, or something?'

'Yeah, his name is Archer, he went on a trip with our Uncle Dawson,' Lux said, a little stiffly.

'Don't worry, no need to be fearful of me, I've learnt never to cross a lady on a mission,' Sticks said almost sweetly.

'What's this trip for anyway, Winslow wouldn't send us with you for no reason, especially when the whole bloomin' towns under attack. He also wouldn't send just anyone to the *Gauntlet* unless he trusted them,' Sticks added.

Mason slowed down, turning around to hear the answer.

'He and our uncle are friends, they trust each other. Dawson, our uncle made him promise to look out for us in his absence,' Hudson explained.

'Right… and where are we off to?' Mason added.

'That's because of me. It's hard to explain really, but I need to find an island, apparently it can help me…' Scarlet trailed off, not really sure how to explain.

'How long do you have to find what it is you're looking for?' Mason asked.

'I don't know,' Scarlet said honestly. Not knowing how long until she fully lost control over the strange things happening to her. Scared and frightened yet encouraged by the trip ahead to finally find answers.

'There's plenty of time, let's just keep on moving,' Hudson said. He could hardly look at any of them. Scarlet knew Lux would have looked just as concerned as he did, even in the rain.

Patters of rain endlessly rang on their coats through the night. Slushes of mud covered their boots, and the dirt-turned-mud was only harder to trek through, making their journey difficult as they stuck to the coastline through trees and cliffsides.

It was the middle of the night when their exhaustion took over, and their feet ached, the rain finally eased when Mason called them to a stop for the night.

The roaring fire glowed like an orb through the fog over the cliffs.

Scarlet's gaze was captured deep into the centre of the flickering embers of fire as she sat right by it. On the far side of the fire Lux was fast asleep, not even getting a chance to eat something before she'd dozed off.

The boys sitting further behind Lux talked away. She listened as she gazed; not minding the heat one bit. Sticks was telling Hudson how busy Winslow's had been recently with more and more travellers arriving every week. Winslow had been prepared for the Guard to soon arrive. The alleyways in town have become overcrowded, and Winslow had instructed him and Mason to make sure nothing went pear-shaped in town. They kept people as calm as they could, slowly letting people know it was time to move on.

'What's happened, why are there so many more people coming into town?' Hudson asked.

'Winslow said it's because more and more towns are being turned inside out by the Grinnwick Guard, says they've been searching for something. They've become desperate and reckless in their actions because of it,' Mason stated in his brooding and sullen manner.

'What are they searching for?' Hudson asked.

'Well, I don't know if you've heard but the princess is officially dead, their last connection to the line of the Grinnwick royals. That apparently having her in Commander Van Helms grasp made it a big win for the old families who are his allies – but without her, he needs something to rally his allies back behind him, to remind them why he is in charge. Rumours are that they are searching for a new source of power, greater than Cor-Marinium. Theres ever swirls of rumours going on about the supposed Heart of Grinnwick – ha.' Sticks laughed. 'People will believe in anything these days. No such thing in my opinion, there's nothing that powerful.' Sticks quipped, like the whole thing was one big joke.

Scarlet turned from the fire, over to them, 'What are they searching for then? What is it?'

'Who knows?' he replied, 'but whatever it is, the Guard have the resources to find it. I hear their bounds ahead in emerging technologies, things we couldn't even imaging. Make old junkpile movers look beyond basic.'

Scarlet tried to imagine the mechanisms that the Grinnwick Guard had in their possession, it was undoubtedly such sight of sleek steel like structures, the inexplicable nature of movement, possibly even flight, she nearly felt eager to see such things; only to remember that the Grinnwick Guard weren't the type of people she'd like to meet. While the stories of the Heart of Grinnwick were possibly just as intriguing, if not legendary. A myth, a bedtime story at most. The Amari had spoken of it at times, like it created and balanced this world. Yet specifically she recalled her book *The Star and the Sea* had spoken of it; the Heart was said to be like that of a star. A bedtime story to be sure. Then again, she more than most people should know better that some myths were true, what with the strange things that had befallen her.

'-trying to get anyone with some valuable information to help them out, eager to please the Commander Van Helm. But you know the Guard, they'll take any reason to pull a place apart.' Sticks had continued as he took out some fresh bread and passed some to them all.

'So, what's the deal with your sister?' Sticks asked Hudson, just as Scarlet joined them.

She took a piece of the bread, adding some of the meat Mason had cooked on the fire onto it.

'Well, she just had her first proper date literally before we fled, but I guess any hopes of that got met with a green bullet,' Scarlet a little too bluntly, she wasn't even sure if Alwynn had been shot or not, but their chances of finding out seemed pretty thin.

'Well, that's not awkward at all…,' Sticks started, 'Guess she could be looking for someone to fill that void though,' he said turning the awkward silence around. Scarlet laugh, she enjoyed Sticks' refreshing manner. His goofy laugh and sweet nature was more of the down to earth person Scarlet would have hoped for Lux.

As the night went on eventually Lux woke up to eat. Scarlet couldn't help but smile as she watched Lux enjoy Sticks antics as well; he childishly ate his food, getting it caught in the gap between his teeth, making silly faces, as well as poking fun at Mason and Hudson for their constant serious faces.

Scarlet joined in when he pulled out his own concoction, a sharp drink that burnt as it went down.

'What's it called?' Lux winced as she took a swig.

'Throat Snatcher,' Sticks said proudly. 'Obvious name really, but it'll have you blind as a bat before you know what hits you.'

'He's not kidding either. He shared it at around Winslow's a month ago, I don't think anyone got out of bed for days. So, let's not crazy on this stuff tonight eh. Tomorrow's another big day,' Mason advised.

'Don't be ridiculous, we'll save the rest of it for the *Gauntlet*, I'd rather be unconscious for most of that trip,' Sticks said.

'Why's that?' asked Hudson.

'You've not been on a boat have you? Sea sickness is an awful feeling. Trust me you'll see. That's not to say you'll get it for sure, after all the *Gauntlet* isn't any old boat – it's incredible – beyond imagination – ahead of its time in all aspects, considering how old it is. I mean there aren't many ships like it around – to be fair I haven't seen any of the Grinnwick Guards ships, but still, there's something special about the *Gauntlet* – in its own league that's for sure.

'In all honesty I prefer to keep my head down with the strange things that are said to happen onboard, but never mind me you'll see it for yourselves in no time,' said Sticks.

'Here,' he offered one more sip of the Throat Snatcher before they all headed off to sleep for the night. It was just enough to ease Scarlet off to sleep. She dreamt of herself on the ship, a swaying of the ocean before her and a light in the distance a glow that got closer and close – but woke to find heat of the morning sun beaming above.

Squinting her eyes, she started to wake properly. Hearing the others already making movements to continue the journey, and just as usual she wished she could stay sleeping. The light from the sky not bothering her one bit, it would be so easy just to close her eyes for a little longer…

'Scar, come on,' Hudson gently rocked her back awake, 'the fog lifted, and the path ahead clear.'

He helped her up, but she felt nearly cross at him for it.

She could see now where they were; the clifftops they'd been walking along were much higher than the ones at home. The sea below looked further away from this height than ever before, the calm water she'd been used to seeing and swimming in was no more as they now saw a savage ocean, crashing far below against the rocks by the cliffs. The trees around them had also thinned out. As they started their days journey they too came to a complete end, and the red rock earth was all that could be seen.

The trek was dull, and even though they were in the heat of the day, Scarlet was glad for her jacket as the ocean breeze blew endlessly. Irritated and tired, feeling her feat starting to blister Scarlet knew she had no choice but to keep going. She felt akin to Mason who seemed to be quietly keeping his eyes on the path ahead, while Hudson, Lux and Sticks chattered every now and then in high spirits. Hudson passed out some of the food that Nicholas had given them before they set off to continue.

As the midday sun past and their journey continued, a town in the distance started to come into view. The town look dishevelled even from afar. It was a small port that was encased in a cove, the cliffsides all around it. A couple of speckles in the water would be the ships – one of them was exactly what they'd come all this way for. Their trek began the descent on a rocky narrow track that led to the town. The track embedded into the cliffside restricted their view of the town below.

***

This could hardly be called a town Scarlet thought, as the track finally brought them to their location. There was one street only and it was lined with several townhouses that looked like they'd been either burnt down, or falling to bits; roof tiles missing, tarps used to create the illusion of an exterior wall, some even had the windows nailed in with wooden planks, it was cold and uninviting to say the least.

'The port got hit years ago by the Grinnwick Guard,' Mason noted, 'you might remember the smoke nearly eight or so years ago. So, the town itself isn't much anymore – practically cleared everyone out. Just a stop for ships when they need one – and you can't see it yet but just wait till we pass this lot, the *Gauntlet* should be in the dock.'

'Should be?' Hudson asked, 'What will we do if it's not?'

'It'll be there,' Sticks said with confidence, 'Winslow use to sail with Captain Grey; he got messages from the Captain every now and then, updating him on their route in case Winslow was ever enticed to join them on the sea again – he's his own leader now though so never did. Anyway, before we left Winslow said that last he heard they were headed this way, if not it'll be the next port down… but I don't think we need to worry about that.'

'Why not?' Scarlet asked.

'Why,' Sticks replied smiling, 'because I can see something shiny reflecting just above the pub inn.'

Scarlet looked way up. The Inn and pub were practically the same thing, and together they were wide and large, at the end of the street, blocking out any sight of the cove behind them, most noticeably was that they were rebuilt exquisitely since the attack years ago. With a combination of metal and bricks the structure looked practically advanced in comparison to what must have been older styles they had in Bellevue Point. Scarlet found herself wondering for the first time in a long time that there were still so many things about this world that she didn't know. After all she'd heard of cities but just assumed they'd be larger versions of home, perhaps they were more than she had thought to imagine.

Looking at the top of them Scarlet too noticed a glimmer of reflection from something on the other side.

***

A large dragon shaped figurehead was mounted at the bow of the ship, which in turn was also made completely of a bronzed, and golden hammered metal. The dragon was all Scarlet could fixate on, the long teeth and the sharp scales that had separately been moulded together to form its skin, with black metal eyes that made the whole thing seem too real. It was a fierce warning to any other ship to be sure. To be fair this was her first and only viewing of a ship, but from stories growing up at the Amari, and even in the books at Monroes they were generally made of wood.

Its detailing even continued across the front of the ship, the scales fading into the curve of the bow. Walking along the dock she couldn't keep her eyes off the structure. The way the rest of the metals were panelled to look just like a wooden vessel was incredible. The sheer weight of it; how could it float?

A great pounding of metal echoed, tearing her gaze away from the dragon to a great metal gangplank that had just crashed down to the dock. Half a dozen men walked down it to the dock, each of them as dangerous and brutal looking as the last, carrying weapons with not one drop of emotion on their faces. Scarlet stared as they passed, not wavered by them, but intrigued by the lives they lived on the seas.

The second one of the men slowed as he passed them, blatantly staring at Scarlet. She went to turn away from his gaze, but felt as he slowed the others did the same. Instead, she nodded hello, feeling even more awkward while trying to pass them.

Mason on the other hand used their attention to his advantage.

'Hi. We are looking for Captain Grey. Could you tell us where he is?' None of them seemed to appreciate his interruption. Each of them glared at him, and their dark eyes nearly sent shudders down Scarlet's spine.

'The captain doesn't just see anyone lad,' the tallest and thickest of them said as he grasped onto his gun at his side.

'Please,' Scarlet said, interrupting the tension the best she could. 'We were sent to see Captain Armistice Grey by our friend Winslow. He said that the captain would help us, if you could point us in the right direction that's all we need,' Scarlet said, feeling the quiver in her own voice.

Their look fixed back on her.

The unease inside was overwhelming; she'd noticed people's glances before but never as intent as this.

'Look, we have this,' Scarlet said, pulling out the stone Winslow gave them.

The one at the front, the shortest of them all, put his hand underneath her palm, bringing the carved stone closer to him.

'Boys, get the last of the supplies. I'll take her up to the Cap,' he said. He waited for them to leave; each one did exactly as they were told while taking a brief closer look at the stone.

'I'm Knox, follow me,' he said turning back towards the gangplank. his broad shoulders were covered in a heavy leather jacket, he walked like a stout man even though he was quite lanky.

'Welcome, to the *Gauntlet*, he said. A most unexpected formal manner for a man of the sea, thought Scarlet. As he continued to speak, the roughness of his exterior faded, and in her eye's, he softened, becoming much more of a gentleman, offering his hand to her to help her, as well as Lux onto the gangplank, and then up the stairs.

He was balding and rough to be sure, but there was also a politeness that she didn't expect to find.

Walking up the stairs to the main deck of the *Gauntlet* was just as impressive as her first gaze at the ship. Two floors stood high above deck towards the bow and columns of fire kept the windows and walkways lit. down the hallway to the upper and lower levels.

There were nearly thirty men at work on deck, it was a busy to say the least, and every bit of it shined nicely against the haze of setting sun. Each one of the crew on deck either wound up ropes or were setting gear into place. There were a lot of barrels and boxes, none of which were labelled, and most of them getting moved below deck. An old cook, frail yet cheerful stood over a cooktop near the stern piling up endless meat and shoving them into rolls. His assistant, a small, rounded lady, who was just as weathered, handed out the rolls to the men walking past.

'This way,' called Knox. 'Don't dally, trust me. There are places aboard this ship even the men refuse to go, so you don't want to get lost.'

Scarlet turned to Hudson who looked just as overwhelmed and in awe of every part of the ship as she. She went first up the stairs after Knox. Metal goblet sconces lit up with flames as they made their way higher. They stopped at the first floor and turned down a hallway. The floor was a dark brown decking with a rather long fine maroon carpet in the centre, and the door ahead was inched open.

'Captain,' Knox said softly as he knocked.

Hudson held Scarlet away from the door, but she pushed his arm down and tried to inch closer into view.

As it was flung open, none of them expected to be greeted by the man before them.

'Knox. I told you no interruptions.'

The captain held the door partly closed, with a large grin on his face. From what Scarlet could see the man wasn't dressed, his long hair passed his shoulders in a mess, and a lot of sweat came from his brow. He would have been in his mid to late thirties, and was rather dashing in a dishevelled sort of way. He was younger than she would have expected. The scruff of a beard growing atop of his sharp yet soft jawline.

'Yes Captain, I know. Sorry to interrupt. It's just—' Knox started.

'Spit it out. You know perfectly well we aren't at port every day,' the captain said expectantly.

'Of course. We have visitors, to see you,' Knox cautioned.

'Visitors?' The captain peered around curiously, looking at them all behind Knox. He sighed. 'Give me a minute,' he said, before closing the door in their faces.

Standing awkwardly for a few moments, Scarlet peered around at the paintings on the wall; there was a seascape painted, and for a split second she was sure she could see the ocean in the image moving as the tides of the sea do. It was only ever so softly, but in the blink of her eye it had stopped, and as quickly as it stopped the captain's door opened.

It wasn't him greeting them this time; a woman in a fine silk gown came out. Her cheeks as flush red as her frizzled hair. Her bare leg slipped out of her gown, as she excused herself to get past them all. Another woman was out next – she was still giggling as she left the captain's quarters and looked as though she still had stars in her eyes as she made her way downstairs.

Finally, Scarlet thought, as the door opened again, but this time it was another man, his dark features still dripping with sweat. Wiping his brow with his sleeve, still doing the buttons of his top up.

Sticks and Hudson were doing their best to contain their admiration for the captain. Knowing too well that if they could, they would be cheering him on for such an accomplishment in their eyes. Scarlet in truth had never seen or experienced such ladies or men in a state like this. But she understood completely that they were more than enjoying themselves.

'Welcome, I assume there's a good reason for this,' Captain Grey said, opening his arms and welcoming them into his quarters, the afternoon sunlight from the stained coloured window seeping in. He was still only wearing a robe, and a fine one at that. He took a seat in an armchair that was next to his rather large bed which was still a mess.

'Yes, sorry about that Captain Grey. My name's Mason; Winslow sent us to you for help,' Mason said.

'They have a stone of the Three Brothers Captain,' Knox said. 'Pass it here girl,' he added ushering her to show him the stone. Scarlet passed it to him, feeling as though her hand shook as she did.

'Winslow gave this to you?' Captain Grey asked curiously.

'He gave it to us for our task,' Hudson said.

'No boy, he wouldn't give this stone to just anyone. He put it in her hand specifically, didn't he?' Captain Grey questioned.

'What if he did?' Mason said.

'You see, Winslow, like me, is a descendant from the knights of the Three Brothers. A stone like this hasn't been used for nearly a century – a call to aide. We know the importance of such things, and it has been a long time since anything has warranted that. What makes you so special miss?' Captain Grey said, moving out of his chair and closing in on her.

Hudson stepped between them. 'Nothing. Winslow made a promise to our uncle, that's all. He knew that this would be the way to make sure that promise could be kept.'

Scarlet pushed Hudson aside. 'Look, I don't know what a knight of the Three Brothers means, but I know that you think this stone means something. Here and now, all it means to tell you is that we can be trusted; that you should help us no matter what. That's all we want. If you don't help, that's fine, we'll get there another way,' Scarlet said.

'What do you want?' Captain Grey asked.

Pulling out the map from her bag she unrolled it for him; she could feel him looking her over – an unsettling feeling to be sure, like she was caged for his enjoyment.

Laying the map down, shifting his gaze, she pointed to the island that lit up, but only to her; she knew that he couldn't see the path just like the others.

'We want to get here,' she insisted.

'That's not possible. Winslow would have told you that. We are pirates, not magicians,' Captain Grey laughed, delighted at the comical idea.

'Please, you have to try,' Scarlet said.

'I don't have to do anything. There is no point. A stunning creature like yourself has too much to live for, the pleasures of the world await you. Why don't you just let me show you them instead,' he cheekily grinned, charming and exciting to be sure. Scarlet could hardly pull herself away from returning his grin but knew it would only distract her from what she wanted.

'Trust me, you don't want to waste your time with a perilous journey like this, your doom is all that will be waiting for you; and every other soul on this ship if we get too close,' Captain Grey said, as he softly pressing the back of his hand down her cheek, trying to convince her otherwise. A charming man he was, Scarlet couldn't deny that as she stared into his eyes, floating into them. He could nearly convince her to change her mind, but her heart said otherwise. But his words although soft, made her feel small, as though he saw her as nothing more than a something to be enamoured by.

'If you could only get us as close as you can, we can take a smaller boat from there if you'd be so kind,' Scarlet said, giving him every ounce of sweetness that she could. A trick of her own, using whatever it was that engaged men like him to do her bidding.

'Those seas aren't travelled by man; they belong to the creatures of the deep and the swirls of storms that surround them. It'll be your end. But if it's what you wish, I can get you as close as I can,' Captain Grey agreed.

Scarlet went to pass him the map, but he refused.

'You hold onto it; I know exactly where those waters are my dear miss...?' Captain Grey said, waiting for Scarlet to introduce herself.

'Scarlet Rivers. Thank you, Captain,' she said politely returning his cheeky grin. She could see Lux in her side vision and could tell she was nearly stepped forward to introduce herself too, possibly wanting the same treatment by the exotic captain – she was a woman who was used to such attention, but was noticeably cut off.

'-Knox, get them into the guest quarters below deck, and return to me for some appropriate clothing for them,' Captain Grey said. He took Scarlet's hand and walked her back to the door.

'I will see you all for dinner to be sure,' he spoke mostly to Scarlet. 'Please make yourself at home,' he kissed her hand, leaving them in the capable hands of Knox. Scarlet felt oddly red as she exited the door. Knox took them back down the stairs and down another hallway which led to the stairs below deck.

There were two rooms for them with three beds in each. Scarlet took one with Lux and Hudson while Mason and Sticks slept in the room across. Scarlet washed her face in the sink of their room looking into the golden framed mirror, absolutely exhausted. She pulled her hair back into a ponytail and dragged off the heavy jacket, placing it on the edge of her bed.

'Is it just me or is everything about this ship more than we could have imagined. These guys are proper pirates, I mean this is real,' Lux said taking a seat on the bottom bunk bed.

'We don't know that their pirates.... But I think even to regular people who grew up around ships, this ship is pretty out there. I mean you saw there were a couple other ships in the dock, but they didn't look anything like this, they were more those wooden ones we'd seen in books. I think there was another one that used metal, but it was less than half the size and more of a cargo sort of barge, nothing fancy' Hudson said.

'Do you think we are safe on here? – when Knox said that some of the crew don't wander in certain places, it sounded a bit peculiar,' Scarlet said.

'Well, you saw their captain, he's a bit odd himself. He probably has a few rooms for his extra curriculars, you never know,' Lux said, laughing. 'He took a real fancy to you as well, you might just get a tour by the captain himself,' she teased. Scarlet couldn't help but laugh.

'You're just jealous cause your used to getting all the boys in towns attention,' Hudson poked back at her.

Lux looked a little annoyed but ignored him, as she went to say something-

'-Hello,' Knox said as he opened their door. 'Hope you find the room comfortable. I'm just dropping off some clothes the captain wished for you to have,' Knox said, leaving some clothes on the end of Scarlet's bed before dropping some to Mason and Sticks.

Both Scarlet and Lux had been given dresses, both of which fitted perfectly. Scarlet's was a pale blue sheer silk dress with short sleeves and a small collar, with a slip underneath. Lux's was navy and buttoned up the middle, with a white hem that made the darkness of her skin stand out.

Hudson's pants were tight black with a form fitting shirt and emerald velvet jacket, that matched his eyes. Scarlet pulled on the soft white gloves she had been given that kept her hands warm. Looking in the mirror, she thought she had never seen herself wear something so fancy.

Lux was at home as she tied her hair up in a sophisticated bun, while Scarlet did nothing but pull out her ponytail and pull her fingers through the tangled waves of her golden hair.

They met Mason and Sticks, who looked just as dapper as Hudson, both comfortable in their new threads. Sticks was doing a happy dance as he greeted them, being ever the clown to break any nerves they might have had.

Following behind Knox when he arrived, he led them up to the dining room. It was lit by a dozen sconces across the walls and Captain Grey sat at the head of the table. He was dressed in a long brown jacket, with a dark brown vest underneath, his hair tied back. A cane rested against the table beside him. Scarlet hadn't noticed him use it earlier, but presumed he was a man of character, and it was just a part of his costume for the evening.

'Here you are. Lady Scarlet, please take a seat. You look lovely,' he said holding out the seat next to him. Scarlet sat down nervously.

'Please everyone, take a seat. Apart from Mister Mason what are your names?' Captain Grey asked.

While they went around the room introducing themselves, Scarlet noticed that there were still three empty seats.

'Knox, send the others up as well. Then get the ship underway,' Captain Grey ordered. Knox nodded and exited.

'Is this a pirate ship?' Hudson asked.

'Pirate ship? Now that's an interesting question... We're not savages if that's what you're asking. But do we steal things from time to time, then yes,' Captain Grey responded, it wasn't a clear answer that was for certain.

'Captain, how long do you think it will be until we're there?' Scarlet asked.

'On the *Gauntlet* it should only be a couple of weeks, less if the seas favour us. I'd like to try and warn you against this trip again, if I may,' Captain Grey said to her. He spoke with such refinement that Scarlet had nearly forgotten about the activities he'd been up to not too much earlier.

'Do you think there's no hope at all then of us making it to the island?' Hudson asked him.

'Hope is a strange mistress; you can hold onto it as tight as you want, but at the worst of times you might just lose it. In saying that I do hope that you find what you seek, the question Hudson is – is what you're looking for worth the risk?' Captain Grey questioned.

Scarlet could see across the table that Hudson wasn't sure. The reality of their journey into the unknown had undoubtedly crossed his mind, just as they did hers; for him this trip wasn't fated with reclaiming control of his life as it was for her.

'Many have tried to get through those waters, and I don't believe one has ever come back out to tell the tale. The Endless Sea isn't a place to be tested, but some just can't help themselves.'

'What is the Three Brothers, and what makes you a knight of it?' Lux spoke up, making her presence known as she beamed at the captain.

He sat in thought for a moment – 'The Three Brothers, it's a brotherhood of knights from a time long before this. A time where the High King Geoffrey ruled, along with his two brothers, Rainor, and Theo.

Stories to people these days, yet generations of families have held onto memories and honour to the royals, and through the knights of the Three brothers their memory lives on.

'– Welcome Gentleman.' Captain Grey spoke over himself, turning from the conversation to the two people who entered the dining room. 'Friends, I'd like you to meet Rick Walsh and Manny Sturges. Take a seat gentleman. Let me introduce you to Mason and Sticks, two of Winslow's boys accompanying the handsome Hudson and his twin Lux. And, next to me is the charming Scarlet Rivers. They will be dining with us for the journey ahead,' Captain Grey said proudly.

Manny took the empty seat at the other head of the table; his height filled the space of the dining room immensely and a look of disinterest set upon him. Mr Walsh on the other hand was already chatting away and seemed unable to shut up.

'Call me Walshy,' he insisted to them all, shaking every one of their hands before taking his seat.

'Well Armistice, the *Gauntlet* is looking in fine form I must say. A tight ship you run indeed. Must be nearly five years since I've been on board,' Walshy boasted.

'The *Gauntlet*'s hard work Rick, don't take to thinking it's as easy as it looks,' Captain Grey responded seriously.

'Well not that I'd think that I could handle it. Not that I wouldn't give it a good go, if you ever decided to step down one day that is,' Walshy added cheekily.

'You could try; I'll tell you a secret old friend… the *Gauntlet*, she has a mind of her own, she would sink not only the man who took her helm unwarranted, but the whole ship, only to rise up alone, and victorious,' the captain advised.

'What about if a lady took it upon herself?' Lux asked.

'As long as their character is strong, the *Gauntlet* respects them; man or lady may take the helm,' The captain added.

'Well no doubt, she will remain in your hands for many more years to come,' Walshy said, 'I also wanted to thank you again for allowing Manny on the journey with us. He has been eager to get to the outer districts just as much as I.'

'A Grinnwick Guard, eager to escape his own. That is a sight you don't see every day, and a welcome one at that,' said the captain.

'Is that not a tattoo common to a Grinnwick Guards creeping up his neck? I mean I have no bother moving a deserter, as long as you give me full honesty,' Captain Grey spoke directly at Manny.

Scarlet observed the tall man, his high buttoned shirt hid most of his tattoo, but she could make out two stripes either side of a word that ran down the left side of his neck that started with VAN. She watched as he pulled it down to reveal the full word – VAN HELM. It didn't mean much to Scarlet, she recognised the name, the commander of the Grinnwick Guard. The stern look of disgust on the captain's face showed just how much he didn't agree with it.

'You may not approve sir, but there were marks that I had to make; a name I had to commit myself to, just to prove I was one of them. Rick will tell you I have been a spy for many years, but my time in the thick of it is over. My mission done; I'm just a ghost to them now,' Manny said, his heavy voice defeated.

Scarlet couldn't help but feel bad, it seemed whatever he'd been a part of had taken more than a toll on him. He was a man who had lost more than a part of himself.

'Stay clear of trouble good man and give me no reason to judge you and we will get you both to the Isles of Andromeda and into the city of Peregian. First, we will be heading into more dangerous territory however, getting these ones to the Endless Seas, where they'll aim to find nothing but misery,' Captain Grey mused, as thought it was almost funny. 'Still, the weather is favouring us, and it is better to head straight there than delay with any stop. So, Rick, Manny you're stop will have to wait.

'Now, everyone enjoy the meal,' Captain Grey held his hands up. Allowing the theatre of it all to be taken in by them, as three cooks brought out half a dozen dishes of food onto the table in front of them. As they began their meal their ships movements below could be felt through the ship around them as the dull sound of an engine was set into gear. Captain Grey assured them the tones of the engine would be something they would all get used to, and turned their attention back to the food as there was nothing spared before them.

Finishing off her pumpkin, Scarlet was still trying to thwart the captain's advances; she excused herself after the main meal before he could continue, not even staying for dessert. Taking to the hallway and out to the deck for fresh air.

The night was oddly still, as the ship had started its trip north, as the coastline in the dark could just be seen as they moved. The crew on deck were quiet as they manned their evening posts. A few glanced her way, but they did their best to keep to themselves as she moved from one side to the other of the ship, looking to the horizon; the pale moonlight a torch across the waves of the sea. Sitting on the step on the side of the ship feeling the movement beneath her as she looked out to the water, a part of her wished she was home at Bellevue Point, that Dawson and Archer had never left, that they'd all be back together. Her inner desire to hide was greater than whatever was waiting for her at the map's end.

Staring out at the horizon, she felt drops on her shoulders, finding flower petals laying there; hundreds of white and summer pinks rose petals were falling from the sky. Knowing they weren't real, Scarlet tried to ignore them; the breeze of the sea blew them down the deck towards a couple who appeared further down the ship. Their outline swayed as they stayed in each other's arms, a sweeter sight she hadn't seen in such a long time. It was a memory she hoped was real, breaking out of her mind before her. A blissful sense of love fell through her as she felt herself sway along with them.

'Ahem.'

Scarlet turned from the shadows, the petals fading, facing Manny who cleared his throat behind her.

'Sorry to interrupt you miss. You seemed somewhat distant,' he said.

'That's fine. Must be tired, I should probably head in to sleep,' Scarlet said.

'Of course. I didn't mean to startle you.'

Before Scarlet went to leave, her curiosity got the better of her.

'Were you really a Grinnwick Guard?' she asked.

He nodded.

'Why?' Scarlet said.

Manny laughed. 'I tell you it wasn't something I was aiming for in life. I was a spy in their midst to begin with. I guess, my intimidating presence helped the Guard to believe I would be one of them with ease.

'It was only supposed to be a short bit of recon, to see what info I could get before I got caught. I found someone who in the end I couldn't help, but who needed me there. I guess I wasn't really thinking about me, or what I looked like to the world; all I thought of was them,' Manny disclosed.

'You must have really cared for them,' Scarlet answered, she had a feeling his emotion regarded a woman.

'I did. I always will, she was something special,' Manny said.

'Why did you leave her?' Scarlet asked. 'I don't mean to pry. It just seems like you too are distant, like a part of you is lost, perhaps left behind.'

'I lost her, she lasted in this world longer than she ever should have. But her light was gone, the glow she brought not just to me, but to the world now gone. The strange thing is, until now nothing has reminded me more of her, than you. A part of you, perhaps your grace and beauty, as though you captivate those around you. It's as glowing as hers once was, if not more. I guess it is nice to be reminded, that the world is not lost to gloom now she is gone,' he said, looking at her hopefully.

'I am sorry for your loss. I don't know how, but I'm glad to remind you of someone who sounds so important to you. The truth is I'm no one, no family, nothing. Not even a memory of them, whatever you sense that is because of the people who love me now, the courage, the confidence they've given me to go on and explore the possibilities in this life. To be happy.'

Scarlet smiled gently at him before wishing him goodnight. She had lost people before, knowing exactly what it was like to see a reminder of them in another. A smile, or way they laughed, and suddenly it was like they were not gone, and never forgotten.

Secrets that Lie Below

Scarlet woke the next morning the sounds of sea washing against the metal of the ship. The motion of the sea rocking her as she tumbled her way out of bed with no idea of the time, holding onto the bed post to keep her straight.

At the foot of her bed swung an outfit; a dress made of a thick maroon material with a low neckline and a black bow around the waist. She wrapped it around herself, tying up the bow, it was heavier than she expected, stiff yet cosy.

Lux and Hudson were both out of bed already – not shocking in the least thought Scarlet. They'd always been early birds.

Wandering the dimly lit halls Scarlet had an eerie sensation that she wasn't alone, as if in the corner of her eye she felt like there were shadows around her moving, but there was nothing when she turned around.

Ignoring the feeling, she wandered up to the dining room, in search of the others, hearing from outside of the double wide door a loud booming voice.

She opened it slightly, peering inside.

'Should have started him on the *Throat Snatcher* as soon as we got aboard, he would have been passed out for the whole journey,' Sticks joked. Scarlet wasn't sure what he was talking about but felt uncomfortable as they all turned towards her as she entered.

Mason stood up instantly at her arrival, as did the other men at the table. Scarlet felt odd, it seemed like a strange thing to do. Looking to Lux, who also seemed a little confused, half prospering herself up to join them.

'You've finally arisen,' Captain Grey beamed as he walked through the doors behind her. This morning he seemed a lot less formal as he wore a button shirt blue pants that were a wide fit, with belt like straps up across his shoulders.

'Dress suits you perfectly,' he commented.

'Thank you, Captain,' Scarlet said, as she followed him to the table, sitting down in the seat he'd pulled out for her. Turning to Lux, then noticing that Hudson wasn't there.

'He's fallen ill, the motion of the seas taking its toll,' Lux said when Scarlet questioned her about his absence.

Scarlet now understood why Sticks was joking about the throat snatcher drink, although she couldn't help but think that would have only made matters worse.

'I've just taken him to a room on his own up at the bow. Keep the scent of bile as far away as possible, hopefully that room should be a better location to ease his sickness,' Captain Grey noted. 'Now Miss Rivers, there isn't much left at the table, but did you want something whipped up for you?' he asked.

'Scarlet asked for some bread on butter only, not wanting to make a fuss. But when her plate was delivered to her by a crewman, she was met with a plate full of fresh fruits, bread, eggs and ham.

It was soon after breakfast that she realised that mealtimes where the most entertaining thing to do on the ship. From wandering up to the deck, to not going walking down the hallways of the ship, to checking on Hudson who looked pale and exhausted in his new bed, a bucket by his side that even though empty stunk of what had been emptied from it.

Scarlet found herself trying to learn from the crew. Remembering knots she'd learned with the Amari, she found herself hitching the ropes of the sails, and climbing up the metal mast, with the grey clouds all around her, and the view of the mainland so far away it blended in with the horizon.

Days passed and Hudson remained bedridden, unable to hold much down other than the odd piece of bread and fluids as the seas became too unbearable for him. The wild winds outside had increased, and the churning of the ocean was a wicked combination that only slowed down their journey as the *Gauntlet* fought against not only the tides and current, but the increasingly fiercer winds and the menacing waves that crashed overhead. Everyone was soon warned against going on deck until the weather cleared.

Scarlet and Lux had found themselves spending hours throwing knifes at targets and borrowing swords from the crew to practice skills neither of them had tried for what seemed like years.

It was late in the afternoon when the rampaging ocean and the seemingly never-ending violent swells rocking the ship suddenly died down.

The captain announced that afternoon that they would have a dinner outside with the crew to make sure everyone finally got a bit of well-deserved fresh air. Especially with deadlier storms on the horizon, meaning they were about to reach the Endless Sea and the pattern of chaos in the ocean would turn fearsome to say the least, but at least in Scarlets mind the northern isles would soon be in reach. Still for now, the glowing sunset of oranges and pinks burning up the thinned clouds made for a dazzling spectacle, and relief of a calming sea brought together a festive evening.

Music played as they ate, drank and danced well into the night. Hudson even felt well enough to leave his bed. He sat on the edge of the dancing, clapping along to the tunes a few of the crew managed to muster.

Scarlet danced with the captain as the music rang; he whisked her up and down the deck and she couldn't help glow, not remembering ever dancing like this. She laughed with him as she trampled his toes, but he didn't care one bit as he twirled her around. When the music slowed Scarlet moved to stop, but the captain pulled her in closer.

He had his arms around her tightly, moving with a soft sway, intensively staring into her eyes.

'Tell me my lady. Do you know this song?' he asked.

'No Captain,' Scarlet said.

'It is a sweet melody, made for two lovers. It used to be played all the time.

You had no place in this heart of mine,

No place on my mind.

Now all you have's the best there is of me, every time you smile.

Cause when you smile, and you laugh,

Like the first time over and over again…'

The captain sang the tune aloud.

'It is about two loves who aren't meant to be. A tale felt by many,' the captain mused.

'You must promise me something, my lady.'

Scarlet nodded, 'depends on what it is Captain,' she noted, feeling a tad childish and embarrassed by her playful tone.

'One day all the confusion I sense in you will fade. You will find whatever answers you seek; you will truly be comfortable and confident in yourself. But make sure on your way you don't forget love and all its beauty. Don't forget to have fun and take this world by storm. Most importantly don't forget to live the life in front of you, not just do what you think you should do. After all, you only live once – make it marvellous.'

Scarlet couldn't help but be enamoured by the captain for a moment, she had grown accustomed to his presence during her time aboard.

'Captain. May I ask you something?' Scarlet said, swaying along with the dance.

'But of course,' he said staring off into the distance, enjoying his dancing like he was performing for a theatre.

As she turned to the crowd, she felt the presence of more than those aboard, seeing in twirling around the top of the ship glowing feathers, like that of her first steps in the Corazon Forest, a sense of magic.

'What is the exact nature of this ship?'

He pondered for a moment before he replied, 'It holds a bit of magic, bestowed on it centuries and centuries ago. Why do you ask?' he said.

'I wondered; it seems as though the ship is trying to talk to me. I have memories of the same sense and connection that I had long ago when I first stepped into the Corazon Forest,' Scarlet noted.

'I believe Knox told you there are places that the crew don't go. I myself don't mind the odd presence. There as some ghosts however that will draw the attention of the crew, some even tricking them.

'We all have a history, Miss Rivers; this ship is no different. I took up the reins knowing that it was a vessel that already belonged to others, as those before me did, but this is and always will be the home to a force to be reckoned with; the walls of the *Gauntlet* hides an army, that is controlled by no man. Like I said earlier, the ship chooses the captain, they allow them to guide them, for as long as their heart is true. I keep their lives peaceful, and they allow me the ability to take control of the *Gauntlet*. But mostly they are memories, to one as sensitive as yourself I can only assume, they felt comfortable being open around you,' the Captain said.

'I did also see a couple on the deck covered in roses. Perhaps from long ago, a wedding maybe,' Scarlet said.

'That is one I have not heard before. That doesn't mean it wasn't one of my ghosts; when this ship was in the royal guard, I believe it would have seen true love like that often. I am glad, someone was able to see the inner beauty that it beholds, after all it does not show its soul to many.'

'May I ask you something?' the captain requested, to which she nodded.

'What are you?' he said ever so simply, as though it were so obvious that she was different.

'I, I guess a bit like your ship there's a bit of magic in me too,' she responded.

'But you are no witch, and stories of fae have been nothing but legend… is that what you are?' he asked.

'I'm not sure captain, but when I find out I'll let you know,' she surmised.

Scarlet said no more on the subject, she danced slowly in the captain's arms, unprepared as he kissed her. His soft lips pulled her in, and she couldn't help but kiss him back. It was only for a moment before he stepped back, let go of her hand, bowing to her above all others. It stopped her in her tracks for a moment until Sticks led a group dance, singing his own merry tune.

They continued the celebrations until the early hours of the morning where she passed out to the rock of the waves.

Nearly halfway through the following morning they were still in bed, sleeping off the mounds of ale they drank and the aching of their feet when the rolls of the storms began to hit harder than ever.

Scarlet in a deep sleep, tossed and turned not even noticing the fierce rocking of the ship. Lost in a dream; Dawson standing at the foot of her bed.

She got up and wrapped her arms around him, no need to tell him how much she missed him. He reached out for her hand; Scarlet took it with ease. Looking up at him, he looked tired, but happy.

Then he pulled away and walked out the door into the hallway of the ship.

Scarlet woke with a jump, she'd been thrown from her bed as the swell from the storm grew larger, and the smash of the waves against the metal echoing.

He had been here. Dawson had been here.

Scurrying to her feet, she pulled on a dress and large green jacket. She ran into the hallway looking for him, falling into the walls of the hall as the ship rocked her about. He was nowhere to be seen; she wasn't dreaming anymore, the emptiness filled her.

Turning back defeated, she wished beyond anything that it hadn't been a dream. That somehow Dawson had found his way to her. Needing him to tell her what was going on, where he'd been. Needing him just to be there.

The darkness of the hallway suddenly became extinguished with a light. Similar to the one from the map, the same one she'd seen earlier atop of the ship and years ago in the Corazon Forest; the floating leaves. They lit up the hallway, its fine strands glowing bright. Just as when Dawson had said that it led to the path ahead and the confidence she had once felt in their guiding light, Scarlet felt that warm feeling of power and confidence in its presence yet again. It was utterly ridiculous to trust in such a notion, she knew that this was absurd – yet the feeling that this was a calling for her couldn't be ignored.

Scarlet followed their moving light up the stairway, rocking with the ship and feeling the intensity of the storm rise, finding her way up towards the entrance hatch that opened up to the deck.

Why would the light lead her here? The raging weather outside of this door would be madness, the flicker of lightning and racket of ropes and barrels could be heard banging around - she wasn't anywhere near experienced enough to handle it.

Still the leaves dropped before the door of the hatch, while others floated through to the other side, she could see their light outside. Holding onto the handle she felt an additional strength, a confidence on top of her own hand to twist the handle and opened it wide.

The wind knocked it wide open, and the ice-cold seawater that had been crashing over the deck whipped across her and the wind made it hard to hold onto the door.

'Scarlet,' yelled Mason from behind her at the bottom of the stairs. 'What do you think you're doing?' He was holding onto the railing as the ship continued to hammer about.

'Stay here, I'm okay,' Scarlet called back. As foolish as she knew it was, she had once trusted Dawson and the magic of the Corazon Forest, she needed to trust in it again. This was what she had to do.

Behind Mason she saw Knox running towards her, and Captain Grey in his wake, both horrified trying to reach her.

Pulling herself up, while the hatch swung shut with a bang behind her, ignoring their screams, holding onto the rail on the deck as tight as possible. A blast of water came across her, and she watched as the three men tried to open the hatch with no luck, and odd occurrence as she had done it with such ease, but it was best that they didn't follow her.

Even with the high walls above the lower level of this deck, waves tumultuously washed over.

Wind soaring past her, the entirety of her body was completely saturated before she took a proper breath. Her clothes stuck to her, and her hair all over her face as she braced against the waves and the wind. She looked at the captains terrified face one last time through the hatch window before she was swept off her feet by a wave, it carried her across the deck.

Screaming, her body hit the deck hard and her shoulder and hip both were struck, but her cries were drowned out by the pounding thunder and cracks of lightning. She had a feeling that this would be as close as Captain Grey would get the *Gauntlet* to the island of Perdita.

Scarlet tried to gather herself as the sheer force of the weather worked against her. She was relieved at the sight of the leaves that had led her out here, their light now came closer towards her; an old friend that had been waiting. There were now dozens more, increasing with every moment, adding to their light as they grew closer.

She gasped for air as another pounding of water forced something that had been on deck into her ribs. A stool from what she could tell. Scarlet pulled herself up one of the side rails trying her best to hold on, arguing with her own desire to retreat as she tried to reach out for the light.

It didn't matter, the light itself reached out for her. The ocean rose over the walls of the deck in a rampaging fury, its sheer height and force more alarming than ever. Coming straight for her Scarlet panicked holding on to the rail as tight as possible with both hands, knocking her head this time into the side of the deck walls leaving Scarlet struggling to breathe, her entirety now fighting the sea that rose over the deck, she tried to keep her head above the water as she felt to weary to stand. The light began to consume her, like a bubbling forcefield from the might of the ocean, it carried her amongst the waves, and while completely submerged the reality of danger faded from the warmth of the leaves as she eventually passed out in its clutches. Completely unaware she was being carried up and over the walls of the Gauntlet.

Leaving not one bit of light left of on the deck of the Gauntlet, all except for the entrance hatch where a desperate Mason, Knox and Captain Grey continued pounding at the hatch stuck inside.

Sinking into the depths of the Endless Sea, carried by light in a deep sleep, Scarlet was lost to them.

Down with the Ship

Perdita was burning.

A thick haze of smoke drew towards Bastian.

He hadn't meant for this; he hadn't meant to be a part of any of this. The last of the men he'd followed to the island ran ahead into the thick of it. What was he thinking, he was an absolute fool to do this, there was no way they would reach the Heart of Grinnwick.

The excitement was building. Bastian's eyes were set on the ruby, sparkles glistened on its edges under the light from above. He wanted it. A treasure to be sure. He tried to hide his enthusiasm and delight. The game should have been rigged, yet it need not matter if he won or lost, the stone would be his.

Putting down his cards to show two black trees and a burning man, he cursed as his opponent showed a winning hand of one golden arrow, a white wolf, and dove. This game made no sense to those outside their wall, but in the Arena, sense was lost.

Making a scene, throwing his cards down, he cursed old gods he didn't believe were real. All while his gold-toothed opponent collected his winnings.

'You've got to be kidding me,' he barked. 'This is ridiculous. I should have won that. Bloody gods of the past tormenting me. Curse them; curse the lot of you. Who do they even think they are... the father of Darkness, and the sisters of the sky. Blasted imbeciles. I thought I had it. It was a fluke. Today is just your lucky day,' he tormented the winner; a rather dull bloke who looked just about ready to pound him in.

'How could I fucking lose it though. That was stupid,' he spoke mostly like himself, a little lunacy inside him acting out, he had grown accustomed to having a flair for drama in the sense.

Bastian finally walked away after walking up and down, acting the part. Only to be handed the Ruby by a scrawny miner not two moments later. While his scene drew his opponent's eyes, the little lad who Bastian had favour with picked his pocket.

***

Hiding out for about four years at his grandfather's request amongst the savage miners of Sildor, Bastian's life had been consumed by their ill-tempered world. As he was getting close to reaching his twenty-fourth year he had come to find himself settled in amongst their ways. He was his own man now, long ago were the days when he was a part of a team and all of his actions guided by the thought of the Guardians. Here he had to look out for himself.

Since he had arrived all those years ago, he had been taken under the wing of Kerry, an older Guardian who had been placed here as a sleeping agent many years ago, who had taken to calling him 'Little Crackler'. A newbie term for miners, which Bastian personally hated. However, it seemed to stick, even after the years that had passed. Bastian slept in a shack out the back of Kerry's' unit, it wasn't fancy, the bed basically a trundle with layer of blankets to give it padding. To be fair there wasn't any fancy sleeping in Sildor, dirt and soot covered everything. It was more a place to rest his head. Kerry made it a sort of home that Bastian had grown used to. And while he taught him the ropes at the mines which Bastian took on easily enough. It was Kerry who first introduced him to the underground lifestyle of Sildor, the Arena.

Kerry was not at all the guardian that Bastian had originally taken him for; he had really taken his post as one of the miners with ease from what Bastian could tell; his scruffy grey haired, completely covered in dirt from the mine, and a desire for nothing but money – telling Bastian how he sent part of it back to the Guardians to help their funding, but Bastian soon saw the truth that he loved the enjoyment of counting his coin, whether it was from working or betting in the Arena. Bastian himself hardly remembered that he was a guardian, and the two of them had become partners in crime at the Arena.

Kerry would take the high-class travellers who had journeyed from the outer district cities on a tour around the Arena; showing them the tables and games, and eventually introduce them to a lone young man –Bastian, who was often having a drink in a booth and over the years had become much more rugged, and rougher than he used to be, his youthful charisma remained and as Kerry sometimes called him 'the good lookin' one', it had perhaps given him a complex that he could enchant any visitor, and usually he was able to win them over. After he'd take them under his wind and show them the skills of the tables – he'd find they enjoyed indulging themselves in a game of wits against him, finding him delightful compared to the stuffy people they were used to hanging around. Still, they were surprised nearly every time that Bastian beat them with his quick and sly remarks. If he didn't win – a rare occurrence that was known to happen every now and then (unless it was set up that way as a form of distraction), Bastian never let it get to him, he simply ended the games for the night. After all, as good as the treasure was only half the fun of getting it.

Understanding life was a strange adjustment in the beginning; the miners favour of greed and strength and using it to their advantage was pivotal to his survival in Sildor. He set himself up as someone that could be trusted. He was smart; smarter than the common man thanks to his training with the Guardians, yet he found it took a certain charm instead of smarts to gain favour among the miners. While each of them only cared about making more money than anyone else they valued others who they could trust.

Spending his days in the filth of the mines, pounding in the dirt-filled caves gasping for breath and coughing up the dirt he spent inhaling all day. Part of him felt that he'd never truly be rid of the dirt that lay on him, it had imbedded itself into the crevices of his skin and his hands always looked and felt tough. He thought if he looked into a mirror his skin would appear dirtier than it ever had before.

His reputation amongst the men soon turned into something similar to what it used to be back in Bellevue Point, as the outsider not to be messed with.

What he found most that won everyone's favour over the years was the simplest acts. Small notions of kindness solidified his place amongst them, he was always seen helping others in the caves; the older miners get water and sharing their load of wheeling around dirt. While guiding the younger ones on how best to take aim in the caves. The kindness was natural to him, the talking even better. Bastian's need for entertaining conversation and his own charm made him talk with ease. He knew when to talk nonsense, and when to keep his mouth closed – the later a much-needed token for any miner who wished to stay out of trouble.

The main drive that brought miners to Sildor was Cor-Marinium; the minerals that were embedded in the cliffs was what kept them all here. Its value to the Grinnwick Guard and Van Helm himself was insurmountable in comparison to any other power source. The Cor-Marinium was extracted from shiny aqua-green coloured translucent stones. This was the largest area of Cor-Marinium known and it was isolated to the coast of Sildor, and was sold to the Grinnwick Guard in majority, but some leaders of the outer districts also came to stock their cities.

Days ran like they were on repeat after some time, with no time or energy to listen for whispers of a long-forgotten myth – the notion of the "Heart of Grinnwick" had become a distant memory, perhaps of why he came to Sildor, but his live had adjusted to living like this, and his advances on its whereabouts had met too many dead ends for him to focus on anything other than live the life before him.

Sometimes though Bastian found himself thinking of Verne, and just how angry he would be with him. The same could be said of Gertie and the others. He would be grouped up in their conversations with the same distrain that Verne held for Felix when he left.

Bastian's deep desire was to know how they reacted after his grandfather's letter reached them about not returning. Did they know if the Guard had finally taken control as his grandfather had predicted? Were any of them even safe?

Soon these thoughts drifted from his daily life, but found him when he woke up at night, sweating.

***

It was a cold night as a large storm belted heavier than usual off the shores when Bastian found himself at the Arena. One of the miners' named

Davies was delighting a small group of them with his tales as they sat around one of the larger booths as they drank the heavy dark ale that was a staple of the Arena.

'It was the largest creature I ever saw – a sea dragon I swear it,' Davies claimed, quite dramatically in fact.

'It was the early hours of the morning, and I saw the side of it by our boat; scales of silver, blue and purple reflecting from the water.'

Bastian laughed with the others; he had studied enough to know that no such beast existed; on record. However, he had also been taught by his grandfather that there was a possibility of anything in Grinnwick, and to keep his mind open. This information struck a small bit of interest, especially now as he'd lived among men for quite some time and had begun to find there was no end to the miners' greed, a feeling that was rubbing off onto him. That mixed with his thirst for adventure made him see the potential beast as treasure, and the journey to find it even more enticing. Even one scale would hold enough weight in the right group of people. Part of his mind drifted off into thought about leaving this place. So, he listened intently right up until Kerry came by him.

'Little Crackler,' Kerry beckoned, 'Let me introduce you to Mr Rick Walsh,' Bastian turned to see a sharp man, a little short but standing proud. He looked as well-groomed as any pompous man who presumed they were better than the regular participants of the Arena.

'Nice to meet you,' Bastian stood up to introduce himself. 'What brings you to Sildor? It can't be us lovely folk.'

But before Mr Walsh even had a chance to reply, Bastian stepped in.

'No, let me guess. You've come to add to your fortune, take a hand up against the fighters, the savages of our small town.

'No, I doubt that very much, not in such fine clothes as the ones you wear. Maybe your desire is to only place a bet on them. Or you're only passing through and it's been weeks, or perhaps months since you've felt a woman's warmth on your skin,' Bastian quipped, leaving a pause to see if he answered. Sometimes he was too much, he didn't want to scare the man away. Something told him this man didn't mind being stirred up a little.

He laughed his desire for an answer off, 'Why don't you sit and have a drink with me, and we will start our night with a full belly, and entertain ourselves in the pleasures of this place?' Bastian suggested.

'You speak my language boy. You sound like you are not from this neck of the woods yourself? And the task of understanding this place is quite perplexing if you do not know it. I give you credit, you seem as to have found yourself in a world full of, well, animals,' Mr Walsh laughed.

'As kind as it is to have Kerry and yourself tend to take me under your wing. I know this place, and I know it well.'

Bastian felt shocked for a moment; never had one as well-groomed in etiquette been familiar to the wild ways of the Arena.

'Well – how's about a drink anyway, between like-minded friends,' Bastian asked calling to a waitress to bring a jug of ale to them. Helping him to sit down in a small booth just next to his friends. 'What brings you here?' Bastian pondered, 'Or back here?'

'I've been travelling. Our ship hit a storm, we needed to make port before deciding on our next move.'

Bastian had heard of a ship that had arrived in the afternoon. A ship that no one had apparently disembarked; seemed the rumours were wrong, or not up to date. It would hardly have been noticeable as a recent increase of Grinnwick Guard ships had landed in the port only a week before. The

411

ship however was grander than even the Guard's, while they had sleek styles and technology ahead of anyone else, the ship had was apparently in a league of its' own. He had planned on going out to see this ship himself the next day, after word of its unique qualities reached him.

'Word is no one has exited that ship. I mean clearly they're mistaken if you've come offboard.'

'The captain is a friend. They keep the *Gauntlet* under high security, including any secrets she may hold. I am trusted to keep its secrets, as I have always done,' Mr Walsh said proudly.

'So, you will not divulge any to me, I mean after all you placed me as a fish out of water among the animals, surely I can be trusted?' Bastian provoked. He saw the glimmer of the thrill of gossip lurk in Mr Walsh's eyes, he was hooked, Bastian knew it.

'Boy, you are quite daring I must say. But alas my secrets stay with me.' Mr Walsh added – Bastian found his presence one that was much more acceptable to being in the company of a younger, and as Kerry noted "good looking" man like himself. It was clearly his preference, and Bastian wanted to play on that heartstring of desire as much as he could, giving Mr Walsh an eye of intrigue, of desire. Bastian would never follow through with such antics, but he knew how to play the game – the smallest gesture would lure a man like Mr Walsh in enough – that and the rest of his ale.

As they drank and spoke, and Bastian allowed him to get closer and closer, so much so that he detected a scent he had not smelt in years, a blossom in fact – perhaps one that his mother had grown long ago. Bastian felt himself breath it in as a now loose-lipped Mr Walsh spoke.

'I can tell you this bit of information boy; there is something strange in the seas out there. I have half a mind to remain here with you animals rather than return to the ship,' Mr Walsh advised.

'Strange like a sea dragon?' called out Davies, who was still playing at the booth across from them. Davies usually spent more time in the fighting ring than on the card tables, not that it mattered right now; Bastian was intrigued at the question he posed.

Mr Walsh looked from Davies and back to Bastian. 'The small-minded world of men. I have forgotten your blissful simple revelations. A sea dragon,' he scoffed but mildly entertained by the interaction. 'That would more than likely get me back into the sea with the worth of simply a sighting.

'The truth is our ship came into port only because we lost a member of the ship overboard, poor Miss Rivers. "Reasons unknown" says the captain. But something strange, why was it she was on the deck in the thick of the storm. One has to wonder.

'The captain is fixing a plan as to find her, truthfully, I don't know why. I'd say she's in the belly of the beast, lost to the seas along with many others – but what would I know?' Mr Walsh contended. 'Not to worry, because if the sea didn't get her, that fleet of Grinnwick Guard ships will.'

Bastian said nothing. News of a loss was never good no matter the circumstances. And of a lady out at sea, what was she doing there?

'Those soldiers are everywhere. They're an absolute nightmare. Think they own the place. Been nice that they're finally started to move their asses on,' Kerry added, trying to steer the conversation away. 'Heard from a friend that they're chasing something else, something new, something more powerful than the minerals we've been digging for, and they were going after it soon.'

Bastian's ears prickled at this; he had not heard Kerry mention it before – what was it they'd heard? – was this the sort of rumour he'd been waiting for? Memories of his stressed-out grandfather talking almost non-stop about the Heart of Grinnwick, and its power. Was this it?

'What did you hear?' Bastian quickly asked Kerry.

'Ezekiel, you know him from the mines boy. Broad, and scruffy red hair, bit older than me, but definitely bigger than me. Works up on level two as their conductor. Anyway, he told me word of a myth that might just be real. Said its source was from the island offshores, not that far away.

'He said that the Grinnwick Guard wouldn't send their newest fleet if they didn't think it was for anything worth their while. He knew a couple of miners who had been listening in, wanting to steal it for themselves. Oh, and that Mr Walsh's ship here, is probably after the same thing, is that right Mr Walsh?'

Laughing, or more giggling from a drink or two too many, Mr Walsh gathered himself. 'The *Gauntlet* is many things, holds many secrets; but believe me if it were following a myth into dangerous territory I would know. And the captain made it perfectly clear all we were doing was making our way through.' Still seeming agitated by the question Mr Walsh excused himself and left for another table and found another younger, yes questioning miner to cosy up to.

This had been exactly what Bastian had been biding his time to hear. After losing himself to the ways of Sildor and the Arena it was like a part of his mind that had been switched off turned back on. Bastian had no choice but to follow this lead, the possibility that this was it, the power source these men searched for must have come from the rumours his grandfather heard about the Heart of Grinnwick so long ago.

***

After enquiring to Ezekiel, Kerry helped Bastian to connect with a group of miners.

Their leader, a stern man with dark skin and deadly features of ink across the side of his face and a long scar going up from his right eye and the stench of smoke and rum radiating off of him, his name was Ulysses.

They met in a container ship on the outskirts of Sildor. The container was one amongst dozens, most of which were packed with Cor Marinium for delivery – others with food that had been delivered to them. This one looked to have just been emptied but for some reason it smelt of wet animal, and the heat of the bodies around him made the air thick. The scent of dirty men wasn't anything new to him, he'd grown accustomed to it in Sildor. The meeting had been set up to be clear from prying eyes.

Kerry had warned him that Ulysses and these men would be worried about the Grinnwick Guard catching wind of their plans. Squashing their efforts before it even began.

Bastian wasn't sure how much impact the Grinnwick Guard had on the mines – there was no guard soldiers in their presence, at least ones who enforced any work. It was usually visitors to their shores by ships. They still had not managed to break through the Corazon Forest – so they were a rare sight in the outer districts. But the port to Sildor was one of the largest, and most accessible in the outer districts, so with all their advances in machinery it was no wonder they were able to reach the northern most point of Grinnwick.

Ulysses and his men seemed intent on keeping their meeting from whoever watched over them. And by the way Kerry gave Ulysses a quick nervous wave before sneaking off once introducing Bastion, he was clearly fearful someone was watching.

'Welcome boy,' Ulysses noted, not emotive at all as Bastian walked into the container towards another miner. This one a bit taller, and around the same age as Bastian, perhaps a little unfamiliar with regarding other people's personal space as Bastian found himself stepping back from him, noting the distinct stench on his breath.

'It's cause of the Guard,' he said almost at a whisper, 'got most men scared these days around here, afraid of every lil' thing they say and do. Those vultures never used to stick their noses around here so often, till now.'

Bastian went to reply when Ulysses cut in.

'Deacon's right Bastian, and we will not take their entitlement lightly. You hear me. If we want power, we need to take it, this is the outer districts after all, and they have no true power here. They don't know the capabilities of the cities to the north, they have forgotten the world, tangled up in the power of their own creations,' Ulysses roared. Bastian had taken to realise he wasn't just talking to him anymore but every man in the container ship.

'Grab what we can and don't hold back. So, when the Guard realises what we've done, they'll be at a loss, and we, we will make more gold than our hearts could desire. This is our job, our chance. Whatever is out there is ours to mine, and ours to control just like we do with the Cor-Marinium,' Ulysses claimed.

Bastian followed suit. 'This is our time,' he boomed, encouraged him, and everyone roared in agreement.

During the cheers and bustle of excitement Bastian finally grasped the full concept of the plan.

Ulysses had found out that the Grinnwick Guard were piling into Sildor's port as a base before heading through the treacherous seas to find their new power source. Most of their ships had already started for the offshore island. Some ships supposedly too big for the port, they stayed offshore and were spotted by some of the sailors who'd come in.

Ulysses had beckoned the miners to follow him to take the source for themselves and leverage it against the Grinnwick Guard. That if the Guard wanted it badly enough, they would pay top dollar.

Nearly every miner Ulysses' gathered was as deadly and greedy as the next. If not in Bastians view they were a little easily led down a con of a rabbit hole. Each one of them more eager than any miner Bastian had met before. If it weren't for the link to a possibility of the Heart of Grinnwick Bastian wouldn't have even given it the time of day.

The looks in the eyes in each of the ragtag group of men that matched the dark desire for power that Bastian had ever seen in a soldier of the Grinnwick Guard's. It was their all in or nothing rough attitude that made them all the more intimidating.

Ulysses ran them through the plan once the men all quietened.

'We'll meet in two nights at the docks,' he stated from a map he'd aggressively stuck to the wall, with two knifes at the top of each end holding it up.

Bastian saw the map Ulysses spread on the table; it was a dodgy version of the one his grandfather had given him. A map that he'd hidden long ago under his bunk, it had been so long that he wondered if it was still there. Ulysses' map was drawn in pencil with a vague guide as to where they needed to go.

Bastian spoke up amongst the group, 'where's the map from?'

'Ahhh boy there's always a rat who'll pay handsomely to enjoy the ladies of Sildor, when their coinless this far from home,' Ulysees noted.

Bastian laughed, knowing that his own map would have helped them ten times over. Part of him wouldn't let him speak the words aloud, feeling it best that he kept it to himself. He'd have to admit to them that he knew more than he let on. To them he was here for the same reason as them, not his own solo mission.

From here Ulysses' plans started to quickly unfold.

He sent out the request for a ship, promising them a cut in the riches to lure them to voyage into the deadly waters.

Ulysses' right-hand man Credence, a heavy man with squinted eyes and leathery skin and a red moustache that covered over his mouth, and even with his lack of height he had muscles bigger than any man amongst them, was organising some of the crew to move all their weapons, and drills, and shovels to the ship, along with food and drink. He had the ship stocked and ready to go well before the two nights' time.

Kerry sat by their small window as Bastian went to leave.

It was odd way to part, as Bastian in silence went over to pat him on the shoulder.

'This is foolish boy,' Kerry said to him, 'those seas aren't safe for any man, no prize is worth the trip.'

Bastian knew he was right, the uncertainty of the voyage was playing on his mind, but he had to try, 'I have to give it a go, as looney as it all seems. I've practically ignored the mission; I mean it's not like I've gone too far out of my way to find word about Perdita–,'

'—Well, why start now, you've got a good life here.' Kerry noted.

Bastian realised this was more about Kerry wanting him to stay. They had both grown use to each other, which was funny now that Bastian thought of it.

'Why don't you come with me, you can't live this life forever,' Bastian said, partly in realisation to himself. As much as he'd be found a sense of fun and routine in this life, it wasn't enough.

'I can't go with you, that journey would be my end, I'm sure of it. Probably much like your grandfather, I'm too old for it.

Na kid, my life will end amongst the rubble of this hideous place. It doesn't matter what role I play anymore; I'm not a guardian anymore, haven't been in a long time.'

- 'I don't think I am either… not really.' Bastian responded, 'this was Grandfathers mission… think that's the only reason I'm going to try and see it though.'

'You're no rule follower like them that's for sure, not anymore… but you've got heart boy, and you've got a sharp mind too… so don't sell yourself short, right.' Kerry assured Bastian.

***

The dock was quiet. The Guard's ships had gone. Mr Walsh's ship had left too. But the one Ulysses had acquired named the *Running Arlo* lay in the port waiting, a foolish captain waiting to lead them, none of them aware that they would soon wish they'd never agreed to such a journey.

'Men, do not dwell, for this night we drink as the seas ravage the ship. When the morning comes, we will do what we must, we will upturn every rock, dig out every trench and pull the island known as Perdita apart until we find the treasure.

'Every last one of us will leave all the wealthier. And, if the Guard wants to get their hands on this new power source, let them find a hefty sum to pay us for finding it first, I say,' Ulysses asserted, beaming at the cheers he received from every last miner. Passing around cups of ale to each one of them, he encouraged them to enjoy their down time because it would be all work once they got to the island.

Bastian slowly drank his ale, the stench of ale that had been spilt in the sitting quarters of the ship was strong, as was the smell of damp cloth, no doubt from the aging maroon cushions on the seats that had been built into the quarters. As the other miners downed their drinks quickly, and continued to fill their glass through the night, many of them passed out as the *Running Arlo* took a thrashing from the seas.

There were two others Bastian noticed in his observations that didn't even touch their drinks, their stayed hooded the whole time, and he was intrigued by their quietness. Bastian didn't think they were a part of the miner group seeking the power source. He could see their darker skin underneath, and one who had long locks – a woman. He was shocked. She wasn't the portly sort who whored through Sildor, but a lady dressed in trousers to slightly disguise herself – a smart move amongst a ship of miners and sailors.

Hours seemed to pass, and the light of dawn started to break through one of the port circular windows. But it was no burst of orange light from the sun, but just the darkness of night lifting to notice the heaviness of the harrowing clouds, and the rain and waves that swept up against them as the boat rocked from side to side.

Bastian was keeping tabs on everything even with every motion and thrash that knocked them around, cautious that the ship may just not make it. He could see the lady take hold of her companion's hand as he too vomited into bucket.

Ulysses now stood by the door, holding onto the doorway as he lent from one leg to the other, going with the ships flow.

Bastian listened in as Ulysses spoke to a runner issuing updates from the captain.

'We are ten hours from Perdita's location sir…'–

'The winds have increased up 90 knots with gusts coming through up to 150, brace the men…'–

'Visibility is low, navigation still on route, but we are dragging with the winds…' –

'The captain can't see, his navigation is lost, he's doing his best to steady the course…' –

'The back hull has been breached; the pressure is building up. Wake all the men.'

Ulysses woke every drunken and sleeping man, that was if they weren't already woken from the chaos, his bellowing voice causing the right amount of alarm needed.

Each one of them sobered up pretty quickly as the ship continued to knock them around. A few of them struggled, still quite full from their night on the drink.

Bastian offer to help with the leak but was told by the young messenger boy that there was nothing he could do. The lower levels would be blocked off, in hopes they would prevent it spreading.

Bastian kept his own head level, focus was paramount – and he needed to get to Perdita. Pushing away the doubts that entered his mind; was he now just a forsaken fool along with the rest of them – giving up his life at someone else's request? Was the Heart of Grinnwick worth his life? Could he not be back with his friends, spending time away from the world on Verne's farm? If that was where they still were, or if they'd returned to the Guardian compound, if they had to face the spies from within, if it still stood now.

He hoped beyond anything that they were okay. If this voyage didn't go well, he may never know.

'Land is in range. Gather your men to take the lifeboats. The captain is sure we are close, but the ship is dragging from the water it carries, and it will not make the rest of the journey,' the young boy cried, then ran off into the shadows of the hallway; this was the first time he actually had genuine fear across his face.

As he made his way out the door, Bastian couldn't help noticing the steady stream of water that was now flowing down the hallway towards them and the piercing noises of pressure from the hull around them building.

Every last miner was gathered to head up to the top, each grabbing a yellow weather jacket.

Before they even had a chance to get through the hallway to ascend to the deck the young boy returned.

'Brace yourselves,' he yelled.

'What is it boy?' asked Ulysses, but before he got another word the ships swung and smacked into something, knocking them all to the floor and into the hallway wall. Bastian still in the room was on the ground with many others. And before he even came to stand a flood of water crashed in from behind the young messenger, like a great force pushing they were all scrambling to fight against it.

Bastian's had been pushed all the way to the back wall, his arm was hit by the iron of a bed base; wincing he used his other arm, and he pushed the base off with all his strength. He screamed not only from the strength he exuded, but as he felt gashes at his leg which must have been cut by the broken glass from the empty ales.

As the water continued to fill the room, Bastian used all his might to ignore the injuries and push though the room to head up to hallway and to the deck like he saw others doing. Bobbling next to him was a mop of head from a lifeless miner – Bastian couldn't see who but tried to lift the man up but saw a great amount of blood coming from his forehead. Dropping him back down into the water he moved on. Bastian part swimming part using the force as a brace to go against the water flow, pushing himself through the chaos, as others tried to do the same all around him. Splashes of water washed over his face, and the water was filled with objects he couldn't see, pounding into his body as he swam.

The young boy, the messenger crewman of the *Running Arlo* screamed from behind them all, amongst the rush of water at the other end of the room. Bastian turned to see his face crying in pain as the water quickly rose; something was keeping the boy down, keeping him from breaking free. The urge to head straight out was overwhelming, but the boy's cries pierced him.

He rushed back as quickly as he could, the force of the water pulled him in every direction now as it swirled around the room. Dodging every bit of floating debris from the rushing water.

'It's okay,' Bastian gasped through the water as he reached the boy.

The boy took quick breaths but as the water rose above his mouth he panicked.

Diving down Bastian found a set of ropes had wrapped around his leg. The coil of the rope was held down by one of the bed bases that had rolled over.

Bastian grabbed a knife from his pocket and cut away at the rope, freeing the boy's leg.

Together they reached for the surface of the water and gasped for air.

'Thanks,' the boy murmured.

'Come on,' Bastian said; there was less and less air to breath in the small room and they still had to get up the hallway and out to deck.

Even worse, Bastian had no idea if their little room was only an air pocket in a ship that may already be well under the sea. Still, he had to keep swimming, now using the slats across the roof to pull him along. Keeping the boy close Bastian moved against the current of the waters, manoeuvring himself around a floating barrel, trying to ignore multiple knocks and scratches to his sides by the debris that washed underneath the water. Wincing in pain, Bastian continued; he was determined that this wouldn't be their end.

The hallway was completely underwater, they'd have to swim for it. The adrenaline and fear mildly excited Bastian for a moment; he realised he was half smiling at the concept of such a difficult challenge. Being in Sildor such a long time he had nearly forgotten the rush an adventure like this gave him.

'Are you ready?' Bastian asked the young man, trying to hide his enthusiasm.

'I, I don't know if I can,' said the boy.

'Look you don't have a choice. Just hold on to me and we will get through,' Bastian said, wishing he believed his own words.

On the count of three they pushed off into the hallway. Bastian couldn't see anything, but felt his way around. It was maybe ten metres until the stairs. The pressure of the water coming at them made it hard to swim forwards, and he held onto the rail and pulled up. Going as quickly as he could, feeling for the young boy behind him, holding onto his pants as they finally reached the stairs.

Both of them broke free of the surface, reaching the deck that was partially underwater, and the weather outside was still wild as ever. Dragging themselves up onto the decking they held on as the storm whirled the ship around. A rage of anger thrown from the skies, and them in the heart of it below.

'Oi. You two, Jump in.'

Bastian turned to see Ulysses on a lifeboat, with seven others who he couldn't make out.

'Let's go,' Bastian called out to the boy, ignoring the dangers around him, focusing only on the boat ahead.

'Go,' Bastian said, partly pushing the boy off the ship toward the boat, not even waiting for the splash when he sprung off the deck and out to the blackened sea below.

The storm still ravaged as they sat in the lifeboat. Bastian felt sickened seeing the ship in its final moments disappear amongst the waves and into the depths, knowing that there were many others that didn't make it.

Tired and worn out every last one of them, the aim to get to Perdita faded in them all except for Ulysses.

'We may be few. But we will not fail. We will carry on men, we will strive for what is ours, and continue on for those we have lost,' he said.

This time it wasn't as a loud speech but in soft spoken words, tears running down his cheek. There was a real sadness to him. He had cared for some of the men he had lost. Bastian had noticed Credence and Deacon his right-hand men weren't aboard. He wondered how long they must have known each other, not just them but many of the others.

Still his words were enough to get everyone paddling, get the lifeboat moving towards the island.

Against the rain the waves the pelted over the lifeboat they all pushed and pulled at the paddles, unsure if they were moving at all Bastian tried not to fall out of sync. He noticed the woman and her partner behind him, now both unhooded; the lady in pants now so obvious as the rain washed across her face – but her strength at the paddle just as strong as any man there.

***

Bastian paddled and paddled, with the saltiness of the water continuously splashing over him, and the breeze from the wind icy against his damp clothes, the chill was almost unbearable. His arms grew wearier, and the ache of his arm only increased with every motion. His head heavy from exhaustion, Bastian continued with his eyes closed, but at some point he passed out. Dreaming; his mind wandered off far away to his home with his Mother and Sticks. Caring about nothing but the small adventures that they once thought to be large. Climbing trees to see the largest views and racing home before dark.

'Your close my friend, closer than you think,' Sticks said to him, patting him on the shoulder before walking off inside Bastian's old family home chatting gleefully with his mother.

Bastian woke.

The darkness of the sky had gone, the blue above him was bright, and the glare caught his eye. His mouth dry from the flavour of salt and thirst struck him hard. Their boat was washed onto the sand of a beach, knocked up on its side, he still lay inside of it, along with eight others. Bastian looked off to the sea and could still see the storm swirling steadily past the shoals offshore.

Ulysses was crouched next to something on the beach; he had a bag so big that Bastian wasn't too sure how he had missed it before.

Unsteadily getting out of the lifeboat, and making his way to Ulysses, Bastian asked 'How did you manage to get that out of the ship with everything going on?'

'You think I'm going to let a little shipwreck get the best of my outcome? You hardly know me boy, I will do everything I can to gain whatever powers the Grinnwick Guard has their heart set on. It will be mine, and if they want to use it, it will come at a hefty price,' Ulysses growled.

'Where are they?' Bastian asked, noticing that many of the others had gathered to hear the conversation. A silly question as he felt the rumbling of machinery in the distance deep within the forest on the island.

'Well, I'm betting it won't take too long to find them with that racket,' Ulysses advised.

'Do you know where to look for the source?' One of the crew asked, at this moment Bastian felt the presence of the young boy now at his side.

'All anyone knows is this island is the source. No one knows what kind of form it takes – we'll hear the Guard sure enough the closer we get,' Ulysses answered.

'Well let's get looking,' Bastian prompted, trying to be encouraging. Even though he unlike the others had surmised that they were marooned on this island, with no way home and no means to contact the outside world, the only way was forward instead of sitting on a beach forever.

'Before we head off take one of these guns. They're top grade and run on Cor-fuel so the water won't have damaged them. And besides, you don't want to be caught off guard if we run into any unfriendlies,' Ulysses said, handing out the weapons to every man (and woman) on the beach, and throwing the bag over his shoulder before leading them into the forest.

Questioning how on earth Ulysses managed to get the guns onto the lifeboat was nearly pointless, Bastian knew if there was a way Ulysses would find it. He was clever like that.

Bastian took an arrow gun, even though he knew they'd need them sooner or later he felt uncomfortable about having it. Knowing that this was a bad idea, that an outright attack on the soldiers would undoubtedly lead to the soldiers walking over them full steam ahead.

Part of him felt that it wasn't the only problem, as he stood on the beach a feeling of uneasiness as though the island itself swept through him. A warning, it was as though it was conscious and sending out signals that it didn't want them here. He was unable to explain the sense, only that his gut told him this place was home to something more curious than the Grinnwick Guard, but he decided to keep it to himself.

He had followed the others. In front of him were the lady and her comrade, who Bastian suspect to be family from the similar darker tone of skin. They both inspected the guns in their hand.

'Here, let me show you,' Bastian spoke up to the two who seemed a little flustered that he spoke to them.

He showed them the trigger, and the on off switch – 'just make sure you point it towards anyone attacking us, not yourselves alright.'

They thanked him, but didn't say much else. They walked strangely Bastian thought, lighter than the other men in front of them.

Their presence while odd only meant that they were after the same thing as the Ulysses and the miners, the Heart of Grinnwick. Each one of the miners, and crewman too – bar the messenger boy, was rough and more deadly than your everyday criminal, part of him had put out of his mind how far they would go to obtain something none of them could possibly understand. The Heart of Grinnwick wasn't meant to be in the hands of the Grinnwick Guard, yet it shouldn't be with people like this either. Bastian needed to be smart – he needed to get himself in a position where he could claim the stone, or jewel, or whatever it was, under the radar, keeping it safe from everyone.

The Race for Perdita

The darkness lingered as Scarlet's mind woke, she had no strength to move. She felt the water washed up against her toes and the sand beneath her sticking to her bare arms and legs. She opened her eyes to find she wasn't alone.

A dozen or more men stared down at her in the night, each looked as though a combination of grey like a rock as well as dirt, their skin looked just as hard as a rock would be. Their eyes looked out through the cracks in the rocky crevasses of their face, and each one had protrusions of what could only be wood, or perhaps roots to be more particular coming out of their heads and shoulders. Whatever they were, they weren't human, that she was sure of. It had been a long time since she'd been amongst fae, but just maybe that's what these people were.

Scarlet propped herself up taking in the sight of the strange men, as curious as they seemed not one of them looked to be aggressive. Still not one of them said a thing.

'Hello. My name is Scarlet Rivers. Who are you? What is this place?' She asked, finding it hard to stand, bracing her feet as the ground shifted, exhausted – her head still thundering and a deep ache in her ribs.

Each one of them stared at her curiously, like she was a monkey in a cage. She understood that compared to them she was extremely different, whereas to her they were otherworldly.

With every moment passing Scarlet felt even more uncomfortable as they continued to stare at her.

Ignoring them as best as she could Scarlet looked to her surroundings properly. The endless pale beach was lit up by the bright moonlight which mirrored across the calm seas, with the calming brushes of small waves that rolled in. Further out to the sea the skies were dark, the storm that she must have been brought through. Up ahead where the beach ended was the edge of a tropical forest, an isolated paradise. Even against the moonlight it took her breath away. Scarlet could only wonder how the lights had managed to bring her all this way, they had only entered the Endless Sea when she was called to them, but they brought her through the storm, through the chaos of the seas safely. This had to be it, this had to be where her answers were.

The men around her suddenly stood back making a path for her to walk through. At the end an elderly man with a short yet fluffy beard, almost like moss but of grey instead stood waiting to greet her. His rock skin had started to crack in many places.

'What is this place? Who are you?' Scarlet asked him directly, feeling herself breathless; the journey through the sea must have been rougher on her than she realised. The man however didn't respond. He took her hand, looking down at it as if to check every inch of it, then he looked up at her, staring just as intently as any of the others around them.

He went to talk, his voice rusty and weary. 'Do not fear,' he said, his accent was deep as he spoke.

'You came looking, and you have found. We must hurry,' he said simply.

'What have I found?' Scarlet asked. She wasn't sure of anything, or of how safe she was with these people. Still the feeling of trusting in the bright leaves that guided her here had trusted in this path. If as Dawson had said long ago, they would truly guide her, being here must be where she needed to be.

Nothing she had learnt with the Amari, or from one of Monroe's books had prepared her for a situation, even for a girl who grew up in a time bubble, she hadn't any idea about these people, who they were, or what they were. Welcoming her was one thing, asking her to follow was another, to what ends would she need to go to find out answers?

The old man sensed her insecurities and held her hand. 'You are in Perdita. The home of the Heart.

'My people live in service to the Heart. As we have from the beginning. We are one of the original people of this land,' the Elder said, taking her hand and leading them all into the forest.

'My name is Jesa W'Anto. With joy we all welcome you,' Jesa said, his hands warm even as they felt like stone.

'What's the Heart?' Scarlet asked. She was given no reply only a childish laugh, which seemed almost sweet coming from someone of his age. He led her off the beach and into the trees. Palms and vines surrounded them. Squarks of birds and the rustling as they flew off while they walked along a hidden path. For over an hour they walked, and eventually came to a narrow stream that they too follow, with no water and still sore from her thrashing around on the deck Scarlet felt herself slow, but oddly was comforted as the men all slowed with her – no one seemed bothered by the lack of pace. The stream eventually led them to an opening, a valley of green rolling hills, full of brightly decorated huts, people and animals that all were going about their activities, their home.

Every one of them was smiling and chatting as they carried out the duties for the evening. Their gentle and easy-going nature only added to the serenity and the gentle peace within them all. The women sang by the stream as they washed their small children and gathered water. Many of the men were working on their fishing spears, and piling up the ones they'd already made. They were laughing about something as far as she could tell. In the middle of the valley, at the centre of the village of Perdita embers burned with a large pig beginning to roast on top of it. It seemed almost tribal, something Scarlet hadn't seen before. But the way they worked together was not unlike the Amari, everyone had their place.

Many people came up to them as they arrived, all watching over Scarlet as she passed them.

A younger lady moved quickly through the crowd and greeted the troupe that had arrived. She wore a long green dress, and her hair bun was wrapped in wooden stems that grew from her head in a way that somehow looked refined. The lady carried herself with grace amongst everyone else, greeting the others with words Scarlet didn't understand only before bowing her head towards Scarlet. A rushed motion from that point saw the same lady bring her away into one of the huts.

The hut was made out of all sorts of vines, branches, palms, and woods. The inside was just as colourful as the outside with weaves of material flowing in and out, along with feathers decorating the roof in blues, greens and yellows. It had a distinct scent of fresh rainfall inside. A platter of fruits, and sweet buns were laid out on a tray.

Famished, Scarlet went straight for them, eating a tangy berry bun within seconds.

Slightly embarrassed Scarlet turned around to the girl who she noticed had small purple flowers growing down the side of her face. She gulped down the last bite in her mouth before taking a breath. 'It's okay. Eat,' she said, encouraging Scarlet.

'Thanks. Can you tell me where exactly am I? What's going on here?' Scarlet asked, not expecting as much as a few strings of sentences pulled together, but was pleasantly mistaken.

'You're safe, I promise. My name is Cara W'Anto, I am the Chief Jesa's granddaughter. You are in Perdita, an ancient island off of Grinnwick's mainland, this valley here is our home,' Cara said.

'Nice to meet you, I'm Scarlet. What exactly are you?' Scarlet asked, trying her best to remain calm , her frustrations at being clueless starting to dawn on her.

'It is our responsibility to help you. We will keep you safe,' Cara assured her.

'Why? You don't know me,' Scarlet questioned. Taking a brush Cara went to brush Scarlets hair ignoring her question, forcing Scarlet to sit still; this was not the time to be brushing hair, what a ridiculous thing to do.

'Please, tell me.'

'We are one of the original people of this land. It is truly important for us to have you here. If we cannot guide you in time, no one will ever be able to guide you,' Cara advised.

'Guide me where?' Scarlet asked.

'It is curious that you do not know. This place, it is a part of you after all. Do you not know who you are?' Cara asked curiously. 'It has been a long time since the Heart has returned to us, and even just looking at you, I can feel what is inside you, like a wave that washes over those you meet; we can all see its strength.

She finally left Scarlets' hair, and then began unfolding what looked to be a black dress onto the bed.

'Cara,' Scarlet said, interrupting as she unpacked. 'I don't understand, I'm sorry. I know I'm different, I get that. But I truly have no idea what that means. All I know is I felt myself being guided off my ship, the light; an instinct, something inside of me.

'I know logically that I'm here because my brother left a map for me, a map that only I could see the path on; a map that was supposed to lead me to answers.

'But why is this all happening, why do I feel this connection? All the strange and peculiar things that have happened, the things I've seen, and done. None of it has really made much sense, some of them would confuse some pretty wise people. Really, all I want to know is why, why am I here?' Scarlet asked, feeling her own desperation in her voice.

Cara sighed with a sense of disappointment.

'Nothing is wrong. Well perhaps something – you are more lost to yourself than any of us could have predicted. You are here because this is where your people come from, it is the place of your blood. It has been a long time since a presence such as yours has returned to Perdita. It was well before my time, and even before my grandfather's earliest memories that a Heart needed us.

'What has been passed down to us is to expect your arrival. You see our people have never left Perdita, and never will. We are of the old world and forgotten to man. A being different from the others of Grinnwick as you can tell, we are a part of this land. We are connected to it; in a way just like you. And so, we have lived here in service to the Hearts of Grinnwick when we are needed—'

'The Heart of Grinnwick's here…' Scarlet asked, butting in, more than a little shocked. She had heard tale before, but just that – tales.

'Yes. It is here,' Cara mused, her eyes wide with admiration for Scarlet.

Scarlet was more confused than ever, how was it here?

She didn't question though, instead she let Cara continue.

'Now, even from here, far from the mainland, it has been evident for centuries that the flickering of the Hearts light has been waning, the magic growing faint and the hope that it brought with it. Not only seen as part of the more brutal storms that have ruined much of the islands around us, more so protecting us from the darkness, keeping the home of the Heart safe for when needed. I suppose it is not only here that more crops are dying off because the land is less fertile, we use to have multiple valleys, but the land couldn't sustain it, many were lost. The days too are shorter than the years before.

'A dark figure covers this world now, biding its time in the shadows, it's plan going too well as it lurks ready for the light to be completely extinguished and open up the chance for creatures below to return to the surface.'

'Deep inside you that spark is strong. A possibility for bringing hope and magic back into this land once again resides with you. Somehow, it's been hidden inside of you, pushed down to a place you have forgotten. Unseen to the land itself, a binding of sorts. Only, by coming here and following the path waiting for you will you be able to embrace it. Even if you don't seem to know yourself, who you are, or what you can be. At the rise of the next full moon the pool will be full, and you will see; you will finally know, and it will all make sense,' Cara said.

'What dark figure?' Scarlet asked.

'You may not remember but you've felt his power; his evil before when you were a child. It was the darkness that he held that tore your family apart. He bled hate into the people who took their lives. As long ago as that was, his presence has been hiding, biding his time to get his claws back into our world, and once he senses your power – into you,' Cara cautioned.

'A weakened Heart of Grinnwick, a scared soul of this world can be targeted by the dark magic such as his. Don't allow him to take you my child, if you ever feel his darkness think of the light, think of love and that will ground you. Many speak of the mind and the heart separately from each other, but if one is affected the other is open to illness. It is in your best interest as the Heart to hold onto all that is good, as it will be your key to your strength. If you faulter, you can be manipulated and eventually fall towards the tempting depths of the world.'

'The Heart of Grinnwick…,' Scarlet pondered.

'I'm the Heart… I can't be the Heart. I'm a person. Besides it's a bedtime story, not a real thing.'

'Is that so, you will see. You are the Heart.'

Scarlet wondered in silence for a time.

From the moment she had left the safety of the Amari she had tried to ignore strange occurrences, her connection to Grinnwick, through the shadow people, the plants, the forces of nature that she felt in touch with. Maybe she wasn't so different from the witch Dawson once mentioned of the Corazon Forest.

'Let us not worry right now about what might be; Tonight, you rest. your tea will let you sleep for days through until the full moon, your body will be restored, and you will be ready for the path ahead,' Cara finished.

Scarlet looked at the tea before her, she was exhausted and sleep would be a welcome treat, she sipped on it slowly and sat quietly in thought.

Her knowledge of the Heart of Grinnwick was small, and if Mason was to be believed it was exactly what the Grinnwick Guard was looking for; she was their prize, the source that was being searched for; she was the Heart of Grinnwick… apparently.

She tried to remember any knowledge from the Amari about the Heart. Stories she had once loved, now she couldn't quite remember them. Only that the Heart was a part of the beginning of all that was. A star, a spark that broke through the world and brought magic – life. The idea that she was connected to such an object, a long-lost myth was past her wildest dreams. How could something so strong and powerful be within her all these years? Were they going to get it out of her? Whatever the dawn would bring, it could only have more answers and no doubt more questions.

Cara had insisted that she continue to brush Scarlet's hair before she sleep. Leaving her with a fluffy version of her usual waves, Scarlet was thankful as it felt softer than it had in such a long time. Before she knew it though her eyes were closed, and the peaceful rest had taken over.

***

Jesa and Cara woke her together; however rested she was, Scarlet felt shocked. They both seemed off, something was wrong.

Cara got out a sheer black dress, with silver and pink patterns weaved along its finishes. Perhaps a little revealing, but she didn't feel comfortable enough to refuse.

Scarlet, enamoured by its beauty as the soft material slipped through her fingers, allowing Cara to help her get into it and help with her hair. The mid sectioned was double lined so it gave some sense of decorum.

Scarlet could see the darkness of the night through the opening of the hut – why would they wake her now? How long had she actually slept? She was sure it had been more than a night's worth.

Blasts could be heard in the distance, causing her to jump.

'What's happening?' Scarlet asked them.

'The moon is rising… No time to delay, we must go NOW bad men are here –' Jesa warned.

'Who? What?' Scarlet asked, following them outside only to find herself faced with the full force of the rock people of Perdita, each of them waiting for her outside her hut, still in the dead of night.

Scarlet soon realised that all was not as it seemed. The reality before her was quickly beginning to dawn; there was a commotion on the island. Flames could be seen in the distance, and abrupt echoes of explosions reached them, and the vibrations shuddered through her.

'They've been here for days, searching for the Heart – the source – you.' Cara said as Scarlet stood uncomfortably in front of the hut looking to the distance.

'The Grinnwick Guard,' Scarlet said.

Even after coming all this way, fear trickled into her mind of what she just might find at the end of this path, here in the furthest corner of the world.

Was it all worth this mayhem? How could the answers she had longed for, for all this time, really be at the centre of dangers that gained on them all? Was what she was searching for really that important that the people here would risk their life for it?

Chief Jesa walked her past his people, completely ignoring everyone that waited and watched her. He was not able to shield their faces of concern as Scarlet walked by.

'Wait,' Scarlet said, stopping in her tracks turning to everyone. 'I know I came for answers. Do you really believe I am the one who needs to take this path, after all this time you've waited? I mean, you found me on a beach; I could be anyone. What if you're honouring the wrong person?' Scarlet questioned, taking a step back from where the chief guided her.

Chief Jesa looked to Cara. 'You explained?' he looked confused.

'Yes Chief,' she responded, looking embarrassed while the whole tribe stared at them.

Chief Jesa turned back to Scarlet.

'Girl, you long for family. This place holds their biggest secrets,' he spoke clearly, making sure she understood.

'In you, I see it. You beam like the stars in the sky, and it has only grown with rest, you are like a sun to this world. No one can look away. My people are concerned, because your overall path is much bigger than the one you are about to go down. Your future is uncertain as is the fate of each and every one of us before this night ends.

'They do not wish to see harm come to one that we serve; and they fear that the darkness will reach you before you reach the path,' the chief said.

'I don't like this,' Scarlet said. 'Whoever, whatever is coming towards us is too close, the fires, the explosions. I can't leave you all; I can help, I can defend you,' Scarlet pleaded.

'You do not yet know how, and the world of Grinnwick is much bigger than just us,' he replied.

She knew too well that without her, without allowing her to help there wouldn't be much hope for these people. That their spears and muscle, while strong, wouldn't be a match for fire and machines fuelled by the glowing green Cor-Marinium.

'Sometimes girl, you must let go to allow for something much more glorious to grow. My people will keep the world at bay, several lifetimes have passed but we have waited to do all that we can. Do not fear for us, we are stronger than we seem. Follow me now and you will find the path. You will also find the life you deserve,' Chief Jesa said. He spoke so clearly, that Scarlet could tell he had practiced it.

'Please child, take my hand,' Chief Jesa said, his voice calm and soft.

Scarlet looked at his hand and stepped towards him. He would not give her more answers than that she was certain. Cara stood at her other side as they walked away from the valley and their people, as they headed up the hill into the thickest part of the forest.

Ignoring the echoes that were drawing closer to the valley as best she could Scarlet tried to walk with her head high, she couldn't help but feel wrong as she left everyone behind.

It didn't take long down the path for her worries to turn to her current predicament however as they reached further inland. She was taken aback with the change to the air. It was lighter and filled with a thin mist. And with every step Scarlet took, the ground beneath her reacted – she hadn't noticed at first. The soft dirt turned before each of her steps, changing into brightly coloured blooms, lighting their path, touching softly against her toes as she walked along. She was unsure when they first appeared but after an encouraging nod from Chief Jesa, she continued along that path up towards the peak of the island. The walk was like a dream, the bright colours against the deep black of night; breathtaking.

'This is where we leave you Scarlet,' Cara said, her breath heavy and her sweating face exhausted, causing part of the wrinkles on her cheek to crack. The thinning air was taking a harsher toll on the others than what it caused Scarlet. Chief Jesa too looked extra weary, and leant onto a nearby tree to keep himself up.

Scarlet hadn't noticed how badly the air up here had affected them; how long had they continued like this, wanting to stay on with her. She felt it in her breath but with no real struggle to continue. Moving to Chief Jesa's side to help him stand upright.

'Follow the path, it will continue to light the way, this is how you will know where. If you choose to visit us again, we will be here when you need, no matter what happens tonight,' Cara said, where her grandfather failed to speak.

'I'll come back to you straight from the path, I'll help against the people who are attacking,' Scarlet said.

She didn't know what Cara meant; she had nowhere else to go, and there was no way she would leave them to face the intruders alone. She knew that they wouldn't allow her to stray from this path, but they couldn't stop her from returning to their side.

'Sadly,' Cara gasped as the lack of air cut her off for a moment. 'You will not need us. And if the stars are right you are better off going on,' Cara said, taking her grandfather's hand.

'We wish you happiness,' he said, struggling with his words but gathering what strength he could to give Scarlet a hug, before Cara helped him to return down the valley.

Scarlet watched as they departed, knowing if she got through the path ahead quickly, she could return to them, to help them from the attackers.

Anxiously turning ahead, she was ready.

Fight for Perdita

'Hello there.'

Bastian looked up, returning from his thoughts as he followed the crew into the forest. The young crewman from the ship seemed to be even more intimated and shy as he approached Bastian.

'Hi,' Bastian said.

'I'm Pug,' the boy said most awkwardly. He was now like a drowned squirrel, or rodent of sorts; his smell left a gross taste in Bastian's mouth.

'It's the nose,' Pug added, pointing to his nose, drawing Bastian's eyes to his pig-like facial features.

'What's your real name?' Bastian asked.

'Darcy, Darcy Moriarti,' the boy replied.

'Nice to meet you,' Bastian said. 'Call me Harker.'

'I, I just wanted to thank you for um, saving my life Harker. I mean, you didn't have to, but you did. And, anyways, thanks. Also, if you need absolutely anything, just let me know – I'm your man,' Darcy aka Pug trembled. He was enthusiastically polite. Not something that was going to be useful in a situation like this. Still, he reminded Bastian of a twiggy young Russ, so it wasn't hard for him to take a quick liking to the little guy.

'Thanks kid, but I'm guessing you probably didn't think you were coming on this part of the journey, did you?' Bastian said, waiting for him to shake his head before he continued.

'What you can do for me is, look out for yourself. I have a feeling this place is more dangerous than anyone really understands just yet, don't let anything fool you. The Guard's going to be much more relentless than

Ulysses or any of these men are even prepared for. So just keep an eye out, okay.'

Darcy nodded, promising to do exactly that.

'Actually Darcy, do you know who those two are?" Bastian pointed at the dark-skinned man and woman who would've been similar in age to him.

'I didn't think they were miners.'

'Them?' No, they're not. The captain from the *Gauntlet* organised for them to come aboard. Their friend apparently fell from the ship, they're hoping to find her… don't think they're able to face the truth if I'm honest, they lost her on the edge of the Endless Seas, and that's multiple days of sailing to reach up here' Darcy noted.

Bastian looked at them curiously, then caught up to them.

'Hi, sorry, I don't mean to intrude but who are you both exactly?'

They both looked at each other for a moment before turning to him. He couldn't help noticing now that he was up close just how stunning they were, like an even symmetry of beautiful features. Only the male and female version from one another. Their darkened features soft, and their eyes both green, a contrast not seen very often. Had they been in a city, they would have been of high-class family, they looked refined in that sort of way he thought. Bastian has never referred to a man as stunning before… but he was. He felt an odd sense of calm from them, even though they seemed tightly strung in the moment. He could only pinpoint to the way they breathed, like to a different beat – slower perhaps.

'What's it to you?' replied the girl, her snappy demeanour a little off putting.

'I just think I ran into your companion from the *Gauntlet,* Mister Walsh,' Bastian answered, 'He said you lost someone overboard.'

'Oh, yeah we did.' The boy didn't look like he wanted to talk all that much.

'It's just you came all this way, you're risking your lives, do you really think she survived?' He didn't know why he was curious, but something seemed odd about why anyone would come so far, how could they even suspect she'd be here of all places? It was impossible to reach by boat.

'Look you don't know us, and you don't know our friend. This is where they were heading, and we know she'll turn up. We just do,' the boy replied... lost in hope more than anything Bastian thought.

Bastian didn't push further, he pulled back to continue walking behind Darcy.

**

Bastian had an eerie feeling that they weren't alone. A feeling he hadn't entirely been prepared for. As he peered around himself into the trees, it was like he was seeing the whites of the eyes blending into the forest around him, but in a blink, they vanished.

Darcy, who stood beside him rambling about how before he had come to work on the *Running Arlo* he'd always wanted to go get his own bit of land in the outer districts and have a quiet life, and that the *Arlo* paid pretty well. That this was supposed to be the big job that landed him a pay check so he might just do that, if he got out of here that was.

Distracted, Bastian hesitated, staring into a set of fierce eyes he'd locked onto in the distance.

'Run,' Bastian whispered to him quietly, signalling for him to tell the others.

He remained steady as Darcy told the crew ahead to run on. He realised that the one pair of eyes were not the only ones, dozens surrounded them.

These people weren't the Guard either; they were wild, non-human, and unlike anything he expected.

He knew that the Grinnwick Guard would not be far from them, he had expected them, knowing that they would have people on the lookout. What he didn't expect were locals on the island; a fateful mistake to be sure – naive and stupid on his behalf. As the first visitors to the island in a long time, their presence would undoubtedly be unwanted, and from the looks of them he was right.

How long had these people protected these lands, how long had they kept prying eyes from what lay on the island? When Bastian was first sent on the mission, he had no idea, how could he be so stupid not to investigate more on the island. Possibly these people, these being were doing exactly what he was, protecting the Heart of Grinnwick, they were the main defence.

If the storm that brought them all here hadn't killed them, the locals certainly would give it a good try. With a closer look he could see their skin was harsh, hard and cracked, a grey colour with horn like branches sticking out of their heads, their eyes fierce like bulls. He only hoped there was the same intensity being delivered by them to the Grinnwick Guard.

Up ahead shots were heard. Bastian's attention turned towards the sound; he could no longer see his crew; they had followed Darcy and run for it. Bastian held onto his weapon and raced forward; a mass of trees surrounded him. Searching for the sight of one of the others, his gaze finally found one of the crew, nodding to let them know he was there. He could see them move forward.

Smoke filled beneath the trees, and vision of the others became difficult. Moving from tree to tree as he heard more shots fired. As he moved along hoping the others were okay, he came into a manmade clearing. Where the trees were either cut down from the base or burning.

Explosions began to rattle the ground beneath him. He ducked for cover behind a boulder, peering around to the scene below. The smoke was clearing – unfortunately for him at the far side of the clearing were a couple of hundred soldiers from the Grinnwick Guard, covered in protective wear, each holding guns as large as the next.

They had large machinery dug deep into the ground that looked perfect for digging up the land. Clearly, they hadn't had a problem reaching the island with all their gear intact.

They had already burnt a large patch of trees and cleared the land down to a small gorge.

Having the soldiers walk through the cleared land with detectors sensing any motion of power sources. It was these soldiers who'd been shooting into the mass of the trees, at the rest of his crew. Other Grinnwick Guard soldiers were setting up explosives to clear away sturdier, rockier terrain. It was the dust and smoke of the explosives that covered the trees around him.

Darcy caught Bastians gaze amongst the trees, and made a motion for him to move closer to the rest of the crew. The pair from the Gauntlet were with him too, they were all miming at him to quickly move, the Guard must have noticed the miners running and shot before asking questions.

A standard Grinnwick Guard procedure, Bastian thought to himself. Shoot before questioning. Trying to move on towards Darcy he found himself behind a tree, stuck; two soldiers were heading their way and would see them both if he cut across.

Pointing to them to go on ahead without him, as he then nodded towards the soldiers who'd see him if he came across.

He had a sinking feeling in his stomach as he watched Darcy's shadow slip into the darkness. Then followed yelling and shots being fired coming from the same direction they had gone. He hoped beyond hope that every one of them were okay.

Bastian prepared his gun as the smoke around him thickened; the soldiers were lighting more fires, clearing the land. Bastian ran as soon as the smoke masked his escape. Running across the forest as far as he could, the heat of the blaze burning around him, make the sweat from his brow drip constantly. He heard shots in the background as he drew further and further away. He didn't stop, he panted and felt the bone in his arm ache in pain from being hit back on the ship, still he continued moving ahead. The trees thickened around him if that was even possible, and the smoky haze began to clear. Catching his breath, he froze.

Again, he wasn't alone.

Whack.

He awoke in a natural clearing, tied to a tree, his arrow gun on the ground near a fire. The locals of Perdita were sitting by it, glaring at him as he came out of his daze. They were under the dark night sky and his pounding head only made it harder to see the men before him, making out mostly their silhouettes like shadows against the fire. There were at least six of them.

'Excuse me,' Bastian said, still a bit groggily. At these words, a particularly grindy type of rock man came by and knocked him back over the head.

Waking up for a second time, it was nearing dawn, and there were only three men by the fire. As his mind came back Bastian decided to remain quiet – he listened in, but they did not speak any English.

He sat there in silence, until one of them came over with a cup of water for him to drink.

'Who are you?' the rock man asked, this local man of Perdita didn't seem as fearsome as the others, in fact even as he spoke aggressively Bastian could see the sorrow in his eyes.

'I'm Bastian Conway,' he said, hoping to be as truthful as possible.

'You do not belong,' the man said. Bastian could see as he spoke parts of his rocky skin had fallen away, and there was a limp to his step that was no doubt from already fighting the intruders on their land.

'No, I don't,' Bastian agreed. He was looking over the man's shoulder to see if the knucklehead who knocked him out was still there; part of him uneasy that a wrong answer could land him with another blow to the head. As far as he could see the buffoon of a man had gone.

'What do your people want?' the man continued, his accented a thick broken English, just manageable to understand.

'They are not my men. They came for a power source, a stone of sorts,' Bastian said, only to be responded with laughter from all of the men, a moment of joyful relief even as they looked exhausted from whatever forces the Grinnwick Guard had put up against them.

'What's funny?' Bastian asked them.

'Men, always looking for trinkets and treasure. Your people will never find what they search for with such small minds.'

A clue, thought Bastian. The Heart of Grinnwick wasn't what it seemed; these men knew its secrets; they were the defence. He was merely a backup.

'What is it then? Please tell me,' Bastian said.

'We will die before you know any more,' the man said before spitting on the ground beside Bastian.

'Please, I'm not with those men. I'm not fighting, I didn't want to burn down your home, I don't want anything to happen to you. I want to keep the Heart of Grinnwick out of the hands of anyone else here. I'm a Guardian, have you heard of our people? All I want is to keep it safe. It's my mission,' Bastian tried his best to explain, hoping that they understood. None of them said anything however, they returned to their fire.

Screams of an impending army, as well as the people of Perdita's forces cries loomed as the sun began to rise. Their cries could be heard against the clashes of guns, along with more explosions. As the sound spread across the forest it was clear to Bastian that the Grinnwick Guard were indeed taking full control. The men before him would either perish, or would be left with the ruins.

They didn't look alarmed however, they spoke in whispers to each other over the fire for what was more than a few minutes before returning to him.

'You. You are a Guardian.'

Bastian nodded.

'I don't trust you, but it is not my place,' he said, his English broken. Unhooking Bastian from the tree and tugging at his sore arm; Bastian cringed in pain. A hood was placed over his head, and he was pushed forcefully down the path.

Walking for a long time in silence, he didn't know if this was a good or bad thing. The rock man gave him a drink of whatever every half an hour or so as they walked on. After a time, he heard people speak, again in words he didn't know.

His capturer forced him to his knees, removing his hood to face an elderly man of Perdita whose rocky face looked ancient like the cliffs that bared their walls by the sea, constantly bashed with the turning tides.

'You are a Guardian. What is your name?' the elderly man said.

'Bastian,' he replied.

'You look like some of the enemy, an enemy who is surrounding us now. Sometimes… Appearances are deceiving. You can go. But you must leave this place and never return,' the elderly man advised.

'That's it? You're just letting me go? Why?' Bastian kicked himself for questioning freedom, yet the intrigue pulled him in.

'Because, you were found running up the mountain path. A path that would consume the minds of any man who dared enter, air too thin for any mere mortal. Yet you boy were not bothered by it, you did not even notice the toll it should take. This is something that I cannot ignore. You are just a man, but perhaps a man who needs to continue up the path – So we will leave you here, to continue up the path while the last of us go to fight for this island; and I will tell them that the Heart has already been claimed; claimed it seems by you,' the elderly man said.

'This makes no sense. I don't even know what the Heart of Grinnwick is. And you're just giving it to me because I was able to walk up a path?

452

That seems ridiculous… How am I going to find it, I don't know what it is? Aren't you people supposed to be defending the bloody thing.'

The elderly man laughed.

'We guided the Heart back to their strength. Strong yet pure, innocent to the world. It needs protecting. But this is not their home. The island suspects you are worthy, and as we fall in the face of fire, I must trust in those that will continue on. I suspect you will know what the Heart is in time. And, if we leave you here you will find it.'

'Please sir, if you go back and face the Guard you will die, all of you will. Why don't you run, find a way out?' Bastian pleaded.

'Our people may not survive today, but tomorrow is another day, we will grow from the ashes. We do not fear what is to come,' he said proudly, putting his arm on Bastian's shoulder, nodding to one of his men to cut him free, and another who threw Bastians arrow gun to his side. Bastian stayed on his knees as he watched them disappear into the trees, the sun now fully spread across the trees around him.

Taking a breath, he got rid of the loose ropes around his hands and got to his feet.

The hilltop was covered with haze from the smoke – not as thick as it was around the valley, but it was spreading. The noise and commotion of gunfire and explosives eventually dissipated. An emptiness filled the whole island.

Bastian knew that even if the soldiers found out that what they had been searching for had been taken it wouldn't affect them one bit, they would retreat only after knowing they had covered every last inch of the island, and destroyed everyone who called it home.

As the air cleared Bastian decided to continue the path high up towards the peak, to find out what the Heart of Grinnwick was, it was not what it seemed; the men wouldn't be looking for something unexpected, their eyes were all fixed for rocks and jewels. He felt safe knowing that the leader of Perdita would face them and tell them they had failed, but that didn't mean the Heart of Grinnwick didn't need his protection. He himself still had to search.

A mist of hazy smoke now followed him upward, the heat of the fires started by the Grinnwick Guard seemingly spreading quicky – going to wipe the sweat from his brow as the first speckles of rain fell across his face – as though from a light spatter to a down pour Bastian sheltered his eyes to see the path ahead.

He found himself walking along the edge of a cliff, as he moved around to the east, he could see a small bay came into sight. Bastian stopped in his tracks, through the rain and smoke haze he could just make out the bay was where the Guard had landed their vessels, there were more than one – an army. Their soldiers were scattered all over the shore, many of them still returning in groups out of the forest. Their vessel was unlike any others, a ship that could submerge itself completely under the water; Bastian had never seen such machinery. He knew that The Grinnwick Guard played with contraptions, with versions of movers, much like the air-lift mover that the Guardians had so long ago – but something this vast, this unique it seemed unimaginable, and notably the force that it must have to control it, to keep the entire thing from sinking. Made of silver and bronze amongst steel cladding, with golden curved beams across the side. Undoubtedly the quickest and strongest one in all of their forces to make the trip in the rough seas, imagining that it was probably just as treacherous to journey below the water. With armour like that though it was no wonder their underwater ship clearly made it through the feisty seas and storms without worry.

A blast of green light brought his attention to the shore. Bastian caught sight of the soldiers; their guns pointed at twenty people.

He moved quickly. Getting himself close as he could to the edge of the ledge, half climbing into a tree that stuck out from below to see the scene down below. Squinting he saw that four of them were part of the crew he arrived with. One was of them was Darcy, the small piggish boy, the pair from the Gauntlet, and another miner.

Stopped in his tracks he watched the scene on the shores. His heartbeat faster, frustrated that he couldn't help any of them, it was just too far.

He watched as the soldiers forced them towards the sub.

Then they lined up the elderly leader and some of the people of Perdita, along with a few others he only assumed were from his ship. Bastian watched as the old man was spoken to by one of the Guards.

A split second was all it took.

The blast echoed all the way up to him. Goosebumps crept up his back and a sadness with it.

The Heart of the Pool

The bright light shone upon a tiny clearing. Ahead was a stone wall that formed part of a cliff edge. And in the middle of the clearing was a small circular pool of vibrant blue water as though there were light underneath. Trickles of water fell out of a crack in the wall and into the pool.

Scarlet stepped closer, in her gaze she stared into the pool. The full Moon directly above reflected off the pool back at her.

Looking into the pool there was no bottom to its depth in sight, but the water inside began to swirl, starting off slow but then became quicker and quicker forming a whirlpool. Inching her hand again to its edge she touched the water, and voices from the shadows called out all around her. Like the ones she had heard many times before, flickers of memories talking, ghosts of the past reaching out. She flicked her eyes around the clearing as they got closer. Confusion started to strain her head.

The sound of a young girl singing; the voice of children running through the trees; a man calling out, but for who she couldn't tell; cries of many all around her.

They stopped as swiftly as they came, a small relief.

Only as a voice she recognised called out; Flynn, a ghost, a memory of him. She saw him plainly as he called to her arms reaching out. Scarlet wanted to go to him, but remained sitting as another strong breeze caused him to disappear.

Scarlet wasn't alone anymore; she felt the strength from those who had whispered within her over the years.

As the water continued to whirl, a quick breeze swiped behind her from what Scarlet thought was an owl in flight, but as she turned towards the other side of the pool there was no bird; but a young girl, of maybe ten years old. Her pale freckled face smiled back to Scarlet, and she put her feet into the swirling edge of the water.

'You've been missed,' the little girl said, her voice distant and gentle. 'We thought we lost you a long time ago. Seems you lost us too, didn't you?' said the little girl giggling.

'Who are you?' Scarlet asked, keeping eye contact with the child who was dazzling to behold.

'You have seen shadows of us all, of the lives that were lived and are soon to be told. It is not common for a Heart to be ripped from who they are supposed to be, to not understand what they are at the core. Your shadows, your ghosts and your inner self calling out to you, trying to break open the light within. It has been a long time since Grinnwick has been beholden to one of us at full strength, and a long time coming for you too to feel whole having its strength in your grasp.' While she spoke the little girl seemed distracted. She was playing with a butterfly that had landed on her hand.

'I don't understand what you mean, I came here because I need answers; I've been losing control. My eyes are bleeding, and well, that's not normal! I don't know how I even do the things that I've done, but it seems to be getting stronger. I get that I'm being reminded of things I've probably forgotten, but does it need to upturn everything I do,' Scarlet ranted.

The little girl's expression changed; her focus was still on Scarlet, but her vagueness had gone.

'Nothing is easy, do not forget that. The people of Grinnwick; our people, your people, they turned on us, they took down the Heart unknowingly, yet remnants of it remained. You remain.

'Still, with your absence and powers locked away, and your sister diminished to a fraction of her true strength Grinnwick fell as the light of the Heart wasn't there to guide it, and it has kept plunging into darker days. Magic has hidden away, and the memory of what was if forgotten. That is, until now,' the little girl said, peering into Scarlet as many had done before. Assessing her in a way.

'*You* are the Heart. Every part of you, it is your entirety – you make up something so beautiful, yet you don't even know it,' she laughed.

'And you have the strongest light I have ever seen. In you is the power to control Grinnwick and its wonders, and all will bow before you,' the girl said, her enthusiasm great and full of wonder.

'Bow before me? I don't want that. All I want is my family back, I want to find Flynn, Archer, Dawson. To have my family all together. And to know my old family. Also, I'd like to be able to control whatever is happening inside of me. Didn't you hear what I was saying, I'm losing control.

'The strange things that happen; magic, or powers – whatever they are – if it is because I am the Heart, I don't really care. Just let me be in control of it all, for once, so I can live my life once again. If it's the magic that's causing me to be different, then get rid of it, please,' Scarlet asked.

'I can't change what you are. Who you will be is up to you. Your growing lack of control is because even though you are the Heart of Grinnwick, your heart has been supressed, you've been hidden; kept safe. Usually, one is brought up knowing what they are, and their mothers nurture those powers as it begins to outgrow her own. For you it has been kept deep down, sporadically forcing itself out over time. Now that the other Heart has died, her light gone. It has sparked your powers to have broken free, the worlds need to be connected to it, to you.

'You lost your mother too young. This is why you needed to come here. The binding that will make it easier to understand your power; the transference of all our knowledge, all that of what was and what could be. Like a starter spark to let you take your true form. Without knowing how you are bound to this world; I couldn't even begin to understand how confusing it must have been. The bleeding eyes happen, but only in moments that bring true pain,' the little girl said.

'You mean my mother was a Heart too, is that why Flynn wanted to follow this map? Is he one? Did he make it here? Was he the other Heart?'

The little girl sighed. 'No one has visited this place for a thousand years. And your brother has not journeyed up this path, and he would not find what he needed here anyway. The Heart is you; it is what you are. Your brother is but a fraction of that. Sons do not take up the power as daughters do, he does not have the strength within him to connect to Grinnwick as you will. Most sons contain some powers of the Heart, one is even known to hold many. For your brother it could still be a mystery to him. It is the same for those we love, we share with them a piece of our light, it in turn gives them unimaginable strength, but it can be lost in the event of our death.

'The only real reason for his journey here would be to know all that he could so he could help you.

'Now. You being here and the moments to come will be the beginning of your journey, as it was the beginning for the first Heart that gave strength to the world that is Grinnwick. So, you'll understand why Grinnwick needs you; why it needs its Heart. I will tell you all that I can, before the next step.

'Thousands of years ago, a star fell right here in this spot forming this pool. Now you may think a star is nothing more than a fiery ball of gas. Which is true for some, but the one who fell was so much more; she held magic and life. A true gift of the gods. This star was more than a burnt-up rock that had landed at the bottom of this hole, it was the first Heart, named Aviary.

'Mother to us all. From her arrival a light was sparked and Grinnwick was guided out of the fiery world that it once was, where monsters and dark shadows had free rein. It was in a flash her magic intertwined at the depths of this pool bonding herself and the world forever. It formed her fate, and she brought out the beauty in Grinnwick. The people of Perdita were the original people who found her alone and afraid of the new world, but it was them who saw what she could first do. She breathed energy into them, bringing them to life, to prosper. They saw that she was nothing but energy that was sent to bring Grinnwick back to life.

They saw her grow trees at the touch of a finger; breathe life back into creatures; calm the wildest seas; she was gentle and kind to them, and a natural leader as she brought peace between all those within Grinnwick. It was the stem of her power that faes were born to the magic of the lakes, forests, rivers, and more. Her power, her being was their source, their guiding light. Creatures who came to life because of her, because of the spark she gave to this world. There were those who were sceptical of course, but with this they met the fiery force that she wielded. Since that first day the Heart has been bound to the world of Grinnwick, and the two have been inseparable since. Back then she was a goddess to all those who followed in her wake, a star, a light for them to follow.

You have that same connection to Grinnwick. A bond that can't be broken, a magic that burns bright. Being hidden to this world kept your powers from forming, but you must understand they are yours, and now yours alone. Find courage inside of yourself and don't faulter to those who would use you for evil,' the little girl warned, stern and steady as she spoke with the wisdom of an ancient, rather than the child who Scarlet saw.

She allowed a moment before she softened. 'As the Heart, don't forget that there is so much beauty in Grinnwick. If you keep finding it and allow it to connect with you, the stronger you will be. Don't be drawn to the dark shadows, not by others or within yourself, don't confuse them with memories that come to you, your protective light, your ghosts. For you have been protected, but that also comes with a naive sense of the world. Be strong, be smart.'

'So, what is it I can do?' Scarlet asked. 'What do you expect of me?'

At this the little girl stood up and walked over to Scarlet, taking a seat by her side, her hand on her shoulder. 'Look in the pool.'

Scarlet did as she was asked, looking down at the ripples to her reflection and the girl beside her. Looking over to the girl's reflection, the face that she saw was different. A woman stared back, her face kind and warm with deep green eyes and long brown hair at her sides. Scarlet looked up to the girl, who had changed before her.

Shocked and confused, Scarlet had no words.

The girl, who was now a woman, cupped Scarlet's chin in her hand, looking lovingly into her eyes.

'My darling. My daughter.'

Scarlet felt breathless, this was madness, this was insanity, but she was so real before her.

'I could not be any happier with the young woman you have become. I cannot take this form for long; the light has allowed me access to you for such a short time.

'I want you to know I expect nothing more than for you to be happy and follow your dreams, do what you will, make sure you do it for yourself. I hope you are surrounded by love, as it will fill you to be stronger each day,' the woman said, her mother said.

Scarlet looked at the woman, hope flowing through her, and she was sure beyond anything that this was the woman from Flynn's drawing, it couldn't be anyone else but her mother. She wrapped her arms around her without thinking.

'I've wished I could have known you for so long,' Scarlet said, her shock suppressed the realisation that her face was covered in tears, again blood red.

'I've always been a part of you. I've always watched over you,' her mother said, her voice soft and gentle like a songbird.

'What happened to you?' Scarlet asked.

'It is a long, sad tale. The beginning of so much horror. A man I should have seen coming took me from you, he took so much from us all. My heart broke into so many pieces that night. There is no pain like the loss of one's children.

'You survived the madness with your brother, my two beacons of hope left. Alone and separated from the world you called home, the world that is yours. I wish I could have been there to guide you through this life but seeing you now, having this place bring me back to you, it's a blessing I couldn't have dreamed of,' she said.

'What is it my sweet?" her mother said.

'You really are my mother, aren't you?' Scarlet said.

The woman's face turned to disappointment. 'You do not recognise me at all?'

Scarlet shook her head. 'I don't know any of my family, just Flynn. I lost those memories long ago. Flynn used to say I was blessed by the bump to the head I received when I was young. That I wasn't haunted by the memories he had; I think he was wrong; he gets to remember you. Keep part of you with him. Still, sometimes I don't think the memories have left me; I hope the voices I hear, the ghost-like memories that I can't reach are part of you,' Scarlet said, feeling the tears across her cheek.

Taking a deep breath in, her mother said, 'Never has there been a child like you. No Heart has grown up the way you have, free of the burden of knowing what they are; of having to protect themselves.

'You need to do that now though, protect yourself. Be safe my sweet.'

Scarlet hugged her mother one more time. 'What am I supposed to do now?' she asked.

'This path is not over, I'm only here to guide you. A friendly face sent to make sure you understand, the steps you now take will open your eyes to your world, bringing out the strength inside of you.

'Unfortunately, with this you will also feel the pain if something happens in the world. Whether it be caused by nature or inflicted by man, you will feel the emotions of the land. In return too it will feel yours, your tears and your joy. You are now the true Heart of this land, only you. Remember to be brave, that the light runs deep, and know with these

463

connections you will never truly be alone,' her mother said, now looking to the depths of the pool and then back to the Scarlet. She grabbed hold of Scarlet's hand tightly.

'I will be with you. All you need to do is dive into the pool and all that connects you to Grinnwick will finally make sense.'

The scary truth was that Scarlet felt that this all may just be too much for her. She wasn't ready for any of this, unsure that she should have chased after these answers. Feeling an eerie sense that her caretaker Ailsa's fears for her all those years ago had been rightly placed. Part of her wished she had never left the Amari, and the safety that the small village had provided her.

'It'll be okay,' her mother promised.

'There isn't a choice here my love, you were never supposed to be disconnected from this world as you were, it has unbalanced you, and Grinnwick as a result has paid the price for centuries running on just a flicker of our flame. It has unbalanced everything. Once you take the leap, you will truly be capable of anything. A gift and a curse, but I believe in you. I know you hold the courage to carry on in this world,' she said.

Scarlet felt every bit as nervous as she was sure she looked. Still gripping tight to her mother's hand she turned to face the pool.

'Will you stay with me?' Scarlet asked.

'I will always be with you my little River,' she said softly, before turning to the pool. 'On the count of three.'

'One, two, three,' they both said, standing and taking a step forward into the whirlpool in the centre of the pool.

Falling deeper into the pool, Scarlet felt her mother's hand still holding on. Water rushed all around her. She held her breath until the pressure of the water was too much.

Squealing out to stop it, Scarlet was left with nothing but a mouth full of water. She choked, feeling it slowly fill her lungs as she fought to go against the whirlpool that kept dragging her down.

Scarlet closed her eyes, trying to ease the panic she felt. To make it as peaceful as possible, feeling her mind stop.

Gasping one more time, her final time.

Feeling her mother's hand in her own she squeezed it tightly, and a calm that eased her spread. As she eased, it brought back her thoughts, feeling of her heart still beating thudding inside. Like a spark in her mind Scarlet saw the first explosion of light spread throughout Grinnwick from the first heart. Her mind whirled like a puzzle being completed in her head formed by visions of powered light connecting to all living things within Grinnwick. A connection that spread from her heart through her blood to every part of her body. She saw vividly the same connection imbedded in Grinnwick; the Haliroot that Dawson had first shown her when they left the Amari. It ran deep through their world as they magic did inside of her. Yet hidden, just as her magic had been. All that was; all that could be in this life began with her blood.

The very first Heart, a golden light that rose from the pool. A Goddess, a woman. She felt every bit of the magic that once flowed through the first Heart in herself.

Scarlet felt the thousands of Hearts connecting to her, drawing a power from inside of her that was only combined by each and every Heart. The forces of nature that they controlled, purely by their emotions. She felt the ocean tide in her veins; the earth force; and the fires of the deep. Powerful, yet delicate and each one before her were warriors in their own way. Through them they allowed the land to grow, to light up with magic. Hundreds of thousands of years building up the connection. Some were feared, others respected, some even stayed to themselves, but to Grinnwick they allowed life and happiness to spread.

She noticed as she drew in more knowledge that the mark of the Heart had been missing from the world. This explained why she thought it only a myth, a bedtime story. The powers they had hidden from the world; scared for their lives and the lives of those they loved. Men taking hold of what they thought belonged to them, and them alone. Feeling every bit of fear and the caution that those before her endured. Grinnwick had forgotten the beauty that once was brought by the Hearts before her. So many still would never comprehend just how important they had been to Grinnwick; how important she was.

As the whirlpool eased so did the pieces in her mind, Scarlet was finally given the sight of her mother and sister. And like so many of the others who had been the Hearts of Grinnwick they looked otherworldly; enchanting to behold – Scarlet couldn't understand how she was related at all, if anything in comparison she was simple.

Her sister, a young replica of her mother, the woman who stood by her side. Both of them just as breathtaking as the first Heart was, the light that was in them shined bright.

The sight of them in her mind's eye brought the touch of another hand on Scarlet's other side as she floated. She knew it had to be her sister. A warming welcome of an embrace.

Understanding finally her blood tears were a trait of a true heart when they were either parted from their true love, or struck by loss of a loved one. The distant memory of losing her loved ones when she knocked her head too, the noises and screams she'd heard in her mind must have been theirs. Those moments of pain, of terror that they must have felt, Scarlet felt for the first time that her missing memories may just be as her brother had once said, a gift.

Most importantly she began to realise the importance of the knowledge she'd been given meant nothing compared to the love she started to remember. Flickers of visions of herself with her sister in a large playroom that was grander than any Scarlet had been in before. The panelling of wood half-way up across the walls, and the pictures of animals atop of it on a green backdrop, with toys and a large canopy of whites and golds at the centre of the room. The light of their mother's face embracing them both as they sat on the window's ledge, playing with a puzzle. A small memory, but it was so much more than Scarlet had ever hoped for. A memory that sparked the courage inside of her, knowing that she wasn't alone; that she had never truly been alone.

With every bit of magic, of power Scarlet felt running through her veins and the Heart bursting inside of her, full of wonder and possibilities, the water inside of her lungs dwindled, and she breathed once more unbothered by its presence.

Never in her life had she felt so sure, so happy. Aware now that she was still in the depths of the water Scarlet opened her eyes to look up around her. The water was still swirling but it now looked slower, as though time around her had slowed down making it that much easier to reach out ahead; glowing sparking lightning connected all around her, but it didn't scare her. She looked to the light above the surface that was ready and waiting. Drawn to it; ready to face whatever was next ahead.

The problems and concerns of the world had drifted away, and she had forgotten that she wouldn't be coming up to a peaceful place. The hands of her mother and sister were gone, but she still felt their strength as she reached up and swam to the top.

Scarlet knew that the responsibility was now hers, and hers alone. To be kind, to give courage and to look after the world that was now in her control, and whose fate could control her own. A balance; a baring of the weight of the world but a light inside her that finally felt free. Being the Heart of Grinnwick was a gift. That original star, that being that fell, the being that entwined itself into all others; that became Grinnwick. It was now her power.

Breaching from the surface she found herself beaming, a light that had been switched on in the darkest corners of her mind. She finally felt alive, and the excitement was intoxicating.

The feeling lasted mere moments as the reality of her surrounds dawned on her. The light still remained but her need to survive was heightened. It poured down with rain, as hear ears echoed with vibration from blast in the distance. She wanted to help, she *could* help, it was what she was meant for. She heard screams, gun shots and the green haze of the Cor-Marinium fuelled shots lighting the misty skies. She wanted to help the people of Perdita so bad, but was warded off by a mound of flames that was consuming the rainforest around her, forcing her back towards the pool.

She'd find another way down to the fighting, another way to help.

In a moment she heard voices, shots being fired. Her instinct told her to hide, as much as she wanted to fight. She didn't know how to control her abilities yet, so she looked for a place to hide while they passed. Scouring around the pool area she tucked further around to the side where there was a cave that rainwater trickled down in front of creating a veil to mask whatever was inside.

The Missing Piece

For one moment the silence of the island around him was deafening as the elderly man's life was taken. He didn't hear the rain that fell around him, the breeze had stopped. The elderly man's body was thrown back onto the shore. As though reality all come spinning back together Bastian heard the screaming in horror from the remaining locals – their wails of such a high pitch the ground beneath him quaked. Clearly ignored by the soldiers of the Grinnwick Guard as they were being dragged off towards the submarine.

If only he'd had the Ravens with him, if he'd had Verne and Gertie to help him plan, and Russ and Mandy to operate a communications system for this mission and even Felix for his useless sense of supporting him. If he'd had a weapon, he'd do his best to help, to make sure that something like this didn't happen. He may not have been able to take down the whole sub of soldiers, but he'd give it a good crack. But he had none of that, and his task was simple to find the Heart.

If his time wasn't so precious, he'd give them all he had, but this wasn't a time for rash thinking, he needed to be smart. The locals of Perdita had left the Heart of Grinnwick here, hidden. Their leader trusted him, leaving him alone to find it; protect it.

He moved on from the bay side of the cliff's ledge – trudging through the mud higher up the mountain path, the rain now pelting down.

It wasn't until he came across a pool of water at the end of the mountain path that he heard anything out of place.

The pool was at the foot of another cliff edge, some of the rock crumbling down towards him moving back away from it as the rain flowed down the rocky wall. And the sound, a faint echo, of someone treading through the mud, further around the bend of the cliff.

He followed the cliff face around unsure what was going to be around the corner as the wall beside him continued to curve around. He was pulled in this direction; he had no idea why. As he inched closer the sound of rushing rainwater, heavier than before as he saw small trickling waterfall in front of a hidden cave.

As he moved closer Bastian found himself faced with a veil of water covering a small opening. The water flowed from the top of the cliff, and flowed gently and onto the rock at the bottom of the opening, washing away down it as it curved off the rocks and fell below.

Grabbing tight of the weapon, he turned it towards the veil in case something unexpected was lurking behind it.

Initiating the gun so that a light at the end of it allowed him to somewhat see. He used the nose of it to break apart the veil of water, slowly entering the cave inside.

The light at the tip of his weapon lit up part of the cave as Bastian moved under the waterfall.

Feeling his side being kicked in, forcing to the ground as he was caught off guard. Holding his weapon tightly to shine the light on his attacker, he shot before he even saw what was in front of him. A move of the Grinnwick Guard, he hated himself as soon as the shot left the gun.

Shocked and confused, Bastian held the weapon up to use for light to search for his attacker. What he saw wasn't what he expected to find. Of all things on this island, she wasn't what he expected.

The light from the gun shined directly onto her. Snuck up to the wall of the cave, damp and startled, looking pained from the shot. She wore a black dress that was almost sheer, it stuck to her leaving her shivering. He dropped his gun, and the light from it shone across the wall of the cave towards her.

***

Footsteps grew closer from outside of the cave. Scarlet moved up against the wall into the shadows pulling her hood up.

A light shone through the veil of water - she paused. Caught in fear, but not allowing it to grasp her, she picked herself back up, and with the smoothest of motions prepared for an attack.

She took aim, and as if a reflex she swiftly moved her leg through the air, kicking the intruder to the side. The first time in years she'd done a defensive move. Breathing in deeply as she landed her feet back down — but as they settled to the ground she felt a searing pain cross her side.

Clenching it tightly with her hand, ignoring the light of the intruder's weapon that glared on her, Scarlet stepped back against the wall of the cave taken back by the pain.

Since she'd stepped out of the pool the world of Grinnwick had been in her grasp.

Every movement of the land around her felt like the breeze was blowing down her neck; there were senses she had never experienced coming to life inside of her. The feeling of energy ran inside of her body, as it connected to every bit of her surrounds.

Noticing the veil of waterfall's every particle of water that it was made up of; she could have moved the whole veil if she liked. Or the rubble of rocks on the ground, if she wanted to force their weight upwards, flying, right into the intruder's face she knew she could have.

But in this moment, her highest sense was the throbbing at her side, wounded.

Scarlet sensed the sweat from her intruder brow. The slight pant to his breath – and something else entirely, the overwhelming sense that he meant her no harm; still Scarlet found no reason to trust the person who just shot her.

As he stepped into the light of his own weapon, coming clearly into her view.

Caught in his gaze, she cautiously stared at him. As if she was waiting for him to come at her again, but his gentle eyes engaged every part of her energy, like a flicker of fire ran through her. Warming up the chill of cold, deep inside her; unable to do anything but gaze back at him.

All that she had felt before that moment was the force of Grinnwick, the rush of everything around her. Now her fixation turned wholly into his eyes.

Drawn to him; the man that shot her.

Was she mad? The feeling made no sense.

Was the overwhelming senses of being the Heart embracing her to see more than she once did?

It had to be more than that. This feeling had to be more than that.

Looking into him, he slowed down the world around her, of her thoughts of Grinnwick, of the power inside of her, of being the Heart.

Time stood still. With every slight breath she felt her pain decreased too. Looking into his blue eyes, she saw the most peculiar soft glow form around them.

***

'I'm so sorry,' Bastian panted, incredibly distressed by what he'd just done. Dropping his weapon. She reached down for her side where the dress was torn, the arrow had grazed her, but there was still a bit of blood.

She fell back against the wall, her gaze going from her wound up to him.

Her gaze had caught him; he felt frozen where he stood.

His breath caught; his mind fixed on her. Silence filled the cave. It even seemed like the veil of water stopped flowing, drawing him deeper into her eyes. Bastian knew this was no regular girl; or more so, woman. It wasn't that she looked strange like the Perdita locals, there was just something else about her. He knew at this moment that he would give her the world.

The green mix in her eyes were dusted with hazel and yellow speckles, he noticed every single detail in them.

Pulling away from his gaze as she winced, she sat herself down so she could catch her breath. Ripping a part of the skirt of her dress off, she wrapped it around her waist, applying as much pressure as she could.

'I truly am sorry, it's just that I thought you were a monster or a creature, or maybe a soldier from the Guard,' Bastian explained, not sure why he was so flushed.

'I'll be okay. It's just a small nick. Really,' she assured him.

'If I was some sort of monster though, I don't fancy your chances of survival with an aim like that,' she laughed, putting Bastian at ease that she wasn't badly hurt.

'I'll catch my breath, and I'll be out of your hair,' she said calmly.

'No,' Bastian said a bit too quickly, trying to reign his expression in, 'I mean, where will you go? …Wait. What are you doing here?' he added. He had completely forgotten that he didn't know this girl, he didn't know where she was from or why of all places, she had found herself here. Most concerning, if she was a part of the Guard… A spy… but they would never allow a woman to take such a position. None of that really seemed to matter to him, he only found himself feeling an array of warmth for this stranger.

'I'm not sure exactly. I expect my friends will be looking for me though. I should find them, but I don't know where we'll go now,' she said, lost in her thoughts.

'Well look, why don't I help you? I'm here looking for something, but I don't think I'm going to have much luck,' Bastian offered.

'Give me time to rest, and let me finish bandaging this, and then if you like I can help,' she said, smiling at him. Her face glowed with a gentle warmth from a girl he had never quite experienced before. Not even Gertie.

'Thanks, I think we better get you proper help first and foremost,' he commented. 'Why don't you tell me what you need, and I'll go fetch it, I've had a little experience with botany before, maybe there's something around here that might help with the pain,' Bastian suggested.

Her face changed, from warm to intrigued, 'are you one of the men who attacked Perdita?'

'Me. No, I never. That was the Grinnwick Guard, I followed them with a crew of miners. I've been laying low amongst their mine for some time. Been biding my time to hear of any news of well... a myth really. Doubt you've ever heard of it. The Heart of Grinnwick, it's called.'

She leaned towards him. He wasn't sure why he was telling her this, it was like she brought the truth out in him.

'What do you want with it?' she asked.

'Nothing, in truth I barely believed in its existence, until recently. But I guess I never would have believed in people like the ones I found here either. Anyway, my grandfather was the one who sent me on this wild goose chase. He believed that this was where it would be. Where it comes from. He wanted me to protect it. He and I were Guardians, but I doubt you've heard of those either. Anyway from the rumours of a power source, and the peculiar local protection alone, this island is harbouring some form of secret. And I think it might just be the Heart.'

He was met with a blank face at this; she clearly had no idea of who the Guardians were, which was how it should be he supposed. For some reason he wished she did know about them, about the secret squads that helped keep Grinnwick at peace. But truly, Grinnwick hasn't been truly at peace for centuries.

But he wanted her to know anyway, to be in awe of him perhaps. Bastian wasn't exactly sure why. Maybe if she knew she would feel comfort in their dire situation. Most of all he was still stuck on why he was spilling everything he knew to this girl; continuing to do so, unable to help himself.

'Anyway, I had no way of getting to Perdita. My grandfather told me to join the miners of Sildor and listen out for word of the Heart, it being the closest point on land to where the isle of Perdita was supposed to be located. If I heard anything, follow the whispers in hopes of protecting it where others might use it for evil.

'It took years before any word came through Sildor. But rumours about a mighty power source on Perdita came to me.

'I joined a group of miners who were dead set on finding the power first, and holding any sort of leverage over the Grinnwick Guard. Now that I'm here though I fear if the locals of this island can't protect it, what hope do I have,' Bastian said, feeling himself overwhelmed by emotions but still holding himself together. He didn't want to look weak, but saw the look of concern on her face.

'Chief Jesa? Cara? The rest of the people of Perdita?' she asked him.

Bastian's heart sank; he knew the elderly man's fate. He assumed that the leader must have been the chief, but had no idea of the woman named Cara, presuming she was one of the lifeless bodies in the valley.

'I don't know about Cara, but some were taken aboard the Guard's sub, hopefully she was one of them, or perhaps she escaped prior. I think the chief, was killed. If there are more, I don't know,' Bastian admitted, his voice low, hating that he had to be the one to give the news.

'It's all my fault,' she said, small tears dripped down her face.

'It's no one's fault apart from the Guard's. No one could have stopped them once they decided to come here.' Bastian couldn't help but want to make it better for her, to make it easier for her. She was quick to gather herself however,

'I'm Scarlet Rivers,' she finally said.

'Bastian,' he replied. 'Bastian Conway, but some call me Harker. My grandfather's last name – you probably didn't need to know that,' Bastian mused at himself.

Scarlet laughed slightly, 'It's okay really. It's nice to have someone to talk to. Look, I think I'm okay. Really. I'd help you find what you were looking for, but have you thought maybe it's not worth the trouble? Something so powerful as you say should just stay hidden, don't you think? How's about we just try and get out of here,' Scarlet asked.

Bastian knew the Heart of Grinnwick was still here somewhere. Part of him felt that this girl knew what or where it was, after all she knew the people of Perdita. If she too had come all this way like him, maybe she was protecting it all the same. His trust in her strange yet he felt like she was his path, with no sense of why.

'We can do that. First, can you tell me why you are here? How did you get here?' Bastian asked.

Scarlet turned to him nervously, as though she was considering her words.

'My family sent me here, much like yours. They wanted me to find something too,' Scarlet said. Bastian saw she held onto a necklace that was around her neck.

'I came on a ship, the *Gauntlet*. But I didn't arrive with them, I don't think they could get here if they tried,' Scarlet said.

Surprised, this was the woman Mr Walsh spoke of. How was it possible that she stood before him.

'Then how?' Bastian asked. Not believing that this was the missing girl from the ship.

'Magic,' Scarlet mused. Bastian didn't believe her, but in the same note there was no other way. Still he didn't press any further.

'And the people of Perdita, they welcomed you as a friend?'

'Well, looks like I wasn't the only one. They would never have allowed you up here, I mean they themselves can barely come up this way. Didn't it affect you?' Scarlet asked curiously.

But Bastian shook his head.

Finding the Heart

'You coming then?' Scarlet called out once she had cleaned and bandaged her wound properly. She knew they couldn't go back outside, the smoke had been too thick, and there was no way of following a safe known passage.

A sense inside her turned her stance towards the inside of the cave… and as if a sign her glowing leaves appeared to dance further down into the cave from one side to another until it blew around the bend.

'Where are we going?' Bastian asked, as Scarlet begun to lead further into the cave.

'It's just the ship I came in on is at the bottom of the sea. And, as you said your people didn't make it here.' Bastian said, picking up his arrow gun, shrugging of the twinge of annoyance, following her, lighting up the darkness.

'I don't know. But sometimes you just have to trust in something more than yourself, you know,' Scarlet said. She was still curious about him, and his interests in the Heart of Grinnwick, if he really meant to protect it – her.

'So, we don't know where we are going. We have no way off this burning island. I guess I can hold onto a little hope that something good can happen,' Bastian commented. 'Why don't you tell me then about your ship, the *Gauntlet*. You know I had hope to catch view of it at port in Sildor,' Bastian said.

'You've already seen it?' she questions. Time is a strange thing. She hadn't even known how much time had passed off or on the island, how long the tea that Cara gave her allowed her to sleep for.

'Who did you see, did anyone get off?' Scarlet turned to him. His knowledge was now valuable.

'Mr Walsh. He said they lost a girl overboard. You, I'm guessing.' Bastian noted to her.

'And a pair, they came here with me. Kept to themselves – never got their names. They were cloaked most of the time, that was until we got here. But we got separated, the fire – the smoke – the gun shots. I did see them before I ran into you, down below in the bay, captured by the guard.'

Scarlet didn't say anything. They'd found a way, they got here. Scarlet wasn't sure how they'd managed, but all she hoped was that they were okay – somehow, she'd get there, to the underwater ship that they'd been taken on, and get them out.

They walked in silence for a time as the sound of trickling water once more began to fill the echoing caves As the trickle turned into a heavy stream of water Scarlet came to a halt. She felt Bastian bump into her.

It was like she saw the path ahead through the water, how it fell and flowed on towards a light, an opening.

'You up for it?' Scarlet smiled cheekily as his light shone on another wall of water.

'For what?' Bastian questioned.

Scarlet pointed down to a great wide hole in the ground where water flowed down from the roof above.

Curiosity and adrenaline rushed through her, it was the first time in a long time she felt the joy in something so ridiculously wild and adventurous.

***

Bastian didn't know how comfortable he was with his choice to follow her down this rabbit hole. Surely this would only end badly, part of him imagined it like one of his early tasks with the Guardians.

'One,' she started,

'Two.

'Three.'

Spray from the water washed over them and the bottom of his stomach flipped as they dropped.

The hole around them widened as they fell, rocks from the hole scraping down their sides, knocking them about. Bastian reached out for Scarlet as they dropped together.

Splash.

The force of water around them came bursting out the other end below, rocks fell with them as they were plunged deeper under the water of a below cavern. Bastian struggled against the force of his plunge, doing his best to reach to the top.

***

Scarlet breached the surface first, gasping for breath before making her way to the water's edge. She lay down catching her breath on the hard ground with her eyes closed, hearing her new companion pull himself onto the hard ground next to her.

'That was the most incredible rush,' Bastian gasped pushing himself to sit up next to her, 'how did you even know it would lead down here?' he said with a softness in his voice.

Scarlet sat up next to him. Slightly disappointed that they were in yet another cave – this one vastly larger, but now there was no light, at all. And it had seemed like Bastian's weapon didn't make it out of the water with him – keeping them completely in the dark.

'Well, I hoped it would have gotten us closer, but I guess not. Sorry about that,' Scarlet said.

'Scarlet. I don't know why you're saying sorry, less than an hour ago I shot you,' Bastian laughed. 'Besides, we're not done searching. We'll find a way. I always do.'

Scarlet's was oddly smoothed by his optimism,

'Tell me again?' she asked him.

'Tell you what?' Bastian asked.

'Why did you come here?' Scarlet asked.

'I told you; my grandfather sent me on the mission to protect the Heart of Grinnwick,' Bastian said, a little uneasily.

'And what do you know about it?' Scarlet asked.

'The myth?' Bastian asked.

Scarlet nodded.

'The Heart is connected to Grinnwick, it holds the balance of our world. They said that the Royals over a thousand years ago used to hold it in their possession. But it predates their history too. But they say that they controlled it to keep peace within Grinnwick. That with it they allowed magic and life to blossom. But with their death, the Heart was lost and so darkness reigned, and forces like the Grinnwick Guard were able to take control.'

'What would you do with it?' Scarlet asked.

'I don't know. I wouldn't want to hide it away, lost to the world as it has been for so much time. Yet, I wouldn't want anyone to know of its true existence. I would use it for small things that could make a difference, I

482

mean I don't really know what it's capable of. I'd keep it safe from prying hands that would use it for evil,' Bastian assured.

'Do you think it is good?'

'I guess it depends on who wields it… but how could it not be?'

Scarlet pondered what he said, it brought about an inner strength, a calmness. Somehow forming clarity through her new energy force that powered through her. Forming a happiness, and glimmer of hope in her – not that he knew that.

A flicker of lines connecting inside her mind, Scarlet pushed on them – seeking. The light of the glowing leaves flowed within her. Pushing her force outwards she saw the cave around her, lit up in her minds' eye.

'Follow me.'

They twisted and turned down a winding narrower cave that she foresaw. Taking one diverted turn followed by another, quickly moving sporadically at every corner. Scarlet quickened her pace, ignoring the pain at her side as she moved through the tunnels. Soon enough a flicker of light reflected off the rocks ahead of them at the next turn.

Bastian raced ahead of her but halted at the exit.

Scarlet caught up, but stopped dead in her tracks.

Her heart stopped.

A valley before the bay – still smoking from the drowned-out fire. The lush green rainforest that had once been all over the island – blackened. And in the centre of the valley a lightly burning pile. Scarlet fell to the ground.

Piles of the Perdita locals lay on top of one another, burning.

She ran to go closer, but Bastian pulled her back.

She turned back to fight him, she had to see if there was a chance for some of them. But she saw in his eyes his own anger at the scene before them.

'We can't help them now,' he said so simply. As if their loss meant nothing, but it did they had meant it to save her – to give her the opportunity to escape.

'If we get to the bay, we can escape this,' he said intently, with such caring, helping her to her feet.

'The Grinnwick Guard seem to be packing down the last of their things.'

Scarlet moved to peer out beside him. Wiping the tears from her eyes. There were still men everywhere. She could see that they had multiple ships, oddly shaped being that they were fully enclosed, including the roof. Some of the digging machinery was still on the shore, getting ready to be loaded aboard.

'Scarlet. This is our way off,' Bastian claimed. 'We have to stay quiet. We have to stay undercover. They cannot be allowed to see us.' He instructed.

Scarlet understood. She hadn't had much to do with the Guard, but she knew not to trifle with them.

Bastian held out his hand.

'Follow me,' he said, as Scarlet grabbed hold.

Together they ran past the burning pile, the stench reaching scarlets nose, like that of rotten eggs but worse, so much worse. Gaining on the Guard, hiding behind rocks, and charcoal tree stumps, getting closer, jumping behind diggers, explosive piles all until they found their way into back of one of their wagons. It was only a couple of minutes before the door opened, and the rustlings of a soldier with his key to drive the mover ignited the engine. It was slowly driven onboard one of the vessels. Which one they didn't know.

Scarlet snuck open the back curtains, looking out at Perdita, and the ruins that the Guard had left it in. The people she had met had to lay their lives down for her. She felt empty looking at it.

Tears ran down her face, just as another shower crossed the bay. Bastian pulled her back down. His face echoing her sadness, but his hand reached for her face, wiping away the blood tears that rolled down her cheeks.

Remaining calm Bastian whispered, 'You're okay. Look at me,' he was deadly serious. 'They will pay for what they've done to your friends here.'

'I feel like their cries are bleeding into my bones. As though I can still hear them. The pain, the anguish, the fear. What was worse was I felt like I have heard it all before,' Scarlet said. It was the first time she had said it out loud. She wasn't even sure if that was a strange memory of her past, or something she had seen in a dream.

The journey was smooth and quiet unlike both their trips there. Bastian told Scarlet to sleep and that he would keep his eye out.

She was awoken by the change in pace of the ship, a large jolt alerting her to where she was.

'I thought you were still sleeping,' he mused as she slightly opened her eyes. 'Since you're awake, we're nearly back. We need to move before they find us.'

Nervous but ready for their next move Scarlet pulled herself together, she held her side where her wound was, the blood had stopped, but the pain lingered, like an ache, draining her. Doing her best to ignore the pain.

Jumping out of the wagon Bastian moved them swiftly through the mover carrier towards the exit, but stopped in his tracks.

'What is it?' Scarlet whispered. She saw what he was looking at. One of the movers held an encaged prison on its tray. Bars squared around the tray, and inside some of the Grinnwick Guards Prisoners. She wasn't exactly sure why he was so excited to see them though.

'Lux, Hudson… How'd you get here?' Scarlet started.

Bastian ran up to the mover. 'Darcy!'

They all turned around in the cage. They were with another miner, but none of the people of Perdita were in sight. Perhaps they were being held in another compartment, Scarlet hoped at least.

'Thought I told you to stay out of trouble kid,' Bastian said mocking the young boy inside the cage. Seeing a Guard coming their way, Scarlet grabbed Bastian's arm, forcing him to wince. A quick wash of guilt crossed her, but he didn't seem to bothered once he saw the Guard soldier.

'Get out of here Mr Harker, Sir. They will capture you too. They will,' Darcy repeated himself.

'Yeah get out of here Scarlet, hurry!' Hudson ordered her.

'Wait here,' Bastian replied. 'You,' Bastian pointed at Scarlet.

'Me, what?' Scarlet said abruptly, unimpressed with being ordered around.

'Get under their mover now,' Bastian insisted. 'Please.'

Scarlet jumped under quickly, holding her breath as she watched events unfold.

The Guard had spotted Bastian.

'You. What's your name?' said the Guard in an official tone.

'Harker is the name.,' he said handing them something that Scarlet couldn't see. I was on downtime soldier, sorry to surprise you. I just left my meds in my bag and my sea belly's acting up again.'

'Well don't let me see you out of quarters like that again or I'll take you to Captain Archbank himself for disciplinary action. Be quick about it, we'll be in port soon enough,' the Guard advised before moving on.

'Yes, Sir.'

'Wait….' The guard turned back around. 'There's meds in the infirmary if you find you need something stro—' the guard started before he caught glimpse of Scarlet's head under the van. Scarlet nearly shouted a warning as she saw the guard, quickly move to pull his gun out and fire, but Bastian knocked him off balance and the shot just missed him.

He took the gun and fired back at the soldier, and the man dropped to the ground in front of Scarlet.

'Hudson?' Lux said.

Scarlet scrambled out from under the mover. Hudson was down, his shoulder red.

'Look at me,' Lux yelled, pleaded, 'help him!' she cried.

Bastian rummaged through the dead guard's clothes for keys. Grabbing the ones in his front pocket he used them to open the cage on the back of the mover.

Scarlet ran to him; he was still with them, but barely.

'Are you okay?' Hudson whispered.

Scarlet nodded, tears rolling from her face.

'You're not hurt?' he said confused,

'Why on earth did you go up on deck, we thought you were dead,' he scolded even through his pain.

'I'm so sorry… It, it was like a haze; a dream. I can't explain it. I thought I saw Dawson. Then this glowing light – it kind of wrapped me up and swept me out to sea. Took me straight to Perdita... I'm so sorry,' Scarlet cried.

'So, you got answers then…' Hudson asked.

'Yes,' Scarlet smiled.

He smiled back at her.

'You'll be more than okay, you'll be amazing. Look after each other,' he breathlessly said to both Scarlet and Lux. Bastian moved them both out of the way, as Hudson went in and out of consciousness. Scarlet watched as he assessed Hudson. Her breaths were short, and her pain was only increasing the stress inside of her.

'He has a pulse, he's still with us,' he assured her.

***

Bastian moved quickly; he had dressed the gunshot best he could. Then he grabbed the dead guard's uniform and put it on himself. He felt detached in the moment, like it was his fault for stepping out of the way of the shot. It could have just as easily been him lying on the ground.

'We have to go,' pleaded Bastian. He moved the body of the soldier into the cage, and pulled down the covers so no one would see what was inside.

'Everyone hop in the back. Do. Not. Make. A. Peep,' Bastian ordered.

'Where are we going?' Scarlet asked through the heaviness of her breathe, jumping into the caged tray that was now fully enclosed with the lifeless body of a soldier next to them.

'We are driving out of here and getting your friend help.' Bastian said confidently.

Silence fell over them as Guards flowed from their quarters into the movers around them.

Not wanting to draw any unwanted attention. She released a breath she didn't realise she had been holding as they finally drove down the ramp onto dry land, and out of the sub. Both Scarlet and Lux held onto Hudson as they drove.

***

They had been following the line of cars from the Port at Astoria for nearly ten minutes when Bastian finally managed to take a side road. Bastian hadn't been to the port before, there were a lot of different paths that he was entirely sure where they lead. The road had been paved with white square stones, forcing the mover shook all around him.

They were still in Astoria's walls, at least he knew one place if any that would be safe for them – only how would they get there without warranting any unexpected attention.

Bastian eventually pulled off to from the parade of movers that had disembarked the ship. Spotting a small of road where there were three or four unattended movers. He pulled the mover to a halt. He wanted to be rid of the car quickly.

Ripping open the caged but to see a Scarlet holding onto her friend – he was pale, he was weak.

Bastian grabbed hold of Scarlet's hand and pulled her out, Bastian jumped in as the miner and Darcy jumped out.

Bastian pulled Scarlets friend off the tray, holding him up.

'What your name?' Bastian asked, trying to keep him alert.

'Hudson,' he replied.

'Look I'm going to get you help, it'll be alright,' Bastian assured him, 'I know a place.'

It was in that moment that he also caught a glimpse down at the side of Scarlet's dress, and blood was leaking out of her bandages. He had almost forgotten that she'd hurt herself, but the blood dripping put him on edge – he didn't want anything to happen to her.

***

Silence. A busy sort of silence. Down in the western end of Astoria, away from the high towers made of glass, far from the lives of the elite. Where the green liquid of the Cor-Marinium was still seen pumping through the power lines in the rustic and working-class side of city. Bastian had guided them down alleys until they arrived The Half Hound. For some reason, it seemed like the right place now.

The innkeeper already had someone tending too Hudson, who he rushed up to a room without any question. Bastian took a seat with Scarlet, and her friend, unconsciously they all sat together on the same side of the booth without even thinking.

'What's your name?' Bastian asked her friend.

'Lux,' she responded, but didn't seem interested in talking, her focus was what was happening up with Hudson, her eyes darting upstairs constantly.

'I'm sorry. This isn't the sort of place you should be in,' Bastian apologised, mostly to Scarlet who was sitting quietly, looking rather exhausted.

'Don't be,' she said almost too softly for his liking. 'It's nice here; familiar in a way, and besides I like their music.' Scarlet added, 'I see they have a piano too. I've only ever read of them; it would be great to get a chance to play.'

'Please do. She is b-e-a-utiful and sounds like a gift from above, given the right player,' Wilbur the innkeeper said, as he passed them by on his way to get himself a seat for another table.

'Are you alright?' Wilbur asked Scarlet, the sound of politeness didn't quite suit him, sounding way too proper than his usual self, thought Bastian.

'Maybe just some fresh bandages, if you could… and an update on our friend,' Scarlet politely asked. She seemed quiet, oddly so.

'Actually, do you have medicine? Or a doctor to look at her wound too?' Bastian interjected, making his concern clear.

'I know your face don't I?' he questioned Bastion for a moment. 'Yes, Manny's friend. Of course, I won't be a moment,' Wilbur replied and rushed off quickly.

'You know I've only met him once, but I don't think he's taken to anyone so well,' Bastian said, trying to distract Scarlet.

'He seems nice,' Scarlet noted. Before turning to Lux, 'you sure you don't need anything?' she asked her.

Lux shook her head. Bastian had come to understand that Hudson was Lux's brother. That the three of them were like family. He couldn't even begin to know what to say. He felt himself give them space while they waited for Wilbur.

'Look, Bastian I need to tell you something,' Scarlet turned to him.

'It's okay, I know,' Bastian said, he could tell her pain was getting worse – he sensed it in her somehow.

'You know?' Scarlet asked.

'How could you possibly? I haven't said anything,' Scarlet said uneasily.

She swayed for a moment in her seat, looking lightheaded.

'You'll be okay,' Bastian reached out for her shoulder – 'Wilbur,' he called, feeling the on urgency in his voice, he lifted her hand – it felt clammy and her face getting paler by the second.

'I'm fine. I need to tell you…' she started, almost breathlessly not trying to continue. Lux had even taken notice as Bastian noticed her moved to help Scarlet.

'What you were looking for,' Scarlet began to stutter. He saw her grimaced with pain, and at the same time the fireplace burst out with flames beside them, leaving the barmaid screaming as it singed her dress.

Scarlet looked around in horror to the fireplace.

'I'm sorry, I didn't mean it,' Scarlet fretted, her voice near breathless.

'What are you sorry for? It was probably just a log from pile combusting,' Bastian said. 'Happens all the time.'

'Not like that,' Scarlet said.

'Scarlet, you need to lie down,' Lux interrupted.

'I know, I will but I need to tell him… I need to tell you,' she pulled towards him, 'you found what you were looking for.'

'The Heart of Grinnwick?' Bastian question, confused by what she meant.

Scarlet nodded.

She was holding tightly onto his arm, as he came closer to her. She quickly passed out into his shoulder.

Wilbur rushed over, 'Let's get her upstairs to lay down.'

Wilbur helped him pick her up, and for the first time Lux seemed interested in something other than her brother.

'What's wrong,' she asked.

'She's wounded…' Bastian noted.

'Might be infected,' Wilbur added, 'I've got just the trick, but she'll need rest.' Wilbur helped him take one of her sides as they moved her upstairs.

A whirlwind of motions seemed to quickly pass as they lifted her up to a room next to Hudson's. Wilbur whipped together some green goo, smearing over her wound before freshly wrapping it. Only to then cover her in warm blankets.

Bastian stood by the door, watching her pale skin, looking – hoping for a tinge of colour to come back to her cheeks.

What did she mean he'd found the Heart. What did she know. He looked more intently to her, finding himself moving closer to her side, taking a seat in one of the armchairs by the bed. Knowing he would not leave her. Thoughts racing around his mind. His grandfathers words from years ago coming to him, *"it is not what it seems.",* the memory of it sparking something in him as he looked at Scarlet. She wasn't what she seemed, he felt it, she was so much more. But she couldn't be, could she.

'Leave her rest boy,' Wilbur said, interrupting his train of thought. Patting him on the shoulder, as if to say he'd done his bit. Bastian didn't move, this was exactly where he needed to be. Whether she held in her possession the Heart of Grinnwick, was indeed the Heart herself, or perhaps no more than a girl in the wrong place at the wrong time, it didn't matter. What mattered to him more than anything right then was that she simply wake.

www.ingramcontent.com/pod-product-compliance
Lightning Source LLC
Chambersburg PA
CBHW021212260626
47172CB00002B/383